Until Soon

Maya Indigal

Yellow Rose Books

Nederland, Texas

ISBN 1-932300-31-7

First Printing 2004

9 8 7 6 5 4 3 2 1

Cover design by Donna Pawlowski

Published by:

Yellow Rose Books
PMB 210, 8691 9th Avenue
Port Arthur, Texas 77642-8025

Find us on the World Wide Web at
http://www.regalcrest.biz

Printed in the United States of America

Acknowledgments

This book may have started as a thought in *my* head, but there are many people whose guidance and support made this final copy possible. I will forever be touched by their kindness and am truly grateful for their assistance.

The many authors in cyberspace and in print who share their talent for the genre have been a great source of pleasure and inspiration to me. Their passion—both for and in their writing—motivated me to try my hand at the craft.

Kim Linonis and B. Iraca Smith offered positive support and critical feedback during the early stages of this manuscript. Lori L. Lake provided an invaluable source of advice and encouragement in getting this book published. Additionally, her careful editing of the manuscript greatly improved the final product. By sharing her knowledge and talent, and by teaching me to become a better writer, she has given me an invaluable gift. I also appreciate the assistance of those who proofed the final drafts, including Sue, M.E., Kim Linonis, and Eleanor German.

The wonderful people at Regal Crest, especially Cathy LeNoir, deserve my heartfelt thanks for believing in me. Kudos to Donna Pawlowski for creating a wonderful cover design, as well as to Sylverre, whose copyediting was first-rate.

I am also grateful to my cousin, Básia, who provided expert optometric advice.

Last on this list, but certainly first in my heart, is Sue, my partner and best friend. Our life together is my greatest source of joy. Her faith in me makes me believe that I can do anything.

~ Maya Indigal

For Sue

My heart beats for you

Still, what I want in my life
is to be willing
to be dazzled—
to cast aside the weight of facts

and maybe even
to float a little
above this difficult world.
I want to believe I am looking

into the white fire of a great mystery.

~Mary Oliver, excerpt from *The Ponds* (1990)

Chapter
One

"ANDI! SO GLAD you could make it," Dean Robarts bellowed. The middle-aged man, head of the small New England liberal arts college, stepped to where Andrea Marlow was standing and greeted her with a warm smile. He shook her hand, patting her shoulder with his left hand. "We're happy that all the departments are so well represented on this special occasion." As he spoke, his eyes darted quickly around the large room then back to meet hers.

"I wouldn't have missed it, Dean," Andi said. *More accurately, I didn't have a choice about missing it.* Her Chair insisted that all members of the English department be there, including the graduate assistants. Wearing dress trousers and a silk blouse that accentuated her broad shoulders and narrow waist, Andi cut an impressive figure as she stood in the doorway and scanned the room; however, she would have much rather been sitting at home on her overstuffed sofa and wearing sweat pants instead of hobnobbing with big buck donors. *These donors help fund my tuition and stipend. I should at least be social.* "Excuse me while I mingle," she said. She left Dean Robarts and moved away from the crowded entrance.

She wandered through the banquet room toward the string quartet in the corner. Most of the two hundred or so guests she didn't recognize, but she smiled politely at the few familiar faces of other graduate assistants and professors. The perimeter of the room was lined with small, round cocktail tables. Tuxedoed staff milled around with champagne and hors d'oeuvres. The noise of a hundred voices in conversation buzzed in her ears. In spite of the vaulted ceilings, she felt claustrophobic.

"Don't *you* look nice!"

Andi smiled and turned toward the familiar voice. "Hi, Martha. I haven't seen you in weeks." She and Martha had been friends since their student days at Northeast Valley College where they now worked. Andi had been happy when Martha took a job in the Registrar's office after graduation. She hugged the short, dark-haired woman.

Martha smiled broadly and returned the hug. "Happy New Year, girlfriend! When did you get back on campus?"

"Two weeks ago. I visited my mom until the seventh. It's good to be back, though."

"Why didn't you call? You're not still moping around, are you? I told you, I've got a few friends I can fix you up with. Just say the word." She paused to look appraisingly at Andi. "Mmmm, you look good, girl."

"It's my recycled Christmas outfit, and thanks for the offer, but no thanks." Andi appreciated her close friend's concern about her happiness and her social life, but she wasn't interested in Martha's matchmaking. "I'm glad you're here, though. I hate these forced social functions."

"Me, too, but at least the food's good, and you never know who you might meet. Come on, let's get a drink and mingle." With that, Martha turned and headed toward the bar.

Andi moved to follow her, then spotted Jen across the room. *Shit. I'm definitely not in the mood to deal with her.* She turned abruptly and bumped into someone, spilling half the woman's drink onto her sweater.

"I'm so sorry," Andi stammered. She stopped a waiter and took several napkins from his hors d'oeuvres tray. "Here, let me help." She was making an attempt to blot at the spill when the woman spoke.

"Really, it's okay. It's only seltzer. It won't stain."

"I'm terribly sorry," persisted Andi. She looked away from the spill and found herself face to face with a young woman matching her nearly six-foot frame. The woman had short, wavy blonde hair and an attractive, androgynous face that looked decidedly more female due to the skirt, sweater, and heels she was wearing. Andi looked directly into the woman's green eyes. "I hope you're not one of the donors," Andi said, smiling sheepishly. She brushed back her shoulder-length ebony hair, revealing her striking face and clear blue eyes.

"Do I look like I have a million bucks to spare?" The woman laughed, her voice hearty and warm. "I'm a guest, but not one of the guests of honor." She extended her hand. "I'm CJ."

Andi accepted the firm handshake and returned CJ's penetrating gaze.

"I'm Andi. Pleasure to meet you."

"Andi?"

"Andrea, really, but my friends call me Andi."

"Nice to meet you, Andi."

"So, CJ, if you're not a million dollar donor, what brings you here?" She looked at the woman before her, guessing her age to be near her own twenty-three years.

"Social obligation. The AD asked the captains of all the sports teams to show up and pay homage to the guy who wrote a check for the new athletic facility," CJ said. "So, here I am. And you?"

"My department Chair got the same memo as your AD, so I'm paying my dues, too."

"Are you a professor?"

"Graduate assistant, English. I take classes part-time and do work in the department part-time."

CJ smiled. "How long have you been doing that?"

"I'm into my second year now. And you? You didn't say what team you played for."

"Basketball."

"Wait a minute. Are you the Cara Jane Lipinski I've read about in the school paper? The basketball star?"

CJ blushed, seeming a bit uncomfortable with the compliment and the attention. "Basketball is a team sport, and the entire team is doing well," she said. "I'm a senior — the home stretch."

"You must be looking forward to graduation."

"I'm hoping to end up in grad school, actually."

"What major?"

"History."

"My second favorite subject," Andi said. CJ still hadn't looked away from her eyes. Andi admired someone who could lock eyes with her and not pull away. Most people were intimidated by her intense eye contact. "So, CJ, since you're now wearing your drink, thanks to me, can I at least get you another one?"

"I should probably get back." She looked at her watch, then back at Andi. "I've got a project to work on."

"It's still early. How about one refill first, my treat?"

"Your treat to get me a seltzer at the open bar, huh?" CJ grinned. "Okay, big spender. You talked me into it."

They made their way across the noisy room and over to the bar. Andi ordered two seltzers, then handed one to CJ. She raised her glass and held it up until CJ did the same. "Here's to mingling with important people." She clinked her glass against CJ's and raised her eyebrows. CJ grinned, then lowered her glass.

They moved away from the bar and stood near a window overlooking the campus. The light from the room filtered through the glass, casting shadows from the bushes onto the snow-covered ground. Across the way, the lights from the other buildings glowed in the darkness.

Andi asked, "So what kind of big project are you working on?" She wondered if this attractive athlete had brains to match her good looks.

"A paper on little-known yet important women in post-Civil War America." CJ paused. "I saw you stifle a yawn."

"Not at all! In fact, I'd love to read it."

"That won't happen any time soon. I'm knee deep in journal articles but don't even know how I'm going to turn all of that information into a cohesive paper." She slowly shook her head. "All I have now is a jumble of notes."

"If you need some help, I could show you a method I've used. In fact, I've taught it to other students and have gotten positive feedback from them."

"I could use all the help I can get. You sure?"

"No problem. It's the least I can do after dousing you with a drink. My office is in Woodcliff Hall, second floor. Stop by sometime."

"I might just take you up on it. But don't feel like you owe me anything. After all, you did buy me a refill." She smiled at Andi. "And now, I really do have to go." She put the glass down on a tray, then turned back to Andi and extended her hand. "I enjoyed talking with you tonight."

"Likewise." She shook CJ's hand firmly, looking once again into her beautiful emerald eyes.

"Good night," CJ said.

Andi watched her walk across the room and disappear into the hallway. She stood by the window for a few minutes, thinking about how nice it was to actually enjoy one of these receptions for a change. *Martha was right. You never know who you might meet.* She found herself still smiling, remembering, of all things, the dimple in CJ's cheek.

Chapter
Two

ANDI SAT GRADING papers behind her desk when she heard a knock on her half-opened door.

"Come in," she called, not taking her eyes from the paper before her.

"Am I interrupting?"

Andi looked up and saw CJ standing in the doorway. The blonde wore faded jeans and a basketball sweatshirt; a backpack spilling over with books hung from one shoulder. She offered a shy smile, and Andi grinned in return.

"Not at all," Andi said after a moment. "Come in." The smile that greeted her, accentuating that prominent dimple, was warm and friendly. Andi rose from behind her desk.

"Remember me?" CJ asked.

"Of course. It's only been a week. You look a bit more comfortable now, though. And not nearly as wet." A hint of a grin brightened Andi's face.

CJ, green eyes twinkling with amusement, laughed with an easy comfort usually reserved for close friends. "I hate heels and hose with a passion. Jeans and sweats are far more comfy."

"I agree," Andi said. She held her arms out to her sides, indicating her own clothing, a neatly pressed white cotton shirt tucked into tan pants, and added, "It's either chinos like these or jeans for me." A braided leather belt completed the casual outfit.

CJ slid the backpack off her shoulder and set it on a chair, then glanced away from Andi toward an Emily Dickinson poster hanging on the wall behind Andi's desk. She stepped toward the bookcase that filled the wall on the right. "Mind if I look?" CJ turned her head to read titles on the book spines. After a moment's reading, she pointed to a book of Mary Oliver poetry on the shelf and then looked over at Andi. "She's one of my favorites."

"Mine, too." Andi was more than a little impressed that CJ even recognized the contemporary poet.

She continued reading titles, then after a few moments looked again at Andi. "You have a great office. It's very...welcoming."

"I wondered if you'd stop by."

"We had two out-of-state games, so I wasn't around much this last week. When I got back, I wanted to find some more journal articles so I'd have a lot to show you." She moved to the other side of the small office. "What's this?" A plaque leaned against books on an upper shelf. CJ removed it, then silently read the inscription. "I'm impressed. Looks like I'm not the only one who's had her name in the paper."

Andi felt her face flush as she became uncomfortable with the attention. She looked away from CJ toward her desk. "Now I'm simply an ex-swimmer drowning in paperwork." She waved her hand over her desk, indicating the pile of papers covering it. "Speaking of papers, how's yours coming along?"

CJ sighed and set the plaque on the shelf. "It's stalled. I have plenty of references and I've taken pages of notes, but it all sounds muddled. It's not blending together seamlessly, and that's the problem."

"That's actually a common problem in research papers," Andi said. She walked around to the front of the desk, facing CJ, and leaned against the front edge. "Ever bake cookies?"

"Cookies?"

"Writing a research paper is actually similar, in a figurative sense." CJ looked at her skeptically, but smiled. "Think of your sources as ingredients, like milk, eggs, flour, sugar, peanut butter —"

"Peanut butter?"

"I *love* peanut butter cookies," Andi said. She rolled her blue eyes toward heaven.

"Continue." CJ smiled as she spoke.

"So you mix all the ingredients together and put it in the oven, and when you take them out for the first bite, you no longer taste milk or eggs or flour. You get a cookie! It's a product of the ingredients, yet doesn't taste like the individual parts anymore." She paused. "Get it?"

"Actually, I do." She smiled sheepishly at Andi, impressed by the simplicity with which she explained the concept. "Maybe my brain's not a hot enough oven."

"I doubt that's the problem," Andi said. "Want to try what I do?"

"Sure."

"Here's what you do. Get 3-by-5 cards and take notes on them."

"I already have pages of notes on notebook paper." CJ reached for her backpack but the grad assistant's grimace caught her eye; she half-expected what she heard next.

"No good. Too hard to blend the ingredients that way."

CJ tilted her head back and sighed.

"Sorry, I know those notes took you a long time. Consider them a sacrifice to the Paper Writing Goddess. Trust me. This will be a lot easier."

"Do *you* ever trust someone who says, 'Trust me'?" CJ asked.

"Rarely, but I hope you will this time." She continued to explain the process to CJ, who listened attentively, occasionally stopping Andi to ask a question. By the time Andi finished explaining what to do, she knew CJ was convinced that it would work. Andi said, "When you've done all this, we'll meet again and I'll tell you the next step. How's that?"

"Great." CJ stood at attention, clicked her heels together and smiled. "I'll work very hard, coach. I promise." She saluted with her left hand.

"I'm sure you will." Andi enjoyed the fact that CJ could slip from serious to funny, yet still stay focused on what had to be done.

CJ retrieved her backpack and moved toward the doorway. Andi followed, and they both paused at the threshold.

"I really appreciate your help." CJ's smile was genuine and sincere, with no trace of the silliness left over from the salute.

"It's my pleasure," Andi said. "I enjoy working with anyone who responds so positively to my suggestions."

"Can I stop by again, if I have any questions?"

"But of course. And, even if the note taking is going smoothly, drop in to give me an update on your progress."

"Thanks. I will." CJ looked at her watch, then back at Andi. "I've got to run to class now. Thanks again." She smiled, and then walked quickly down the hallway.

Andi remained standing in the doorway, eyes trailing CJ until the other woman turned and headed down the staircase and out of Andi's view.

Chapter
Three

ANDI CURSED UNDER her breath as she struggled to balance the overhead projector. *Next time, remember to fill out the AV work order form in advance,* she reprimanded herself. The machine itself hadn't seemed that heavy when she picked it up in the AV office a few moments ago; however, its weight increased significantly with each step across campus. As she got to Alexander Hall, her book bag was slipping off her shoulder, and she didn't have a free hand to open the door. *Shit.* She paused for a moment, deciding how she was going to pull open the door without dropping the projector.

"I'll get the door."

Andi, relieved, rebalanced the projector again as the Good Samaritan bounded up the stairs. Too weighted down to turn her head, Andi didn't recognize her savior until she pulled the door open wide. "CJ! What perfect timing."

"Here, let me take that." CJ took the projector from Andi's hands.

Once relieved of the heavy object, Andi let her hands drop, then sighed.

"You sure you've got that? It's heavy."

"I'm fine. Where do you want it?"

"Right down the hall in 106." Andi walked ahead quickly to unlock the door, which she held open for CJ, then flicked on the lights to illuminate the empty classroom.

"Where?"

"On the desk is fine," Andi said.

CJ placed the projector on the desk carefully, and then turned to Andi.

"Doesn't the school hire football players to do the grunt work around here?" She smiled and shot Andi a teasing look.

"Yes, they would have, if I had filled out the work order in advance. The operative word there being 'if.'" She dumped her book bag on the desk next to the projector. "I was running late, and decided to carry it myself. You came along at just the right time. Thanks." She turned and smiled appreciatively at CJ.

"Timing is everything. Glad to help." CJ sat on top of one of the student desks, swinging her legs, as Andi unpacked her book bag. "You teaching a class now?"

Andi looked at her watch, then back at CJ. "Assisting, actually, in about twenty minutes. I came early to set up the overhead. Do you have a class now?"

"Nope. I was just heading to the library to work on my paper."

"How's that coming?" Andi continued to organize her papers on the desk, looking up frequently as CJ spoke.

"Quite honestly, I haven't done much work on it since we spoke last," CJ said sheepishly. Andi looked up, surprised, as CJ raised her hands in protest. "Don't be mad. We had an away game over the weekend, and this is the first opportunity I've had to get into the library. Some schoolwork I can do easily on the road, but I needed to work on this project here." Andi regarded her with a skeptical smile. "Really, Andi." CJ's tone became serious. "I don't want you to think I'm a dumb jock —"

Andi stopped what she was doing and gazed directly at CJ. "I don't think that for a minute."

"Good, because I hate that stereotype." She looked at Andi and smiled again. "I really do appreciate your help, and I want you to know that I'll work very hard on this, I promise."

"I have complete confidence that you will."

"Complete confidence, huh?" She slid quickly off the desk and stood in front of Andi. "Then I better get to work. I don't want to disappoint you."

Andi opened her mouth to speak, but changed her mind. The timing didn't seem right to remind CJ that her goal was not to avoid disappointing Andi, but simply to learn a new method. CJ stood there, so eager to impress Andi with her hard work and dedication. Andi couldn't help being flattered. She smiled and walked around to the front of the desk, facing CJ.

"Don't ever worry that you'll disappoint me, CJ." She spoke softly and sincerely. "Just be yourself, and there'll be nothing disappointing in that."

"Thanks, Andi." She looked into her blue eyes and smiled. "Oh, can I still stop by your office if I have any questions?"

"I'll be there."

"Great! Have a good class." CJ smiled and waved as she backed out the doorway.

Andi returned the gesture. She was still smiling when the first student came into the classroom ten minutes later.

Chapter
Four

ANDI LOOKED ACROSS her desk at the undergraduate sitting in the chair. "So, I think with a minor adjustment in your thesis statement and additional supporting evidence that directly defends your thesis, your paper will be much improved." He nodded his head, agreeing with her assessment. "Do you have any other questions?" He shook his head, thanked her, and rose to leave. "See you in class next week," Andi added. "Send the next person in on your way out, okay?"

Andi turned in her chair and opened a filing cabinet behind her desk as he exited the office. She sorted through files, scanning for the last student's name, then added some papers to the folder before turning around to face her desk again. There, sitting in the chair right in front of her desk, was CJ. The unexpected guest surprised her. Andi's head snapped up, eyes open wide.

"He..." CJ stammered, pointing out the door, "that guy who just left told me to come in. I didn't mean to startle you."

"Not startled, pleasantly surprised." She smiled warmly at CJ. "I've been meeting with freshmen from English 101 most of the afternoon, so you're a nice change of pace."

"I can come back, if this isn't a good time." She stood and grabbed the handle of her backpack.

"Sit, please." She motioned for CJ, who sat down again. Several days had passed since CJ had helped her out with the overhead projector, and Andi had wondered when she would stop by the office. Seeing CJ's smiling face on the other side of the desk was a nice way to end a long Friday afternoon. "It'll be good to talk with someone who's crossed the two-decade mark in age." She shook her head. "Those freshman keep getting younger and younger." She paused and looked quizzically at CJ. "You have crossed that two-decade mark, haven't you?"

"Yes, I'm twenty-two." CJ sat back and crossed her ankle over her knee, a worn pair of high-tops poking out from beneath her faded jeans. Her arms rested casually on the arms of the wooden chair. "I feel the same way about freshmen sometimes, especially the noisy ones in my dorm. They get a little taste of freedom and they carry on like fools."

"Ah, yes. Life in the dorms. I don't miss that or cafeteria food. Which dorm do you live in?"

"Grayson Hall."

"Hey, that was my dorm, senior year. A single?"

"Ah...yes." CJ paused. "I am single." A hint of crimson blushed her cheeks, yet she kept her eyes locked on Andi.

"No, I, uh, I meant do you have a single room. There's a couple on the third floor reserved for seniors." Andi felt the warm tingle of a blush on her own face as she stumbled to explain.

"No, unfortunately I don't. I'm in a triple; we each have our own space but we share a bathroom. My roommates are other athletes, so we pretty much keep similar schedules. It's not that bad, really, but I'd rather have a single." They smiled, each aware of the flush of pink on the other's cheeks.

Andi, feeling a little self-conscious, picked up a pen from her desk. CJ watched as Andi's long, elegant fingers twirled the pen from pinky to pointer and back again with a fluid, graceful motion. Short, neatly trimmed nails accentuated sensuous, long fingers and hands. To CJ, Andi's hands appeared delicate yet strong and certainly beautiful. Andi then grasped the pen gently between her pointer and thumb, tapping it lightly on the desk, gliding her fingers slowly to the bottom, inverting the pen, and sliding down again. CJ found herself staring almost hypnotically at Andi's hands until her blush reemerged. She pulled her eyes away to meet Andi's eyes once again.

"So, how's your week been?" CJ asked.

"Long, and I'm glad it's over. And you? How'd you do at the library?"

"Great, actually. I put a big dent in the work you gave me."

"Is it working out okay so far?"

CJ paused to think, her brow furrowing as she considered Andi's questions. "It's different, and it took me a while to get used to it, but now it's pretty smooth."

"No problems? Questions?"

"Nope. I just stopped by to touch base, as you asked. And to say hi."

"Well, I'm glad you did." Andi's smile lit up her blue eyes. CJ stood and retrieved her backpack, slipping it over her shoulder. As she moved toward the doorway, Andi followed. Not aware that Andi was so close, CJ turned abruptly and stood face to face with her, CJ's emerald eyes focusing on Andi's. She paused for a few seconds, inches away from Andi's face, before speaking.

"Thanks again, for everything." CJ's smile was genuine and heartfelt. She looked, unblinking, into Andi's piercing blue eyes.

"I'm glad to help you, CJ. You really don't have to thank me," Andi said. She maintained the eye contact, intrigued by the intense look.

"We have a home game next Tuesday. Want to come?"

"I don't think I have any plans."

CJ watched Andi's brow furrow as she paused to consider the offer. She hoped that Andi wouldn't suddenly remember a pressing commitment that would cause her to reject the invitation.

"Sure," Andi said.

"Great! I'll leave tickets for you at the door." She hesitated, not tearing her eyes away from Andi's gaze. "Will you need one or two?"

Andi responded without breaking eye contact. "Just one."

"You've got it." CJ smiled, and stepped back to the open door. "I've got to run to class. Thanks again, and I'll see you on Tuesday." She raised a hand to wave, then disappeared down the hall.

Andi paused in the doorway with her hand on the knob. Slowly she closed the door and leaned against it, facing her desk. She crossed her arms over her chest and smiled. "Well, Emily," she said, addressing the poster, "you were the one who said, 'I dwell in possibility—a fairer house than prose.'"

Chapter
Five

ANDI STOOD IN line at the ticket window, absorbing the sights and sounds of the noisy gymnasium. Students gathered in bunches, wearing t-shirts and sweatshirts emblazoned with their college name and emblem. Parents with young children in tow held bleacher mats, those butt-saving inventions so necessary for a few hours on the hard, wooden seats. Boyfriends and girlfriends, locals from town, the opposing team's fans, all milled around the lobby waiting to get into the gym.

The buzz of chattering and the tension before the competition brought back bittersweet memories for Andi. She glanced off to the left of the lobby at the foggy windows overlooking the pool in the basement below. She could practically smell the chlorine and feel the humid air of that pool area, a place where she'd spent years of her life. The pool bleachers used to be crowded with students, family, and friends, just like the people in the lobby now, all there to cheer on the team, her team. She pictured herself walking across the pool deck, feet slapping against the wet tile. Two steps led up to the starting block. She took deep breaths, as she always did to steady her nerves.

"How many?"

Andi was startled out of her daydream. She turned and faced a guy, most likely a student, behind the ticket office glass.

"How many?" he repeated.

"I'm picking up one that was left for me."

"Name?" He reached over and got a file box, then looked dully back at her.

"Andrea Marlow."

"Marlow, Marlow," he mumbled. "Here it is." He slid the envelope under the glass to Andi. "Next," he called out, looking over her shoulder before she had a chance to move.

Andi stepped out of the way and opened the envelope. The ticket was folded inside a neatly printed note, which read: *Hi,*

Andi, I'm really glad you're here. Can I meet you in the bleachers after the game? CJ

Andi smiled and slipped the note into her pocket. She walked across the lobby, then handed the ticket to the collector at the door. She climbed the bleachers filled with the home team fans and found a seat halfway up at center court.

Both teams were running through their pre-game warm-ups as she settled into the seat. Two at a time, the players bounded toward the basket, one dribbling the ball, then shooting, the other getting the rebound. The two lines of players stretched back to half court. Andi recognized CJ standing toward the end of the far line.

When CJ removed her warm-up suit, Andi was pleasantly surprised and duly impressed to see her well-developed body. Neither the outfit that CJ had worn at the donor reception nor the sweatshirt and jeans she usually wore hinted at a physique that was so taut and well defined. Out on the court, in her sleeveless uniform and shorts, CJ's body was displayed in action. Her heart-shaped calf muscles flexed as she ran up and down the floor. Strong shoulder and arm muscles, curving and defined, were visible to Andi from across the gym as CJ dribbled, passed, or shot the ball. Far from being masculine, CJ's muscle tone was beautiful, and Andi enjoyed watching her in motion.

The officials moved out to center court, blowing their whistles to signal the end of warm-ups. The players, a few still dressed in their blue and white sweats, jogged over to the bench. As CJ headed off the court, she looked up into the stands and spotted Andi. Surrounded by her teammates near the home team benches, the basketball star smiled and waved. Andi waved back.

Then Andi spotted Jen. The assistant coach had been sitting off to the side of the bench. Evidently, CJ's wave caught Jen's attention as she looked over toward the group of players circled together around the head coach. Jen glanced up into the bleachers just in time to notice the wave Andi was returning. Jen glared at Andi and frowned, then turned her attention back to the court. *Shit,* Andi thought, *so much for blending into the crowd.*

The spectators were on their feet, clapping in unison faster and faster as the din rose to the rafters. The players from both teams stood in tight packs, getting last-minute instructions from their coaches. CJ leaned into the middle of her teammates. The officials blew the whistle to bring the players out onto the court. A muffled cheer broke the Bobcat's huddle, then the players took their places around the circle at center court. CJ felt her palms sweating as she paired up with her opponent and waited for the ref to get set for the tip-off. She thrived on competition and expected her team to win this game tonight, but the anxiety she was feeling was new to her, and she realized it was not game-related. She thought of Andi sitting up there in the bleachers watching her and smiled.

Thoughts of the beautiful, blue-eyed woman had crept into her mind quite often since their last meeting in Andi's office a few days earlier. CJ found Andi's intelligence very attractive, a bonus added to the physically appealing package of an engaging face and lithe body. She was mature and confident, which CJ admired. CJ enjoyed being around women who knew what they wanted and were strong enough to make it happen. She sensed that strength in Andi. She glanced up to the bleachers once more, then, hearing the official's voice, returned her attention to the the players on the court. She shifted emotional gears and got focused on the game. The playful smile CJ usually wore was gone, replaced by a determined look that was all business. The moment that ball was tossed into the air, CJ played with a single-minded focus. Whether she was shooting, dribbling, or encouraging her teammates, CJ was resolute. Recognizing her passion, her teammates looked to her as their driving force.

To Andi, it seemed as if CJ was everywhere on the court, filled with boundless energy. She sat at the front of the bleacher whenever CJ got the ball. She joined the fans with rousing cheers when CJ scored. By halftime, CJ and the home team held a ten-point lead. Andi watched the players jog off and disappear into the locker room.

Andi stood to stretch, moving out of the way as others in the stands filed past her toward the lobby and concession stand. As she stood, she noticed Jen leaning over the scorer's table, reviewing the stats book and discussing it with the team manager. Andi quickly sat and shifted over to the left, dodging behind two men standing in the rows in front of hers. She hoped that, if Jen didn't see her again, she'd forget that Andi was there.

The grad assistant thought back to September when she and Jen went on their first and only date. She had tried to explain to Jen that she wasn't looking to get involved, but Jen persisted and took personal insult when Andi wouldn't go out with her again. For two weeks she bombarded Andi with notes and phone calls, then stopped abruptly. A few weeks later, when Andi saw her walking across campus she waved, to show that she wasn't completely cold-hearted, as Jen had accused. Jen saw her, but turned her head away without any acknowledgment. From then on, Andi avoided uncomfortable moments by avoiding Jen.

A few minutes into halftime, the players, clad in sweats, emerged from the locker room and then shot baskets to stay loose before the game resumed. Shortly after, the refs blew their whistles to signal the start of the second half.

The opposing team returned to the floor with a renewed sense of purpose, quickly cutting the home team's lead to two points. The change in the game's tide seemed to ignite CJ's drive to win. With a nearly single-handed effort that was more resuscitating than selfish, she jump-started her team through her passing, scoring, and defensive intensity. Andi looked on admiringly at CJ's passionate efforts. She watched as the star player stepped up her own game while simultaneously inspiring her teammates to give more. Andi could tell that CJ was enough of a team player to know that she couldn't carry her team to victory alone, but she knew just what to do and say to draw the best out of them. With ten minutes still remaining, the home team went on a scoring run that increased their lead to fifteen. By the end of the game, that number had increased to twenty-one, with the home team victorious.

After the game, Andi remained in her seat as the bleachers emptied. Within moments, the loud buzz of the thousand voices in the gym became a faint hum in the lobby. Clean-up crews began their work of sweeping out popcorn and soda cups from between the rows. For a good fifteen minutes, she watched their ant-like work as they wove in and out of the bleachers. Movement across the gym distracted her from the workers. She looked over to see CJ walking across the floor. Andi sat up in her seat and returned her wave.

CJ climbed the steps and sat down, straddling the wooden seat to face her.

"Thanks for waiting. I hope I didn't keep you too long," CJ said. Andi shook her head, returning the smile. CJ's blonde hair was wet and much wavier than usual, with clusters of hairs forming ringlets all around her head. She wore sweats and sneakers and smelled pleasantly of shower gel and conditioner.

"You were great!" Andi said. "No wonder your name's always in the paper." Andi noticed a hint of blush redden CJ's cheeks as she dropped her green eyes to look down for a moment, clearly embarrassed by the compliment.

After a moment, she met Andi's eyes again. "The team was great, that's why we won. I'm just part of the team," CJ said.

"You're too modest."

"It helps me remember that there's always more improvement and more work to be done," CJ responded. "Speaking of which, I've been working on those note cards. I followed your directions exactly." She sat up straight and saluted Andi.

"First you dazzle me with your prowess on the court, now you want to further impress me with your note-taking skills?" Andi said, and then paused. "You amaze me." She watched as CJ averted her eyes and blushed deeply at the comment.

"To amaze is a good thing, although I'm really not deserving of that compliment, either." Her green eyes sparkled as she smiled. "I am anxious to get your feedback, though, just to make sure I'm doing the right thing. Then, I need to know what to do next."

"I'm sure what you're doing is fine. Once you finish notes on all your sources, then you'll be ready for the next step."

"I hope to finish up with note-taking by Thursday."

"Good." Andi was discovering that CJ's determination to succeed was not limited to the basketball court. She admired CJ's ambition to do well and was equally flattered by CJ's desire to follow through with exactly what Andi told her to do. She wished that the students in her classes listened so attentively. "Let's meet again on Friday, then. Think you'll be ready?"

"Definitely."

CJ's confidence made Andi smile. "Okay. We'll meet then." She stopped a moment to think. "My office is too small to spread out and work." She paused. "Why don't we meet at my place? It's much less cramped than my office, and we can work on the dining room table. How's that sound?"

"Perfect." CJ grinned broadly, accentuating her dimples. "Where's your place?"

"On the other side of campus. I live on the second floor, above the administrative offices in Sanford Hall. Know where that is?" CJ nodded. "Ring the second floor bell on the front porch, and I'll come down to let you in." She stood slowly, stretching a bit. "I better get back," Andi sighed. "I've got a pile of papers to correct. You're probably tired after your game."

CJ stood, still facing Andi. "I'm actually pretty up now. I always feel pumped after a good game." She moved out into the aisle and waited for Andi. Together they walked down the stairs, footsteps echoing in the empty gym. Few people were left in the lobby. One or two students lingered by the doorway while the people at the concession stand wiped the counters and cleaned up for the night.

CJ stopped when they got to the front doors, waiting while Andi zipped her jacket. The "click, click, click" of heels on the floor drew their attention across the lobby. Jen had emerged from the coaches' office and was making a beeline for the exit on the other side of the lobby. CJ waved, but Jen, walking quickly, continued to look forward, then disappeared out the doors. CJ shrugged. "She's usually happy after we win." The door banged closed and they both turned back to face each other.

"Well..." Andi stalled, hands stuffed into her jacket pockets.

"Thanks so much for coming." As she spoke, CJ reached out and touched Andi, resting a hand for just a moment on her forearm. CJ's lively green eyes shone in the dimming light of the lobby. Andi returned her smile, and then the basketball star removed her hand. She opened the door and held it as the grad assistant passed through.

"Until soon," CJ said. She locked her emerald eyes on the other woman's.

"Until Friday," Andi said.

Chapter
Six

ANDI SPENT MUCH of Friday afternoon straightening up her place. She never let it get dirty, but frequently it was cluttered with textbooks and notes, students' papers and her own schoolwork, as well as the occasional magazine or newspaper that she left out to finish later. She even dusted the bookshelves, a chore she hated, because she thought CJ might browse the books here as she had in Andi's office. She debated about removing her collection of lesbian books by Katherine V. Forrest, Radclyffe, Lori L. Lake, and the rest of the "writin' gals," as she called them. *Don't bother*, she told herself. *You know she knows, even if it's yet unspoken.*

She dusted off a picture of Martha and her partner, Karen, embracing on the porch of Martha's family cabin by the lake. The three of them had spent a weekend there in August, before school started up again, and had a great time. *I owe Martha a phone call.* She hadn't seen her old friend since the night of the donor reception, the night she met CJ.

She smiled, envisioning CJ's emerald eyes, so expressive when she spoke. *Admit it. You've been looking forward to seeing her again. You don't dust for just anyone.* She chuckled. *It's not just her eyes, or that dimple that deepens when she laughs — although there's nothing wrong with any of that, that's for sure.* She paused and looked through the window toward the lights across campus. *It's her openness and sincerity that's so inviting, and unfortunately so rare in a world where we're afraid to trust.* She sighed and shook her head slowly. *Don't get caught up in this. Be careful, Andi.* She tossed the dust rag into the hamper, washed her hands, and settled onto the sofa to catch the end of the TV news while she waited.

The doorbell rang promptly at 6:00. Andi bounded off the sofa, then headed down the stairs to unlock the door. Standing out on the porch was CJ, jacket unzipped, dressed in jeans and a Cape Cod sweatshirt, backpack slung over her shoulder. She was smiling, hands behind her back.

"Come on in." She held the door open as CJ brushed against her in the narrow door frame. "Up the stairs," she indicated, directing CJ to her apartment. CJ stealthily moved what she was carrying behind her back to the front and marched up the steps. She waited on the landing for Andi to open the door. As they moved through the doorway, CJ presented Andi with the package she was hiding.

"For you," CJ beamed. She held out a small brown bag.

"What's this?" She was flattered by the gift.

"Close your eyes, open the bag, and smell," CJ said.

Andi looked at her skeptically, but did as she was told. She breathed deeply into the bag then moved her face away slowly, smiling.

"Peanut butter cookies! You really do amaze me." She reached inside the bag and pulled one out. Glancing at it, then at CJ, she took a bite. "Mmmm. These are great! How'd you make them?"

"There's a small kitchen in the dorm," CJ said. "I love to cook and bake. It's a hobby, sort of. It relaxes me."

"You're very thoughtful." She paused and looked at CJ. "Look at me, hogging them all to myself. Want one?" She extended the bag.

"They're all yours. Enjoy."

"Let me take your coat," Andi said. She finished the remainder of the cookie as CJ removed her jacket.

While Andi put the coat away, CJ glanced around the room.

"This is a *great* place. How'd you luck out and get an entire second floor of this house? It's warm—and so comfortable."

"Come on. I'll give you the nickel tour. This is the living room." Andi waved her hand in front of her. A Berber rug covered the wood floor in the center of living area near the sofa, but the remainder of the floor was bare oak. The wall closest to the door held floor-to-ceiling bookcases, filled with books, pictures in frames, candles, and vases. Two large windows faced the front of the house, overlooking the distant lights of the campus. CJ turned to face a brick fireplace on the wall opposite the bookcases. Instead of a fire, five candles were burning in the hearth. "Unfortunately, the flue is sealed up," Andi explained, noticing CJ looking at the fireplace.

"Your bike?" CJ asked. She pointed to a mountain bike suspended by a hook from the ceiling in the corner of the room. Behind it, skis and a large backpack leaned against the wall.

"My toys," Andi said. "Old houses definitely do not have enough storage space." CJ smiled and nodded, admiring the charming place. "Here's the kitchen," Andi continued. She set the brown paper cookie bag on the counter. "It's small, but it'll do. Over this way is the bathroom." She flicked the light on, then off. "This is my bedroom." With her hand, she motioned for CJ to enter. The small room, neat and orderly, had very little furniture. A double bed with a flannel comforter was set up on the far wall, and next to it was a mirrored dresser. Ribboned medals hung around the corner of the mirror.

"Lots of gold here," CJ observed. She touched one of the medals and turned to look at Andi. "Still swim?" Andi dug her hands deeper into the pockets of her jeans and shook her head, indicating no. The basketball star thought she noticed a tinge of sadness color her azure eyes, but in the next instant it was gone. Andi paused for a moment, then turned toward the bedroom door. CJ followed her out into the living room. *This is a place I'd love to come home to*, CJ thought.

"That's it," Andi said. "It's not real big, but it's home." She stood facing CJ, hands still in her pockets. A large burgundy corduroy shirt, untucked and half unbuttoned, covered a white t-shirt. She wore slippers on her feet.

"I love it!" CJ exclaimed. Her green eyes danced as she spoke enthusiastically. "It's like your office, only better. It's so... you. It's great."

"Thanks," Andi said. "Can I get you a drink?"

"Seltzer would be great."

"In a glass, or should I pour it directly from the bottle onto your sweatshirt?"

CJ laughed out loud, a hearty belly laugh so spontaneous that it was contagious. Andi laughed, too.

"I'll take it in a glass," she said.

"Coming right up. Make yourself at home." Andi walked into the kitchen. CJ moved toward the bookcase and browsed in front of the titles and pictures. She was right in front of Martha and Karen's photo when Andi returned from the kitchen with her drink.

"I thought you had a lot of books at your office," she noted, taking the drink from Andi. "You have twice as many here."

"It's great until you have to move them," the grad assistant said. "So, how's your project going?"

"Notes are done." She walked over and picked up her backpack.

"Let's spread out on the table. The next step is to organize the cards." She took the thick stack of 3-by-5 cards that CJ had removed from her backpack and explained how to sort them. "Here," Andi said. "I'll take a few to help get you started. We'll work together." She handed the rest of the cards back to CJ.

"So we're mixing the ingredients, right?" The younger athlete grinned.

"Exactly. You obviously listen very closely."

"You *did* ask me to trust you, remember?" She looked at Andi and smirked. It was true that she trusted Andi, which was unusual at such an early stage of getting to know another person. CJ trusted her own instinct, though, and that led her to trust Andi.

The two women began sorting, leaning over the table and placing their cards in piles. They worked silently, reading the cards and distributing them. Now and then, CJ held up a card for Andi to read. After a quick glance, Andi pointed to a pile while CJ smiled and nodded, indicating that she understood. They worked closely, often touching as one leaned across the other to place a card. After nearly a half-hour of sorting, CJ reached past Andi, her hip pressing against Andi's side. After a moment of contact, she followed it up with a playful bump that shifted Andi off balance. CJ laughed as Andi looked at her, surprised.

"What was that for?" Andi said, grinning.

"For fun," CJ said. "All work and no play is no fun. There's nothing wrong with a little fun, is there?"

"Nope." Andi smiled, then looked at her watch. "Fun's over. Back to work." She feigned a serious look and resumed her pile sorting while CJ followed suit. A moment later, Andi leaned her hip over and bumped the younger woman off balance. She laughed out loud at CJ, whose surprised look turned into laughter, too. An easy, comfortable energy flowed between them.

Once the piles were completed, Andi explained how to sort the piles, subdividing as necessary. "Each pile represents information in one paragraph. So, you've got to sort the cards within each pile, and then you have to order the piles. Understand?"

"Completely." The process, initially confusing and completely new to her, was becoming clear. It was as if clouds around her head suddenly blew away, and she could see the end of the road in the distance. She finished her sorting while Andi, her personal guide, looked on, overseeing her work. Finally, the sorting was complete.

"I'm starving," CJ said. She glanced at her watch. "Geez! We've been at this for two hours."

"Time flies..." Andi said. "How about a pizza?"

"My treat, I insist. It's the least I can do to thank you for giving up your Friday night to help me."

"Giovanni's delivers on campus. I'll call." Andi stepped into the kitchen to find the phone number, stuck to her fridge with a magnet, then turned back toward the living room, pausing in the doorway. With both palms flat on the table, CJ was leaning over her piles, looking at the last of the cards. Andi stared at her, remembering how supple and defined CJ's body had been as she bounded up and down the court. She envisioned CJ's arm muscles under the sweatshirt, flexed and taut as she leaned her weight forward on her hands. Her jeans hung loosely over her rounded glutes. *She's a student, Andi. Don't look at her that way.* Just then, CJ turned and caught her staring. A flush of red colored Andi's cheeks. CJ looked at her and grinned.

Andi stammered, "I...was wondering if you wanted anything on your pizza?"

"Plain is fine," CJ responded. She smiled, and then finished picking up her note cards. Andi stepped back into the kitchen to call.

Once the pizza was ordered and Andi had taken a couple moments to compose herself, she meandered into the living room. "How about some music, now that the serious concentrating is over?" Andi asked.

"Sure," CJ said. She was sitting on the sofa, sneakers off, with her feet crossed in her lap. With the business of the paper done for the evening, she felt completely relaxed. She and Andi connected easily on the teacher to student level, but CJ was eager to establish a connection on another, more equal plane.

"Any preference?"

"But of course."

"Like what?"

CJ opened her mouth to speak, then changed her mind. She paused. "Never mind. Whatever you pick is fine."

Andi replayed the innuendo in her head while she searched the CD titles. *Don't go there now,* she warned herself. *Just let it drop.* She put in a disk and returned to the sofa. She sat sideways on the cushion, only a few feet from CJ, with her back leaning against the heavily padded arm. The song, "Fugitive," rose through the speakers in the background.

"I recognize this," CJ said.

"Indigo Girls, *Swamp Ophelia.* Are you a fan?"

"Yes. I have a few of their CDs. You a fan?"

"A big one, actually. I've got all their albums as well as a pretty good bootleg collection."

"Why so enthusiastic?" CJ asked.

"They sing with passion and they write lyrics that speak to my heart. They don't mold their image to fit anyone's expectations, and on top of that, they support a number of important causes. And if that's not reason enough, they both studied English in college, too!" The doorbell rang. "Probably the pizza guy."

"I'll get it." CJ leaped off the sofa before Andi could protest.

"I'll refill your seltzer," Andi offered. She went into the kitchen, returning with the drink, paper plates, and napkins just as CJ walked back into the apartment. "Lay the box on these magazines," she directed. The flaxen-haired woman placed it on the coffee table near the sofa. They resumed their previous seats, eating from plates balanced in their laps.

"So, CJ, how'd you end up coming to school here?" Andi asked.

CJ finished chewing her pizza before responding. "The basketball coach recruited me. She offered me a good package so I came to look at the school."

Andi nodded. "Scholarship money is a dangling carrot." She reflected on her own college athletic days, and continued to eat as CJ talked.

"You said it. I'm the youngest of four, so my parents couldn't afford to send me any place where the tuition was high. In fact, they wanted me to stay more local so I could live at home and commute to school." CJ shook her head slowly, then silently stared out the window. Andi noticed a subtle change in CJ's body language, a slouching in her shoulders and sadness in her eyes. CJ continued. "But, I really needed to get out on my own and live my own life, so I didn't really consider that an option, much to my parents' disappointment." Her eyes returned to Andi's again. A half smile tugged at the corner of her mouth as she tried to shake off the memory. "Once I got here, I liked what I saw, so I signed."

"And the rest is history, including your major." Andi grinned.

CJ rolled her eyes and smiled. "I thought English majors were too creative to be corny."

"Sorry. I'll try to be better." She reached over to open the pizza box, then motioned for CJ's plate.

"Sure," CJ said.

Andi slid another slice onto her plate, then took a piece for herself. "And what about after graduation? It's right around the corner." Although Andi had known CJ for only two weeks, she almost felt sad at the prospect of her graduating and leaving. In such a short time she had come to enjoy her cheerful smile and optimistic attitude. *You're also flattered by her attention, admit it.*

"Grad school, I hope. I'd like to teach or coach at the college level."

"Any prospects?"

CJ rolled her eyebrows up and grinned at Andi. "What kind of prospects?" she asked playfully.

Another double entendre. Just ignore it. "Where have you applied?"

"A school near my parents, about three hours from here, two schools near here, and another on the West Coast, but that's kind of a last resort."

"What about here?"

"I spoke to my advisor last week about that. It may be another option."

Andi felt almost relieved.

"So how come I've done all the talking?" CJ asked. "How about you? How'd you end up here?"

"By the time I was a senior here, I'd decided I wanted to be a college professor. I looked around at the teachers I had here, and their jobs looked pretty appealing to me. Besides, I liked the idea of working in an academically stimulating environment all the time. It's fun to learn new things and to share that with students."

"Here, here!" toasted CJ. She raised her glass and clinked it against Andi's. "I think you're a great teacher."

"You didn't think I was so swell when I told you to redo all your notes," Andi teased. She balled up a napkin and tossed it at CJ.

"I've seen the light. You've saved me from the eternal damnation of research papers without focus, of unblended information and muddled facts. You, Andi, have made me a believer." She placed her hand over her heart and bowed her head in mock reverence.

"You should have been a drama major." This time CJ threw her napkin at Andi. They both laughed playfully, followed by a few moments of silence. Strains of "Power of Two" drifted from the speakers.

"This is such a great song," CJ said.

"It's actually one of my favorites."

"It's exactly how a relationship should be when two people love each other."

"Unfortunately, life and love are never that simple," Andi said.

"I believe that they can be. Don't Amy and Emily sing about the hardest things to learn being the least complicated."

"Oh, brother! Now who's being corny?"

"I thought you'd appreciate the song reference, being that you're a big fan. Hey, how about popping in one of those bootlegs?" CJ asked. "I'd like to hear one."

"Sure," Andi said. "I've got a couple of really good concerts." She got up and chose a disk from her collection, then put in the CD. She returned to the sofa just as the music rose from the speakers.

All the while they talked — about life, school, family, future plans — a familiarity developed between them. It was a comfortable and surprisingly safe feeling of talking and being open with another person. They discovered that they had many similar interests, which made clear why they enjoyed each other's company. Andi hadn't felt this relaxed in a long time. CJ, with her legs stretched out across the sofa and nearly touching Andi, also seemed to feel completely at ease.

CJ stretched when the music from the last track ended. She glanced at her watch. "God, Andi! You'll never believe what time it is."

"Tell me," she said. She reached out her arms in a big cat-stretch.

"It's nearly tomorrow."

"No way!"

"Way."

"See, time does fly."

"I'm sorry I kept you up so late."

"Don't worry about me. Tomorrow's Saturday and I can sleep in. How about you?" Andi asked

"Early practice," CJ said.

"Then I'm the one who should apologize for keeping you up so late."

"Not at all. I had a great time." She swung her legs off the sofa then stood. Andi got up as well, facing her. "So, got any big plans for the rest of the weekend?" CJ asked.

"Let's see...food shopping, two loads of laundry, a few chapters of reading, and a workout. That's the extent of my exciting life. And you?"

"Aside from practice and study session, I have plenty of schoolwork, including this paper."

"Here," offered Andi. She picked up a note card from the coffee table and wrote something on it before handing it to CJ. "Take my home number, in case you have any questions. I'll be around most of the weekend." Andi looked at her and smiled warmly. They walked toward the door. "I'll go get your coat."

Andi walked down to the porch door with CJ. "Thanks again for those great cookies." She looked at CJ, standing so close, her green eyes shadowed by the dim porch light.

"It was my pleasure." She focused on Andi's blue eyes as

she spoke. "Thank you for all your help with this project." In a few hours her alarm would be ringing her off to practice, but she was completely wide-awake now. "I'll call you."

"Ring once tonight, so I know that you were okay getting back to your dorm."

"Sure." She looked at her watch then back at Andi. "I can jog that half mile in under five minutes."

"I'll be waiting."

CJ smiled and paused, looking directly at Andi's eyes. *I could get lost swimming in those pools of blue.* "Until soon," she said.

"Yes, until soon," Andi said.

Andi held the door open and CJ brushed by her. She closed the door as CJ reached the bottom step on the porch. Quickly she bounded up the steps to her apartment and then over to the windows just as CJ jogged across the green and out of view. She leaned her palms on the window ledge and continued to look through the glass until her breath fogged the pane. Motionless, she remained there until the phone rang once. Then she picked up her journal and began to write.

When I opened the door this evening and she was standing there with that mischievous grin on her face and those dancing green eyes, I'll admit that my heart fluttered a bit. And then she whipped out this bag for me and told me to close my eyes. I can't even remember the last time someone brought me a surprise, but to present it to me with my eyes closed... Well, shutting down that one sense seemed to heighten my other senses, that's for sure. How could I not like someone who makes me homemade peanut butter cookies? Her warmth and sincerity are infectious, and I find myself smiling when I'm around her, or even when I think of her — which is becoming more frequent...

Chapter
Seven

CJ NEVER MINDED attending the mandatory athlete study sessions her coach required of all the basketball players. She herself was disciplined enough to do her schoolwork without supervision, but she knew many other athletes who were not. In any team sport, it was important for all the players to do well not only on the playing field but in the classroom, too, since poor grades resulted in academic probation and playing restrictions.

Male and female athletes filled the long tables in the study lounge. Textbooks and notebooks were spread over the workspace as the athletes busied themselves with their studies. Several students worked in small groups, discussing their assignments in hushed whispers. Two graduate assistants, employed by the school to supervise the sessions and to provide help for students, sat at desks in opposite corners of the room.

CJ sat at the far end of one of the long tables. To her right was Joanne, a senior on the lacrosse squad. She had met Joanne during freshmen orientation, and they became fast friends and frequent off-season workout partners. CJ knew that sitting near her would probably result in more chatting than studying, but she was eager for some information and knew Joanne might prove helpful. She looked up from her book and spoke. "Is there a group going out tonight?"

Joanne paused from her writing and looked at CJ. "Probably. It's Saturday, so I would guess."

"Where?"

"The usual, Oasis, I think. Kim said she heard they have a girl band playing this weekend."

"Kim?"

"You know, she's a junior on the lacrosse team, plays middie. Not real tall, dark hair..." CJ nodded, recognizing the description. "Well, she's sweet on Sarah, who hangs out with the softball gang who goes to Oasis. She wanted some of the lacrosse gals to go, too, so she could see Sarah there. I haven't talked to her since Wednesday, though, so I'm not sure what's up."

"You going?"

"If everybody else is. Should be a fun time if the band is playing. Why? Need a ride?"

"Maybe. I haven't made plans yet." CJ smiled at Joanne. "So, Jo, since you know everybody who's anybody on campus..."

Joanne grinned broadly at the compliment. She put her pen down and placed her elbows on the table, chin in palms. "At your service."

"Do you know many of the grad assistants on campus?"

"Plenty! Obviously, I know Sue from the lacrosse team, Courtney with the softball team, and a bunch from other teams who go out with us sometimes." Joanne leaned closer to CJ and whispered. "You talking about someone in particular?" She grinned mischievously.

"Maybe, but keep this to yourself." CJ spoke quietly yet firmly, and pointed a finger at her friend. Joanne put her finger to her lips then crossed her heart. She leaned in closer as CJ spoke. "I've seen this woman around campus. I found out that her name's Andi, and she's a grad assistant in the English department, used to be a swimmer here a few years ago. Tall, shoulder-length dark hair, attractive—"

Joanne interrupted. "Uh huh! Sounds interesting."

"Yeah, it kind of is. Does she sound familiar?"

"Not really. Jen might know her. Did you ask?"

"Jen's been a real bitch lately. I don't want to ask her, nor do I want you to ask her, okay?"

"Fine. I'll check with my sources."

"Only if you're not obvious about it. I don't want it to get back to Andi or anyone else."

"What! You can't trust me?" Joanne asked, faking insult.

"Of course I can. You're the best at this kind of thing, which is why I'm asking you." She winked at Joanne and smiled.

"So what do you want to know?"

"Find out if she's family, and if she's with anybody. Think you can do that subtly?"

"Piece of cake. There'll be plenty of people out tonight who I can chat with, and, after a couple beers, they'll sing like canaries and then won't remember we even had the conversation. Consider it done." She smiled and ceremoniously brushed her palms together three times.

"Great. Thanks, Jo." She looked at her watch. "My time here is up. Call me if you go out tonight. You talked me in to going." She packed up her books and stood quietly.

"See you later." Joanne continued her writing as CJ left the room.

ANDI SLEPT UNTIL nearly 9:00 on Saturday morning. Her journaling had kept her up long past the time when CJ left; although she was tired, she had needed to write. Sorting out her thoughts and feelings on paper had become therapeutic for her. When she first entered college, she made time to write several days a week. It got her through homesickness, her grandmother's stroke, swimming injuries, and a painful break-up. She wrote about everyday problems, simple pleasures, unusual places, and interesting people. Last night she wrote about CJ.

She was out the door by late morning to start her errands. At the Laundromat, she read through three chapters in her literature book as she waited for her clothes to wash and dry. The constant whirring and humming of the machines drowned out the noise of the people coming and going, making it surprisingly easy for her to concentrate. After a stop at the post office, then the bank, she pulled into the parking lot of the grocery store.

The store was typically bustling for a Saturday afternoon, yet Andi was uncharacteristically patient among the crowded aisles. Thoughts of CJ's laughter made her smile, helping her to ignore both the child screaming at the end of the row and the woman who had clipped her heels with her cart twice already. She walked down the produce aisle grinning, then stopped to pick out a cantaloupe, which was on sale.

"Hands off my melons, toots!"

She popped out of her daydream and turned toward Martha's familiar voice. Andi laughed, then embraced her in a big hug.

"I've been thinking about you," Andi said, smiling.

"Good things, I hope."

"Always. How's Karen?"

"Too busy at work, but other than that, fine. I haven't seen you since the reception. How've you been?"

Remembering the reception evoked images of CJ, and a warm blush suffused her face. "Pretty good," Andi said, grinning.

"What's with that goofy grin?"

"Nothing. I'm just happy."

"Come on, Andi. Spill it."

"There's nothing to spill. Can't a gal be happy?"

"Of course, but can't a friend know the source of that gal's happiness? Come on. I haven't seen you smile dreamily like that since..."

Martha stopped short of saying the name, but they both

knew she was talking about Liz. The happy expression on Andi's face quickly faded.

Martha, obviously regretting her words, reached out and touched Andi's arm. "I didn't..."

"You didn't have to." Andi frowned. "We both know who you meant."

"I'm sorry, Andi. It was so long ago, and you never really mention it anymore. I didn't think you thought about it."

"I didn't, until you mentioned it."

"Forget it, then. Tell me about what or who was making you smile. Please?"

"Another time, maybe. I've got to get back."

"I'm sorry, Andi. I didn't mean to make you upset."

"I know, Martha. I'm just being overly sensitive, I guess."

"How about coming over for dinner next week? We've missed you."

"Sure, that would be great." She forced a smile.

"Call, okay? Even if you just want to talk."

Andi nodded.

ANDI CLENCHED THE steering wheel until her hands grew cramped. Martha's mention of Liz brought back to her heart all the painful memories with a full-force crash. Her initial annoyance at Martha faded, but she grew even more annoyed at herself. *Liz hurt me once, and I couldn't control that, but if I continue to let it hurt me, then it's my own damn fault.* Nearly three and a half years had passed since their painful break-up but obviously her heart wasn't completely healed. As she drove, hypnotized by the lines on the road, she was unable to prevent her thoughts from going back to Liz, and for the hundredth time she relived those horrible weeks.

For so long up to that point, her life seemed complete and happy in every way. She was pulling mostly A's in her schoolwork, proving to her mother and herself that academics were top priority in spite of the heavy demands placed on her as a scholarship athlete. She was voted captain of the swim team by her peers. During her junior year, she broke all the school records in her dominant stroke, the butterfly. She was later named All American for an unprecedented second year in a row, the first time that ever happened to any swimmer, male or female, at her school. She was also in love, for the first time in her life.

She and Liz had been involved for nearly a year and a half. They met during the second semester of her freshman year and quickly became friends. Liz, a junior, knew all the ins and outs of college life, like how to sneak back into the cafeteria without using a meal card, how to duck out of the athletes' dorm during pre-game curfews, and how to get into the pool for a midnight skinny dip. She also knew the most secluded spots in the library, the lookout spot near the lake, and a dozen other out-of-the way places where she took Andi. There they talked, laughed, teased, and had many heart-to-heart discussions about feelings, and about love.

It was in one of those spots, about three months after they met, that Liz first kissed her. It was Andi's first kiss ever by another woman and the first time she felt completely alive in her life. That feeling intensified a few weeks later when she spent the night with Liz in her dorm.

"I'm so nervous," she told Liz. "I've never been with a woman before."

Liz kissed her. "You'll be fine. Besides, practice makes perfect," she added, grinning.

Whenever Liz's roommate was away for the weekend, Andi stayed with her new lover and quickly became comfortable with both of their bodies.

From then on, her life revolved around three things: school work, swimming, and Liz, but not always in that order. Never before had she been so happy. For a year an a half they hung out together, went to movies, worked out, and planned for the day when Andi, too, would graduate and be able to move into the apartment with Liz. Then the accident occurred.

Andi had just finished an especially difficult pool practice and was heading into the locker room. She had walked across that deck hundreds of times, but this time she slipped on the wet tiles. She still remembered the feeling of vertigo, of being out of control for an instant, as the ground rose up toward her startled face. Turning slightly, she tried to catch herself, but as her palms hit, they slid out in front of her and she landed flat out on the deck, the air whooshing out of her painfully.

At the moment of impact, she screamed so loudly and was in such pain that she felt outside of her body, as if it was someone else lying there on the deck and she was hovering somewhere above, simply screaming. She moved her left arm in an attempt to get up, but the least movement in her body brought excruciating pain through her right shoulder.

Her coach and the trainer came running across the deck, directing her to remain still. She whimpered softly, wracked with pain and fear. The whole episode, only a few seconds in duration, moved in slow motion. Her coach's words were slow and muffled, the trainer's directions foggy in her head. When they stood her up, another cry, like that of a wounded animal, escaped her lips. The slow motion moved back into real time when the trainer popped her shoulder back in place with one jerky motion. She let out a third cry right before she blacked out, collapsing like dead weight into the trainer's arms.

A trip to the orthopedist revealed that her worst fears were true. The difficult workout prior to the fall had left her muscles tight and fatigued; consequently, instead of stretching as she fell, they tore. Three of her four rotator cuff muscles ripped completely away from the bone, leaving her arm dangling limply in a sling. The pain was excruciating.

"I'm afraid I have some bad news," the doctor said. Surgery was scheduled three days later.

Andi was devastated by the diagnosis and heartbroken by the prognosis. The doctors told her their goal was to restore functionality to her shoulder so she could return to normal activities. Swimming competitively wasn't on the list. Her coach and her mother were especially supportive to her, but she turned to Liz during this time of crisis. She believed Liz would be there for her, be her comfort and support, and help her deal with not only the painful surgery and rehab, but also the realization that her athletic career was over. For a while, Liz did fill that role, but then things changed.

Physical therapy sessions three times a week and severe limitations on her activities followed the difficult surgery. For the first few weeks, Liz seemed happy to give up her free time to hang out with Andi. They rented movies, ate Ben & Jerry's pints, and talked; however, after a few weeks Liz acted restless and distracted whenever she was near Andi. She asked, "When will you be able to do things again?" Her voice was tinted with impatience.

"Soon, I hope," Andi said. "I'm sorry to be such an anchor. If you want to go out dancing with the girls sometime, that would be okay with me. I'll understand."

Andi did understand why Liz might want to go out and have the kind of fun they used to have, but she was a bit hurt the following Friday night when Liz took her up on the offer and chose to go out to the local bar with some friends instead of hanging out with her. The next week, Andi asked if she could go, too, so they went together, but the jostling and crowded bar made Andi uncomfortable. She asked to leave the smoky hangout. Liz clearly acted inconvenienced, and grumpily took her home. She didn't invite Andi to go dancing again.

Over the next few weeks, Liz frequently made other plans

and spent less time with Andi. The injured swimmer rationalized and made excuses that Liz shouldn't limit her life just because she had to, but she was deeply saddened by Liz's choices. Then a whole week went by without a visit from her lover. Andi phoned and left several messages asking her to call or stop by. Finally, when Liz did, she came by Andi's room, clearly uncomfortable and distracted, and told her that she didn't think things between them were working anymore. Andi was devastated. She reminded Liz of the plans they made for their future together, but Liz said coldly that things changed and she didn't feel the same.

"Don't you love me anymore?" Andi pleaded.

"Not in the same way," Liz confessed. "I'm sorry. I never meant to hurt you."

Andi began to weep, and Liz made a feeble attempt to put her arm around her shoulder, then hesitated when she remembered Andi's injury. The gesture turned into a few pats on the back, which were worse comfort than no contact at all.

"I'll call you," Liz said as she walked to the door. "In time, you'll see that this is the right thing to do."

All this time, and Andi still wasn't sure if it had been the right thing to do. What she was sure about was that it still hurt, still bewildered her. She didn't like to think about it, but Martha's pointed reference had taken her into the past more thoroughly than ever before. Andi didn't know how long she sat in the car outside her apartment after having driven home, lost in that remembrance. She took a deep breath and slowly exhaled. *I'm better off without her, if that's how she treated my heart,* she reminded herself for the hundredth time. *It's true, I need to be with someone who loves me for who I am, unconditionally, and who will accept my love in return.* She rolled her eyes. *I'm pathetic. I could win first prize in the Corny Lyrics Contest.* She slowly shook her head. *I've got to stop listening to love songs and become a character in one again.*

She carried her groceries up to her apartment and set them on the counter. From across the room she could see her message machine blinking. She walked across the room and hit the play button and was greeted by Martha's friendly voice.

"Hey, girlfriend! Karen's decided to cook a feast on Wednesday, and we'd love to have you join us for dinner. In fact, we won't take no for an answer. How's 6:00 sound to you? Bring your appetite and a bottle of wine. Call us when you get this message, okay?"

Martha's cheerful voice helped to squeeze out those memories from Andi's mind, and she smiled. She unpacked the rest of the groceries before sitting down on the sofa and calling her friends back.

Chapter
Eight

ANDI DROVE THE three miles from campus to Martha and Karen's house with a growling stomach. She had worked through lunch to free up time for tonight's dinner, which she had been looking forward to all week. Karen was a wonderful cook and, based on past experience, their promise of a feast would indeed be accurate. She pulled into their driveway at 6:05 then walked to their front door with wine bottle in hand. She rang the bell and was greeted by Martha.

"Welcome!" Martha said. Andi stepped into the foyer and was enfolded in one of Martha's bear hugs. "We're so glad you came." Andi handed her the bottle. "Thanks. Let me take your coat." Andi had known Martha since their college days, when Martha had been the manager of the swim team. Although Andi was somewhat reserved back then compared to Martha's outgoing personality, she had taken a liking to the outspoken Martha, who was always the first to start cheering at meets. Even though they were the same age, Martha, who to Andi seemed so settled in life, was like a big sister figure, protective and always looking out for her. Andi had a great fondness for Martha. She smiled warmly at her friend.

"Hi, Andi!" called a voice from the kitchen. Andi could see Karen wearing a cook's apron and standing in front of the stove . "I'm in here," she added.

"Smells wonderful!" Andi enthused as she made her way into the kitchen. Pungent and spicy aromas greeted her nose as she stepped into the room. Karen turned from the stove to greet her guest. Although she was nearly six inches shorter than Andi, she was stocky and strong. The grad assistant knew that beneath her stalwart exterior was a soft heart. Karen gave her friend a hug that nearly crushed her. "I've missed you," Karen proclaimed. Andi had met Karen through Martha, and had quickly grown to enjoy her friendship.

"Me, too," Andi said honestly. "Thanks so much for inviting

me tonight." Unable to resist the temptation, Andi turned toward the stove and lifted the lid on one of the big pots. With the steam rose a wonderful aroma, which Andi breathed in deeply. "Ummmm," she hummed happily.

"Homemade chili, with corn bread and salad," beamed Karen. "And a surprise for dessert."

"As much as I hate to see Karen stressed at work," noted Martha, "we all benefit from her cooking to blow off steam." She stood next to Karen and wrapped one arm around her waist, then planted a big kiss on her cheek. Andi knew that Karen's job as a lawyer in juvenile court was as difficult as it was stressful. In this, her second year on the job right out of law school, Karen was still optimistic about helping those kids. Andi admired her spirit and big heart.

"You gals are lucky I don't blow off steam by hightailing it to Las Vegas to gamble away my stress," Karen teased. She tried to keep a straight face, but laughed out loud at herself. Her smooth, round face was glowing pink from the stove's heat.

"You're not the gambling type," scoffed Andi. She smiled at Karen.

"I took a chance with Martha, didn't I?" Karen joked. She grinned and winked at Martha, whose arm remained around her waist.

"And look at what a great payoff you've gotten for the past four years," Martha said. The three friends laughed, the hearty and comfortable laughter shared with longtime friends.

"How about some wine?" Martha asked. She removed her arm from Karen and motioned toward Andi.

"I'll wait 'til dinner. I've got an empty stomach now and I'll be a mess after half a glass."

"Well, we're ready to eat now," offered Karen. "Martha, why don't you pour the wine, then you gals can have a seat while I bring the food out."

"What can I do?" Andi asked.

"Here." Karen handed her a large salad bowl and a bottle of dressing. "Pour some on, then mix the salad for me, will you? Salad bowls are on the table. Fill them up when you're finished mixing."

As Andi worked on the salad, Martha poured wine, and Karen brought out the rest of the food. Sounds of upbeat jazz music drifted into the dining room from the stereo in the living room. Several candles were clustered in the center of the table, around which the chili, cornbread, and salad were placed. Andi settled into a seat and breathed in deeply. She was famished and could hardly resist diving in. She waited while Martha and

Karen took their seats.

"Before we begin, a toast," Martha said. She raised her glass and looked first at Karen and then at Andi. They, too, raised their glasses, waiting for her to speak. "Here's to wonderful friends, a gift to the heart."

"Here, here!" Karen cheered. The three clinked glasses. "Now dig in!"

Bowls were passed and plates were filled. Lively conversation filled the room as they each discussed their jobs and told stories about events or people at work. Martha, who had quite a sense of humor, had them in stitches with her stories about life in the Registrar's office. Andi and Karen were laughing so hard that tears ran down their cheeks. Martha laughed along, too, then let out a big sigh as the chuckling faded. Andi smiled at both her friends. She hadn't had this much fun in a long time, and she had forgotten how good it felt to laugh so heartily that her stomach hurt.

After a round of seconds for everybody, they each pushed their plates toward the center of the table and leaned back in their chairs. Andi patted her stomach a few times.

"I'm stuffed," she announced.

"Me, too," Martha said. She glanced at Andi's lean, athletic body, sighing deeply and shaking her head slowly. "I just don't know where you put it. I wish I had your metabolism." She stood and began to collect the plates and silverware.

"Here, let me help," Andi said. She lifted the chili bowl and carried it into the kitchen. "Where do you want this?"

"On the counter, near the stove," Karen said. "Martha, just pile the dishes in the sink, and we'll load the dishwasher later. Who wants coffee?"

"Sounds great," Andi said.

"Me, too," Martha added. "I'll get a pot going."

They cleared the dining room table quickly, then Andi stood out of the way near the doorway as Karen and Martha packed up the leftovers and stored them in the fridge. She watched how her friends chatted and worked together, each seeming to know what the other was going to say or ask before the sentence was finished. Their playful and affectionate gestures, a touch or a glance, clearly reflected a deep fondness for one another. Andi enjoyed being in their company so much partly because of their comfortable relationship. Karen and Martha were like a rock amongst their circle of lesbian friends, all of whom admired and even envied their wonderful relationship.

"Let's eat dessert in the living room," Karen said. "Toss another log on the fire, will you, hon?"

"Coming right up," Martha said. She moved into the living room and poked the embers before placing two small logs on the pile. Within minutes, the fire was blazing. Andi walked over to it and held out her hands, feeling the warming glow on her palms.

"That feels wonderful," she said. Martha stood and smiled at her.

"Come on back in here and get your dessert," Karen called from the kitchen.

"What's the surprise?" Andi asked. She and Martha stepped into the kitchen just as Karen handed them each a plate.

"Pineapple upside down cake! Hot out of the oven."

"My favorite!" Andi grinned.

"That's exactly why I made it," Karen said. "You need to be spoiled a little."

"Well, you've both done that tonight." She smiled warmly at her friends.

"Grab a coffee mug and then we'll go back into the living room," Martha suggested. "The fire's roaring."

They lounged in the living room in front of the fire, enjoying their desserts. Martha told more stories and they all laughed again. The warming glow of the fire and the jazzy music filled the room, making Andi so relaxed that she stretched and yawned. She looked at her watch. "Jeez! You'll never believe what time it is."

"Do you have an early class tomorrow?" Karen asked.

"No, but I know that you both have to get up early for work."

"Not to worry. We had a great time," Martha said.

Andi got up and stacked their dessert dishes, then brought them into the kitchen. Martha gathered up the mugs and followed her in. Karen took out a container from the fridge, put it in a bag and handed it to Andi.

"Here's a meal for another night this week."

Andi took it and smiled. "You don't have to feed me twice, but thanks so much. I had a great time this evening. I really appreciate you gals having me over."

"It's our pleasure," Karen said. "We'll see you Saturday, right?"

"Saturday?" Andi questioned.

"Our party," reminded Martha. "I sent you an e-mail."

"Remind me again?" Andi furrowed her brow to remember.

"It's a Hawaiian theme. We all need a hot summer night in the middle of the winter." She grinned broadly at Andi.

"Sure, I'll be here. You having a big crowd?"

"It always seems to turn out that way," Martha said. "Karen

invited a few friends from work, but it will mostly be people from campus, some grad students..."

"Jen won't be here, will she?" Andi asked.

"I doubt she'd come. She knows we're good friends and that you'll be here."

"You're right. What can I bring, and what time?" Andi asked.

"Bring whatever you're drinking, and come at 8:00 for the first round of Piña Coladas!" Karen grinned. "And don't forget to wear your Hawaiian shirt."

After a round of hugs goodbye, Andi drove back to campus with a full belly and a happy heart.

Chapter
Nine

KAREN AND MARTHA'S driveway was full of cars by the time Andi arrived at 8:30. She parked on the street in front of their house in a lineup with other cars that she assumed belonged to the partygoers. Martha and Karen had purchased the house nearly two years prior, moving into the residential neighborhood that housed many of the college faculty. The older homes on the block were all moderately sized with well-manicured properties.

The light glowing through Karen and Martha's windows cast shadows across the lawn. Andi could see people standing and talking in their living room, and she heard the music all the way out in the street. She left her coat in the car and, wearing only a brightly flowered Hawaiian shirt tucked into faded jeans, strode up to the front door carrying a six-pack of beer.

"Well, look who's here!" Karen said as she held the door open for Andi. Karen had on a pink and orange Hawaiian shirt and a grass skirt over a pair of shorts. "Aloha!" She gave Andi a big hug.

"Nice grass," Andi teased. She winked at Karen, then handed her the six-pack.

"How about a *lei*?" Karen grinned mischievously at Andi, removing the flowered necklace from around her neck.

Andi laughed at being one-upped. "Maybe later."

"Feeling lucky tonight?" She smiled at Andi. "Hey Martha. Look who's here," she shouted across the living room.

The furniture had been moved to the perimeter of the room, and about ten people stood talking. Most wore brightly colored Hawaiian shirts, shorts, and sandals. Jimmy Buffet music drifted from the stereo. Andi stepped across the room to greet Martha.

"Hey Andi!" Martha sang out. She was sipping a Piña Colada, which she offered to Andi.

"No thanks. I brought beer."

"So, how was the rest of your week?"

"Busy, as usual. You?"

"Same. I could use the chance to unwind tonight." Martha scanned the room. "I hear there'll be a good crowd."

"Nobody wants to miss your legendary parties," Andi said. "Are some of these people from Karen's work?"

"That group over there," she indicated, pointing to the fireplace. "Come on. I'll introduce you." She grabbed Andi by the arm and walked with her toward the people on the far side of the room. "Hey, y'all. This is Andi, a very good friend of ours. Andi, this is Ken and Albert, Peg and Clare, and Barb."

Andi shook hands with each as Martha introduced them. She noticed that Martha had introduced them in twos, and assumed that the pairs were together, except for the fifth person, Barb. Andi suspected Barb was single and the introductions were Martha's way of making that clear to Andi. Martha often tried to set up Andi with eligible women. Barb confirmed Andi's suspicions by making strong eye contact and smiling. Her hand lingered in Andi's as they shook.

For the next half-hour, Andi listened to juvenile court tales and lawyers' lingo while Barb made her interest in Andi known. The grad assistant could feel the weight of Barb's appraising stares not only when she talked, but when others in the groups spoke as well. Barb offered to get Andi a drink and, after returning with the beer, stood close at Andi's elbow, directing her questions and attention solely to her.

"SO, YOU COMING or not?" Joanne asked. She was sitting on the sofa with her feet up on the coffee table in the communal room of CJ's dorm suite.

"Tell me again about this party?" CJ called out through her open bedroom door. She sat on the end of her bed, putting on socks and shoes.

"It's off campus, on the way to Oasis. From what I hear, a bunch of the girls will be there. You know, the usual crowd. We're going to stop there for a while, check it out, then go to Oasis."

"Who's throwing it?"

"Don't know."

"How'd you find out, then?"

"Courtney told me about it."

"Courtney?" CJ walked into the living room, threading a belt through the loops of her pants.

"Softball assistant coach." She paused and looked at CJ, who nodded her acknowledgment. "She's the one I spoke to about

Andi the other night." Joanne arched her eyebrows up and grinned mischievously at CJ. "She said the women who are throwing the party are friends of this woman Andi."

"You talked me into it," CJ said.

"I thought so." She winked at CJ. "Hurry up, then, and let's get out of here."

AS MORE PEOPLE arrived at the party and floor space became more limited, Andi found herself standing nearly face to face with Barb. Although their conversation was mildly interesting and Barb's dark features were certainly attractive, Andi grew uncomfortable with her exclusive attention. When she noticed Sue, the lacrosse grad student, across the room, she politely excused herself and squeezed through the crowd to catch up with her.

By 11:00 the party was packed with people, many of whom Andi didn't know. As she moved and mingled through the crowd, friends stopped her and introduced her to the people they came with. The list of guests grew exponentially that way, with each invited person bringing at least one other friend along to the party. Andi recognized many other grad students as well as a few college seniors. One or two of the younger professors were there, too.

In keeping with the theme, most guests wore Hawaiian clothing, each offering beer or wine coolers to the hosts. The din of conversation and the music from the stereo echoed throughout the house. The rooms were packed with guests.

"Having a good time?" Karen asked. She was making her way through the crowd with a huge bag of chips to augment the depleted supply in the living room.

"Great, as usual," Andi said. "Is there anything I can do to help?"

"Just eat, drink, and mingle," Karen said. "Can I get you another beer?"

"What I need is the bathroom first," Andi answered.

"You'll have to take care of that one yourself," chuckled Karen as she disappeared into the crowd.

Andi headed to the upstairs bathroom, hoping to avoid the long line for one on the first floor. The door was shut so she waited outside in the hall. She was glad to be removed from the commotion of the party below and sighed deeply as she listened to the muffled noise drifting up the stairs. Still facing the bathroom, she crossed her hands over her chest and tilted her head to the right, resting it and her shoulder against the wall.

She closed her eyes and slowly exhaled.

Suddenly, she felt someone's hands softly on her waist. The person leaned against her back and whispered close to her ear.

"Guess who?"

Andi recognized the voice immediately, and her heart began to race. She turned to face CJ and was greeted by a broad, grinning smile and twinkling emerald eyes.

"What are you doing here?" Andi asked. She was surprised and genuinely happy to see CJ.

"One of my friends, Joanne, invited me to tag along. She said it was a bring-a-friend party, so here I am." She stood inches away from Andi's face.

"What a great surprise," Andi responded.

At that moment, the bathroom door opened and Barb emerged. She nearly walked right into Andi as she stepped into the hall.

"I'm sorry," Barb said. "Oh, hi Andi. I've been looking for you." She stared at Andi for a moment before looking briefly at CJ. "I'm Barb." She extended a hand to CJ.

"This is CJ," Andi noted.

They shook hands, then Barb locked Andi's eyes again. "I'll see you downstairs, okay?"

"Sure," Andi said. She waved half-heartedly as Barb turned and walked down the stairs.

"Friend of yours?" CJ asked. She feigned a casualness she wasn't really feeling. CJ couldn't help but notice Barb's good looks as well as her obvious flirting with Andi. A twinge of jealousy tightened in her stomach for this woman she barely knew.

"We met earlier. She works with Karen, one of the women who's throwing the party."

"She seems interested in your company," CJ noted. She looked earnestly for Andi's reaction. "Am I keeping you?"

"Not at all, CJ," Andi reassured. She placed her hand on CJ's arm for a moment. "I always enjoy talking with you, and I'm glad you're here." She smiled and looked directly into her green eyes, her face only inches away. The grad assistant's heart was still beating rapidly, and she was aware of the tingling in her body that was brought on by seeing CJ. "If you'll excuse me for a second, though," she added, motioning toward the bathroom.

"Of course," CJ said. "I'll meet you downstairs in the kitchen. Can I get you a drink?"

"A beer would be great, thanks. I'll be down in a minute."

Once inside the bathroom, Andi stood at the sink and looked at her face in the mirror. The bright light revealed a crimson blush that she hoped had been obscured by the darkened hallway. She turned on the cold water tap and splashed her face a few times, then toweled dry. Try as she might, she couldn't ignore her reaction to CJ or deny its cause. Something about this woman attracted her attention and touched her heart. She finished in the bathroom then made her way through the crowd and into the kitchen.

"Here you go," offered CJ. She handed Andi a beer then clinked her own bottle against it.

"Thanks," Andi said. "So, how long have you been here?" She leaned against the counter top in the corner of the room.

CJ stood facing her, close to the dining room entrance. "About ten minutes. I saw you in the hallway just after we came in, so I went up to say hi." Because the noise level was quite a bit louder than upstairs, CJ leaned toward Andi in order to speak and be heard. Her body was only inches away from Andi's as she spoke. The basketball player could feel the heat radiating off the other woman's body, which caused her own body to tingle. "I stopped by your office the other day, but you weren't in."

"What day was that?"

"Thursday afternoon."

"I had a meeting with my Chair," she answered. "Everything okay with your project?"

"Oh yeah, fine. I just stopped by to say hi." CJ smiled. Someone walked past CJ into the dining room, bumping her into Andi. "Sorry," she said. She placed her hand on Andi's shoulder to regain her balance. Although she was reluctant to remove it, she casually slipped it into her pocket.

"I'm sorry I missed you," Andi said. Her shoulder tingled warmly where CJ's hand had touched her.

"So, who's your connection to this party?"

"Martha and Karen, the women who are throwing it, are good friends of mine."

"Oh, you're a first-generation invitation," CJ chuckled. "I'm like a second cousin, once removed." Andi laughed with her.

"Everyone's welcome here. Martha and Karen are great."

"How do you know them?"

"Martha was the swim team manager when I was on the team. We've been friends ever since. I met Karen four years ago through her." She scanned the room looking for the women. "I'll introduce you to them, if I can find them."

"Hey, Joanne!" CJ said. She waved above the heads of the people in the kitchen to get her friend's attention. "Over here." Joanne sneaked her way through to where CJ and Andi were standing. "Joanne, this is my friend Andi. Andi, Joanne." They shook hands and exchanged smiles. Joanne gave an appraising look to Andi, followed by a wink to CJ. CJ cringed slightly, hoping that Andi didn't notice.

"I hate to say it, but I think we'll have to head out," warned Joanne. "Someone by the door said that the cops have driven by twice in the last ten minutes. One of the neighbors probably called." She frowned and shook her head slowly.

"What time is it?" CJ asked.

"Eleven forty-five," noted Andi. She was disappointed that the party might be breaking up and that CJ would be leaving.

"Why don't you come out with us," asked Joanne.

"Yeah!" agreed CJ. "A bunch of us were heading out after the party anyway. Why don't you come?"

"Where you going?"

"Oasis, a local hangout," CJ said. "Ever been there?" She paused and looked at Andi, anxiously waiting for her response. Most people on campus knew that Oasis was a gay bar, and CJ wondered if Andi would admit to having gone to Oasis as well as to being gay. She hoped that Andi would trust her enough to be open, and to say what up until this point had been left unsaid.

"Sure, I'll go," said Andi said.

"Great!" CJ exclaimed. Although disappointed that Andi had dodged the question, CJ was happy that Andi would be joining them.

"I need to find Martha and Karen, first," she added. She made a visual sweep of the kitchen once more, then spotted Martha. "Hey, Martha," she waved.

Martha moved through the crowded toward Andi. She looked distracted. "Cops," she noted, and shook her head slowly. "The party's over."

"Sorry to hear that," Andi said.

"Thanks for having us, though," added CJ. She extended her hand to Martha and introduced herself and Joanne.

"Glad you gals could come," Martha said. "Maybe next time we'll plan the party for when the neighbors are out of town."

"CJ and Joanne invited me to join a bunch of them. They're going out to Oasis," Andi added. CJ noticed Martha's knowing look, which was directed at Andi.

Martha smiled.

"Good! Go and enjoy," Martha said.

"Why don't you join us?" suggested Joanne.

"Maybe. First we'll see what kind of shape the house is in after everyone leaves."

"You sure you don't mind?" Andi asked. "I'll stay and help clean up, if you'd like."

"Don't be silly. Go, have fun. Maybe the cops will go away if the house starts to clear out."

"Have you seen Karen?" Andi asked. "I want to say goodbye."

"Not in a while, but I'll tell her for you. Call us during the week, okay?" She looked at CJ and Joanne. "It was nice meeting you ladies. Now if you'll excuse me, I've got to appease the cops." She turned and left the kitchen.

"Do you need a lift?" offered CJ. She looked expectantly at Andi.

"I have a car here, so I'll follow you," Andi said. They made their way across the still-crowded living room and out the front door.

"I'll pull out and meet you at the end of the block," Joanne said.

"Okay," Andi said. She jogged to her car and put on her coat, then pulled out and followed Joanne and CJ to the bar.

CJ AND JOANNE introduced Andi to their friends at Oasis. Several of the women Andi recognized, either by name or by face. Although she'd frequented bars in college, especially with Liz and their group of friends, she went out very seldom these days and almost never by herself. With a group, the bar scene could be fun, but by herself, she felt uncomfortable. The group CJ and Joanne met up with, upperclassmen and grad students, were a lively bunch, and Andi was looking forward to an enjoyable night. She was also glad to see that others, who obviously came from Martha and Karen's party, were also wearing Hawaiian shirts.

Andi stood near the corner of the bar as her eyes adjusted to the pulsing lights of the dance floor. CJ and Joanne were across the room, talking to a group of women whom Andi recognized as basketball players. She hoped that Jen wouldn't make an appearance, and scanned the darkened room to check. As she was looking, an arm slipped quickly around her waist. She turned her head and smiled, recognizing her friend Sue.

"I never see you out, Andi," Sue shouted over the music. She smiled. "I'm glad you didn't change, either." She pointed to her own flowery shirt. "How about dancing?"

"Sure," Andi said.

They stepped out onto the crowded dance floor and moved to the rhythm of the club music blasting loudly through the speakers. Strobe lighting flashed, producing a slow motion appearance of dancing on the floor. Sue was a good dancer, one of the few who could keep up with Andi. They made good partners as they moved rhythmically around the floor. Andi noticed that others nearby were watching them. She and Sue had met two years ago through mutual friends and saw each other often at many school functions. Andi felt relieved that Sue, unlike other grad students, never wanted anything more from her than a casual friendship.

After the second song, Andi could feel herself growing hot and perspired. She thanked Sue for the dance, then headed to the bar and purchased a bottled water. She consumed the small drink quickly and turned back toward the dancers, enjoying the creative display of energy as they moved around the floor.

As she stood watching the dancers, she scanned the room looking for CJ. Over the past few weeks, Andi had sensed CJ's interest when they had been in each other's company; more strongly than ever, she'd felt a connection between them at the party. She thought back to that moment when CJ touched her and whispered to her in the hallway at Martha and Karen's.

"How about a dance for me?"

Andi blinked hard and emerged from her daydream to find CJ standing next to her.

"I was wondering where you went," Andi said.

"Sorry. I didn't mean to invite you and leave you by yourself. I ran into some of my teammates over there." She pointed across the room.

"Don't apologize. I was mingling with the people you introduced me to." It was true that she could keep herself entertained, but she appreciated that CJ was looking after her.

"Yes, I saw you dancing with Sue. You're good! So, want to dance?" She held out her hand.

"Sure," Andi said. She placed her hand in CJ's, and they walked out to the dance floor. CJ squeezed her hand as they shuffled across the bar. Andi felt a warm, tingling sensation radiate from that touch. The loud, pulsing music rocked her body as she and CJ moved toward the other dancers on the crowded floor. Some of CJ's friends joined them and they all danced in a small circle. When the friends moved across the floor, CJ and Andi were once again face-to-face, smiling and enjoying the music.

For CJ, the night was just what she wanted — an opportunity for Andi to see her as a peer, not as another one of her students. Surrounded by mutual friends in a setting other than school, their feelings toward one another seemed to be somehow different. So far, both at the party and at the club, CJ felt that connection to her, and she sensed that Andi felt it, too.

After two club mixes and a retro Madonna medley, Andi was once again in need of a drink. She motioned to CJ, and they walked off the floor toward the bar. Andi bought two bottled waters, one for each of them, then drank half of hers in one long swallow.

"You never did answer my question before," CJ reminded. She moved closer to Andi to hear her above the noise of the bar. She locked onto her blue eyes with an open, questioning gaze, waiting for an answer.

"Which question?" Andi asked. She arched a single dark eyebrow that nearly became lost in the ebony bangs across her forehead.

"Have you ever been here before?" CJ looked at Andi and waited for her to answer.

Andi could see that the expression on her face was sincere, that CJ was not trying to trick her into revealing any secrets or make her uncomfortable. This question was her attempt to create a more open dialogue between them, to speak honestly about what had been left unspoken. Andi looked at CJ and no longer saw the student who asked research questions, but the friend she was becoming. She smiled at her and felt ready to take a chance.

"Yes, I have. I came here a lot when I was in college, but less frequently over the last few years." She felt relieved, as if they were finally speaking to each other face to face instead of talking through a partially closed window. She paused and waited for CJ to speak, and when she didn't, Andi continued. "I didn't think it was a secret, CJ. I kind of figured that you knew, that it didn't need to be said."

"I guess I did know," CJ said. "I just didn't want to assume." She paused and looked intensely into Andi's azure eyes. "I was hoping you felt you could trust me enough to be open with me. Do you?"

"I just did, didn't I?" She rested her hand on CJ's forearm for a moment and smiled as she looked in her eyes.

"Thanks, Andi. It's between us." CJ's eyes remained locked on Andi's.

"There you are!" Joanne interrupted. Her approach broke the trance-like stare between CJ and Andi. Joanne didn't seem to notice and continued talking. "Some of the gals on the team are leaving. They were looking for you to say goodbye." She turned to Andi and smiled. "Can I borrow her for a minute?"

Andi nodded. "By all means."

CJ asked, "Do you mind, Andi?"

"I'll bring her right back," Joanne promised.

"It's fine. I'll meet you back here when you're finished, CJ."

Andi watched CJ and Joanne walk across the room to meet their friends. Joanne's timing wasn't great, but it gave Andi a minute to think about what just transpired between her and CJ. She felt surprisingly comfortable after having just come out to a student. *A friend*, she corrected herself. *She's my friend, and not my student.* She took a deep breath and exhaled slowly.

CJ thought better of reprimanding Joanne for dragging her away from Andi. She didn't want Joanne to know that what CJ presented to her initially as curiosity about Andi had developed into flat-out, head-over-heels attraction. She fought back her annoyance and said nothing to Joanne as they walked over to say their good byes.

As the last of their friends headed out, the DJ called the last dance of the night, a slow dance. CJ disappeared from Joanne's side without her noticing and went in search of Andi. Couples crowded onto the dance floor, locked in embraces so different from the frenetic dancing throughout the rest of the night. The basketball player wove her way around and through the dancers to make her way back to the bar where she was supposed to meet the grad assistant. More than anything, she wanted to end this evening with her arms wrapped around Andi in a slow dance. When she finally emerged from the throng of dancers, Andi was nowhere to be seen.

CJ was crushed. She cursed Joanne silently, annoyed that she left Andi there at the end of what had been a fabulous night. She looked around frantically, scanning over the heads of the women milling about near her. Wondering if Andi got tired of waiting and left, CJ walked toward the exit but didn't notice Andi amongst the crowd leaving the building. She moved back to the bar and leaned against the barstool, annoyed at herself for allowing the evening to end this way.

"I've been looking for you."

CJ looked up quickly and saw Andi standing before her. She smiled, heart racing, and stepped forward toward her. They stood face to face, looking into each other's eyes.

"It's the last dance," CJ said. She held out her hand to Andi. "Want to..." Before she could finish, the song ended. The lights came up, exposing the dancing couples that lingered on the floor, loathe to move apart.

"Next time," Andi promised. She took CJ's hand and squeezed it gently, then smiled before releasing it. "I guess we'd better go."

They walked slowly and silently toward the exit. The lights were up, illuminating the people who funneled out the exit door. Andi walked close to CJ and bumped her hip, throwing her off stride. Andi looked at her and grinned until a smile emerged on CJ's face.

"What was that for?" CJ asked.

"For fun." She winked.

Once outside, the brisk winter air chilled their damp clothing. CJ walked with Andi to her car. They both stood next to it, rubbing their hands on their arms to create warming friction.

"Need a lift back to campus?" Andi asked.

"Joanne will be waiting for me, but thanks for offering."

A long silence lingered between them as they shuffled around, attempting to keep warm. Something had changed between them. A connection was made that each woman felt personally and knew that the other felt as well. Neither knew how to put that feeling into words, however, so with silent eye contact and knowing glances they bridged the space between them.

"Will you be around this week?" Andi asked.

"We're leaving tomorrow for a two-game road trip. I'll be back on campus Wednesday." She paused and looked into Andi's blue eyes. "Can I call you when I get back?"

"Definitely," Andi said. She smiled at CJ, never taking her eyes off the green ones that looked so intensely at her.

"I had a great time tonight, Andi. Thanks so much for being open with me, and for trusting me."

"You don't have to thank me, CJ. I had a great time, too."

CJ leaned toward Andi just as a car pulled up next to them, tooting the horn and coming to a stop. Joanne rolled down the window and smiled.

"Hey, gals! You must be freezing out here."

"CJ was just wondering where you were," Andi said. "I didn't want to leave her here without a ride."

"I wouldn't abandon you here, girlfriend," Joanne teased. "Hop in." CJ locked eyes once more with Andi before moving around her friend's car and getting in. Andi bent down toward the driver's window and waved to the women.

Joanne said, "Get into your car and start it up before we drive away." Andi appreciated her concern and did as she asked. After starting the engine, she gave a thumbs up to Joanne and CJ in the other car. Joanne then rolled up the window and pulled away. Andi followed their tail lights until they turned the corner and exited the lot. She pulled out of the lot behind them and headed back to campus.

Although Andi's body was tired, her mind was wide-awake with thoughts and feelings about the night. She hoped that her journaling would help her sort it out.

I'm really happy, a little confused, somewhat overwhelmed, and a bit afraid. How did this woman, whom I barely know, wiggle her way into my heart so quickly that I find myself thinking about her, daydreaming, and getting warm fuzzies when I'm near her? Lord knows that I've taken enough teasing about being aloof — and I can't deny the truth of it — but around CJ I don't feel that way. I don't want to keep her at arm's length, like I usually do with people I meet (most people, in fact!). I'm surprised at myself, actually. That's also part of what's so confusing and overwhelming at the same time. The way I'm feeling is so not me, but at the same time it feels so natural to be this way around her. It's not a conscious decision — I'm just following my heart. That's the scary part. I haven't had too much success in areas of the heart. In fact, since my last attempt was a complete and total disaster, the idea of a repeat performance makes me want to run the other way. But CJ isn't Liz, and even though I don't know her that well, I get a good vibe from her, a safe feeling. Should I trust her? Should I trust my own heart?

Chapter
Ten

CJ STARED OUT the window of the bus as it wound its way back to campus. The snow had been falling steadily for the last two hours and was accumulating on the road. She hoped it wouldn't delay their arrival. Hypnotized by the falling flakes, she gazed at the blanketed landscape and let her thoughts drift once again to Andi.

She mentally kicked herself for leaving her cell phone in the dorm. Several times over the last few days she thought about calling Andi from a pay phone or the hotel room, but the lack of privacy prevented her from making the call. That, and the fact that she really didn't have a reason to call her. There was always something to talk about, and conversation flowed easily between them in person, but CJ felt somehow uncomfortable about calling while on the road.

The party, followed by the evening at the Oasis, had gone so well CJ found herself wanting more, but didn't know how to make that happen. Something had clicked that night between them, but she feared forcing it would ruin what was going so smoothly. The basketball player waited impatiently to arrive back on campus and call her.

"What do you remember?" Kelly asked. She playfully tapped the daydreaming athlete on the arm three times. "Hey CJ! Did you hear me?"

"What?" Gathering her thoughts, CJ emerged from her reverie. She turned to face Kelly and another teammate who were engaged in a lively discussion. She hadn't even heard them talking all along, let alone heard the question that was just addressed to her.

"Where's your head?" Kelly asked.

"Sorry. I was looking at the snow."

"I said, what do you remember from when you were a kid playing in the snow?" Kelly and Diane looked at CJ expectantly. Although derailed from her train of thought, CJ jumped right into the discussion.

"Sled riding. We had a big hill at the golf course a few blocks from my house, and we used to go there after a snowfall. Not just my brothers and sister, but a bunch of the kids on the block. We'd bring our sleds and snow disks, then spend the whole afternoon sliding down that hill." She paused and smiled, lost in the remembrance. Kelly chimed in with a sledding memory of huge hills and long runs. The story grew animated and laughter filled their part of the bus. CJ smiled as Kelly relived her childhood fun.

"We should go sledding!" Kelly urged in a hushed whisper. Two pairs of mischievous eyes looked at Kelly, then at their coach to see if she heard. When the coach didn't respond, they expressed their interest in silent nods. "Over the weekend, after Sunday's practice," Kelly added. "Just a few friends, you know, so Coach doesn't find out and have a fit. It'd be a blast! What do you say?"

CJ thought about sledding down a big hill just like in her childhood. The image of carefree and unfettered fun was appealing, a relief from the stress of school, basketball practice, and games. She smiled at the thought of piling on a sled and racing down a hill with her friends—or even with Andi. That thought made her heart jump. Sledding was a great way to include the grad assistant in an activity that would align them as peers again, as they were at the party and the bar, instead of as mentor and student.

"Count me in," CJ said. She grinned and nodded. "I'll mention it to a few people who I think will be interested."

"Great!" Kelly said. "We can go to the big hill near Cloud Mountain after practice." She smiled, obviously pleased with herself for coming up with the idea. CJ was happy, too, for it gave her an even better reason to call Andi when they got back to campus.

WITH CJ OFF campus for a few days, Andi was able to concentrate more on her studies. Lately, when she knew the basketball star was on campus, she found herself searching faces as she walked across the green, hoping to spot the younger athlete's familiar smile. Every knock on Andi's office door quickened her pulse with the anticipation that CJ might be visiting. She admonished herself for getting distracted so easily, but she enjoyed thinking of CJ and often didn't chase away those thoughts, even though they kept her from her work.

Both Andi and her students were halfway through the

second semester, and the workload seemed to increase as the end of the school year loomed nine weeks away. In addition to meeting with her students to discuss their midterm grades, she had to meet with her own professors and advisor to chart her Masters' degree progress. She anticipated three more semesters on campus to finish. During the summer and the fall term, she would complete her course work, and then in the spring, a year from now, she would complete her thesis. Her plans beyond graduation were still undetermined.

With books and papers spread out across her dining room table, Andi sat concentrating on the work before her. On days like this, her paperwork seemed endless, and she questioned her decision to pursue a career that promised a future filled with never-ending editing and grading. Her thoughts were interrupted by the ringing phone. Relieved, she got up from the table and settled onto the couch before answering it.

"Hello?"

"Hi, Andi. It's CJ."

"Hey! How are you?" She smiled broadly at hearing the young athlete's friendly voice.

"Glad to be home. Am I interrupting you?"

"Not really. I could use a study break. How was your road trip?"

"One win, one loss. Kind of disappointing, really, because we should have won both."

"How'd you do?"

"I played well, I guess, but not good enough to pull off a second win."

"Seems to me I remember having a discussion with you once about how basketball is a team sport, remember?" A hint of playful sarcasm rose in her voice.

"I know, I know. I take things too personally sometimes."

"I'll be careful what I say, then."

"Please don't," CJ said earnestly. "I thought we agreed upon being open and honest."

"We did, and I will be." Andi paused and thought back to their evening at the Oasis, and of coming out to CJ. She took a deep breath and exhaled slowly. "So, how were the roads driving back? I had to go out earlier and brush off my car."

"The bus did okay, but some of the roads are covered. Hey, speaking of snow, are you doing anything on Sunday?"

"No, why?"

"A bunch of us are going sledding. Interested? It should be a lot of fun."

"Sure." Andi could hear her enthusiasm. She envisioned CJ's

dancing emerald eyes as she chattered energetically on the other end of the phone.

"Why don't you invite Karen and Martha, too? They seemed like fun people."

"That's really nice of you to offer. I was going to call them later tonight, so I'll mention it to them."

"Great! It'll be in the early afternoon, after practice."

"Your coach won't mind?"

"Coaches and parents get information on a need-to-know basis, and this is something I don't think she needs to know. Sledding down a hill is not a high-injury activity. Besides, I could use a little fun."

"So could I."

"Excellent! It's a plan, then. How about I pick you up at one o'clock? Then, we can ride over and pick up Martha and Karen, if they decide to go."

"That's fine. I'll put in a little extra work between now and then so I can have the afternoon free."

"I'm really glad you're going, Andi."

"Me, too."

"I had such a great time last weekend and, well...sledding will be a lot of fun. So, I guess I should let you get back to your work." CJ paused.

"And I guess you have work to do, too, after being away for a few days." She could hear the reluctance in CJ's voice about ending the conversation, and was flattered by her attention. She smiled. "If you're working on your paper and you have any questions, you could always stop by my office. Or, you could just call me. I'd be happy to help."

"Thanks, Andi. I'll call you later in the week to confirm the time for sledding, okay?"

"Sure. Call me any time."

"Well, then, until soon," CJ said softly.

"Until Sunday," Andi said. She hung up the phone and leaned back against the sofa, grinning.

Chapter
Eleven

ANDI'S DOORBELL RANG at exactly 1:00.

"Ready?" CJ asked when Andi pulled open the door.

Andi nodded and stepped out onto the porch dressed in ski clothes and winter boots. She carried something in her gloved hand. CJ greeted her with a big smile and a playful pat on the back. They walked out to CJ's car, an old Volvo station wagon.

"Nice wheels," Andi teased.

"This baby has been in the family for sixteen years now," CJ said, patting the hood with a gloved hand. "She's not shiny anymore, and she has a few dings here and there, but on the inside she still runs great. You can't just dump something that's not perfect anymore, right?"

"Amen to that." Andi's expression became solemn as her eyes dropped to look at her feet.

"I was teasing, but you were not," CJ said. Her familiar smile grew serious as she looked at Andi. "Want to tell me what you were thinking?" She sensed that Andi's remark hinted of sadness deeper than that of an abandoned old car.

"What I'd really like is to get inside this old car and start out on our sledding adventure," she said to avoid an explanation.

"Okay then, hop in." She allowed the comment to drop, not wanting to make Andi uncomfortable before their outing even began. Andi climbed into the front passenger seat as CJ started up the engine.

"I brought my only three Indigo Girls CD's for the ride," CJ said.

"Did CD players even exist when this car was born?" Andi joked.

"After-market, baby! I like tunes when I drive."

"Then you might like this." She looked down at the object in her hand. "It's a bootleg of Indigo Girls at Radio City Music Hall. It was the first time I saw them in concert."

"Your first, huh?" She smiled at Andi.

"Yup." She handed the disc to CJ. "This copy's for you."

"I can keep it?" Andi nodded. "Excellent! My first Indigo Girls boot." She smiled at Andi with dancing green eyes. "Pop it in, okay?"

Andi put the CD into the player then adjusted the volume so she could be heard over the song. "Thanks so much for planning this outing," Andi said. "I've been looking forward to this all week."

"Me, too. Remind me how to get to Martha and Karen's, okay?" Andi gave her directions, and they arrived shortly at Andi's friends' house. CJ tooted the horn twice to announce their arrival. Within seconds, the garage door opened and Martha emerged carrying a sled. Karen followed her after shutting the garage door.

"Got room for this?" Martha asked.

"Sure," CJ said. She got out of the car and opened the rear door of the wagon. "We can put it in here with the toboggan and rest it on the back of the seat." She and Martha positioned the sled and toboggan, slammed shut the hatch, and climbed into the car. "Ready?" CJ asked.

"Ready! By the way, I'm Karen." She leaned forward from the back seat and offered her hand to CJ. "We didn't meet at the party last weekend."

"Hi, Karen. I'm glad you gals could join us," CJ said.

"I'm glad that Andi called," Martha said.

Andi said, "I love sledding! How long is the ride to the slope?"

"About thirty minutes," CJ said. "I know what'll pass the time quickly, though. Ever play 'I love, I hate'?" Andi looked quizzically at CJ.

"I don't know what you're talking about," Andi said.

"It's a game, kind of," CJ continued. She addressed the three women in the car, glancing at Martha and Karen in the rear view mirror. "You sit around, usually in a group, and each person takes a turn saying one thing that she loves, then on the next round, one thing that she hates, then loves, then hates, and it goes on. It's interesting to hear what people feel passionate about, and it's a good way to get to know somebody. When Andi said that she loved sledding, it reminded me of that. Want to play?"

"Sure," Andi said, "but I already went, so it's your turn." She turned a bit in the seat, as much as her seatbelt would allow, to face CJ.

As she drove, CJ glanced off the road now and then to look at Andi. "Hmmm. I love...getting a greeting card in the mail, not just on a special occasion like a birthday or something, but just because the person sending it was thinking of me." CJ glanced at Andi and smiled. "Now Martha goes."

"I love a delicious, home-cooked meal. It's much better than the finest restaurant." She looked at Karen and smiled. "Especially since I live with such a good cook." She put her arm around Karen's shoulder.

"My turn?" Karen asked. "I love a day where everything goes right. No mistakes, no harassing phone calls, no forgotten paperwork."

"How often does that happen?" Andi asked.

"I'm still waiting for the first time," Karen chuckled. "But when it does happen, I know I'll love it."

"Good one," Andi said. "Let's see. I hate...when I rip the cereal box liner trying to open it, then the cereal slips down between the liner and the inside of the box every time I pour it."

"I hate that, too," CJ added.

"You've got to think of your own. No piggybacking," Andi teased.

"I thought you never played this game before? And now you know all the rules?" CJ joked. "Let me see. I hate when people make racial, ethnic, or sexual jokes that are insulting, and someone's feelings in the group get hurt."

"Aren't *you* sensitive," Andi said. *She just keeps getting more impressive.*

"Me?" Martha asked. "I hate when I forget to save something I'm typing on the computer and the damn thing freezes, then I lose everything I've just typed. Cripes! That happened to me on Friday afternoon, just when I was getting ready to leave the office. I had to retype the whole thing."

"That does stink," Karen agreed. "I hate when people drive in the left hand lane with their left blinker on. I mean, where the hell do they think they are turning? Hello? Pay attention and drive."

"Back to I love, right?" Andi asked. "I love when the moonlight casts shadows and makes the snow look blue."

CJ said, "I love to hike up to the top of a mountain on a clear autumn day where the view at the top is 360 degrees, and I love to stand up there, without the crowds and noise and pollution and pavement, and just look out upon the blanket of color and know that I'm far away from the world below."

Andi nodded. "I've had a few days like that myself. I love that, too."

CJ nodded in return. "Back to you, Martha."

"I love finding an outfit on sale, reduced like seventy-five percent or something, and the only one they have left is exactly my size!"

Karen said, "I love putting on an old coat and finding twenty dollars in the pocket. That happened to me a few weeks ago." She tapped Andi on the shoulder. "Now you again."

"Hmmmm... I hate seeing dead animals by the side of the road. It makes me want to cry when I think about how scared they must have been right before they got killed." Andi's smile faded as she thought of what she'd just described.

CJ reached over and patted her leg. "Don't worry. I drive carefully." She paused for a minute, then spoke. "My turn? I hate liver." She shivered at the thought of it. "I mean, how can anyone eat a filter organ, that's what I'd like to know? An organ filled with all the toxins it's meant to suck out from the body? Yuck." She paused and made a funny face, then glanced at the other women in the car. "Did I offend any of you? Do you eat filter organs?"

"I won't be eating them anymore, thank you very much," Andi teased. Unable to maintain her serious expression, she broke into laughter. The other three joined in and they laughed together.

"I hate wasting eight-fifty on a crappy movie," Martha said. "I can't believe that theaters get away with that kind of robbery."

"I hate going to the dentist," Karen noted. "My dentist is very nice and all, but I hate that drilling sound. It gives me the creeps."

"Is it my turn again?" Andi asked. CJ nodded. "I love to lie out on the beach late at night, when the crowds have gone, and smell the salt air, and listen to the waves crashing on the sand, and gaze at the heavens, looking for shooting stars."

"By yourself?" CJ asked.

"It depends." She looked at CJ and arched one dark, expressive eyebrow. "Your turn."

"I love to be touched. Massages, back scratches, hugs, you name it. I love physical contact. It makes me feel close to someone." She looked at Andi for a long second, trying to read her reaction. Andi's blue eyes remained locked on hers. CJ had to turn away first, for fear of driving off the road.

As CJ drove, the four women played round after round of CJ's game while the Indigo Girls rang from the car speakers. When the disc ended, so did their conversation; the women remained quiet for a short time until they arrived at their destination.

"What are you thinking?" CJ asked. She glanced briefly at

Andi before returning her gaze to the road.

What am *I thinking?* Andi mused. *That it's a shame you and I have been on the same campus for three and a half years, but never met earlier.* "Do you believe in fate?" Andi asked.

CJ thought pensively before responding. "I'd like to believe I control my own life through my decisions and actions."

"I agree with you there, but do you ever wonder about the seeming randomness of life, circumstances, people?"

"Like literally bumping into you at the reception?"

"Sure, that's a good example. That's certainly not something that happened as a result of carefully planned decisions and actions," Andi noted.

"Maybe that was just meant to be," CJ said softly.

"WE'RE HERE!" CJ announced as she pulled into a parking lot dotted with a few other cars. The sky was cloudless blue and sunny, and the temperature hovered around freezing. They got out and stretched. "Kelly's here already. That's her car over there, and the one next to it has a campus parking sticker on it, too."

"What can I take?" Andi asked.

"Why don't you help me with the toboggan," CJ said.

"I've been sledding as a kid but I've never been on a toboggan before."

"So you're a toboggan virgin," CJ grinned.

"Yes, but you will be gentle with me, won't you?" Andi answered.

"But of course."

CJ and Andi carried the toboggan, while Martha pulled the sled. Karen walked at the front of the group, whistling. They marched up the path and came to a hill where about a dozen people were sledding

"Here?" Andi asked.

"No, too crowded. There's another place that's usually less crowded because people don't want to walk farther," CJ answered. "Do you mind a little extra walk? That's where the rest of the gang is."

"Not at all," Andi said.

They walked for another ten minutes on a path through the snow, then arrived at the top of a hill. They could hear the sound of laughter as sledders raced down the slope. Andi and CJ put the toboggan down near some logs that served as benches near a fire pit surrounded by stones. Charred wood in the pit indicated it had been used within the last few days.

"What a great spot!" Andi exclaimed. "How did you find it?" She looked around at the hillside blanketed with evergreens and white birch. An expansive white slope stretched out in front of them, leading toward a frozen creek nearly half a mile away. She saw people walking back up the slope, dragging sleds behind them.

"I came to the first spot once and saw some footprints in the snow leading away. I followed them and found this place. I like it much better because it's usually empty, the hill is a bit longer, and the fire pit makes it easy to warm up."

"It's okay to start a fire?" Andi asked.

"No one's ever said otherwise, and I always smother the fire with snow before I leave, just to be safe."

"We're heading down," Karen announced. "See you gals at the bottom." She sat on the sled behind Martha, and they pushed off, accelerating down the hill.

"So how does this thing work?" Andi asked, pointing at the toboggan.

"Easy. Lean right to turn right, lean left to turn left. It's that simple."

"Wouldn't it be easier to go straight?"

"Straight just isn't as much fun," CJ quipped. "And most of the time, you just don't have a choice." She smiled and winked.

Andi blushed at yet another of CJ's double entendres. She looked skeptically at the toboggan and then back at CJ.

"It is easier with two people on together though, more bodyweight, more stability. Toboggan teamwork," CJ added.

"That suits me fine," Andi said, relieved. "I wasn't sure I could steer it by myself anyway. What do you say, then? Let's go!" CJ sat in the front and stretched her legs out, then directed Andi to sit behind her. "What should I do with my legs?" Andi asked as she squeezed in behind her.

CJ grabbed each boot and lifted Andi's legs over the tops of her own thighs so that Andi's boots were in front of CJ.

"Once we push off, hold on to me," CJ said. "That way, we can lean together. Ever ride a motorcycle?" Andi nodded. "It's kind of like that. Ready?" Andi nodded again.

They scooted the toboggan to the edge of the hill until it was gliding on its own. Andi put her gloved hands around CJ's waist. Just sitting close to her was making her heart jump, but putting her hands around her, albeit through many layers of clothing, *too many layers*, she thought guiltily, felt wonderful. They built up speed as they flew down the hill. CJ leaned now and then to avoid bumps and obstacles, and then they glided to a stop at the bottom of the hill not far from where Martha and Karen were. CJ let out a hoot.

"That was great!" Andi said. "Let's do it again."

"But first we have to walk back up." CJ grimaced. They both looked up the long hill. "I hate walking up the hill after a great ride down."

"I hate when someone forgets to turn the shower faucet down, so when you turn on the tap, you get an unexpected spray of cold water on your back."

"They do that in the dorm all the time. I hate that, too. Hmmmm. I love the smell of roses..."

As they took turns pulling the toboggan back up, they continued the game after each ride down the hill. CJ introduced Andi, Martha, and Karen to her friends as the sledders gathered at the top of the slope. Andi recognized some of the women from the Oasis. Inhaling a chestful of the crisp, winter air, Andi smiled as she listened to the sounds of her friends' laughter echoing off the frozen ground as they glided down the hill. She couldn't remember the last time she had such a great time. She felt like a kid again, far removed from the stress of teaching and studying, the pressure of bills, and the tension of deadlines and expectations. For now, there was no place else she'd rather be. As much fun as the tobogganing was, however, it was CJ's company that made the day really special. She turned to the younger athlete and smiled. "Can I be up front for the next ride?"

"Sure, but that means you've got to steer. If I'm sitting behind you, I won't be able to see the bumps, so it's all up to you."

"I was hoping you'd help me out a bit."

"I'm just going to sit back and enjoy the ride." CJ grinned.

Andi got on the front of the toboggan and CJ moved in behind her. Andi felt CJ's body pressed up against her back, and it made her tingle warmly all over. She lifted up CJ's boots and legs over her own and into her lap. The idea of being enveloped by CJ's body made her feel safe, yet excited.

"Ready?" Andi asked. She turned her head slightly and brushed up against CJ's face, so close to hers, and felt CJ's warm, spearmint breath on her cheek.

"I was born ready," CJ whispered near Andi's ear.

Tingles shot throughout Andi's body.

They pushed off and headed down the hill. As they approached the first bump, Andi leaned and felt CJ holding on tightly and leaning with her. The speed of the ride and the touch of CJ's body were exhilarating. As the next bump neared, Andi became tentative, not sure how much to lean or shift her weight.

She finally leaned to avoid the bump ahead, but not in time. The toboggan became airborne over the bump.

Andi hollered and leaned while the toboggan was in the air. It twisted and landed at an angle, tossing both of them off. CJ and Andi tumbled a few yards down the hill before coming to a stop, covered with snow. The toboggan glided to a halt at the bottom of the hill.

Andi, disoriented, got up quickly and looked around for CJ. She saw her about fifteen feet away, lying on her side in the snow. Panicked that CJ was hurt, Andi stumbled over to her. She fell to her knees, bending over CJ.

"CJ! Oh my God, CJ! Are you okay?"

Before Andi could react, CJ grabbed her around the waist, rolled her over in the snow, and sat on top of her, straddling her hips.

"You drive crazy, girl!" CJ teased. "You need to learn the rhythm and balance of being with another person."

"That's the story of my life," Andi joked. She was so relieved CJ wasn't hurt, she couldn't even be mad that CJ had tricked her. Besides, CJ's smile was hard to resist. "Swimming is a solo sport."

"I guessed you never learned synchronized swimming," CJ said. "Sometimes teamwork can be more fun than solo." She smiled and winked at Andi. "Come on." She got up and pulled Andi to her feet. "Let's go get the toboggan."

AFTER NEARLY TWO hours of sledding, the group gathered around the fire pit to warm up and to rest after many walks up the hill. Wet mittens and gloves leaned against the large stones surrounding the pit. The air was filled with the talking and laughter of the dozen friends who were out enjoying each other's company as well as the beautiful day.

"Three cheers for Kelly," CJ called out. "She dreamed up this plan on the bus ride home." The group hooted and hollered as Kelly stood and ceremoniously bowed.

CJ then turned her attention to the pit, watching as Andi started a fire. Her pink-cheeked friend worked so efficiently layering the dry twigs and leaves that within minutes the flame was blazing brightly. CJ marveled that everything Andi did, she seemed to do effortlessly and well. The grad student's smooth confidence, far from being haughty or intimidating, was comfortable to be around. The younger athlete watched as her friend fed larger branches into the blaze. Once the fire was roaring, Andi backed away from it and sat on the log next to CJ.

"How's that feel?" Andi asked.

"Great!" She held her hands out to the fire. "What a great mix of the elements — fire, wood, ice." She smiled and looked around at the group of women relaxing around the fire. The crackling blaze drowned out their quiet talking, yet CJ could see their lips moving and their faces lighting up with laughter. Martha and Karen seemed to be enjoying themselves, talking with two women who sat near them.

"Hey, Andi!" Martha hollered. "How about a song?"

"Yeah!" Karen said. "That'll warm us all up." She looked encouragingly at Andi, then briskly rubbed her hands together in front of the blaze.

Andi felt a blush rise to her face at hearing the request. She glared half-heartedly at her friends across the fire pit then looked down at her feet, hoping their request went unnoticed. Out of the corner of her eye she could see CJ peering at her with a questioning look, her blonde head tilted slightly to the side. Andi sat quietly, holding her breath for a moment until CJ nudged her in the arm.

"You can sing?" CJ asked.

"That's an understatement," Karen hastened to add. "You mean you've never heard her?"

CJ grinned broadly at Andi, whose face was flushed red from the attention she was hoping to avoid.

"She's obviously been holding out on me," CJ teased. "I haven't heard a single note." She bumped Andi playfully in the shoulder. Andi continued to look at her feet. "So how about it, Andi? Will you sing something?"

"Come on," chimed in Martha. The other women in the circle added their encouragement. "It'll be fun."

Andi was uncomfortable with the attention turned on her. Her hands were clasped in her lap while her long legs extended out in front of her, crossed at the ankles. Her eyes were locked on the tips of her boots, which she jiggled vigorously. CJ leaned toward Andi, their bodies pressed together from shoulder to hip. Andi felt CJ's warmth penetrating the layers of her winter clothes and her warm breath as she whispered close to Andi's ear.

"Please?" CJ asked.

Andi's body shuddered at the word combined with the body contact. She turned her head slightly to look at CJ, whose honey-brown eyebrows were raised in invitation while her green eyes pleaded softly. There was no way she could refuse that look and she knew it. Andi let out the breath she was holding.

"Okay," she agreed. CJ reached out and squeezed her arm.

"But only if everybody sings along." She glared at Martha and Karen again but her stare was met with laughing eyes that quickly softened her own.

"We could start with 'Happy Birthday,'" suggested one of the women. "Kelly's birthday is four days from now."

With that, the group of women launched into a rousing chorus of the birthday song. Andi joined in, pitching her voice just loud enough to add to the chorus without standing out. When that song was over, someone else began a song by Mary Chapin Carpenter. By the start of the second verse, the voices of the singers had softened enough so that Andi's rich, alto voice could be heard above the rest. Resisting the urge to turn and face Andi, CJ simply tilted her head slightly and watched her friend out of the corner of her eye. The grad assistant's sonorous voice, so powerful and in perfect key, made CJ's body tingle. After two or three more songs, Andi put up her hands in protest of another round.

"Where'd you learn to sing like that?" CJ asked quietly. She turned to face Andi.

"Just always could, I guess," she said with a shrug.

"You should do it more often. It's beautiful."

The noise around the fire pit died down to quiet conversation. Andi sat silently, staring at the flickering flames of the fire and feeling the heat of the blaze. The warmth radiating from the woman next to her was equally as strong.

Andi looked over at her flaxen-haired friend and smiled. CJ had a way of doing little things that made her feel very special. She was flattered by the attention, really. No one ever made her feel quite like this before. She reached over and clasped CJ's ungloved hand. "I'm having so much fun, I want you to know," Andi said softly. She turned her face to look into CJ's eyes as she spoke. Her companion's emerald eyes, flecked with gold from the fire, returned her gaze.

"I'm glad," CJ said. "Me, too." She leaned toward Andi so that their shoulders touched, then both women shifted their eyes to the fire light.

Andi kept her hand in CJ's an extended moment before removing it to pick up her gloves. They lingered in the glow of the fire.

THE CAR RIDE back to campus passed quickly as they listened to music and talked. Their cheeks were flushed bright pink from the wind and cold. Karen and Martha dozed quietly in the back seat. CJ and Andi were pleasantly relaxed from their many walks up the hill with toboggan or sled in tow. Despite this, neither woman was anxious for the day to end.

Andi turned in her seat to look at and talk with CJ as she drove. "I've got a pile of paperwork waiting for me. I'd much rather be tobogganing down that hill, that's for sure."

"Is that your grad assistant work?"

"Yes, and my least favorite part. Correcting papers is a drag."

"Why'd you choose that route?"

"Financial reasons. I get a small stipend, and I get to take classes for free. If I didn't do it this way, I probably couldn't afford to go."

"That's pretty much why I want to go that route, too. I'll just have to wait and see what kind of deal I can get."

"Would you consider going far away?" Andi asked, hoping the answer was no. She couldn't deny the emerging feelings of attraction to CJ

"Why? Would you miss me?" The basketball player's tone was casual, but her question was sincere.

The older woman paused, then answered. "Even though we've known each other only, let's see, a month and a half...yes, I think I would."

CJ smiled broadly and her dimple grew deep. Andi couldn't help looking at it, or her lips. The younger woman noticed Andi staring at her, but couldn't take her eyes off the road long enough to return Andi's intense gaze. "Well, I'm not going anywhere, yet."

"I'm glad."

They dropped off Martha and Karen first, then arrived back on campus in the late afternoon. The sky was splashed with pink, orange, and purple hues, casting dark shadows across the front of Andi's building. CJ walked with her friend up to the porch. As they reached the door, they turned and faced one another. Even in the dim light of the setting sun, Andi could see CJ's eyes moving, searching her face. Her heart stirred as she looked deeply into her companion's green eyes.

"Thank you for a great day," Andi began.

"It was my pleasure," CJ said. She slowly moved forward with her body then gently put her arms around Andi and hugged her.

The tentativeness of her movement gave Andi ample time to dodge the hug if she wanted to, but she didn't. As CJ drew their bodies together in the embrace, she felt her defenses melt away. The times earlier in the day when she had wrapped her arms around the younger athlete on the toboggan had made her body tingle, but this face-to-face body hug, even through many layers of winter clothing, was electric. Her heart was beating so rapidly that she thought her blonde companion would feel it.

CJ whispered in her ear, "I really enjoy being with you," and squeezed Andi a bit tighter.

They remained in the embrace for a few seconds longer before Andi suddenly remembered she was standing in plain view out on her porch with her arms wrapped around a student. The campus was mostly deserted on Sundays but she still felt uncomfortable. She gently pulled back from the other woman's arms.

"Can I call you?" CJ asked.

"I'd be disappointed if you didn't."

"Good answer." CJ grinned. Her green eyes danced as she spoke. "Until soon."

ANDI WENT UPSTAIRS and changed out of her winter clothes. She boiled water for tea, then sat down in front of a pile of papers, but found herself unable to concentrate. Her thoughts kept returning to CJ, their wonderful day, CJ's innuendoes, the warm tingling Andi felt when they touched. She walked across the room to a window looking out toward the campus. From there, she could see the roof of CJ's dorm.

She's a student. What the hell am I doing? I could lose my grad assistant position and be disgraced! She walked to the sofa and sat down at the edge of the cushion. With her head in her hands she sat for a moment, taking deep breaths, then leaned back against the sofa, squeezing a pillow close to her chest. *I admitted to being gay, but I don't even know for sure if she is.* She thought about CJ's many hints and innuendoes and that unforgettable hug on the porch, then shook her head slowly. *But she certainly acts like she is, unless she's just straight and curious, and if that's the case, forget it. That's a heartbreak waiting to happen.*

She stood abruptly and walked over to the window, arms crossed over her chest. *Things are okay now. I haven't done anything wrong . . . yet. I need to take it slow and see what happens. Maybe I'm just flattered by her attention. It's been a long time since someone's made me feel special. What's not to like about it? She's charming. Why shouldn't I enjoy it, and her company? It's nice to have a friend who has similar interests. I need to give things time. Maybe nothing more will develop and then I'll feel foolish that I let myself get all worked up over how to avoid a problem when there wasn't a problem to begin with. Why complicate my life unnecessarily? God, I think too much.*

"ANYBODY HOME?" CJ called as she entered her dorm suite. The aroma of Chinese food wafted through the halls, greeting her as she removed her coat. She was starving from her active day outdoors, and the wonderful smells made her mouth water.

"In here."

CJ followed the sound of the voice into the kitchen. There, sitting at the kitchen table, were Kim and Maria, her two roommates.

"Hungry?" Kim asked.

"Starved!" CJ said.

"Like you had to ask?" Maria said, looking at Kim. She added, "She's always hungry." Maria turned toward CJ and addressed her again. "You're just in time for dinner. Get a plate and grab a seat. There's enough for one more."

"Is this from Ming's in town?" CJ asked. Her eyes flashed with anticipation.

"Of course," Maria said.

"We needed a break from cafeteria food," Kim added.

CJ brought a plate and fork to the table and joined her friends. Maria offered her a small white carton filled with vegetable fried rice and then returned to eating. CJ took a spoonful of the chicken lo mein Kim passed to her, then leaned over her plate and breathed in the fragrant aroma.

"So, where you been all day?" Kim asked.

"Actually, I went tobogganing." CJ spoke matter-of-factly and didn't look up from her bowl, hoping her remark would go unnoticed. Kim and Maria, clearly shocked by the disclosure, stopped chewing and stared blankly at her. CJ kept on eating, trying to ignore their surprise. She finally responded to their silence. "What?"

"Coach is going to kill you," Kim said. She shook her head, then ate another forkful of food.

"Oh, she is not," CJ said. She tried to sound nonchalant, then looked up first at Kim and then at Maria. "It's not like skiing or anything. Injury risk is practically nonexistent." She looked back at Kim. "Does your coach tell you that you can't go for a bike ride during swimming season?"

"Honey, my coach doesn't let me do squat during the season, or before." She pointed at CJ with her fork for emphasis. "My body belongs to the team during the season."

"Ain't that the truth, you heartbreaker!" CJ teased.

Kim poked CJ playfully in the arm with her fork. "Don't you go changing the subject. You know what I'm talking about."

"A couple rides on a toboggan are not a problem," CJ insisted.

"Uh huh," Maria muttered. "So, I suppose you told that to your coach before you went?" She paused and looked at CJ, who stared back at her silently. "Thought so," Maria said sarcastically. "Otherwise, Jen wouldn't have called here looking for you this afternoon." She grinned at CJ, then dug her fork back into her dinner.

"What'd she want?" CJ asked.

"Didn't say. Just asked if you were around. She didn't leave a message," Maria said.

"Okay," Kim interrupted. "Let's forget all that and get down to what's really important."

"Fine with me," CJ agreed. She pushed some rice onto her fork and took a bite. Kim grinned at Maria and rolled her eyebrows up.

"So, who'd you go with?" Maria asked. The basketball star paused in her chewing, then looked first at Kim and then at Maria. She swallowed slowly. Both Maria and Kim put down their forks and stared at CJ.

"Kelly and some of her friends, Martha and Karen, who I met at a party last week, and...and that's about it."

"Who else?" Kim asked. "I can tell you're withholding info."

"Just a friend," she said.

"We're your friends, and we know all your other friends, so tell us who!" Kim said. She planted both her elbows on the table and rested her chin in her palms, staring at CJ. Trying not to act bothered by their prodding, the basketball player scooped another forkful of rice and put it in her mouth. Kim and Maria silently waited for a response as she chewed.

"Well?" Maria asked.

"Listen," CJ said. She put down her fork and looked at both women. "It's no one you know. In fact, she's someone I'm just getting to know, so let's leave it at that, okay?" She picked up her fork again.

"It's not that cute new shortstop on the softball team, is it?" Kim asked. "Maria, I don't know how you're going to concentrate out in left field with that view in front of you." Kim shook her head slowly and smiled.

"Is it?" Maria asked.

"No, it isn't, but no more questions, okay? Let me just keep this to myself for a while. I hate when everybody else knows my business."

"I can't even remember the last time you had the hots for somebody, and now that you do, you aren't going to tell?" Kim said. "Besides, we're not everybody." She crossed her arms over her chest and frowned.

"You know what I mean, though." CJ looked pleadingly at Kim and then at Maria. "It's like a big little circle, and everybody in the circle knows everybody's business. You know it's true, too." She smiled at her friends. "Listen, give me a little more time on my own with this and then I'll share some of it with you both, okay? It's kind of special so far, and I don't want to mess anything up."

Kim looked skeptically at Maria, and they exchanged silent eye communication while CJ looked on. After a few eye rolls and a head nod or two, they both agreed.

"Okay, as long as you tell us first. Deal?" Maria insisted.

"I promise. And do me a favor? Don't say anything about this to anybody else, okay? I don't want people bugging me about it."

"We're not bugging you, we're just looking out for you," Kim countered. "There's a difference."

"I know, and that's why I love you gals." She reached over and touched each of them. She grinned at her friends until they smiled back at her. She knew she could trust them to keep her secret, for now.

Chapter
Twelve

ANDI WAS WORKING at her office desk when she heard a knock on the half-opened door. "Come in," she called without looking up.

"Hey!"

Andi recognized CJ's voice before she looked up and saw her. A few days had passed since their tobogganing adventure, and Andi had missed her cheerful smile. Their occasional phone conversations were enjoyable but didn't take the place of seeing her expressive eyes and her lively bearing.

"Hey, yourself." She smiled broadly as CJ entered then stood in front of her desk.

"I brought you something." CJ whipped out a bag from behind her back.

"What?" Andi moved around to the front of the desk and leaned against it. The blonde woman stood facing her, an arm's length away.

"A mocha latte from the student center, quite tasty on a cold day like today." CJ grinned.

"Perfect! I could use a blast of caffeine, too." She removed the cup from the bag, opened the lid, and took a sip.

"Well?" CJ asked.

"Wonderful, really," Andi said. "You're very sweet." She raised the cup as if to toast her and winked.

"Coming to the game tonight?"

"Would you like a fan in the stands?"

"If you're the fan, then yes."

"Then I'll be there. I've got to meet with my department Chair first, so I may not be there 'til the second half. Is that okay?"

"Whenever you get there is fine." CJ grinned. "Your ticket will be at the door."

ANDI ARRIVED DURING the last few minutes of halftime, when both teams were back out on the court warming up. The home team was up by fifteen points, and the bleachers were half-empty. She chose a seat in the same section where she had sat during the previous game she attended, then removed her coat and took her seat. The players were still wearing their warm-up suits, taking random turns shooting the balls near the basket. CJ glanced up toward the bleachers, scanning the seats. When she saw Andi, she smiled broadly and waved. The grad assistant returned her smile and gave her the thumbs up.

When the refs blew the whistle to end halftime, Andi glanced around the gym and over to the visiting team. As her eyes moved back toward the home bench, she made eye contact with Jen, who appeared to be staring directly at her. Andi, trying not to notice, pretended to be looking casually across the gym at something past Jen. However, she could still make out Jen's hostile glare. Andi turned and looked away.

The whistle blew and the second half of the game began. Nearly an hour later, the final buzzer sounded with the home team victorious. Both teams jogged off to the locker rooms as the fans exited the bleachers and milled about in the gym. While Andi waited in the bleachers for CJ to emerge from the locker room, Jen left the scorer's table and climbed up to where the grad assistant sat. She stood in front of Andi, arms crossed, and looked at her coldly.

"So, have you become a fan of the basketball team, or just of one person in particular?" Jen sneered.

"I was invited," Andi retorted.

"You didn't accept any of my invitations."

"Jen, let's not go there. That was months ago."

"Employees of the school can date each other, but they can't date students."

"I don't need rule reminders, Jen."

"Since you didn't come to this game to see me, I'm guessing that you do. Just how much is that grad assistant position worth to you?" She glared at Andi before turning and walking down the bleachers.

Andi's heart sunk to her stomach. Even though she hadn't crossed the line with CJ or done anything wrong, she felt like a guilty child who was being reprimanded. To be admonished by Jen, of all people, made her feel even worse. She didn't trust Jen, and now she had reason to fear her a bit, too. Andi's good mood had been snuffed out quickly, replaced by an uncomfortable, anxious feeling.

CJ came out of the locker room just as Jen descended the last

Maya Indigal

few steps. The assistant coach walked across the court and into
the coaches' office without acknowledging CJ, who simply
shrugged as she passed by. The basketball player climbed up the
bleachers to sit next to Andi.

"Do you know Jen?" CJ asked.

"We've met at some grad school functions," Andi said
halfheartedly. She looked distracted and lacked her usual warm
smile.

"And what do you think?" Her tone, like Andi's, was
serious.

"I think you played one heck of a game!" She straightened
up quickly and smiled at CJ, trying to brighten up her voice and
mood.

"Not about..."

"I especially like that behind-the-back pass to Thompson.
Very slick."

"You're the one who's slick, if you ask me."

"Come on. Let's get out of this gym and take a walk." Andi
stood and pulled on her coat.

"Could we go somewhere and talk?" CJ asked.

Andi, too, was anxious to leave the gym and go anyplace
where she could avoid Jen's accusing eyes and push Jen's
warning from her mind. She had been in such a good mood for
the last few weeks that she'd nearly forgotten about the real
world of hurtful people like Jen. *Don't let Jen ruin this friendship
because she's bitter*, she lectured herself.

"How about my place?" Andi asked.

"That'd be great."

They walked silently across campus.

"I'LL TAKE YOUR coat," Andi offered as they entered her
second floor apartment. "Can I get you a drink?"

"Seltzer would be great," CJ said.

"Sounds like déjà vu," Andi joked. "I'll be back in a
minute." She disappeared into the kitchen.

CJ sat on the sofa in the same place where she sat that Friday
three weeks ago. She thought about that night often as an early
turning point in their friendship. She sensed that Andi had
opened up to her that night, that they interacted not as a teacher
helping a student but simply as two friends.

And now they had had that strange exchange at the gym.
Andi had dodged a few of her questions in the past, but CJ never
took it personally. CJ had been told that her forthright manner
made some people feel uncomfortable, but she preferred the

direct and honest approach right from the start in a friendship. Since that night when she confronted Andi in the Oasis, she thought that their interaction had been more open and honest. However, at this moment she felt a bit concerned with her blue-eyed friend's earlier demeanor. She wondered about Andi's connection to Jen.

CJ enjoyed their laughter and their long talks, which had grown in frequency lately. She also noticed Andi making more intense eye contact with her, not just looking at her — although she noticed Andi doing that too — but looking into her, as if her eyes mirrored her soul. CJ was drawn into those beautiful pools of blue. Something inside her stirred when Andi looked at her that way. It was that wonderful feeling she wanted to talkabout with Andi.

"How about some music?" CJ asked as Andi returned with her drink. She was nervous about bringing up her feelings, although she was pretty sure that, at least on some level, they were mutual. In her typical direct approach, however, she was determined to make her feelings known to Andi and hoped to spark a reciprocal response.

Andi sorted through her CDs and inserted one into the player. She adjusted the volume, then sat on the sofa near CJ. Her shoulders were tense, and CJ could see she was clenching her jaw, even though she looked like she was making a conscious effort to relax. She took a few deeps breaths, rolled her head from side to side, then exhaled slowly.

"You okay?" CJ asked.

"Long day."

"Why don't you let me work on those tight muscles? Here." CJ put a pillow on the floor in front of her. "Sit here and I'll loosen up your shoulders." Andi, still distracted by thoughts of Jen, did as she was told. CJ placed her hands slowly on Andi and began to massage her tight shoulders. The feel of her hands on Andi's body was electrifying. She worked slowly and deeply, kneading Andi's muscles with strong and confident fingers. With long strokes, she glided her thumbs up and down on either side of Andi's spine to loosen her stress. Andi responded with deep sighs, still aggravated by something.

"So, we can talk to each other about anything, right?"

"Sure."

"Good. It's important to me that I can be open with you. And honest. Are you comfortable with that?"

"Of course I want you to be honest. Are you having a problem with your paper? You can tell me if you are."

"No. It's nothing like that. Nothing bad. Just the opposite.

It's something good. At least I hope you'll think so."

"You got a grad assistant offer?"

"No. It's nothing like that either. If you'll stop guessing, I'll just tell you."

CJ paused to make sure Andi wasn't going to fire any more questions at her. She couldn't believe her friend was so clueless regarding what she was about to tell her. This thought made CJ panic a bit. *Maybe I misjudged her feelings.* She squeezed out the rising doubt and took a deep breath before speaking.

"Well?" Andi asked.

"I've really enjoyed spending time with you lately. Not only all the help that you've given me on my paper, but just getting to know you. I feel like I can be myself around you."

"You can."

"Good." With her hands still draped on Andi's shoulders, CJ leaned forward and kissed her softly on the cheek. Andi, startled and completely off guard, jumped up off the floor.

"I...I can't." She stepped to the window, still shocked at CJ's kiss. Visions of Jen's threat flashed in her head. Her heart was racing and in panic mode, as if she had just been caught doing exactly what she had been warned not to do.

CJ sat with her hands over her face. Obviously embarrassed to look at Andi, she spoke with her face covered. "I'm sorry. I didn't mean to make you uncomfortable. I thought...I didn't mean to assume..."

Andi moved back over to the sofa and gently moved CJ's hands away from her face. She longed to look into CJ's green eyes, but CJ would not look at her.

"It's not you, CJ. I just can't because..."

"Please don't." She got up quickly and grabbed her coat off Andi's bed.

Andi followed in her footsteps. "Where are you going?"

"I need to leave."

"CJ, please don't go."

"I've embarrassed myself enough for one day." She ran down the steps and paused as she reached the porch door. "I'm sorry, Andi." The door banged shut before Andi could descend the flight of stairs. As she reached the bottom, she could make out CJ running across the green, then fading into the night.

She slowly shut the door and dragged herself back upstairs. She sat on the sofa, head in her hands, and wept.

Chapter
Thirteen

"THAT'S QUITE AN earful you're laying on me," Martha said. Andi had just finished telling her about CJ, beginning with the night of the donor reception up through the previous night's fiasco. "It doesn't surprise me all that much, though. I could see the way she looked at you when we were sledding." She finished the last bite of her sandwich, then sipped her coffee. She looked at Andi over the rim of her mug.

"I feel horrible, Martha." She pushed the uneaten portion of her lunch around the plate. Her eyes welled up with tears as she stared at her food. If she looked up at Martha, she feared her eyes would overflow and she'd sob uncontrollably as she had the night before. She took a deep breath and slowly exhaled.

"Why didn't you talk to me sooner? Why'd you let it get to this point?"

"It got to this point last night. Before that everything was fine."

"She was still a student before last night, Andi. Isn't that why this is a problem?"

Martha's comment hit the bull's eye and Andi knew she was right. Andi wanted to believe the situation wasn't her fault, that it wasn't anyone's fault; however, she reflected on a conversation she'd had with CJ once, about fate versus personal control, and she knew she had to shoulder the responsibility. Martha was right. She should have seen this coming.

"But we were just friends," Andi said in a weak attempt to justify her position.

"Come on, Andi. You said you were developing feelings for her. So nothing happened between you two—yet, but from what you were describing, it was just a matter of time." She put down her coffee cup and leaned forward with her elbows on the table. "What happened last night was inevitable. The problem was, you weren't expecting it at that moment."

"So now what do I do?" She pushed her plate to the middle

of the table and rested her forearms on the space in front of her.

"You thank your lucky stars you didn't cross the line and get caught, especially by Jen, that's what you do. I don't trust that bitch as far as I could throw her. She'd march her behind right over to the dean and tell all kinds of stories, and then your grad assistant position would be as good as gone." Andi could see Martha was getting herself worked up as she spoke. Her face, usually happy, was red and frowning. The napkin was balled up in her fist.

"But what about our friendship? I've grown to really enjoy CJ's company." She thought of CJ's surprise visits at her office, the wonderful day tobogganing, and their long conversations. The idea of having those things taken away ripped at her heart.

"Well, then this emotional distance will allow you to work on that friendship—"

"If I haven't already ruined it."

"If it ruins that easily, maybe you should wonder how strong it was to begin with." She reached across the table and rested her hand on Andi's forearm. Martha's eyes softened, and she spoke kindly to her. "Listen, girlfriend. I don't want to see you get hurt again. Take things slow. If CJ really likes you, she won't run away. In three more months she'll graduate, then she won't be a student here any more. Give your friendship that much time to grow, and see where it leads." She patted Andi's forearm before moving her hand away. "You've got a lot to lose, Andi. Think long and hard about what you're going to do."

Andi looked at Martha's concerned face. She offered a sad smile to her friend, then sighed. She knew Martha was right. Martha's insights and support had helped see her through the Liz crisis. Martha knew Andi like a sister, yet she offered the advice of a close and loving friend.

"Thanks so much for meeting with me, Martha."

"You know I'm always here for you." She smiled, then looked at her watch. "I've got to get back to the Registrar's office now, though. You okay?"

"Yeah, I'm fine."

"I think fine is pushing it a bit." Martha smirked, trying to get a smile from Andi. "Things will get better. They always do." She stood from the table and put on her coat. "Call us, will you? And don't wait until the sky falls in, okay?"

"Okay." Andi stood and faced her friend. "Thanks again, Martha." She gave her a long hug, which Martha returned sincerely. They walked out of the diner together then drove off in separate cars.

Chapter
Fourteen

KIM LEANED AGAINST the door frame of CJ's room. "Why don't you come with us?"

"I'm just not in the mood," CJ said. She lay stretched out, belly down, over her blanket bedspread, arms hugging the pillow balled up underneath her face. She looked over at Kim, but made no attempt to move off the bed.

"But it's Friday and the whole gang will be going. It'll be fun."

"Thanks, but I'll pass."

"It'll do you good to get out and have some fun, CJ. You've been moping around for the past two days."

"I just don't feel like it."

Kim walked into the room and sat on the edge of CJ's bed. She placed her hand on CJ's back and rubbed it lightly up and down, as one would rub a puppy. The basketball player sighed deeply but said nothing. Her sad eyes focused on nothing in particular across the room. Kim sat quietly with her for a few moments, apparently hoping CJ might open up, but she remained silent.

"Want to tell me what's bothering you so much?"

"I don't really feel like talking about it."

"You know you can trust me, don't you, CJ? We've been friends since freshman year and I've cried on your shoulder more times than I can count. I hate to see you so sad. Won't you talk to me? What happened?"

CJ listened as Kim spoke and appreciated her friend's concern. It was true Kim had turned to CJ often to discuss relationship problems in Kim's Heartbreak-a-Month Club, but CJ had always taken on the role of the strong advisor. Now she felt weak and hated to appear that way to anyone else, even her friend, yet Kim's interest was sincere. After bottling up her emotions for the last forty-eight hours, CJ was ready to burst.

"Rejection," CJ divulged. That was all she could bring herself to say before her eyes welled up with tears. She didn't want to break down into a sobbing mess, so she stopped after that one word and squeezed her pillow harder.

"Someone rejected you?" Kim rubbed her friend's back again. "I'm sorry, CJ. I know how bad that feels. Do I know this person?"

"Let's not talk about that, okay?"

"Sure. I guess it doesn't matter. She's a bad judge of character, that's all I have to say."

"I'm the bad judge."

"What do you mean?"

"I really thought things were going well, that we clicked. When she looked at me or when I looked at her, I could see something—or at least I thought I did. Maybe I just wanted so badly to believe it was happening." Tears flowed from her eyes, and she turned her face away from Kim. "I feel like such a fool."

"Maybe it's not you, CJ. Don't get me wrong, I'm not trying to defend her or anything, but maybe she's just not ready now."

"Obviously."

"I mean, are you sure she's gay?"

"Yes, that I know."

"Maybe she just got out of a relationship. You sure she's not seeing anyone? Maybe she's just not emotionally available right now. Maybe—"

"Maybe I thought it was meant to be, and it wasn't."

"That might be the case, too," Kim acknowledged. She spoke softly and rubbed CJ's back gently. "Should I quote you, and give you the advice that you always give me?"

"Go ahead. I guess I deserve it." CJ turned to face Kim.

"Time. You've got to give it time. Then, when you step away from it, things come back into perspective."

"Remind me not to give you any dumb-ass advice anymore." She poked Kim playfully in the leg and forced a sad smile.

"You can give me advice anytime, girlfriend. You've always been a good listener, so thanks for letting me return the favor."

"Don't tell anyone what I told you, okay? If anyone asks where I am tonight, tell them I had a splitting headache."

"You sure you won't change your mind?"

"I'll just stay here and give myself some time, just like you said I said."

"Okay, girlfriend." She tussled CJ's blonde hair as she got off the bed. "If you need anything, I'll be around over the weekend."

"Thanks Kim. Have fun tonight, and please, keep this between us." Kim faced her and put her finger up to her lips, then crossed her heart. She waved, then left the dorm room.

Chapter
Fifteen

"HELLO?"

Andi had been trying unsuccessfully to reach CJ for the past five days. When she finally heard CJ's voice on the other end of the phone, she was more surprised than prepared.

"Hi, CJ. It's me, Andi." She paused, listening attentively not only for her reply, but for the tone in her voice. She longed to hear the cheerful and peppy response she had come to enjoy from CJ. Closing her eyes, she anxiously held her breath and waited.

"Hi," CJ said. Her tone was flat and lifeless. It lacked the spark, the enthusiasm that usually characterized her voice.

"I've...been trying to reach you."

"I was out of state. We had a game."

"How'd you do?"

"We won."

"When did you get back?"

"Saturday night."

Andi had called her Saturday night, as well as Sunday. CJ was either screening her calls or simply not answering the phone. Andi's heart sank. She wanted to cry. "How are you?" she asked.

"Very sad and quite embarrassed, if you really want to know." Her voice was soft and sounded hurt, not angry.

"Oh, CJ. I'm so sorry. Can't we meet somewhere to talk?"

"I don't think I'd be comfortable with that right now."

"Please? Just for a few minutes? There are things I want to explain to you, things that need to be said." There was silence on the other end of the phone, and Andi waited anxiously, hoping she'd convinced CJ to see her and talk. She could hear the younger athlete take a deep breath and sigh. Holding her breath for an answer, Andi waited.

"No, I can't. Not now."

Andi, anticipating a more positive answer, exhaled and slumped in her chair. She felt a lump rising up in her throat and feared that she'd start weeping soon if she continued to hear CJ's sad voice.

"What about your paper? We could meet to talk about that."

"I can't see you about that either, Andi. Don't you get it? I feel vulnerable and exposed around you. Even just talking to you on the phone is difficult—"

"I just want to help—"

"Then give me some space."

Andi had heard that request before, and she was crushed. In her experience, space led only to further, unbridgeable distance. Her attempts to patch up and save their friendship were failing miserably. Short of begging, she didn't know what to say. "Is there anything I can do? I'll do anything that you ask because I want us to be friends." Her entreaty fell just short of outright begging.

CJ was totally crushed to hear Andi say that she wanted them to be friends. After she had poured her heart out and felt romantically rejected, did Andi think it would be so easy to forget that hurt and slip back into their comfortable friendship? Clearly, friendship was all Andi was looking for. What little glimmer of hope lived inside CJ simply burst upon hearing Andi say that.

"You can give me time and space. I just need to think."

"Oh, CJ—"

"Please Andi. You asked me what you could do and I told you. I've got to go."

"Wait! Don't hang up yet. Will you call me...when you're ready?"

"I can't make any promises."

"Until soon?"

CJ heard Andi borrowing her expression. It hurt her to think about how excitedly she herself had said it not that long ago, how it could never have been soon enough before she saw the beautiful, blue-eyed woman again. She paused before speaking.

"Bye, Andi."

Andi heard the phone line click and go dead. No longer could she contain the floodgates of emotion that welled up in her heart. With sobs that rocked her body she cried, tears streaming down her face. She rocked and sobbed on the sofa until she had no more tears to cry. With eyes so puffy she could barely see, she sat down at the table, took out her journal, and began to write.

Dear CJ,

I want so badly to talk to you, not on the phone or in a note, but in person. I need to see your beautiful green eyes looking into my eyes and into my heart so that you know how I really feel, and how much I miss you. Words are inadequate, but I know that if we could meet, face-to-face, our hearts would reconnect...

Chapter
Sixteen

"PARDON ME. EXCUSE me." Andi felt like a salmon swimming upstream as she tried to make her way against the tide of people emptying from the gym. She was determined to speak with CJ, and she knew she'd find her here after the game.

More than a week had passed since their last awkward phone conversation, and she had been totally miserable because so many things were left unsaid. She missed her new friend terribly, too. Even though the basketball star had asked her to give her time and space, Andi believed that, if she could just see her and talk to her in person, CJ might understand. She needed to look in CJ's eyes to see if that spark was still burning or if it was extinguished. She hoped she wasn't too late.

The bleachers were nearly empty as she entered the gym. Her heart thumped wildly as she climbed the steps to her usual spot in the stands, hoping CJ would notice her as she left the gym. It also gave Andi a good vantage point to spot the blonde athlete, in case she wasn't looking into the seats. She fidgeted with her keys, nervous about seeing CJ again. With eyes fixed on the locker room door, she sat almost trance-like, waiting for her to emerge. She was so distracted she didn't hear the footsteps approach until someone was standing right beside her. Startled, Andi turned to find Jen.

"What the hell have you done to her?" Jen spoke in a hushed, jaw-clenched whisper. Her face was snarled in a frown. Her arms were crossed on her chest. Andi was so taken aback to see her that Jen's words didn't immediately sink in.

"What?"

"To CJ. What did you do?"

"Jen, I don't—"

"You know exactly what I'm talking about. CJ's been distracted, moping around. She's not concentrating and her game is off. Even her teammates noticed." Jen uncrossed her arms and leaned forward toward Andi. She pointed in Andi's face as she spoke, barely able to control her voice. "You've done this to her. You're playing with her head like you tried to play with me."

"You're wrong."

"You've disappeared. You haven't been to a game in almost two weeks. That's exactly how long CJ has been a mess. What kind of games are you playing with her?" Her voice was increasing in volume but Jen didn't seem to notice. Andi, uncomfortable with the accusations as well as Jen's tone, glanced around the gym, hoping no one else was witnessing the scene. She knew she needed to end the confrontation before it got louder and uglier.

"You have no right to accuse me of anything." Her voice was rough yet hushed. She hoped it would help to lower Jen's volume as well. "And I resent the implication that I've done anything to her." Jen's accusations were sinking in, along with the guilt of hearing that CJ was an emotional wreck and knowing that she was the cause.

"The hell you didn't."

"You don't know what you're talking about, Jen. I know CJ didn't tell you this."

"She didn't have to. I have two eyes. I can see for myself."

The admission that CJ hadn't spoken to Jen was a relief, and fueled Andi's anger at her accusations. She was beginning to realize Jen's tirade wasn't only about the star player being distracted.

"You're making assumptions that aren't true," Andi countered. She didn't want to say specifically what Jen was accusing her of, since CJ clearly hadn't told Jen anything to begin with. Any details Andi mentioned in her defense, Jen might turn around and use against her.

"Then why is she talking about going to grad school out West? She always considered that a last resort, and now it's tops on her list. Why is she running away?" Jen's hands were on her hips, her voice under control once again.

"That's her decision, Jen. Butt out."

"You're the one who needs to butt out, Andi. If you start bothering her again, I'm going right to the dean." She turned and took one step, then looked again at Andi. "Consider yourself warned." She stomped down the steps.

Both Andi and Jen were too angry and distracted to notice CJ's head peeking through the locker room door, slightly ajar. As Jen turned and stomped away, CJ closed the door quietly. The basketball star could not make out clearly what they were saying, but their aggressive tone was unmistakable. She stood alone in the locker room for a few minutes, deciding what to do, before she turned and went out the back exit, disappearing into the night.

Andi sat in the bleachers until the clean up crew shut off the gym lights.

Chapter
Seventeen

CJ STARED AT the 3-by-5 card piles spread out on her desk. Like pieces of a puzzle laid out in front of her, they just didn't seem to fit together. No matter how she tried to arrange them, parts were missing. That seemed like the pattern of her life lately, too. No matter how she tried to distract her thoughts or busy her time, an important piece was missing there as well. That piece was Andi.

She thought back to Andi's analogy of the ingredients and the cookie, trying to make sense of the formula she was attempting to follow to complete the paper. However, her mind and heart were stuck on the words and images of Andi herself, not on the concepts the grad assistant tried to explain, and CJ couldn't seem to focus on her work. The harder she tried to block out thoughts of Andi, the stronger her presence became.

The argument between Andi and Jen the previous night also piqued her curiosity, but she had no way of finding out its origin. She wondered about Andi's connection to Jen. Clearly, one existed between the two women, although Andi had brushed it off as a casual acquaintance between grad assistants. Jen had been grumpy lately, and CJ didn't feel close enough to the assistant coach to speak to her about personal matters. Lately, in fact, when Jen commented about CJ's noticeable distraction, the basketball player just brushed it off as playoff pressure.

Frustrated with the paper and her inability to concentrate, CJ pushed her chair away from her desk and got up. She walked over to the small dorm fridge in the living room and pulled out a soda. When the front door opened, she turned to face Kim.

"Greetings!" Kim grinned. "Check this out." She held up a bio lab report with a red B+ in the upper corner. "Pretty impressive, huh?"

"Way to go," CJ said. She plopped down on the sofa and raised her soda can in a mock toast. "I'm glad you're doing well."

"Still struggling with that paper? Why don't you go down to the English department and ask for some help? They're pretty good about that kind of thing."

"I'll work it out." She sipped her soda as Kim removed her coat and tossed it onto her bed in the other room. Kim walked back into the living room and sat in an armchair across from CJ.

"You're still down, aren't you?"

"I guess not enough time has passed. You did say that was the answer, didn't you?" A hint of sarcasm rose in her voice. "Well, I'm still waiting."

"Maybe you should do something to get if off your mind."

"Get if off my mind! Do something? Shit, that's all I've been trying to do is get if off my mind!" She slammed the soda can down on the end table next to her. "Do you have any idea what I have on my mind? Do you? How about playoff pressure." Her voice rose in volume and intensity. "We're into the first rounds of the playoffs, something I've dreamed about my whole career. What a perfect way to end my senior year, with a tournament bid. We're ranked in the top three, and that means we're good enough to take it all! The coach, the team, they're all counting on me to be at the top of my game because when I'm flat, we lose. That's a lot of fucking pressure, you know? I obviously don't make the right decisions all the time, and now's not a good time to mess up. And, on top of that, I've got commitment deadline for grad school positions. A school on the West Coast needs a final yes or no by the end of the month. They're offering me a great package, but do I want to pick up my life and move across the country? Some days I think so. I just want to run the hell away from here as far and as fast as I can go. But I don't want to make such a big decision like that for the wrong reasons. And if I ever finish this stinkin' paper, maybe I can impress someone around here enough to get a position for next year. But do I want to be here? I don't know. It's familiar, it's comfortable, but where's it leading me? Do something? What the hell should I do?" She paused for a moment and looked at Kim. Her green eyes were sad and her voice softened. "Tell me, Kim, how the hell do I get her out of my heart?"

She sat back against the sofa and took a deep breath, then exhaled slowly. Tears ran down her cheeks. Kim moved from the chair and sat next to her on the sofa, putting her arm around CJ's shoulders. They sat in silence for a few minutes while the basketball player fought back her tears.

"Sorry I unloaded on you," CJ said.

"It's okay," Kim said. "That's a lot to deal with and I know that you've not been yourself lately." She shook her head slowly.

"You really got it bad for her, don't you."

"So now what?"

"One step at a time, one day at a time. Concentrate on the playoffs, since that's going on right now. You've trained years for this, CJ! Focus on it and enjoy it. Just go out there and do your best. That's all your coaches and teammates expect of you, not perfection. Regarding the grad school out West, let them wait 'til the end of the month. Tell them you're in the middle of the playoffs and you've got other things on your mind. They don't need to know all of what those other things are. As for the mystery lady who broke your heart, give that more time. Who knows? Maybe she'll come around. She'd be crazy not to." Kim bumped her playfully and winked.

CJ forced a small smile. "You're right, Kim. What you said makes good sense, but it's easier said than done." She stood, then walked across the room and tossed the soda can in the trash. "I'm really sorry I yelled before."

"Don't worry about it. My coach yells at me all the time, so I'm used to it."

"You're a good friend, Kim. Thanks."

"What do you say we head down to the cafeteria for dinner. Wednesday is pasta night and I could use the carbs. Practice has been killer lately."

"Sure. Just let me get my coat."

Chapter
Eighteen

"KNOW WHAT BOTHERS me?" Andi said. She slipped off her shoes and sat cross-legged on the sofa near the fire.

"What's that?" Karen asked.

"I'm afraid CJ thinks that her kiss freaked me out that night. She didn't know about the conversation Jen and I had after the game, or that I was worried about Jen's threat. What freaked me out was Jen, not the kiss." She looked at Martha and Karen, who were sitting on the loveseat facing her. "Actually," Andi added, sheepishly, "the kiss was really nice."

"What are we going to do with you?" Martha asked.

"I'm sorry to make you hear all this again. I just don't know what to do. You gals see the whole picture more objectively than I do. Any suggestions?"

"You tried calling her, right?" Martha asked.

"Yeah, but her voice was cold and distant. I didn't feel comfortable, and I didn't get the feeling that she'd be too receptive."

"How about e-mail?" Karen asked. "Better yet, how about a letter? You could send her a good, old-fashioned love letter to melt her heart. You're good with words and —"

"No letter!" Martha insisted. "If that letter gets into the wrong hands, we might as well stick a fork in you 'cause you'll be done. You can't have that kind of evidence floating around. First, you don't know she'll get it, unless you hand deliver it, and that's probably not an option. Second, and I hate to say it, she might not be receptive to the letter and might be so mad at you that she gives it to the dean or something just to get you in trouble —"

"Martha!" Karen said.

"I'm sorry to be blunt, but she's got to weigh all the risks."

"CJ didn't seem to be the kind of gal to be running to the dean," Karen said.

Martha shook her head. "Heartbreak makes people do crazy things. You work in a courtroom, Karen. How many cases a day do judges see that have to do with love gone bad?"

"Girls!" Andi interrupted. She put up her hands to stop their bickering. "Enough about a letter. I get the idea." She sighed deeply and shook her head. "So, no phone calls, no email, no letter. What communication option does that leave me?"

"Why don't you just try to talk with her again in person?" Martha said. "You've got nothing to lose. Maybe she'll soften up a bit and listen. Be prepared, though. She might just tell you in person what she said on the phone. Are you prepared for the kind of rejection that CJ felt?"

"I'm getting to the point where I have to try something," shrugged Andi. "I'm driving myself—and you gals—crazy. I can't concentrate on my work, and my studies certainly have suffered, too."

"Aside from talking to us, which you're always welcome to do," Karen said, "are you doing anything else to manage your anxiety over this? Meditating, maybe, or working out?"

"Working out, definitely. I've also been writing, actually. It's always been my outlet. In fact, every night I've sat down at the end of the day and written in my journal. Writing helps me sort out my feelings, you know? It forces me to think about one thing at a time while I write, even though my head is swimming with a million things at once." Andi looked up and smiled sadly at her friends. "I wrote my first entry about CJ shortly after we met at the reception back in January. Lately, I've been writing entries to her, like in a letter. I guess I'm practicing what I'd like to say to her, if she'll ever talk to me again."

"CJ will talk to you again," Karen assured. She got up off the loveseat and sat next to Andi, put her arm around her shoulder, and gave her a hug. "I'm getting a good vibe here," she added, pointing to her heart.

"Well, good vibe or not, don't lose that journal," Martha muttered. She shook her head slowly. "You really fell hard, didn't you?"

"It sneaked up on me, that's the funny thing. Her warm laughter and dimpled smile, a surprise visit, homemade cookies..." Andi's voice trailed off at the remembrances of CJ, and her eyes welled up with tears. She sighed deeply.

"One way or another, things will be okay," Karen promised. "Things usually have a way of working out, but sometimes not as quickly as we'd like. That's the hard part."

"Whatever you need, we're here for you," Martha added. "Just be careful, Andi, okay?"

"Thanks, and I will." She leaned back and rested her head against the sofa, then stared into the blazing fire.

Chapter
Nineteen

ANDI CLIMBED TO nearly the last row of the bleachers before she chose a seat far off to the left of the court where the visiting team's fans were gathered. She pulled the baseball cap low over her eyes so she wouldn't be recognized, especially by Jen. For the last few days, she'd struggled with the decision about how to speak with CJ, and this game seemed like the best option.

She had hoped their paths might cross on campus, as they had that one day when she was struggling with the overhead projector, but CJ was not around. Andi even spent extra time in her office, in case she decided to stop by, but that too led to nothing. With the conference tournament finals playing in the gym that night, she knew exactly where she could find the basketball star. Andi was optimistic the team would win, which might put CJ in a more receptive mood.

Having made the decision to speak with her, no matter the outcome, Andi felt relieved. For weeks Andi had been talking to the younger athlete in countless dialogues in her head as well as through numerous journal entries, and she felt hopeful she could find the words to break through to CJ. One way or another, she was going to meet with her face to face after the game. She settled into her seat to watch and wait.

Although initially distracted by her thoughts of talking to CJ, Andi quickly got sucked into the excitement of the game. CJ's team was seeded number one, but the number six team was putting up a heck of a fight to upset the home squad. Their rowdy fans brought posters and banners and roared with cheers every time their team scored. Andi felt out of place surrounded by fans who where hooting and hollering for the underdogs, but she felt confident she could escape watchful eyes if she stayed amongst them.

As rambunctious as the fans were in the bleachers, the players on the floor were even more fired up. With the score fluctuating no more than three points in either team's favor, every point became crucial. The roughness of the game increased, too, with post players physically shoving and boxing out in the paint, and players diving to retrieve loose balls. Fouls were abundant, yet the refs seemed reluctant to stop the game with foul calls.

CJ was one of the more scrappy players on the court and Andi watched, mesmerized, as the captain pushed herself and her teammates to try and pull out a victory. She could see the desire burning in her athletic friend as she exhausted herself trying to do everything and be everywhere on the court. The challengers knew CJ was their biggest threat, so they double-teamed her, bumping and shoving to try and get the Bobcat's star player out of her rhythm. With every blow of the whistle, the basketball star bent forward and placed her hands on her knees, ribs heaving as she panted for breath. With the score so close, Andi realized the coach was unlikely to take CJ out of the game to give her the breather that she needed.

With less than a minute left in the first half and the game tied, both teams aggressively tried to score in order to take the lead and the emotional edge into the locker room. Closely defended, CJ dribbled the ball to the top of the key before passing it off to the baseline forward. After dishing the ball, CJ cut hard to the basket with an opponent hot on her heels. She received the pass and leaned in for the lay up just as the defender leaped up with both hands to deflect her shot. The two players' arms became tangled, their bodies ricocheting off each other in mid-air. As they twisted to land balanced on their feet, the defender's elbow crashed into CJ's face, knocking her to the floor with a thud. She lay writhing on the ground, hands to her face, as the official blew the whistle.

Andi leaped to her feet as CJ hit the floor. The rambunctious fans grew silent, and all eyes focused on the injured star. Her teammates gathered around her, then the trainer jogged out onto the court. The head coach and Jen also walked out quickly to send the players to the bench as the trainer kneeled over CJ. The officials hovered nearby. The crowd murmured their concern. Andi watched helplessly from her seat in the bleachers. Twelve seconds remained on the game clock, yet several minutes passed in the gymnasium without CJ getting up. Finally, the trainer stood and spoke into a walkie-talkie.

Moments later, rescue squad members burst into the gym rolling a gurney, which they moved next to the injured athlete. They lowered the unit, then surrounded her and in unison lifted her onto the cart. Andi could make out what looked to be gauze packing on CJ's face as they strapped her down onto the bed. They raised the unit and rolled it off the court as the crowd rose to its feel and began clapping. Andi stood and clapped too, yet her knees felt so weak that she nearly fell back into her seat.

The players came back on the court for the final twelve seconds, then the buzzer sounded for halftime. The crowd returned to their feet to stretch or to leave for the lobby area. Andi, still reeling from the effect of witnessing CJ's crushing injury, sat limply in her seat.

Andi's body remained inert, yet her mind was racing. She was worried about CJ's injury, which must be serious to warrant her being removed on a stretcher. Fighting back the urge to run down from the bleachers and across the court after her injured friend, she stood once again on shaky legs and descended the stairs. She walked past the scorer's table and the empty team benches and headed toward the locker room. Fear and worry about CJ's injury clouded her mind as she moved trance-like toward the door. As she reached for the handle, the door swung open, nearly hitting her. The unexpected motion snapped her out of her mental fog. She looked into glaring eyes.

"What do you want?" Jen snarled. Her eyes narrowed.

"How's CJ?" Andi asked. Her voice was pleading.

"Hurt. They're evaluating her now."

"I need to see her," Andi insisted. She reached past Jen and tried to pull open the door but Jen blocked her attempt.

"No one's allowed in there, especially not you. You've caused enough trouble."

"What the hell's that supposed to mean?" Andi tried once again, unsuccessfully, to get into the locker room. "Get out of my way," she snapped.

"Do you really want to make a scene here, with all the school dignitaries in the stands watching the game?" Jen crossed her arms over her chest and stood looking smugly at Andi. At that moment, the door swung open again, nearly hitting Jen, who was standing in front of it. One of the players poked her head out and addressed the assistant coach.

"Coach said to tell you that they're moving her to the infirmary now." Jen, who had turned to face the player as she spoke, nodded and motioned with her hand for the player to return to the locker room. By the time Jen turned around to lace into Andi again, she had disappeared into the gym.

ANDI CREPT STEALTHILY along the shiny linoleum floor of the infirmary hallway, glad she was wearing sneakers, not loafers. The night supervisor was seated behind her desk at the other end of the building, far out of sight, but Andi didn't want to alert anyone else to her presence as she made her way toward the patients' rooms. The glow of the exit signs as well as dim night lighting provided just enough illumination for her to see yet still blend into the shadows as she moved down the corridor.

Earlier that night, she had waited outside for nearly two hours by the back entrance of the infirmary. She lurked behind a cluster of trees not far from the dumpster, waiting for an opportunity to get into the building. Finally, she saw a night-shift custodian hauling out the trash. As he pushed his cart out to the dumpster at the far end of the lot, she skulked out from the trees' shadows and crept inside the back door. She could hear banging as he tossed the bags into the bin while she made her way up the stairs leading to the main floor.

Sneaking into the building this way took her back to her college days, and she smiled faintly at the memory. Liz used to lead similar midnight raids into the cafeteria kitchen. Once inside, she would invade the food pantry or freezer to provide midnight snacks for the gang waiting back at the dorm. Most of the time, she would creep out the door with bags of cookies or a five-gallon tub of ice cream. Now and then, Andi accompanied Liz on these adventures. *Who would have thought that Liz's sneakiness training would come in so handy*, she thought as she continued down the hallway. *Liz.* She stopped abruptly as an image of Liz entered her mind merely by thinking her name. She paused and waited for the familiar heartache to follow, and was pleasantly surprised when it didn't. Her dark eyebrows arched upward slightly as she considered the reason. The image of CJ's beautiful face filled her mind's eye.

Andi continued down the hall past the treatment rooms, storage closets, and restrooms, until she neared the area where overnight patients were accommodated. The first door she approached was shut completely. She dared not turn the handle and make noise that might either alert the floor supervisor or startle what might be the wrong patient inside the room. She hoped CJ wasn't behind that door.

Several doors further down were cracked open slightly, so Andi silently poked her head in each one, looking for CJ's familiar face. The fluorescent light from the parking lot outside the rooms glowed brightly enough for Andi to recognize that none of the persons sleeping in those rooms was CJ.

For a moment she panicked. What if CJ's injury was so serious she had to be transported from the infirmary to the local hospital? During the time Andi spent waiting out back, trying to sneak in, an ambulance could have pulled around the front of the building and whisked CJ away completely unbeknownst to her. She shivered at the thought and shook her head quickly, as if dispelling the thought would prevent it from having taken place. She sighed deeply yet silently as she pushed the next door ajar just enough to peek her head inside the room. There, in the gray-white glow of the parking lot lighting, she saw a person lying face up on the bed, with thick white bandages covering the eyes.

She inhaled so forcefully that she feared the sound of her breath catching would alert someone of her presence. Without thinking, she stepped quickly beyond the threshold then pushed the door back to its original, nearly closed position. Slowly she turned to face the bed once again.

Andi stood perfectly still, conscious of her shallow breathing and her racing heart. As first one, then two minutes passed, her eyes adjusted to the relative darkness of the room. From where she stood, only two paces from the bed, she confirmed that the person lying there was indeed CJ. Her short, wavy blonde hair, pushed back off her forehead by the bandages, spilled out over the top of the pillow's surface. The cotton hospital blanket was pulled up and tucked under her arms, which rested near her sides on top of the blanket. An IV tube was hooked up to her left arm. Andi could see the slow and steady rise and fall of her chest as CJ breathed deeply in her sleep.

A lump rose to her throat as she fought back tears. She tilted her head and stared up at the ceiling to prevent them from running down her cheeks. *Now what?* she thought to herself. *What the hell am I going to do now?* She took a big, silent breath, then exhaled slowly as she lowered her head to gaze at CJ once again. Cautiously she stepped toward the bed until she was standing at her friend's side, looking down at her.

Andi's eyes took in CJ's image lying before her. She resented the fact that those bandages covered CJ's beautiful, dancing green eyes. Andi looked at her friend's nose, remembering how it wrinkled up when she laughed. CJ's lips, slightly open as she breathed, looked dark and soft. Andi remembered how they felt on her cheek that fateful night nearly three weeks ago. *That's why I'm here*, she determined. *She was the brave one the first time.*

Tearing her eyes away from CJ, Andi looked across the room and spotted a chair near the window. She moved slowly so as to avoid making noise and crossed the floor, silently picking up the chair. She stepped back to the bed before lowering the chair noiselessly to the floor next to CJ's bed. Carefully she moved around to the front of the chair and lowered herself into the seat.

Andi cautiously leaned her forearm on the bed next to CJ's

thigh, then reached tentatively to touch CJ's hand. Gently, she slid her right hand in place under CJ's palm before lightly wrapping her fingers around the injured woman's hand. CJ's hand, while warm to the touch, remained motionless in Andi's. She squeezed it gently once and was surprised when the hand she was holding twitched back and momentarily returned the pressure before growing heavy again. Andi sat holding CJ's hand for several minutes, relishing the physical connection that she felt, which she had missed so much over the last few weeks.

"I'm sorry, CJ," she whispered into the darkness. "I never wanted to push you away. In fact, sitting here holding your hand, touching you, makes me realize what I do want." She shook her head slightly and frowned. "I just didn't know how to handle it at the time, and boy did I mess up." She paused and looked at the woman lying there, nearly motionless except for the rise and fall of her breathing. "That's why I came to the game tonight. I was hoping that, after the game, we could have talked. I know you said you wanted space, and I tried to give you that, but I was kind of hoping...if you knew how I really felt...you might not want that space after all." She paused and watched CJ breathe again. After a minute, she continued.

"What I really felt was scared." She hesitated, then continued again in a soft whisper. "Earlier that night after the game, Jen gave me a not-so-friendly reminder that you were a student. She basically threatened my grad assistant position, is what she did." Andi took a breath in, then exhaled slowly. "Her threat was on my mind when you kissed me." She paused and ran her fingers across her forehead and into her hair, rubbing the back of her neck before placing her hand in her lap. Her right hand continued to hold CJ's. "So, instead of returning your kiss, like I've thought about doing a thousand times since that night, I panicked. I hurt you." Her blue eyes filled with tears, which trailed slowly down her cheeks.

"Know what else I was scared of?" She continued looking at CJ as if she expected her to answer the whispered question. As the silence continued, so did she. "How quickly you worked your way into my heart." She smiled at her remembered image of tobogganing with CJ. "I haven't trusted anyone with my heart in a long time, and when you kissed me, wordlessly asking for that trust, I ran." She paused, then continued. "You never gave me a reason to be afraid, but I was. It wasn't your fault."

"But know what scares me even more than all that?" She paused again, as if waiting for a reply. "The thought of losing you, the idea of missing out on something wonderful that could happen between us. That's why I had to see you at the game, and that's why I sneaked in here tonight." She raised her left hand and placed it on top of CJ's, gently sandwiching her friend's hand between her own. "Forgive me, CJ. Please give me another chance."

Gently, Andi squeezed CJ's hand between her own and once again her pressure was answered by a twitch as CJ's fingers momentarily flexed around Andi's hand. Andi smiled sadly, then removed her left hand from on top of CJ's. Her right hand continued to cradle the injured woman's hand on the edge of the bed. Andi slid down the seat a bit so that her head was leaning on the back of the chair and continued to watch CJ breathe. She extended her long legs in front of her, then crossed them at the ankles.

Andi yawned silently, shutting her eyes tightly for an extended blink. *I'm exhausted.* She looked at her watch, which brightly glowed the hour. *No wonder. It's tomorrow already.* Stifling another yawn, she slid a little lower in the chair and fought to keep her eyes open. Within moments, she lost the battle.

CJ WAS DIMLY aware of pressure around her eyes, but the strong painkillers that dripped steadily into the IV in her arm insured that she would sleep through the discomfort. She didn't know where she was, but that didn't seem to bother her. She felt like she could step out of her body and hover in the air above it, knowing that the body below in the bed was hers but not quite feeling like she could control it. Everything felt heavy. In fact, she couldn't even raise her arms or move her feet, but in her mind, for now, that was okay. Something made her feel safe, like she was being watched over. She felt like it didn't matter that she didn't know where she was or that she couldn't move. Someone else did, and she was comforted by that feeling. Now and then some stimulus seeped through her consciousness. Was that a touch? Did she hear breathing? A voice? An indefinable presence surrounded her, wrapping her in a fog of security. CJ's hand twitched as her mind waves ebbed and flowed. A faint smile appeared on her lips as she drifted back into the drug-induced lassitude. Her guardian never noticed.

Chapter
Twenty

THE NEXT MORNING, CJ emerged from sleep as a diver rises toward the water's surface from the depths of the pool. Although vaguely cognizant that she was waking, she remained in darkness. She was conscious of a dull headache and pressure on her eyes, which increased as she awakened more fully. Her skin pinched under the adhesive tape that held the IV shunt in place. Gradually, she became aware of the air, warm and dry, which smelled like antiseptic. A deep inhale reminded her that her body was quite sore. She rolled her shoulders back, pressing her shoulder blades to the bed and squeezing her hands. One of them was not empty. She gasped and pulled it back toward her chest quickly.

"Who's there?" she asked. Her tone revealed fear and vulnerability.

Andi was startled from sleep. She sat up in the chair and quickly removed her hand from the bedside near CJ, clasping both hands in her lap. Shaking her head to clear slumber from her mind, she stared at the blonde lying in the bed. Words stuck in her throat. The events of the previous evening came crashing back to her mind and she sat there, paralyzed by fear and indecision. Her heart was pounding in her chest and she could hear her own shallow, rapid breathing.

"Answer me," CJ repeated, her tone more confident. "Who's there?"

"It's me," she whispered, then added, "Andi."

"Andi?" CJ's voice softened, and she tilted her head sideways on the pillow, the gesture reflecting the questioning in her voice. She lowered her arms to the bedside once again.

"Please don't be mad," Andi pleaded. She shifted forward on the seat and gently placed her fingertips on the top of CJ's hand. Her heart continued to race as she studied CJ's face for a response. She watched the injured woman's chest rise and fall rapidly. CJ's lips were parted as if she was poised to speak.

Slowly, CJ closed her mouth. Her full, dark lips gradually

turned up as a small smile emerged on her face, highlighted by her dimple. Although she could not see Andi, she turned her head toward where she heard the other woman breathing rapidly. Without losing skin contact, she turned her hand over so her fingertips touched Andi's.

The older woman breathed in audibly at the contact, then allowed a half grin to tug at her mouth. "CJ...I'm so sorry that I—" She paused as a beam of light was thrown across the bed. Turning toward the door, she was shocked to see a middle-aged man dressed in green hospital scrubs marching into the room. His name tag read T. Bennett, R.N.

"What are you doing here?" Bennett demanded. "How did you get in?"

Andi stood abruptly and faced the man. His forehead was creased with frown lines, and he held a clipboard in one hand. His other fisted hand was pressed against his hip. The muscles in his jaw were clenched.

"I was just—"

"What's going on here?" The woman who spoke entered the room and stood to the side between Mr. Bennett and Andi. Her white lab jacket with clip-on name tag identified her as Dr. Erroll, M.D. Her kind, brown eyes looked from the nurse to Andi, then back again. She arched her dark gray eyebrows, which matched her wavy hair, as she waited for a response.

"That's what I'd like to know," Mr. Bennett said. He looked at the doctor and continued. "I just came in to check on the patient and found this unauthorized visitor in the room." He turned back toward Andi and glared at her. "It's time for you to leave," he ordered. He pointed toward the door with his clipboard, indicating that Andi should precede him out. Andi hung her head and took a step toward the door.

"Wait!" As CJ spoke, both Andi and the nurse stopped and looked at her. The doctor, too, looked at the woman who up until this point had remained silent. "I want her to stay," she insisted.

"Doctor, this type of intrusion is highly unorthodox," Mr. Bennett said. He spoke loudly and rapidly, indicative of his obvious annoyance. "If people are allowed to just waltz—"

"Nurse—" the doctor interrupted.

"—into the infirmary anytime they like and—"

"Mr. Bennett!" The doctor's tone was a bit louder, but her eyes remained kind as she spoke. "If our patient..." She paused to look at her folder. "If Cara Jane—"

"CJ, please," the blonde said.

"If CJ would like her to stay," she said, nodding in Andi's direction, "then she can stay. I don't have a problem with it."

She smiled at Andi.

"But I do!" the nurse insisted. "It's my responsibility to make sure the rules are followed and I—"

"I'll take responsibility for her being here, Mr. Bennett."

The nurse opened his mouth as if to speak again, then promptly closed it. He glared at Andi, then turned an impassive face toward the doctor before speaking. "I'll be down the hall if you need anything." He spun on his heels and left the room.

"Thank you, Doctor," Andi said softly. She looked into her dark eyes and returned her smile with a slight grin. "I...well...just thanks." She gazed down at her feet.

"Why don't you move that chair over there," Dr. Erroll directed, indicating a spot near the window, "and you can have a seat while I talk with CJ." Andi nodded silently and did as the woman requested. She sat toward the edge of the seat with her elbows on her knees and her chin in her hands.

The doctor moved toward CJ. "Mind if I get a bit closer, CJ?" Dr. Erroll asked. CJ nodded, then felt the bed dip, and she shifted to her left to give the woman more room."That's okay, CJ." The woman softly tapped her patient's forearm three times. "I don't need much room. I just want to get a look at those bandages."

"Were you the one who put them on?" the injured athlete asked.

"I'm the one," the doctor said. "Don't remember me from last night, do you?"

"Don't remember much." Her mouth dipped into a frown.

"Well then, let me introduce myself." She lifted CJ's hand and shook it firmly. "I'm Doctor Erroll."

"Hi, Doc."

She removed her hand from CJ's and gently touched the areas of her head near the bandages.

"Is the pressure from the bandages too tight? How's it feel under there?"

"The pressure I feel is from the inside out, Doc. The bandages feel okay."

"That's to be expected, CJ." She stood and walked around to the other side of the bed to check the IV. "You took a pretty hard hit to the eye, then another hard knock on the head when you landed on the hardwood."

"One eye is hurt, right? So why are they both bandaged?"

"The injury requires rest and no movement, CJ, and since your eyes work in concert, both need to rest. For the time being, anyway."

Andi found herself clenching her fists as she listened to their conversation. Having witnessed the assault herself, she believed it was intentional, designed at least to foul or possibly take out the home team's star player. She clenched her jaw in anger. *I'd like to get my hands on that player. I'd kick her ass into the middle of next week.* She could feel the blood rising to her face and she consciously took a deep breath to wash away her anger.

"Cheap shot," CJ sneered.

"Unfortunately, the cost to your vision might be anything but cheap."

"What do you mean?" CJ asked. A hint of fear rose in her voice.

"You have a Grade 4 hyphema," said the doctor.

"And that means?"

"Well, a hyphema is a bruise in your eye that is bleeding, usually caused by impact. They are classified in Grades 1-4, depending on severity. Unfortunately, yours is the most severe type. It occurred when that player elbowed your eye. Add to that a concussion, which happened when you landed on the gym floor."

CJ remained quiet as the doctor explained the injury. Her heart was beating quickly as the words "eye bruise" and "bleeding" seeped into her consciousness. After a lifetime of athletic involvement, she was used to scrapes, bruises, and bleeding, but she was smart enough to realize that the injury she had now, which had landed her in the infirmary, was quite a bit more serious. She clasped her hands together and rubbed them, an outward sign of her inner apprehension. "Now tell me what all that means," she asked quietly.

"It means that you're not out of the woods on this, CJ." She paused and placed her hand gently on CJ's forearm. "I'll be up front with you. This is a serious injury. Since it's an internal bleed, the blood pools in the eye because there's no place else for it to go. Just as with any bruise, the body deals with that by reabsorbing the blood; however, if your eye continues to bleed faster than your body can absorb the blood... Well, unfortunately, there's a risk of permanent loss of sight in that eye." She stopped speaking for a moment to let the impact of her words sink in, then continued. "It's imperative that the bleeding not only stops but that no rebleeding occurs. The big key to resolving a hyphema is virtual immobility. By that I mean bed rest, period. No walking around, no going to class, no driving in cars, nothing. Even a coughing or sneezing fit could cause a rebleed." The woman stopped speaking and studied CJ's face. The injured woman's lips were pursed together tightly and her jaw muscles clenched beneath the surface of her cheek. Her hands were clasped together tightly, yet remained still.

"I realize that's difficult," the doctor continued, "but it's imperative that you follow my directive if you want to recover fully." She took a deep breath, then exhaled slowly. "Do you live in a dorm on campus?"

"Yes."

"No good. How about your family? Do they live around here?"

"Near Norwich."

"Way too far," the doctor said. She shook her head slightly as she said, "I can't have you riding in a vehicle that long, even if you were lying in an ambulance. Okay then, I'll make arrangements with Mr. Bennett for you to stay here in the infirmary—"

"She can stay with me," Andi offered. The words came rushing from her mouth before she thought about their implications or repercussions. She had been sitting there, listening to the doctor explain CJ's injury, her heart breaking for the fear and anxiety she knew her injured friend was feeling. Andi knew all too well the emotional agony of a career-ending injury. Hearing CJ get the disheartening prognosis from the doctor was like reliving her own career-ending accident not that many years ago. Just as with her own injury, she felt completely helpless, but this time she took the only measure of control she could think of by extending the invitation. Andi looked away from the doctor long enough to notice CJ's head turned toward her. A hint of a smile played on her lips.

"Where do you live?" the doctor asked.

"On the far corner of campus. I rent a converted apartment on the second floor of an administrative office. It's quiet, so she'd get a lot of rest. There's enough room for her. I live there by myself."

"But who'll be available for her during the day, if she needs something?"

"I work on campus. I'm a grad assistant, so I'm always around. I could stop by between classes to check on her. She wouldn't be alone for more than a couple hours at a time." She paused, then added, "I'm sure Mr. Bennett won't be with her 24/7." She watched as her comment brought a smile to the doctor's lips. "I'm perfectly okay with it as long as...well, CJ? Would that be okay with you?" Both Andi and the doctor turned to look at the blonde.

"I'd like that," she said softly.

The doctor said, "I'm not completely sold on the idea." She rubbed her chin and hesitated. "Tell you what. I'll see how your

eye is looking after another twenty-four hours, and then I'll
make a decision. If the bleeding's bad, I'm afraid you'll be
staying right here. I simply can't take a chance of moving you,
even if it is a short distance. However, if the bleeding has
stopped, then I'll consider letting you go."

The doctor turned her attention to the folder she had
brought with her. She made a few notes about their discussion as
well as CJ's condition, then checked her watch. "On my way out,
I'll tell Mr. Bennett to come by to remove your IV around noon
today. If the pain becomes too much for you, buzz him and he'll
give you something to swallow to get it back under control. I'll
be by tomorrow at 11:00 a.m. to reevaluate your injury. Until
that time, I want you to rest, and I mean totally and completely."
She turned to face Andi. "And that includes no visitors. Sorry."
The woman's dark eyes were indeed sympathetic, and Andi
appreciated her empathy. She continued to address the grad
assistant. "You can meet us back here at 11:30 tomorrow, and I'll
let CJ know my decision. And no sneaking in before then," she
added, winking at Andi. She turned to face her patient once
again. "Any questions before I go, CJ?"

"No, Doc, I don't think so."

"Fine. Well then, we'll both be going now and leave you to
rest and heal." She turned toward Andi, tilting her head slightly
to the side as she spoke. "Ready?" She took a few steps across
the room and paused, waiting for Andi at the door.

Andi stood from the chair and walked over to the side of the
bed. She gently placed her hand in CJ's and gave it a squeeze.
Leaning down near her, she whispered softly in the injured
woman's ear.

"Everything will be okay, CJ. I'll be back tomorrow, I
promise."

"Thanks Andi." CJ squeezed the hand she was holding.

Andi moved toward the door where the doctor was waiting.
Before she crossed the threshold into the hallway, she looked
back over her shoulder for a final glimpse of her injured friend.

Then the doctor pulled the door nearly shut before walking
down the hall by Andi's side. "Try not to worry about your
friend," she said softly. "You look like you could use a little rest
yourself." She patted Andi on the shoulder gently and smiled.
"See you tomorrow." With that, she turned to find Mr. Bennett
while Andi left the infirmary.

CJ LISTENED AS the sound of footsteps and voices faded
down the hallway, leaving her alone with her thoughts and

fears. She clenched her fist, now empty after having held Andi's hand just moments ago. Her body and heart ached for that connection again, that feeling of protection. She felt so alone.

Do not cry, she reprimanded herself. *Your eyes are already a mess. Don't make it worse.* She took a deep breath and exhaled slowly. *Besides, you couldn't even find a tissue to blow your nose in. Shit.*

Her head was throbbing and her body sore from hitting the floor so hard the night before. She thought about the game and the play leading right up to her collision with the other player. Envisioning her drive to the basket as well as her attempt to score, she watched a slow motion replay in her mind's eye of the moment of impact as her opponent's elbow came crashing into her face. It was as if she could see it coming but was powerless to move out of the way. She remembered that the room had spun a half turn as her view changed from backboard to blurry ceiling, concerned faces above her peering down. Beyond those few seconds, she didn't remember anything until she arrived at the infirmary. Bits and pieces of voices, images, and sensations flashed through her mind — her coach, people touching her, lying flat yet moving — but none of the pieces added up to a complete picture of the previous night. *I'm sure the coach and the players will fill me in. I wonder if we won.*

She thought about the game and her teammates. *So, this is how it ends for me...my career as an athlete.* She inhaled and held her breath, clenching her fists tightly as she once again fought back tears. *Four long years I played for the championship title, and now this? This is NOT how it's supposed to be.* She breathed in quickly several times and exhaled with such force through her mouth that the breath was audible. *Well, it's not over 'til I say it's over.*

Oh sure. What are you going to do? Just get up off this bed, march your ass out of the infirmary, and join the team for practice? Face reality, she admonished herself. *Just take one step at a time, and one day at a time. Maybe the doctor will give me unexpected good news tomorrow.* She smiled a little when she thought of the kind woman who had so patiently explained her eye injury. Dr. Erroll seemed as if she knew what she was doing, and CJ decided that she trusted her. *Hopefully she'll let me leave here tomorrow...with Andi.* A smile tugged at her lips as she thought of her considerate friend. She had been completely surprised to awaken and find Andi in the room with her. In retrospect, she thought she even had a dream of Andi talking with her the night before, but she attributed it to the drugs as well as missing her new friend. *Funny...for the past few weeks I've felt so embarrassed being around her or even talking to her on the phone that I totally avoided her. Then she shows up here, and I'm so happy that I forget all about that embarrassment. Hmmmm... Maybe she came because she just feels sorry for me.*

She frowned at that thought, not wanting to believe that pity brought Andi to see her. *Then what? You want to think that she likes you. Admit it.*

Of course I admit it. I said it to her with that kiss; I certainly can't deny it to myself. She pursed her lips together as her mind raced with her thoughts. *So now what am I going to do? About Andi? About the playoffs? About grad school? Shit! Grad school... That's one more thing to add to the list of things to think about. I have a feeling that the next twenty-four hours are going to be some of the longest hours of my life.*

ANDI COULD HEAR the phone ringing as she reached the landing outside the door leading to her apartment. After quickly unlocking, then opening the door, she raced across the living room and lifted the receiver.

"Hello?" she said, a little breathless from her sprint as well as the stress of the recent events.

"Hey, Andi," Martha said. "I'm glad we finally reached you."

"I just walked through the door. Well, more like ran when I heard the phone ringing."

"You can disregard our two earlier messages then." Andi glanced at the answering machine, whose red message light was blinking. "We've been trying to reach you since last night." She hesitated, then continued. "Did you hear what happened at the basketball playoff game?"

"You mean CJ?"

"So you know."

"I was there." Andi slowly exhaled a large breath.

"You were at the game?" Martha's voice registered surprise. "We didn't see you in the stands."

"I wasn't in the home bleacher section." Andi hesitated. Thinking about the previous night brought back all the painful emotions of why she was there to begin with as well as the horrible injury she'd witnessed. She spoke softly into the phone. "I didn't want CJ to see me during the game. I was hoping to talk with her in person after the game..." She paused. "I saw the whole thing."

"Jeez, Andi. Karen and I have been worried about her, and about you since we couldn't reach you. She took a pretty bad hit, and then they had to carry her off. I hope she's okay."

"Her injury's pretty serious." Andi spoke barely above a whisper. As she closed her eyes, she could see an image of CJ lying in the bed with her eyes bandaged.

"How do you know?"

"I went to see her last night. She's in the infirmary."

"But how did you —"

"Long story," Andi said. She proceeded to relate the events of the previous twelve hours, ending with leaving the infirmary less than twenty minutes before. "So, I just got back."

"So now what are you going to do?"

"Wait for the slowest twenty-four hours of my life to pass."

"How about some company?" Martha suggested. "You could come over here, or we'll drive to your place if you're not up for going out. How about it?"

"Thanks for the offer, Martha, but what I really need is a long nap. I didn't sleep much last night, and I think I'm just wrung out from seeing CJ like this." She raked her long fingers through her dark hair. "And it brings back such bad memories, too, you know?"

"Sure, honey. I understand. Catch up on some rest. We'll be home all day, so call us later and maybe we can do something, okay?"

"That sounds good," she said. As she spoke, she leaned over and unlaced her sneakers, then slipped her feet out of them. She stretched out her long legs and crossed them at the ankles.

"If we don't hear from you by dinner time, I'm going to call you back. Consider that fair warning," Martha teased. Her tone was intentionally playful in an attempt to lighten her friend's spirits.

"Duly noted," Andi said, with as much reciprocal lightheartedness as she could muster.

"Besides, the time will drag if you're there by yourself." She added in a self-mocking tone, "However, with our quick wit, charming conversation, and convivial humor, the time will simply fly by, and it will be tomorrow before you know it." She chuckled on the other end of the phone.

"Okay, okay. I get the message." She smiled at Martha's thoughtfulness. "You both are such special friends. I hope you know that."

"The feeling's very mutual, Andi. We're here for you."

"Thanks. That really means a lot to me."

"Go. Take a nap and call us later."

"Okay, Martha. Thanks again for calling. I'll talk to you soon."

Andi lowered the receiver back to the base, then sat forward on the edge of the sofa. With her elbows on her knees, she rested her head in her hands and closed her eyes in an attempt to wind down. After a few deep, slow breaths, she pushed herself up from the sofa and headed into the bathroom. She removed her clothes and tossed them into a pile in the corner of the small room. Turning on the water full force, she stepped into the shower and let the hot water cascade over her head and shoulders. For several minutes she just stood there, her tears mingling with the water. Finally, she emerged, dried off, and donned a pair of sweat pants and a long sleeve T-shirt before climbing under the covers of her bed. She slipped into a deep sleep almost as soon as her head touched the pillow.

Chapter
Twenty-one

ANDI WALKED QUICKLY across campus toward the infirmary. The late morning sun was just above the treetops, but its rays did not sufficiently warm the March morning. She turned up the collar of her jacket, then pushed her hands deeper into her pockets as she moved across the green. The chilly air served to clear her head of the anxiety and apprehension of seeing CJ again, as well as of hearing the doctor's report. She breathed in deeply, filling her lungs with the cold blast until her chest tingled from the sensation.

The previous night, once she finally turned in at nearly 1:00 a.m., had been filled with fitful stretches of sleeping and wakefulness. As promised, Martha did call her again around dinnertime, and she and Karen showed up at her door a half-hour later. They brought pizza, beer, and a DVD of *Fried Green Tomatoes* to help her pass the time. While it was true that her mind wandered to CJ many times throughout the evening, Martha and Karen's company proved to be a pleasant distraction. When they left just after midnight, she still wasn't tired enough to sleep, so she journaled for thirty minutes or so before finally crawling under the covers.

She awakened well before the alarm, early enough to spend an hour and a half at the gym. A half-hour on the elliptical trainer followed by an abbreviated circuit of the weight machines took the edge off her anxiety just enough to get her through the morning. After a quick stop at the deli, she returned to her apartment to shower and eat a late breakfast before heading out to meet CJ and the doctor at 11:30.

Entering through the front doors to the infirmary, she approached the nurses' station at the far end of the hall away from CJ's room. Mr. Bennett raised his head, then glared at her as she passed. She smiled broadly at him and waved.

"Good morning, Mr. Bennett," she said with exaggerated politeness.

"I see you're using the front door this time," he sneered.

Andi continued to smile as she walked past him, ignoring his comment. She headed down the hallway toward CJ's room. The corridor looked so different to her in the daylight with the florescent lights glowing brightly and the sun streaming though the windows. It looked warmer and more inviting. No longer did she have to lurk in the shadows to see her friend. She slowed her steps as she neared CJ's room. The door was cracked open enough for her to see a blonde, bandaged head as well as the doctor standing by the far side of the bed. She checked her watch, which read 11:27. Andi took a deep breath, then exhaled slowly before knocking on the open door.

"Come in," the doctor invited.

"I'm back," Andi said shyly. She walked toward the bed and gently rested her hand on the injured woman's shoulder. "Hi, CJ."

"Hi, Andi." She turned her head toward the voice and grinned slightly at her friend.

"You're just in time," the older woman said. "I just finished examining CJ's eyes." The gauze bandages had been replaced by a double eye patch.

"How's it look?" Andi said. She held her breath waiting for a response.

"I didn't get the miracle I was praying for," CJ said, "but at least I don't have to stay here any more."

"The bleeding appears to have stopped, which is why I agreed to let her leave," the doctor added. "From my experience, most patients are more relaxed and therefore heal better when they're in a home environment. Have you made the necessary arrangements for CJ to stay with you?"

"Everything's all set," Andi said.

"Okay then." She scribbled some notes in CJ's file, then moved closer to her patient, resting her hand on CJ's forearm. "Let me be very clear that you are not out of the woods with this injury, CJ. Although the bleeding has been arrested, the problem is still serious. Partial or even complete vision loss is still a very real possibility. Additionally, you suffered a pretty hard blow to your head, resulting in a concussion." She paused to let the severity of her words sink in. "It's absolutely imperative that you rest and remain as motionless as possible. You'll have many restrictions placed on you when you're at Andi's place, and if you don't follow them to the letter, I'll have to move you back here immediately."

"Restrictions?" Andi asked.

"Yes. Like no unnecessary walking around. That means trips

to the bathroom and that's it. No driving in cars. You also can't attend classes for a while. I can give you a note if your professors require one." She wrote on a pad then handed the paper to Andi. "Here, hold this for her." The doctor continued. "No coughing, sneezing, laughing, or crying—nothing that will cause internal pressure on your eyes. I know it sounds nearly impossible to stay emotionally neutral, but that's about what it comes down to. Your two allowed positions are lying flat, as you are now, or lying on a slight incline, with pillows propped behind your head and back. If you need to sit up to eat, that's okay, but don't stay that way for more than thirty minutes. I'll give you a prescription for painkillers that you can take if you need them. It might be necessary for a few more days, especially at night if you can't sleep." She wrote on the pad once again then handed Andi the second slip of paper. "The most important thing you can do is rest, CJ. That means there shouldn't be a parade of people coming and going—"

"I'll be bored out of my mind, Doc," CJ protested.

"No, you'll be giving your body the rest it needs to heal. I didn't say you couldn't have any visitors. A short visit now and then is fine. What I don't want is your entire team, your coaches, your friends all smothering you with so much concern that you won't get any rest. Got it?" Her tone was firm and brooked no compromise. "I have a print-out of restrictions that I'll give to Andi. She'll read it to you later and see to it that they are followed." She looked at the dark-haired woman. "I can count on you to follow these procedures, right?"

"Absolutely," Andi said.

"And, CJ, I can count on you to go along with all those restrictions?"

She sighed reluctantly. "I promise."

"Good. I'll go find Mr. Bennett and have him arrange for transportation over to Andi's apartment. If you experience any problems, call me immediately. Otherwise, I'll see you in my office in ten days." She turned and left the room.

CJ heard the footsteps fade across the room and out the door. For a moment the room was completely silent, and she assumed that Andi had left with the doctor. She sighed deeply and audibly.

"You okay?" Andi asked quietly. She moved to the side of the bed and brushed her fingertips across her friend's forearm.

"I guess. Glad to be leaving here, that's for sure. I mean, they've been very nice to me and all but it's just so...I don't know...lonely?" She paused. "You know, you didn't have to offer to take care of me—"

"But I wanted to," she interrupted.

"Why?" She turned her face toward Andi's voice.

"Well, you said yourself that you'd rather not be here and besides, I...I've really missed you, CJ."

The blonde's heart thumped rapidly in her chest. Her skin tingled from where Andi's fingertips were gently touching her forearm. CJ exhaled slowly and allowed a small smile to tug on her lips. "I missed you, too," she said softly.

Andi's heart jumped at hearing not only her words but also the sincerity in her voice. Dragging her fingers down the fine blonde hairs, she clasped her friend's hand tightly. Their joined touch was warm, comfortable, and safe.

"Thanks, Andi," CJ added. "I really mean that."

The squeaky wheels of the gurney interrupted their conversation. Mr. Bennett pushed the rolling table into the room and right up to CJ's bed before locking the wheels. He ignored Andi as he moved, focusing his eyes on the woman in the bed. "Okay, CJ. I've brought the gurney to take you to the ambulance. Then they'll drive you across campus to the apartment."

"I don't need a gurney," she said impatiently. "I'm perfectly capable of walking."

"Doctor's orders. Besides, this one folds so you'll be riding on it in the ambulance. When you arrive, they'll carry you upstairs on it, too. Doctor said it's not an option."

"Hrrummmfff," she said, clearly annoyed but acknowledging that she had no choice.

"Just scoot over to your right a little at a time and you'll be on it," he directed. He rested his hand on her shoulder and hip to guide her. "I won't let you slide off the other side," he joked.

"I wasn't worried," she answered.

"Your friend can't drive in the ambulance," he said matter-of-factly. His eyes remained on CJ.

"I'll leave now and meet you there, CJ" Andi said. "I'll probably beat the ambulance there anyway."

"That'll be great. Thanks again, Andi," CJ responded.

"See you in a few minutes."

"WHAT ROOM AM I in?" CJ asked. The two orderlies from the infirmary had just left after having carried her up the stairs into the apartment.

"The living room," Andi said. "Last night, Martha and Karen came over to keep me company, and they helped me move the mattress from my room onto the floor in—"

"You didn't have to give me your mattress!" CJ interrupted.

"Letting me stay here is a big enough imposition."

"It's nothing, really," she said casually. "I've spent more then a few nights on the sofa after falling asleep watching a late movie. It's really quite comfortable. Besides, I can keep an eye on you better if I'm in here instead of in my room."

"You really didn't have to do that, Andi."

"Don't worry about it, okay? Besides, I thought you might enjoy being out here in the living room, since you can hear the TV and stereo better. The sun streams though those windows for most of the afternoon so it's really warm. In fact, I've taken a nap or two in just that spot on some lazy afternoons."

"I wouldn't want to take your favorite spot."

"I'm more than happy to share it with you."

The two women paused in their bantering to consider the implications of that invitation.

"I guess I'm going to owe you, big time, after all this," CJ joked. She faced the direction where she heard Andi's voice.

"Then I'll start writing up a list of how you can make it up to me," she teased.

CJ laughed. "Anything you want!"

"Anything?" Andi's voice was playful.

"Yes. Anything."

"Hhhmmmm. I'll have to think long and hard about it, then." She chuckled as she conjured up the list.

"What are you laughing about?"

"Nothing," she said quickly, eager to change the subject. "How do those pillows feel behind your back? You comfortable?"

"Fine, thanks."

"Can I get you anything?"

"Well, I hate to bother—"

"It's no bother. Please, what is it that you'd like?"

"Lunch?"

"Sure! That's easy enough." She rose from the sofa and walked toward the kitchen. "It's a good sign that you haven't lost your appetite."

"Not much makes me lose my appetite," she said.

"I've always been amazed about how much you can eat. You have such a great—" She stopped short of finishing her thought with a slight cough. Her face glowed bright red, and at that moment she was very glad CJ couldn't see her. "I mean, you certainly seem lean and fit." She covered her eyes with her hand, still embarrassed by her thoughts and verbal slip.

"Well, thanks," CJ said. She caught Andi's comment and was secretly flattered that her friend even noticed her body. She wished she could see her companion's face, since she heard her stumble over her words and sensed her embarrassment. She smiled and added, "You're in pretty good shape yourself."

"Thanks," Andi said weakly. Eager to talk about something else, she continued. "So, I stopped at the deli on the way back from the gym this morning. I've got rolls and the fixings for sandwiches. Is that okay?"

"Great!"

"What kind would you like?"

"Anything, really. Surprise me."

"What would you like to drink?"

"Do you have any diet soda?"

"Diet Coke okay?"

"Perfect."

Andi prepared the sandwiches and brought them with the sodas into the living room, putting them on the coffee table near the sofa. She placed CJ's plate in the blonde's lap.

"Here's your sandwich," she said. "Your soda is on the table. Just let me know when you want a drink and I'll hand it to you." She sat down on the floor next to the mattress with her long legs stretched out in front of her, crossed at the ankles.

"Thanks." She took a bite of her lunch and grinned. "This is great! I love that spicy deli mustard."

"I kind of figured you for a spicy deli mustard kind of gal," Andi joked.

The two friends ate in companionable silence for several minutes before CJ interrupted the stillness. "The first night I spent in the infirmary," she began, "I had a dream."

"What kind of dream?"

"I dreamed you were there in the infirmary, talking to me."

Andi stopped chewing and swallowed hard. She quickly grabbed for her soda and took a few sips to clear her throat. She had wondered if CJ had been coherent enough to know she was there that night, but didn't exactly know how to explain to her friend why she sneaked in.

"What were we talking about?" she asked. She held her breath as she waited for CJ to answer.

"I don't exactly remember. I've been trying so hard to remember since then because...I don't know, but whatever it was that I dreamed you were saying made me feel less scared...about everything."

"So I guess it was a good dream," Andi said softly.

"Yeah, it was. I wish I could remember it."

"Maybe you'll have it again," Andi said. CJ considered that thought and smiled, nodding her head.

"Maybe I will, especially now that I'm surrounded by Andi-vibes." She chuckled.

"Andi-vibes?" She, too, laughed.

"Sure. I'm here with you, in your apartment, on your bed, eating your food... I'm surrounded by your energy. You do know that you give off a lot of energy, don't you?"

"Energy?"

"Yeah, energy. I noticed it right away, the first time we met. You practically pulse with energy, this inner strength that kind of flows out of you. It's all beneath the surface, almost hidden, but I can feel it. I know it's there."

Andi didn't quite know how to respond to CJ's observations. Hearing herself described this way was indeed flattering, and she was touched that her friend was so willing to share such a personal feeling with her. "Thanks, CJ," she responded softly.

The younger woman noticed Andi's hesitation and quiet response. A thought occurred to her and she paused, turning her head toward her friend. "Did I just make you uncomfortable by saying that? I'm so used to blurting out whatever I'm thinking or feeling that I didn't even consider how it might make you feel."

"No," Andi said quickly. She placed her hand gently on CJ's forearm. "Your openness is one of the things I like so much about you, so please, don't ever worry about being that way. I can't say I'm used to it, since most people aren't like that, but I really do like it." She paused and continued in a lighthearted tone. "Maybe I'll pick up on some CJ-vibes and learn to be more like you in that regard." She grinned at her friend.

"I'm sure we could learn a lot from each other," CJ answered, laughing.

They finished their lunch quietly, each woman delighting in the thought of the shared intimacy of learning from the other. Andi smiled, then stretched. "Can I get you anything else?"

"I'm good for now."

"Let me clear these plates out of here." She collected their plates and glasses and headed off to the kitchen, then returned to the living room after stacking the lunch dishes in the sink. She sat down on the floor next to CJ and gently touched her arm, as had become her habit, to let the woman know she was there. "Would you mind if I went into my office for a few hours this afternoon?"

"Of course not, Andi. You do what you need to do and don't worry about me."

"I had posted my office hours last week, before this happened, and I really do need to make myself available in case any students stop by."

"That's fine."

"I'll leave the phone right here on the floor by your bed, so if you need me just call. Do you remember my number?"

"Of course," she said, grinning. "I didn't bang my head that hard."

"And the TV clicker's here, too, and the remote for the stereo. For both of them the power button is in the upper right corner." She placed them next to the phone. "I'll leave a glass of water on the coffee table, too. How about I walk you to the bathroom before I go, just to remind you of the path in case you have to go when I'm not here?"

"I suppose that's a good idea."

"Here, let me help," Andi offered. She placed her arm around the injured woman's shoulders and helped her to sit up slowly. "Put your arm across my shoulders so I can help you stand up." She put her arm around CJ's waist. "Okay, ready? One, two, three." The two women rose slowly and stood still for a minute so CJ could orient herself to being vertical. "Now, if you reach out your hand, you'll feel the sofa over here," Andi said. "If you walk slowly for a few feet with your hand touching the back of it, you'll come to one of the kitchen chairs." She walked next to CJ with her arm still around her waist as CJ felt for the objects. When she touched the back of the chair, Andi continued. "I lined up all four chairs next to each other so that their backrests act as an aisle leading you to the bathroom."

"Pretty clever," CJ said.

"I don't want you to wander around and fall. I was trying to make it easy for you."

"You did a great job, Andi. I hope you know how grateful I am, for everything."

"It's my pleasure, CJ. Besides, you told me I can make a payback list, don't forget," she joked. "So, once you get to the fourth chair, just reach your hands straight out in front of you and take one small step and you'll be at the bathroom door." CJ continued to follow her directions and could feel the door frame at her fingers. "The light switch is on the left—"

"I won't need that for a while."

"Oh. Right. Sorry."

"It's okay."

"The bowl is on the left, and the sink is directly across from it. If you take one small step, you'll be right in between both."

"Might as well take advantage of the room while I'm here," CJ said.

"I'll wait outside," Andi said. She closed the door and paced until the door reopened a few minutes later. "Ready to head back?"

"Sure," she said. Andi reached to take her arm. "I should try this once by myself," CJ said. "If I have to go later, you might not be here. I should make sure I can do it alone."

"You're right." She reluctantly removed her hand from CJ's arm. "I'll be right next to you."

CJ felt her way back using the chair and sofa guides Andi had arranged. When she made it back to the mattress, Andi praised her efforts.

"That was great, CJ! I'll feel a lot better being gone for a few hours knowing that you can at least get back and forth to the bathroom."

"Thanks to you." She reached out her hands toward where she heard Andi's voice. "Where are you?"

"Here," Andi said. She stepped toward the younger woman, taking her hands as she moved. CJ squeezed them, then pulled Andi toward her, enveloping her friend in a warm, lingering hug. The full lengths of their bodies pressed together, and Andi felt her heart thumping in her chest. She rubbed her palms slowly up and down CJ's back a few times before gathering up the woman into a deeper embrace. They remained locked in the hug for a few moments longer before Andi sighed and grudgingly stepped back, still holding CJ's hands.

"I'd better go." Her voice was flat, and she wanted desperately to wrap her arms around CJ once again. "Any requests for dinner?" she asked, trying to get her mind off the hug.

"Anything is fine." She smirked. "Other than filter organs."

"Don't worry. I didn't forget," Andi said. "I'll be back in a few hours, okay?"

"Okay. If I'm not here, I'll be over at the gym shooting hoops—"

"CJ! Don't you—"

"Just kidding." She grinned broadly, deepening the dimple in her cheek. "I'll be here when you get back. I promise."

CJ HEARD THE lock click, followed by muffled footsteps.

"Andi?"

"It's just me creeping in." She removed her coat and walked over to the mattress. Squatting down, she reached over and touched CJ's arm. "I thought you might be sleeping."

"Nope. Just hanging out." She sniffed the air a few times. "What do I smell?"

"Chinese from Ming's. Hungry?"

"Silly question. What did you get?"

"Hot and sour soup, General Tsao's chicken, crispy fish with black bean sauce, and vegetable fried rice." She grinned. "How did I do?"

"All excellent choices! You did great, Andi."

"Then let's eat while it's hot. I'll go and make up some plates." She stood and carried the bag of food into the kitchen. "So what'd you do while I was out?" she asked, calling to CJ from the kitchen.

"I listened to MSNBC to catch up on the news a bit, just to pass the time. I also called my parents, to let them know what was going on. I hope you don't mind. Let me know when the bill comes in so I can pay you for the calls."

"Don't worry about a few phone calls, please," she insisted. "What'd your parents have to say?"

"My mom was worried, of course. She always worries. While I was growing up, she always gave me a hard time about being a tomboy. She tried to put me in dresses and frilly clothes — she really wanted a girlie-girl, you know? I wouldn't have any of it, though. My only concession to 'suitable behavior for young women,' to quote my mother, was my interest in cooking. And my only real reason for that was my interest in eating." She shook her head slowly as she thought of her mother. "Mom didn't get the daughter she always dreamed of with me," she added, sighing.

"Don't buy into that, CJ," Andi called from the kitchen. "You're an excellent student, a super athlete, and from what I've seen so far, a really great person. How could she possibly be disappointed?"

"Thanks, Andi. I do think she recognizes all that, but it's still not the way she pictured my life."

"It's not her life to picture," Andi said. She walked into the living room carrying their food and set it down on the coffee table. "It's your life, CJ."

"Yes, that's true. I've been working on that 'letting go' stage since I started college. That's part of the reason I decided to go away to school."

"I remember you telling me," Andi said. "And I'm certainly glad you did. So, what can I get you to drink?"

"Water would be great."

Andi went to the kitchen and returned with two glasses of water. She helped CJ sit up, then propped several more pillows behind her so she could eat comfortably. Andi sat cross-legged on the floor next to the mattress.

"How about we start with soup?"

"I'm ready," she said.

Andi handed her the bowl, which CJ raised up close to her face so as to have a short distance to lift the spoon to her mouth. She consumed more than half the bowl in that manner before switching tactics.

"Would you mind if I just drank the rest?" she asked.

"Go for it," Andi said. "I promise not to report you to Miss Manners."

CJ put down the spoon and dispensed with the remaining soup in a few swallows before lowering the soup bowl to her lap.

"That was delicious," she said. "My tongue's still tingling."

"Here's your dinner." She put the plate on CJ's lap.

"Smells great!"

Andi placed the fork in CJ's hand then looked on as she blindly poked it at her plate in the hopes of spearing a piece of food. The older woman watched as three times the rice slipped off CJ's fork before she was able to get it to her mouth. Andi could see her frustration.

"I'm sorry, CJ. I wasn't thinking when I picked this food." She put down her own plate and shifted to sit on the end of the mattress, facing her friend. She took the fork from the blonde's hand and the plate off her lap. "Here. Let me help you."

"No, Andi. You've helped me enough. You don't have to feed me, too."

Andi could sense her embarrassment at not being able to feed herself, and she knew that she had to diffuse the situation quickly so as not to embarrass her further. "Come on, consider it a decadent indulgence, CJ," she purred. "The ancient Romans reclined as they were fed their meals. Sounds like fun to me. I'll put this on my payback list. Once you can see again, you can return the favor. Deal?"

CJ hesitated. She didn't like feeling helpless or dependent on anyone, especially for something as basic as eating. At the same time, she did appreciate Andi's efforts to lighten the awkward situation. She sighed audibly. "Deal."

"Good." Andi grinned. "So, do you like a mixture of foods on the fork at the same time, or are you a purist?"

"A little of both," she responded. "I'll leave it up to you."

Andi was relieved that CJ was going along with it. She knew this wasn't going to be the only meal her friend wouldn't be able to feed herself, so it would be easier and more comfortable for both of them if they got over the awkwardness right away. She picked up the fork and speared a piece of General Tsao's chicken, then raised it to CJ's lips. The younger woman smelled the food near her nose and opened her mouth. Andi slowly inserted the fork and CJ closed her lips on the utensil to take the food as Andi removed the fork. She chewed several times, then swallowed.

"Ming's makes the best Chinese food," she said. "We order from them every few weeks."

"Me, too." Andi scooped some vegetable fried rice onto the fork and raised it to CJ's lips. "Ready?"

"Part of this 'deal' is that you have to eat, too," CJ insisted. "I'm not going to have you feed my whole meal to me while yours gets cold. We alternate forkfuls, that's the 'new' deal." Her voice was playful, yet insistent.

Andi played along. "You drive a hard bargain, but if you insist..."

"I insist."

Andi lifted the rice to her own lips and ate it. As she chewed, she refilled the fork with the rice and vegetable mixture and offered it to CJ.

"Your turn," she said. CJ opened up and closed her mouth slowly around the fork while Andi unhurriedly removed the utensil. CJ made happy food noises as she chewed the rice. Andi raised one eyebrow nearly up to her hairline as she listened to the sounds emanating from her friend. "You like?" she asked.

"I like," CJ murmured.

The meal continued at a leisurely pace, alternating forkfuls of food. As they ate, Andi told CJ about the students who visited during her office hours that afternoon. Sensing that her friend was eager for any link to the world outside the apartment where she was stuck for the next few days, Andi entertained her with stories of nameless students who sought out English assistance. Before they knew it, CJ's plate and then Andi's were emptied.

"I'm stuffed," Andi said. She stacked the empty plates on the coffee table and patted her stomach.

"Me, too," CJ said. "However..."

"However, what?"

"According to your Roman feast analogy, isn't this the part where you're supposed to peel me grapes?"

"Forget the grapes, kiddo. I've got Ben & Jerry's! Those Romans didn't know what they were missing."

"Flavor?"

"Chubby Hubby," she said. "It's as close as I'll ever come to having a fat husband, I can guarantee you."

"I'll second that."

"Let me clear these plates and I'll scoop us some." She picked up the dishes and carried them into the kitchen. As she got the bowls from the cabinet and began scooping the ice cream, she found herself grinning broadly. *Things are going better than I thought*, she mused. *There's still so much more to say...but at least the door is open now. I wish it didn't have to happen like this, though.* The smile faded from her lips as she gazed out across the room at CJ's eye patch. She sighed sadly. Looking down at the two ice cream bowls on the counter in front of her, she made an impulsive decision. Lifting up one bowl, she dumped its contents into the other bowl. She returned the second spoon to its holder in the drawer then headed back out to the living room carrying one spoon and one bowl loaded with ice cream. By the time she reached CJ, the smile had returned to her lips.

ANDI HAD SPENT the two hours after dinner grading papers and going over her research notes. A mug of honey and lemon tea steamed fragrantly on the table. From where she sat working, she could watch CJ as she lay quietly on the mattress across the room. Soft piano strains from Liz Story's *Solid Colors* CD filled the room with tranquil sounds. The evening was typical, like one of a hundred past evenings spent on schoolwork with instrumental music and a hot mug for company. Only CJ's presence changed the scene.

She put down her pen and paused in her work. Looking over at CJ, she considered how much in her life had changed since she met the attractive blonde. For many years she had been content to be alone. Initially, she had chosen social isolation as a way to heal her broken heart, but after many months of reclusiveness she grew accustomed to her disconnection and built her life around solitude. Schoolwork and grad assistant responsibilities kept her extremely busy, and any free time in between work and school was filled with working out or reading. There was always something for her to do to avoid thinking about loneliness. Even years after Liz, she often rejected dating or any type of social situation simply because she wasn't willing to risk the hurt of trusting and loving another person. In her mind, she had likened her present life to her life as a swimmer. Although her successful race efforts earned points for the team, she considered swimming a solo sport since she had no one but herself to rely on as she powered her way across the pool. Ever since the heartbreak of Liz, her life had become a solo sport.

For years she had existed as emotionally neutral, quietly enjoying her work and classes yet never risking opening her heart to another person. *Have I really been happy?* she wondered. *Well, I wasn't unhappy, but something was missing. Something was always just short of wonderful.* She pondered what measured the distance between seemingly happy and wonderful. Before she could intellectualize the answer, it simply popped into her head. CJ. Andi realized that without the presence of the green-eyed woman, her aloneness turned quickly back into loneliness, and a void was left in her heart.

"Andi?"

Andi blinked hard and shook her head to return her focus from daydreaming. She quickly stood and moved across the room to the mattress, then squatted down beside her friend. "Do you need something?"

"You've been so quiet over there. I was wondering what you were doing."

"Just correcting papers, the usual," she said casually. She smiled as she realized that the mere physical presence of CJ so close by made her heart feel wonderful, which confirmed her previous daydreaming.

"Sorry. Didn't mean to interrupt you."

"It's okay. I could use a break."

"Would you mind if I took a bath? They washed me up at the infirmary, but I think I'd rather soak for a while and wash up more thoroughly."

"Sure. Will you be okay doing that?"

"Taking a bath, yes. Taking a shower, I don't think so. I won't lose my balance if I'm sitting on my butt for a few minutes." She chuckled.

"Did Dr. Erroll say it was okay?" Andi reached toward the coffee table for the typed instructions the doctor had left with her. "Let me check the list." She scanned the directions silently, then found what she was looking for. "It says you can bathe in a tub and wash your hair as long as you don't move around too much."

"Move around too much? How the hell do you move around too much in a tub? Maybe if it was a hot tub..." CJ grinned mischievously.

"I'm just reading what's on the paper." She rose and headed toward the bathroom. "I'll start filling up the tub."

Andi stepped into the bathroom and ran the water. Once the water was comfortably hot, she stopped up the drain to fill the tub. As she stood and turned to leave the room, she nearly bumped into CJ. "Oh! Sorry," she said. "With the water running, I didn't hear you."

"Didn't mean to scare you. Rather than wait out there I thought I'd make my way over. Don't want the water to get cold."

"I'll put a towel on the floor right outside the tub. Can I get you anything else?"

"Could I borrow a pair of sweat pants and a T-shirt? No sense in taking a shower and putting on the same clothes. I'll call one of my roommates tomorrow and ask her to bring some of my clothes over, but until then—"

"Of course! Lord knows I have enough to outfit the whole women's athletic department. I'll be right back." Andi stepped out of the room, then returned shortly with the clothes. "I brought sweats, a T-shirt, and a pair of socks," she announced. "I'll leave them on the side of the sink for you. Let me turn off the water. The tub's just about full." She shut off the knobs and in the absence of the splashing water, the room suddenly became silent. "Anything else?"

"Nope. That's it."

"Are you sure you'll be okay?"

"I'm sure. If I'm not out in twenty minutes, you can send in the scuba search and rescue team."

"Very funny," Andi responded, smiling. "I'll be working at the table. Holler if you need anything." She turned and left the bathroom, closing the door behind her.

Fifteen minutes later, CJ emerged from the bathroom, her blonde hair wet and disheveled from toweling it dry. As she entered the living room, she reached her right hand toward the chair backs to guide herself.

"How'd the bath go?"

She stopped near the row of chairs when she heard Andi speak. "It felt great, actually. Hey, did I put on any of these clothes backward or inside out?" She motioned at what she was wearing.

"Nope. Everything's on the right way."

"What colors am I wearing?"

Andi paused at the question. She looked at CJ, whose head was tilted slightly to the side to reflect the question she just asked. Her hands were pushed into the side pockets of the sweat pants. Andi's brow creased as she considered the seemingly unusual question. "Navy blue sweats with white socks and a white T-shirt," she responded. "Are those colors okay? I mean, they're not our school colors, but—"

"They're fine, Andi. I was just curious." She paused and dropped her head as if she were looking at her feet, then she raised her head and spoke again. "It's hard to explain, but I feel left out of things a bit."

"I'm sorry, CJ." She got up quickly and moved over to where CJ stood. Reaching out, she placed her hand on her friend's shoulder. "I should have asked you what you wanted to wear before—"

"No, it's not that, Andi. I don't feel left out because of that." She stopped speaking as she gathered her thoughts to articulate with words what had simply been a feeling. "It's more like I'm missing things, as if I'm not aware of everything that's going on around me. It feels weird to be standing here wearing clothes and not know how they look. Life is still happening all around me but for right now I'm left out of it." She paused and added softly, "Does that make any sense?"

"Yeah, it makes sense," Andi said softly. "I feel that way sometimes even with my eyes open." She surprised herself at the frank openness of her response. The implications of that admission did not go unnoticed by CJ, who stored them away for a future conversation.

"I knew you wouldn't dress me in wacky, mis-matched colors. That's not why I asked."

"I know that." She gently squeezed CJ's shoulder. "I'm glad you told me how you feel, though. I'll try to be more sensitive to it."

"Please don't think that you did anything wrong, Andi." She placed her hand over the other woman's, which remained on her shoulder. "It's the situation. It's not you." She lifted her head up and smiled at her friend. "In fact, you're making it better than you are probably aware." Andi was glad CJ couldn't see her blushing.

"It's my lucky T-shirt," Andi said. She tugged gently at the sleeve, then lowered her hand from CJ's shoulder. "It's got a picture of Garfield jumping off a diving board in a cannon ball, holding his nose. Martha got it for me right before Regionals."

"How'd you do?"

"I won."

"Well then, thanks for letting me wear your special shirt. I hope it brings me as much luck as it brought you."

"Me, too." She smiled sadly, then reached up and gave CJ's shoulder a gentle squeeze. "It's after 10:30. Are you getting tired?"

"Actually, I am," she said. She covered her mouth as she yawned. She reached out with her right hand and made her way to the mattress using the chair backs and sofa as a guide. Andi looked on as she moved, following her.

"Want me to get you one of those pain pills?"

"I'd rather not take them," CJ said. "They make my brain feel fuzzy even after I wake up. The pain's not real bad and besides, I'm pretty tired and will probably fall asleep without much trouble."

"If you change your mind, let me know and I'll bring you

one. I have a little more paperwork to do, and then I'll be turning in, too. I'll be right on the sofa. If you need anything, just wake me. I'm a light sleeper."

"I'll try not to have to do that."

"Don't worry about it. I'm used to getting up at night. The slightest noises around this old house wake me. I fall right back to sleep, though, so it's fine."

"Thanks, Andi." She lay back on the mattress and pulled the blanket up to her chest. She rested her arms outside the covers and across her stomach. "I really am very grateful for everything you've done."

"I'm happy to help you," Andi said. She squatted and reached out to clasp one of CJ's hands. "I'm here for you if you need anything, okay?"

"Okay. Goodnight, Andi."

"Goodnight, CJ." She gave her hand a final squeeze, then released it. Andi stood and turned off the stereo using the remote. Moving across the room, she resumed her seat at the table and returned to her papers.

For the next half-hour she forced herself to concentrate on her work, but she frequently found herself looking across the room at the woman who reclined on the mattress. Taking out her day planner, she reviewed her schedule for the following day, then added more notes on her to-do list before she closed the book and put down her pen. She pushed away from the table slowly and quietly and walked to the bathroom to prepare for bed, emerging a few minutes later. She padded softly to the sofa, turning out the overhead light as she passed the switch.

When she reached her temporary bed, she turned on the small table lamp. She lowered herself onto the cushions and leaned back against the pillows propped up against the arm of the sofa. With her long legs stretched out along the length of the couch, she reached over and picked up her journal and pen from the table that held the lamp. A purple ribbon marked the page of her last entry, and she flipped the writing tablet open to that spot. She reread her last entry, then bent both of her knees to rest the book on them as she began to write.

The apartment was mostly dark except for the halo of the table lamp, which illuminated Andi's journal. The moonlight peeked through the living room windows, glowing dimly and casting faint shadows on the objects inside the room. From where Andi sat stretched out on the sofa, she could see CJ clearly. The blonde remained on her back with her arms outside the blanket and her hands still crossed on her stomach. Her mouth was slightly open and Andi could hear the cadence of her sleep breathing, which matched the rise and fall of her chest. The younger woman's face, slightly shadowed by the room's darkness, was calm and relaxed. Andi looked with longing at her face, the softness of her lips, the slight crease where her dimple formed. *I miss looking into those beautiful green eyes. I've missed that so much.* She sighed heavily, thinking back to the night in the infirmary when she first saw CJ's bandaged head and worried so much that her friend was seriously injured. Remembering that night in the infirmary made her think back to the conversation she and CJ had over lunch earlier today, when the blonde woman told about her comforting dream of Andi talking to her.

"It wasn't a dream, CJ," she whispered aloud. "I was there that night, just like I am now. But just like then, I'm still afraid." She watched to see if her whispering had any effect on the woman, but noticed no change in the rhythm of her breathing. "I guess the cover of darkness and sleep gives me courage that daylight and wakefulness chase away. I'm trying, CJ. I want to be able to say these things to you when you can hear me and can respond. Maybe by the time you recover your vision I'll recover my courage and I can look into your beautiful green eyes and speak to you from my heart. Until that time, I'll talk to you as you sleep and hope you continue to dream happy, safe thoughts of me. I am here watching over you, as you imagined in your dream. I'll always be here for you, if you let me."

She flipped back a few pages in her journal and opened to a page she had written weeks before. Taking a deep breath to steady her nerves, she exhaled slowly and began to read, her voice barely above a whisper.

> Dear CJ,
>
> I want so badly to talk to you, not on the phone or in a note, but in person. I need to see your beautiful green eyes looking into my eyes and into my heart so that you know how I really feel, and how much I miss you. Words are inadequate, but I know that if we could meet, face-to-face, our hearts would reconnect.
>
> I'm afraid, CJ. I consider myself to be a strong person and it makes me feel weak to admit that, but it's true. Once before I trusted someone with my heart and she broke it. I was so overcome with such aching sadness that I thought I'd never let anyone ever get close enough to hurt me that badly again. Then I met you, and your sincerity and warmth climbed over that wall I had built around my heart and for the first time in years I found myself actually welcoming an emotional

and physical connection with another person. Still, I was afraid, but not of you; rather, it was the ghosts of my past that continued to haunt me.

I'm also afraid of losing my graduate position for being involved with a student, even though you're technically not my student. I've already been warned — more accurately threatened — by someone who suspected my interest in you. That fear weighed heavily on my mind that night you came over, the night when you ran away. My reaction to your kiss that night reflected that fear; otherwise, I would have welcomed your kiss as I did your intense gazes, your warm touches, and your sensual hugs. In my heart, I wanted to take that next step with you, but my head wasn't ready to deal with the consequences of doing so. I'm so sorry that I pulled away and hurt your feelings so badly. I was reacting to my own demons and not your wonderful kiss. I wish I could have said that to you before you left that night, but putting my fear into words isn't easy for me.

Mostly I'm afraid of losing you, CJ. Since that night when we met at the reception, nearly two months ago (how did the time pass so quickly?), I've grown so very fond of you. You came into my life and have become my sunshine. I feel like I'm glowing on the inside whenever I'm with you or thinking about you. You once said that perhaps our meeting was just meant to be. I believe that now, but I don't believe it was meant to end this way. Please say it won't.

My fear has paralyzed me with indecision, CJ, and now I don't know what to do to make things right again between us. There's so much that I want to say, but my words on this page are inadequate. At best, they allow me to sort out my feelings and help me to cope with missing you. I can only hope that they will one day reunite us as well.

She sighed deeply, closed her journal, and replaced it on the end table near the sofa. After turning off the light, she stretched out on her side and pulled the blanket up. From this position, she had a clear view of CJ's profile in the dim moonlight. *She looks so peaceful, almost smiling.* The idea made her happy, and she drifted off to sleep with that image seared into her heart.

SHE WAS RIGHT. It's back. The fuzzy thought lingered in the recesses of CJ's sleepy, subconscious mind. Awareness spread slowly like the circling arcs on water when a pebble is dropped in. *Don't move. You'll scare it away.* She lay perfectly still to fool the dream into staying. Soft whispering pulled her from the depths of a deep, healing sleep. She surfaced hesitantly, motionlessly, as her body and senses slowly became revived.

"...I am here watching over you, as you thought in your dream. I'll always be here for you, if you let me," the voice whispered.

Andi's apartment, Andi's bed, she remembered as the light of consciousness grew brighter. *Andi's voice...* Had her eyes not been covered, they would have flown open at the realization. *She was my dream.*

She emerged into complete awareness yet her body remained motionless. With her heart racing, she fought to maintain her steady, slow breathing so as to remain unnoticed. *Don't frighten this waking dream away,* she warned herself. Her lips parted slightly as if they wanted to speak of their own volition. She willed her voice to silence and her racing heart to stillness as she listened to the voice of her dream.

"...I want so badly to talk to you, not on the phone or in a note, but in person. I need to see your beautiful green eyes looking into my eyes and into my heart so that you know how I really feel, and how much I miss you. Words are inadequate, but I know that if we could meet, face to face, our hearts would reconnect..."

She listened to the whispering, and a lightness grew in her heart. *Can this be real?* she asked herself, yet she knew that her asking simply confirmed her conscious awareness. A slight, peaceful smile spread across her lips as she listened. The moonlight reflected softly on her face and her heart was filled with contentment.

The voice in the dream continued to read, unaware.

Finally, the whispering stopped but the words and the sentiments lingered in CJ's mind and heart. She slipped back to sleep, safe in the reciprocal feelings of her dream.

Chapter
Twenty-two

CJ SNIFFED THE air in a state of half-sleep. *Coffee.* She stretched her arms and legs and yawned as she attempted to rouse her body to wakefulness. Her failed attempt at opening her eyes to greet the morning sun reminded her of her injury as well as her location. Rising up on her elbows, she gradually adjusted to being awake, then moved to a sitting position while shifting her legs off the mattress. She paused to yawn again and pushed off the mattress to stand. After regaining her balance, she used the sofa and chair backs to guide herself toward the bathroom.

She emerged from the bathroom and heard noises to her left, coming from the kitchen. Enticed by the smells of coffee and the sizzle of something frying in a pan, she tentatively stepped in the direction of the kitchen, keeping her left hand touching the wall for guidance. The clanging grew louder as she neared the kitchen, followed by a crash and a muttered curse.

"Shit!"

"Andi?"

"Oh. Sorry. Morning, CJ." She looked up at CJ's disheveled hair and wrinkled clothing and grinned broadly. The blue sweats rode low on her hips, and the white T-shirt was untucked. The younger woman yawned again and stretched slowly, reaching up her arms over her head and exposing her smooth, flat stomach to Andi's view. Dark eyebrows arched up appreciatively. "Did I wake you?"

"Nope. I smelled the coffee."

"Want some?"

"Nah, never touch the stuff. Love how it smells, though."

"Here, let me help you to the stool at the counter," Andi said. She moved toward CJ and grasped the blonde gently by the arm. "You can sit here and keep me company while I finish breakfast."

"You didn't tell me you could cook."

"Well, the jury's still out on that one. I wouldn't exactly call making an omelet cooking."

"Smells great to me."

"How about some juice?"

"OJ is great, thanks."

"So, how'd you sleep last night?" She poured the juice and moved toward CJ, placing the glass in her hand.

"Great." She couldn't stop the grin on her face when she remembered the whispering that awakened her. Hearing Andi reveal her heart in the quiet of the night made CJ feel much more comfortable around the blue-eyed woman. Prior to that midnight confession, CJ could clearly sense her friend's concern about her injury, and she appreciated the offer to stay at her apartment, but she was very glad to discover that Andi's motivation seemed to involve deeper feelings than pity. "I feel really good this morning. Your mattress was very comfortable. But how about you? I feel bad that I displaced you."

"Actually, I was fine on the sofa." Andi wiped her hands off on the dishtowel, then turned to face CJ. "So, are you feeling brave?"

"Hmmmm...depends on what you're talking about," she teased.

"My cooking. Are you hungry?"

"You have to ask?"

"Coming right up!" She slid the mini-omelet out of the pan and sandwiched it between two English muffin halves. After placing it on a plate, she put it down in front of CJ. "Here you go," she announced. "It's my version of an Egg McMuffin except that the eggs, cheese, and bacon are all combined. This way, you can pick up the muffin to eat it without a fork."

"Super idea! Smells great." She picked up the breakfast sandwich and took a bite, then chewed and swallowed.

"Well?"

"The jury's back and a verdict's been rendered," she intoned seriously. "You're a great cook!"

"I'm not deserving of such praise. You'll soon see that after about the third day my meager cooking repertoire will be exhausted, and then the food's all downhill from there."

"Then you should let me help."

"I can use all the help I can get, as long as it doesn't involve you using any sharp knives," she joked.

"Very funny. I could teach you to cook, even with my eyes closed. I've got the recipes all up here," she added, tapping a finger to her head.

"I'll take you up on your offer, then. You're in charge of dinner on Saturday night. You can dictate a shopping list to me, and I'll pick up the ingredients, then you can talk me through the procedures."

"Sounds good to me." She took another bite, then swallowed before continuing. "So, what are your plans for the day?"

"Let's see. I've got to assist with a class at nine this morning, and then I'll make a quick stop at my office before heading back here to meet you for lunch. In the afternoon I have office hours from 2:00-3:30, and afterwards I need to pick up some journals from the library. I should be back here before dinnertime. Need me to do anything for you while I'm out?"

"Not that I can think of. I was going to call one of my roommates to see if she can bring over clothes and some other things. Would that be okay?"

"Of course. I'll leave the bottom door unlocked. Tell her to walk right up." Andi noticed CJ had finished the last bite of the muffin sandwich. "Can I make you another one? More juice?"

"I'm good, thanks," she said. Patting her stomach she added, "I've got to watch what I eat since I can't work out for a while."

"I don't think you have to worry too much about that, CJ. Your metabolism is still in high gear, and you'll be back to your routine in no time."

"Think so?" she asked hesitantly. Her voice was soft and reflected apprehension mixed with a little doubt. Her head was tilted to the side.

"Definitely," Andi declared. "I'm sending you lots of positive, healing energy. You're the one who says I have lots of it."

"You do. And thanks for sending some my way."

"Any time." She looked at her watch. "Cripes! I've got to get out of here." She stacked the dishes in the sink and wiped off the counter quickly while CJ remained seated. Once she finished, she moved next to CJ's stool. "How about I help you back to the mattress, since you've strayed from the marked path? You should be horizontal, or at least reclined."

"Sure," CJ said. She thought she could probably make her way back by herself, but she was actually looking forward to Andi's nearness. She had barely touched her companion at all this morning, and she was eager for some physical contact, especially after the previous night's truths were revealed. She stood and waited for Andi to reach out to assist her. The warmth of the touch tingled CJ's back as Andi wrapped her arm around her and let her hand rest gently on the younger woman's hip. CJ responded by draping her arm around Andi's shoulder. They moved slowly and in unison back to the mattress. CJ noticed how their rhythm and stride were completely in synch. A smile crept onto her lips.

Andi propped up some pillows and helped CJ to recline on the mattress. She sat on the edge of the padded surface, facing her injured friend. Being in the younger woman's company was always so comfortable, and she was reminded again just how much she missed her during their recent lack of contact. *Well, she's here now. I just have to work on keeping her around.* The previous night's journal confession to the slumbering CJ was a warm-up for the conversation she hoped to have with the injured athlete as soon as she was out of the woods with her eye trouble. Andi had admitted her feelings on paper and then dared to whisper the words out loud, so surely those were the first steps to baring her heart to CJ. Whispering it to her in the stillness of the night had definitely made her feel better.

Eager for a connection to the younger woman, she reached out her hand and gently grasped CJ's forearm. Her companion responded by returning the grasp. Andi felt the warm, comforting pressure of CJ's hand wrapped around her forearm, and a smile spread on CJ's lips.

"I better go or I'll be late," Andi sighed. Her voice held a note of reluctance, which CJ picked up on.

"I'll be fine here," she insisted. "Don't worry, okay?"

"Can I get you anything before I go?"

"The phone and the clickers would be great."

"Of course," she said. She leaned over and removed them from the top of the coffee table and put them on the floor next to the mattress. "I'll bring you a glass of water before I go, too."

"Thanks, Andi. Go. I don't want you to be late. See you for lunch?"

"I'll be here."

She gave CJ's arm a lingering squeeze, which the blonde returned. Andi reluctantly stood and moved toward the kitchen, returning with a glass of water. She then headed toward the door, picking up her laptop bag on the way and pausing as she reached the door.

"See you soon," she called.

"Bye, Andi."

CJ heard the door click open and then close, and she was left alone in the apartment. She sighed audibly. Her arm still tingled from the warming contact of Andi's touch. Reaching across with her other hand, she gently rubbed the skin on her arm where Andi had last touched her. A smile formed on her lips. *I know at least one of your secrets, Andi.* She chuckled. *My dream. Hmmmm. How ironic. From the first moment that I looked into your beautiful blue eyes I knew you were the woman of my dreams, and last night you proved that to be true.*

ANDI LOOKED DOWN at her watch as she walked up the porch steps to her apartment. *It's 5:30 already. Where did the day go?* After her morning work, she returned home to have lunch with CJ. Normally she ate lunch at her desk while she did paperwork, but she found herself looking forward to her meal break with her ward. The hour-long lunch passed much too quickly, and she reluctantly said goodbye for the second time that day.

To her surprise, the afternoon passed quickly as well, with a steady flow of students visiting her office to discuss projects or to request assistance. The first time she looked at her watch it was already 4:00, so she locked up her office and headed to the library. She collected the journals she needed, arranged for some materials to be left on reserve for one of the classes, then packed up her bag to head home. Her usual routine might have included a workout before returning home for the evening, but with CJ awaiting her, she didn't feel her usual pull to the gym.

Her long legs mounted the stairs two at a time, and she found herself smiling as she opened the door. "I'm home," she announced. She stepped into the living room and put down her bag.

"Hey there!"

"Hey, yourself," she teased. "How you doing?" Andi made her way across the room with several long strides and lowered herself to the edge of the mattress.

"Better now," CJ said.

"Why's that?"

"The company," she responded. A grin spread across her face, accenting her dimple. A flush of color darkened Andi's face. She reached out and stroked the younger woman's forearm.

"Hungry?"

"Moderately."

"It'll take me a half-hour or so to make dinner. Will that be okay?"

"Whenever you want is fine," CJ said. "Can I ask a favor?"

"Of course."

"Can I move over to the counter and sit for a while? I could keep you company while you're cooking, and besides, it's much easier for me to eat sitting on the stool or a chair than on this mattress."

"But the doctor said that—"

"I've been laying flat or reclining all day. I swear it'll just be for a little while. I'm getting stiff from not moving." She reached out her hand until she touched Andi. Gently dragging her fingers up and down Andi's arm, she tilted her head to the side and spoke. "Please?"

Tingles shot through Andi's body from the fingers gently dancing on her skin. She could no more deny CJ's request than she could deny her own increasing attraction to her. Feeling a bit off-balance as her self-control wavered, she took a deep breath to rein in her emotions. "I suppose it'll be okay for a little while, but only if you promise to rest for the remainder of the evening."

"Deal! Help me over there?"

She swiveled and slid her legs off the mattress. Andi stood and moved in front of CJ, facing the blonde. She reached down and grasped both her hands and slowly lifted the younger woman to her feet. Their hands remained clasped for a moment longer as CJ adjusted to her vertical position. She wavered a bit to her left.

"Whoa," CJ muttered. "Head rush."

"You okay?" Andi asked. Her voice reflected concern. "Here, let me help you." She moved to CJ's side and slipped her arm around CJ's waist. "Just stand still for a minute."

CJ remained still as her head spins abated. Once the threat of falling was no longer imminent, she could enjoy the feel of Andi's arm around her. She moved her arm up, placing her hand on Andi's broad shoulder. "I'm okay now. It passed. Maybe I'm hungrier than I thought."

"No surprise there," she joked. "I'll hang on to you 'til you get to the stool."

CJ was not about to refuse.

CJ sat at the counter while Andi banged around the kitchen preparing dinner. The injured woman heard water filling a pot as well as the grinding of a can opener. Soon after, the enticing aroma of herbs and olive oil greeted her nose.

"What's for dinner?" she asked. She sniffed the air again.

"Pasta. That's one of the few meals I can cook. I picked up a box of shells so you could eat them with a spoon, no twirling necessary. The water's nearly boiling and the sauce is just heating up. Should be ready in a few more minutes." She stirred the pot on the stove. "So, what'd you do the rest of the day?"

"Maria brought over some of my clothes this afternoon. I asked her to put the duffel bag in your room. Is that okay for now?"

"That's fine," she said. "So, I guess her visit was a nice distraction."

"Yeah, it was. She didn't stay long because she had to go to class and then practice. She said some of my friends on the team have been calling the dorm asking for me. They want to know if they can visit."

"Fine with me," Andi said. "You up for company?"

"I think it would be fun to see everybody...well, not exactly *see* everybody." She paused and dropped her head. "You know what I mean," she added softly.

Andi reached over and rested her hand on CJ's shoulder. "Why don't you call Maria later and see if some of the gals can stop by tomorrow. Dr. Erroll said short visits were okay, and I certainly don't mind if your friends come by. In fact, I'll clear out of here for a while so you can be—"

"No! I don't want you to leave. I'm anxious for my friends to meet you. Would you...want to stick around?"

"Sure, if you'd like," Andi said. She was glad to see a smile reemerge on CJ's face.

Shortly after, Andi helped CJ move to a chair at the table. She returned briefly to the kitchen and emerged with their bowls of pasta. Placing both of the bowls on the table, she chose a seat next to her friend. "So, your bowl of pasta is in the middle of the place mat, your water is at the 2:00 position, and the bread plate is at 10:00." Andi smiled, pleased that she'd arranged the place setting in a way that allowed CJ a measure of independence while eating. "Want some grated cheese on the pasta?"

"Sure, a little would be great," CJ said. She slid her right hand up the fabric of the place mat until she touched the water glass, just where Andi said it would be. A slight grin lifted her lips. "This smells great, Andi. Thanks so much for cooking."

"You're on deck for Saturday, don't forget."

"I didn't. So, how was the rest of your day after lunch?"

"Busy, actually. The time passed quickly." She spoke between mouthfuls of food. "I got email responses from your professors about your classes."

"You contacted them for me?"

"Yes. I hope you don't mind, but you seemed worried about missing classes, and I wanted to help. I wrote them about your injury at the game. Most of them had heard about it already—the good and bad news about small campuses where everybody knows everybody's business—and were quick to offer whatever help they could. I asked if they could forward lecture notes to me, so I could pass them on to you. I got the first batch of responses this afternoon."

"I can't believe you went through all that trouble," CJ said incredulously.

"No trouble. I knew they'd send it to me as kind of a professional courtesy. Plus, everybody knows that you're the basketball superstar."

"Stop with the star stuff," she protested.

"It's true. Anyway, I printed out copies at my office so I could read the notes to you later, if you'd like."

"That would be great, Andi." She hesitated, then continued. "Today, when I was sitting around by myself, I got to thinking about how far behind in my work I'll be getting while I lie around waiting for my eyes to heal. There are only two more months before I'm supposed to graduate. I don't want to blow it at this point. If I can at least keep up with the class notes, I'd be a lot less worried about falling completely behind." She smiled at the thought of Andi's kindness and shook her head slowly. "You are just too much."

"It's nothing, CJ. I'm happy to do it for you. I know what it's like to be an injured athlete. I understand the pressures of juggling sports and academics and trying to live up to everyone's expectations." She paused and reflected on a thought, then continued in a softer, more serious voice. "It's during those times that you learn who you can count on and who you can't."

"I didn't know that you were injured," CJ said. "Sounds like there's a story behind that."

"There's always a story, right?"

"Will you share it with me?"

"Sure, but another time, okay?" Andi's tone was nearly pleading, not one of rejection. If she hoped to bridge the distance between her heart and CJ's, she knew one day soon she would have to reveal the ghosts of her past to her younger friend. However, the story of her career-ending injury, with its inextricable link to Liz, was not a topic she was ready to broach yet.

"Okay, Andi. Whenever you're ready. I'm not going anywhere...I mean, uh, unless I'm in your space too much and you need for me to leave." Her voice dropped to just above a whisper.

"No, CJ," Andi assured. She reached out and placed her hand on the other woman's shoulder. "You're not in my space too much." Moving her fingers underneath CJ's chin, she raised her head up. "I really enjoy having you around," she added softly.

"Thanks. You've made me feel very comfortable. I've enjoyed being here."

"So then you were right the first time. You're not going anywhere." She tilted her dark head slightly and arched up an eyebrow as she waited for a reply.

"Okay. I'm not going anywhere. But you've got to promise to tell me if I start to get on your nerves."

"You're a very perceptive and sensitive person, CJ. If that

happens, which I doubt, I'm sure you'll know." She smirked at her friend. "Let me clear away these dishes, then I'll read class notes to you. How's that sound?"

"Great. Can I help?"

"Nope. Time for you to get horizontal again." Andi rose from the chair and helped CJ move back across the room. Her arm began to feel quite natural wrapped around the younger woman's back.

Later that night, as she lay on the sofa watching CJ's rhythmic sleep breathing, Andi wished that her arm was wrapped tightly around the younger woman's body once again.

Chapter
Twenty-three

THE NEXT DAY passed with the same comfortable routine as the previous one. The two women shared breakfast muffins and parted for a few hours until midday when Andi returned. Following a leisurely lunch of sub sandwiches, the grad assistant departed once again with the promise to return by 4:00, when CJ's teammates were due to arrive.

After lunch, Andi returned to her office to review students' papers and to prepare for upcoming lectures. Lost in her work, she did not hear the footsteps that grew louder as they approached her office.

"Knock, knock," Martha called. She poked her head around Andi's partly open office door, smiling as she spotted her friend.

"Hey!" Andi exclaimed. She moved around from behind the desk and greeted her friend with a warm hug. "What a nice surprise," she added, grinning. "Were your ears ringing? I've been thinking about you."

"Honey, my ears are always ringing from the sheer volume of noise at the Registrar's office lately." She held Andi's shoulders at arms' length and looked over her friend from head to toe. "You look good, girlfriend. Much better than the last time I saw you."

"Yeah, well, I was a bit stressed then. How's Karen?"

"Work's still crazy, you know? Some days she comes home frazzled, but for the most part, things are okay."

"You both are workaholics."

"Only nine to five, but when the day is over I leave it all behind. In fact, we're headed up to the cabin this weekend. It's been cool, but we thought we'd open it early this season and hope the weather holds."

"Oh," Andi frowned. "But I won't be able to go and help you if you're going this weekend. I've got CJ."

"Don't worry about it," Martha assured. "We've appreciated your help when you could come, but don't worry about it when you can't. You'll be missing a few good meals, though."

"I'm sure, but I couldn't leave CJ alone."

"Of course not, Andi. We understand. Once things settle down, then you'll come out for a weekend. I'm sure you could use some down time and a little R&R."

"Yeah," Andi said.

"Everything okay? How are things so far?"

"Great," Andi said. She tilted her head and paused, envisioning CJ in her mind's eye. "Everything's been really...I don't know...comfortable."

"Not feeling crowded?"

"No, not at all, actually. I admit I was a little worried about that, since I'm so used to being by myself and having my own space, but I've really enjoyed having her around. I know she's really worried about her eye, and sometimes she gets kind of quiet and I can tell she's thinking about it. But mostly she's smiling and talkative and upbeat—much more so than I would be, that's for sure. We sit around and talk a lot, you know? About her family, and my family, sports stuff, music, movies. She's a big movie fan. So, she's fun to be around."

"While you're doing all that talking, have you talked to her about the kiss?"

"No, I haven't brought that up yet," Andi said sheepishly.

"How come?"

"Lot's of reasons."

"Such as?"

"Dr. Erroll said CJ should stay relaxed and calm. What if I bring up things and she gets upset? I mean, she seems to be comfortable around me now, but what if it's a friendship kind of comfort? What if I tell her how I really feel about her but she's gotten over me and doesn't feel that way any more?"

Martha smirked and said, "Then I think you'll be the one who's upset, not CJ."

"Wise ass," Andi scoffed.

"You know I'm right."

"Yeah, well..."

"Well what?"

"Okay, so you're a little bit right," sighed Andi. "Now that I've admitted to myself how I feel about her, I'd be upset if she's changed her mind and isn't interested in me. There. I've said it, okay?" She glared momentarily at Martha, then softened her eye contact as Martha's expression remained unfazed. "I *think* she still is, but I just can't be sure. Before, when we were spending time together, I could look into her eyes and know how she felt, even if I didn't consciously acknowledge it back then. Now, I listen to her words and read her body language, but that visual key is missing. I need to see her looking back at me to know for sure." She paused, then continued. "Besides, Dr. Erroll really doesn't want her to get upset."

"Chicken shit," Martha teased.

"Guilty as charged," Andi said.

"You really should talk to her, Andi." Martha's tone was kind, with all hints of teasing gone. "Wasn't it only about a week ago you were telling Karen and me how much you just wanted the opportunity to talk to her in person? Well, you've got that opportunity now. Shit, she's a captive audience. Don't you think she deserves to know how you feel? She put her heart on the line, Andi. It's your turn now."

"I have every intention of telling her," Andi said. Martha looked at her skeptically. "Really," Andi insisted. "Every day I spend with her I grow more fond of her. It's sometimes a little scary, you know? I'm not used to feeling this way. I don't know...she makes my heart happy, really happy."

"All right, let me get this straight. You're going to wait until she gets the okay from the doctor before you lay your heart on the line, because you really want to look in her eyes to be sure she still feels the same way you do. Does that about sum it up?"

"More or less."

"Have you considered that she might never—"

"Don't even say it!" Andi interrupted. "She's going to be okay. She'll see again. She's done everything the doctor has asked her to do. Why shouldn't she make a complete recovery?"

"Easy there, Andi. I'm not wishing any bad luck on her, you know that. I'm just asking if you've considered what you'll do in the event that things don't go quite as smoothly as we all hope they do, that's all."

"I can't even think about that, Martha. It won't change the way I feel about her, if that's what you're wondering."

"I didn't mean to imply that."

"Fine. I just wanted to be sure you understood. I—I'm really fond of CJ, and that won't change if..." She paused and looked at her hands. "It won't change, ever."

"Ever, huh?" Martha chuckled kindly. "Sounds like you've got it bad, my friend."

"I don't know." Andi grinned. "I think it feels pretty good."

"What am I going to do with you?" Martha asked, laughing.

"Be patient? You know you're better at this kind of stuff than I am."

"What kind of stuff?"

"You know, talking, communicating, being open— relationship stuff."

"Seems to me that CJ is pretty good at those things, too. You better start taking notes, my friend. Here, give me a hug goodbye. I've got to get back to the office before all hell breaks lose." She stepped up to Andi and embraced her.

"Thanks for stopping by. Your friendship means a lot to me," she added softly.

"See? You're not so bad at it."

"At what?" Andi asked, pinching together her dark eyebrows.

"At talking, communicating, and being open," Martha said. Andi blushed at her remark. "Practice makes perfect, you know."

"I'll try," she promised. "I'm going to miss not going with you gals. Call me when you get back, okay?"

"I will. You'll come next time. Oh, I nearly forgot." She slid her bag off her shoulder. "Karen made some banana nut bread for you and CJ. She knows how you hate to cook and thought poor CJ might need some snacks." She smirked at Andi as she handed over the loaf.

"Easy there," Andi teased. "I've been doing okay so far in the food department. She hasn't complained yet."

"She's way too polite, my friend." She winked at Andi. "I'm just teasing you."

"I know. Tell Karen thanks for the bread. We'll enjoy it for breakfast."

"Bye. I'll call you in a few days." With a wave, Martha disappeared down the hallway.

TRUE TO HER word, Andi walked through the apartment door at 3:50. As she sat on the sofa, sharing her day's events with her companion, the doorbell echoed through the room. "I'll get it." Andi strode quickly across the living room and headed down the stairs.

Opening the wooden door, she greeted the six women who stood on the porch. "Hi," she said. She pushed open the storm door as they responded with hellos. "Right up the stairs." She motioned as she held the door open while they passed through. "CJ's been looking forward to your visit." She closed the doors behind the last of CJ's guests and followed the group up the stairs. As she entered the living room, she heard them greeting CJ, who was dressed in sweats and lying propped up against pillows on the mattress.

Andi walked toward the group. Some of CJ's friends looked familiar to her, having seen them at the basketball games that she attended. She immediately noticed Kelly, the woman who had organized the sledding day. Heading toward her, Andi sat on the floor, cross-legged, between Kelly and the mattress where CJ reclined.

"Hey, Kelly." She extended her hand in greeting.

"Hi, Andi. Long time no see."

"Kelly," CJ piped up, "would you introduce Andi to the rest of the gang?"

"Sure." Kelly pointed one at a time to each and announced names. "This is Sarah, Jude, LaShawna, Becky, and Coop." She then motioned to Andi and addressed the women. "And this is Andi."

They all smiled and waved or nodded their greeting. Andi glanced over at CJ, who smiled at the company. She was glad that the basketball player's friends had come by to inquire about their teammate and to break up the long, boring hours of CJ's day.

"How the hell are you?" Becky asked. "We've been pretty worried about you."

"Yeah, tell us about the prognosis," Kelly asked. "Coach didn't have too many details about your eye."

"Heard you got whisked off to the infirmary," Coop said, "with mean old nurse Whipple and Mr. Bennett. I went there once when I thought I had the flu, but I left there quick, let me tell you. I almost —"

"Coop!" Sarah blurted out. "Let the woman talk, will ya?" She turned to CJ and spoke. "So tell us, CJ."

"You probably remember it better than I do. I got elbowed in the eye, bounced my head off the floor, and next thing I know I'm waking up in the infirmary." Talking about the incident with her teammates who witnessed it made the injury seem all the more real to her. With her friends sitting around her, she was reminded that they were free to leave later and go shoot hoops or walk across campus or go out dancing, while she was limited to lying on her back, hoping the situation didn't get worse. Her spirits drooped.

"So why the patch over your eyes?" Jude asked.

"To rest my eye. I have some bleeding in there. The doctor said I have to keep it covered for a week to ten days and remain 'neutral' as she put it. No laughing, crying, coughing, nothing that would increase the pressure behind my eyes." She felt trapped by her restrictions and suddenly became very warm.

"Or else what?" Jude said.

"I...I could lose..." CJ's voice became soft as her words faltered.

Andi interrupted. "Everything's going to be fine once she rests her eyes for a while longer. That's why she's here, so she can follow the doctor's orders and give her eye a chance to heal." CJ's head was drooping and her mouth no longer held the grin that it had when her friends first arrived.

Andi looked up and made eye contact with each woman in the circle. Her no-nonsense stare offered a silent warning not to press the subject and make her injured friend upset. The women nodded in silent agreement.

"Sure, you're young and in good shape," Coop said. "After a little rest, you'll be fine, I'm sure."

"Coop's right," Becky added. "The doctors who work at the infirmary come from the university hospital near Hanover. They really know their stuff."

"It was nice of you to offer to let her stay with you, Andi," Kelly said. She smiled at the attractive, dark-haired woman, and Andi smiled back.

"I would have been stuck in the infirmary otherwise," CJ said. She turned her head toward where Andi sat. "She's been a great help." She smiled sweetly at Andi, which caused her champion to blush.

Andi stood abruptly. "Anybody besides me need something to drink?" she asked. CJ's guests politely declined her offer. She strode toward the kitchen, anxious to remove her flushed face from the view of six pairs of inquiring eyes.

Sarah said, "Well, the dorm's certainly quiet without you. I miss hearing your goofy stories about your professors, or the bus rides, or that guy who shows up at all the home games with his face painted with the school colors. What's his name?"

"Stanley Limpet," Coop answered. She pinched her nose to add a nasal sound to the name. "But you can call me 'Sly,'" she mocked, her tone still nasal. The women all laughed at her impersonation. Andi returned to the circle with her glass of water just in time to catch the end of the laughter. She looked over at CJ and noticed her grinning, too. She exhaled slowly, relieved that her friend appeared to be a bit more upbeat.

"Did I overhear you gals talking about CJ stories?" She smirked at the women in the group, silently encouraging them to keep the stories casual and upbeat. "I wouldn't mind hearing one of—"

"Oh, no, you don't!" CJ interrupted. "We're not going to talk about me. Come on, gals! Fill me in on what's new. I've been out of the loop for four days now. What's been going on?"

"Well, you probably know we won the game where you got clobbered," Kelly said. "There's no way we were going to let them beat us after what that bitch did to you." Her teammates chimed in their agreement.

"I heard you kicked their ass by fifteen points," CJ said. "That's the best revenge I could ask for."

"But we lost in the Conference Finals," LaShawna added. Her tone was apologetic. "Coach said we probably ruined our shot at a Tournament bid." She sighed audibly and shook her head back and forth slowly.

The smile slowly faded on CJ's face.

Andi shot daggered looks at LaShawna, then around the group once again. She was frustrated that the topics of conversation seemed to keep coming back to subjects that were upsetting to CJ. When the purpose of the teammates' visit was to cheer up their injured friend, Andi was not about to have those friends bring down her spirits. As she made eye contact, each woman looked away quickly, anxious to avoid her stare.

"Coach said to say hi," Kelly said, obviously impatient to fill the uncomfortable silence. "She had a meeting with the AD and couldn't come with us, but she said she'd stop by soon, if that's okay."

"Sure," CJ said. Her voice remained flat and held none of the energy and enthusiasm Andi had grown to enjoy so much.

"Well," Coop bragged, "let me tell you what I heard." The other girls leaned forward so as not to miss any of the gossip. "My roommate's girlfriend does some filing in the AD's office, just a few hours a week. She's on one of those work-study programs to help pay her tuition, which sounds like a good deal to me. I'd like to get involved—"

"The point, Coop," Sarah said. "Get to the point."

"Oh. Right. Well, anyway, she overheard that Jen was offered the head basketball job at some Division III school in western Massachusetts. Can you believe it?"

"When'd you hear that?" Becky asked. "Why didn't you say anything sooner?"

"Yesterday. I forgot until just now."

"Think she'll take it?" Jude asked. She looked around the room addressing her teammates.

"Why not?" LaShawna asked. "Why be an assistant when you can be a head coach?"

"True," Kelly agreed. "You can tell she doesn't like when Coach tells her what to do."

"She doesn't like when *anyone* tells her what to do," Coop said. "In fact, she's been damn moody lately, even though we were winning."

"It'll be interesting to see what she does," CJ said. Andi

could tell by the way the blonde pursed her lips that she was thinking intently about the information she had just received.

"You gals have to promise not to say anything," Coop implored. "My roommate will kill me."

"We won't say anything, Coop," Becky said. "Besides, if it's true, we'll hear about it soon enough."

The conversation shifted to schoolwork, friends, off-campus parties, and the spring sports season. The women made sure not to bring up topics that might cause CJ to get upset. After nearly an hour had passed, the guests stood and began their good-byes. One by one they patted CJ's shoulder or hugged her, then headed for the door.

"Call if you need anything," Kelly said. She lingered by the door as the others walked down the stairs in front of her. "I'll see you in a few days, okay?"

"Okay. And thanks for coming by," CJ called out.

Andi followed the women downstairs and let them out, then locked the door before returning to the apartment. "Your friends are nice," she said. She sat on the edge of the mattress and placed her hand on CJ's forearm.

"Yeah. They're good people. I really miss not wrapping up the season with them." Her voice, tinged with sadness, became soft.

"I can understand your disappointment, CJ. You worked so hard to do well, and it's difficult not to see that through. I wish there was something I could do for you."

"You've already done so much, Andi." She reached out and rested her hand on Andi's leg. "You've made a difficult situation infinitely better. I hope you know how grateful I am."

Andi placed her hand gently on CJ's, intertwining her long fingers with those of her friend. The younger woman's hand was soft and warm, and Andi's skin tingled from the contact. She felt her pulse quicken as their hands lingered in the embrace. An energy connection flowed between them, powerful and alluring. She closed her eyes and focused all her concentration on their interlocked fingers, drawn in by the spirit of the affectionate, emerald-eyed woman. With every rapid beat of her heart, she felt her self-control slipping. An expectant silence lingered between them.

CJ felt Andi's pulse quicken as their fingers remained linked. She smiled. *You've had that effect on me for a long time, Andi.* She gently squeezed Andi's long fingers and felt the pressure returned. In her mind's eye, she could see the blue-eyed woman's hand covering her own, wrapping around her fingers. Many times she had noticed Andi's strong, sensual fingers and imagined how they would feel touching her. The tingling she felt as their hands remained joined only hinted at the pleasure the other woman's touch could bring. *I took a chance a few weeks ago, Andi, but I can be very patient. Next time, the first move will have to come from you.*

After an extended moment, Andi opened her eyes and shook her head slightly to release the spell. "So, have you thought about dinner?" Andi asked.

I have a lot more than dinner on my mind, the blonde thought to herself. "I'm ready when you are," CJ grinned.

THE EVENING PASSED quickly as the women slipped into what was rapidly becoming a pleasant routine. Andi was surprised at how easily she adjusted to sharing her time and space with the younger woman. Dinner was followed by an hour of cable news. Conversation and background music filled the remainder of the evening until yawning replaced talking. First CJ bathed, then Andi showered, and both women settled into their sleep spots to end the long, busy day. CJ drifted off quickly while Andi remained awake for another quarter hour on the sofa, enjoying the rhythm of CJ's sleep breathing. Hypnotized by the cadence of CJ's rising and falling chest, Andi soon fell asleep.

"No! No!"

Andi sat bolt upright as the crying-out reached her ears. She shook her head, temporarily disoriented at not being in her bed, but quickly regained her bearings. Looking over at her sleeping friend, she discovered the source of the noises that awakened her.

CJ tossed around in the bed as if struggling to free herself from a captor. Tormented sounds emerged from her lips as a nightmare haunted her sleep. Andi quickly moved off the sofa and sat down at the edge of the mattress, near the still-sleeping woman. She gently placed her hand on CJ's shoulder and softly called her name.

"CJ," she whispered into the darkness of the room. "CJ, it's okay." The thrashing woman stilled but continued to moan softly. Her body shook and her breathing was rapid. "I'm here, CJ. It's only a dream." She grasped her friend's shoulder more firmly, then gently stroked the woman's face with her other hand. When the whimpering ceased, she removed her hand from the softness of CJ's cheek.

"Andi?" CJ gasped.

"It's me, CJ. It's okay, I'm here."

The basketball player reached out her hands into the darkness until she touched Andi, who sat beside her. Grasping the older woman by the shoulders, she pulled her down into a frantic embrace, wrapping her arms around her back and squeezing tightly. Andi could feel CJ's heart racing. Her warm breath panted against the grad assistant's neck as the younger woman clung to her fiercely. A small cry escaped CJ's lips as her body trembled.

"I can't see!" the younger woman cried out. "It's so dark. Everything's dark. I couldn't find my way. I got lost and couldn't find anybody. I was trying to look for you but I was blind. Forever." Her words became choked off by weeping, and she hugged Andi more fiercely.

"Shhhh. It's okay now. It was only a dream."

Andi's arms, locked down to her body by CJ's embrace, moved slightly to stroke CJ's side. She whispered soothing sounds to the distraught woman in an attempt to calm her. Slowly and gently, her hand traveled up and down CJ's side, over the cotton T-shirt she slept in. As Andi's caresses continued, the rapid rise and fall of CJ's breathing abated and her trembling decreased. Her power-hold on Andi's arms eased enough for the other woman to lengthen the path of her stroking.

"I wasn't supposed to cry," CJ whimpered. She sniffled loudly, then exhaled. "What if I made it worse?" She reluctantly removed her arms from around Andi's shoulders. Lying back, she clasped her own hands tightly as they crossed her stomach.

"You didn't cry for very long, CJ. You couldn't help it. It was a bad dream." Once released from CJ's powerful hold, Andi moved next to her. She reclined on her side and faced the younger woman. With her arm bent at the elbow and her hand supporting her head, she watched her friend.

"But what if—"

"No 'what ifs,' CJ," she interrupted. Reaching out, she covered the injured woman's hands with her own, intertwining their fingers and squeezing gently. "Focus all your energy on healing, not worrying, okay?"

"I'll try," she responded. After a few minutes her breathing returned to its regular rhythm.

"You okay now? Want to talk about that dream some more?"

"No," she blurted out quickly. "Not tonight. Maybe...maybe tomorrow, if I need to."

"Sure. Whatever makes you comfortable." She stifled a yawn. "Ready to try and get back to sleep?"

"I think so," she said.

"Okay." Andi unlaced her fingers from CJ's and began to

rise. "If you need any — "

"No! Don't go." Her hand quickly tightened around Andi's to prevent her protector from removing it. When she spoke again, her voice was soft and almost pleading. "Would you...stay...with me...in case the dream comes back?" CJ held her breath as she waited for Andi to respond.

"Sure," she said kindly. "I'll be here for you." She stroked the top of CJ's hand with her thumb as their fingers once more intertwined. "Try to relax now and rest."

CJ reached down and pulled up the blanket, draping it over both their shoulders. Andi moved an extra pillow under her head. She remained on her side with her hand still holding CJ's. By the moonlight beaming through the living room window, she could watch the rhythm of the other woman's breathing. The muscles in her young face slowly relaxed, appearing to erase her earlier anxiety. Her mouth parted slightly as she drifted back into sleep.

Andi's eyes memorized every feature of CJ's beautiful face, mere inches away. The moonbeams danced off her light skin, highlighting the fine hairs that covered her cheeks. The muscles in the woman's face, so relaxed as she slept, hid the dimple that magically appeared whenever her young friend smiled. Even though the dimple crease was smooth, Andi could reach out and touch the exact spot where it would appear. So many times she had admired it. She breathed in slowly and smiled. CJ's skin and hair smelled slightly of soap and conditioner mixed with the unusual muskiness that was uniquely CJ. Andi closed her eyes to focus her senses. She breathed in deeply one more time, absorbing CJ, then exhaled slowly and relaxed. Her eyelids, heavy from sleepiness, blinked several times before staying weighted down for the remainder of the night. A peaceful smile graced her lips.

Chapter
Twenty-four

CJ AWAKENED TO the smell of coffee. Slowly she emerged from her slumber and stretched, straightening out her legs and reaching out with her arms. As her hand touched the mattress next to her, she noted the absence of her new bedmate. Rolling on her side, she rubbed her hand up and down the mattress where Andi lay just a short time before. She smiled. *Best sleep I've had in a long time. I could get used to this.* She pulled Andi's pillow close to her, then buried her face in it. The aroma of Andi's shampoo, mixed with her earthy scent, lingered on the pillowcase. Pressing the cloth to her nose, she breathed in deeply.

For several moments she lay there, embracing the pillow and burying her face in the material's surface. She reveled in the sensual pleasure of knowing Andi recently slept touching that same pillow. She sighed deeply, wishing she were hugging the person instead of the pillow.

Suddenly she stopped and rolled onto her back, releasing the pillow. *What if she's watching me? She could be standing nearby, watching me hugging this stupid pillow with a goofy grin on my face. How embarrassing.* She breathed in, then exhaled. *So much for playing it cool, CJ. Jeez...You better get a grip and not make a complete fool of yourself.* She lay motionless, hoping to hear a tell-tale noise that might indicate Andi's presence, but she heard nothing. After several seconds, she heard the sound of a spoon clinking against the inside of a coffee cup, and she felt somewhat relieved that perhaps Andi hadn't seen her after all.

She smirked, shaking her head slowly from side to side. *Don't lay it all out there so soon, CJ,* she reprimanded herself. Sitting up slowly, she swung her legs over the edge of the mattress and stood gradually. Using the sofa and chairs as a guide, she made her way toward the bathroom. After a few minutes she emerged, her cheeks pink from the cold water she had splashed on them. She moved toward the kitchen with her hand on the wall to guide her. Before she could take her third step, Andi was at her side. Her guardian gently took her arm and walked her toward the stool at the counter.

"So, how'd you sleep?" Andi asked. She waited as CJ settled herself on the seat cushion. Reaching for a glass of OJ on the counter, Andi handed her friend the drink.

"Much better, after..." She paused. "Thanks for...ahhhh..."

"No problem. I'm glad you slept better."

"I didn't crowd you, did I?"

"No, not at all," Andi said. She smiled. *I rather enjoyed it.* "So, you hungry?"

"I'm sure I could be tempted," she teased.

"Martha stopped by my office yesterday to see how you were doing. She dropped off a loaf of banana nut bread that Karen made. Want some?"

"You bet!" CJ said. "I love nut bread."

Andi brought out the bread and placed it on the cutting board. She sliced several thick pieces and placed two on a plate for CJ.

"Want more OJ with that?" she asked.

"I'd prefer milk, if you have it."

"Coming right up." She poured a tall glass of milk, placing it near her friend's left hand. She refilled her own coffee mug and joined the blonde at the counter, breaking off pieces of the nut loaf and washing them down with her drink. "So, have you thought up a menu for tonight?"

"Yup," she answered, still chewing. She swallowed the bread, then continued. "Let's see... You'll need soy sauce, peanut oil, fresh ginger—"

"Hold on a minute," Andi interrupted. "I'd better write this down." She got out a pen and paper from the junk drawer and returned to the counter seat. "Okay. I think I have soy sauce, but I need peanut oil and fresh ginger. What's next?"

"A package of dried Asian noodles, scallions, fresh bean sprouts, broccoli, peanut butter—"

"Peanut butter?"

"Yes, peanut butter. You did tell me you liked peanut butter, didn't you?"

"In cookies, yes, but I don't think I've ever had it in the main course."

"You're in for a treat, then," CJ assured. "Also get some mirin, that's sweet rice vinegar, and dried shiitake mushrooms, garlic, and red pepper flakes. That's it, I think."

"That's some mix of food," Andi said. "What's this going to be?"

"I'm not sure it has a name," CJ answered. "I call it spicy noodles with shiitake mushroom sauce."

"Sounds complicated."

"Piece of cake. I'll walk you through all the steps." She paused. "Unless you've changed your mind. I don't want to make you—"

"No! I didn't change my mind. I'm just a little intimidated by the prospect of cooking something so elaborate."

"It's really not that bad."

"Easy for you to say," she joked, "but I trust you." She popped the last piece of her nut bread in her mouth, then drained her mug. "Would you like more milk or bread?" she asked.

"Nope," CJ said. "Be sure to tell Martha and Karen I said thanks, and that it was delicious."

"I'll clear these plates and head out to the store," Andi said.

"Wish I could go, too," CJ said glumly. Her head dropped, and the corners of her mouth tilted downward. "I'm getting a little stir crazy just lying around all day."

"I wish you could come, too," Andi said. "But we promised Dr. Erroll you'd follow her directions and rest." She stepped over and stood next to CJ's chair, then placed her arm around the other woman's shoulder. "Just hang in there a little longer, okay?"

"Okay," she sighed. "I'm sorry if I sound like I'm complaining. It's just that, I guess now that my head's starting to feel better, I'm feeling really frustrated that I still can't do anything, you know?"

"I know what you mean. I'm a really bad patient when I'm sick or injured since I usually don't sit still for very long." She paused and thought back to when she had twisted her ankle on an ice patch around Thanksgiving, and how she'd hobbled around campus for nearly two weeks because she refused to be on crutches. Shaking her head slowly, she sighed at her own stubbornness. "But, hey," she added, tousling CJ's blonde hair, "at least today's Saturday and you won't have to be by yourself most of today or tomorrow. Maybe that'll help the time pass more quickly and keep your mind off feeling frustrated."

"You don't have to hang around here to keep me company if you have other things to do. I don't want to monopolize all your free time."

"You're not monopolizing anything. Besides, I didn't have any plans for the weekend."

"You sure?"

"Positive. It'll be fun to just hang out and relax. I don't do that enough." She gave CJ's shoulder one last squeeze, then collected their breakfast dishes, and stepped back into the kitchen. CJ heard the clatter of plates as Andi stacked them in the sink, washed them quickly, and put them in the dish drain before moving back to her companion. "So, did you think of anything else you want me to pick up at the store?"

"That was a long enough list, don't you think?"

"Just checking. How about I help you back to the mattress now?"

"Sure." CJ swiveled toward Andi on the stool, then stood. Andi gently took her arm and transferred her hold to the younger woman's waist. CJ draped her hand over Andi's broad shoulder as they walked.

After a few steps, Andi took CJ's hand as she lowered herself to the mattress. Still holding it, Andi squatted near her friend and spoke. "I'm going to get out of these sweats and brush my teeth before heading out. Can I get you anything before I go?"

"Just the TV clicker so I can listen to news," she said.

Andi placed the remote in her hand and stood. "I'll be back in about an hour, okay?"

"Okay. Well then...until soon?"

Andi's heart danced at the long unheard expression. A smile tugged at her mouth and lightness filled her heart. "Yes, until soon," she said. A smile lit up her face.

CJ RECLINED ON the sofa with her back against some pillows and the armrest. Her legs were stretched out across the cushions and her fingers were laced across her stomach.

"I'll be there in a minute," Andi called from the kitchen. "I just want to unpack the rest of the groceries."

"Take your time. I'm not going anywhere," CJ said. She wiggled her stocking feet back and forth in time to the rhythm of a song she couldn't get out of her head. Suddenly, she felt a warm hand wrap around her foot and abruptly stop moving it.

"Just me," Andi said. "I didn't want to sit on your feet while you were sofa dancing."

"Sorry. I'll move." She bent her knees to make more room at the end for Andi.

"No need." She sat at the end of the sofa and drew CJ's feet back down to where they had been. The blonde woman felt Andi's thighs against the soles of her feet. "There's plenty of room for both of us," Andi added.

Andi's leg felt warm and firm, and CJ enjoyed the sensation

of touching the alto-voiced woman, even if it was only with her feet. She moved her feet side to side again, in the same way she had before, but this time it created a pleasant friction against Andi's denim-clad leg. CJ heard her friend chuckle.

"So, where do you want to begin?" Andi asked.

"How about with Professor Wallington's notes. His class is always challenging."

"Wallington it is." She heard Andi shuffling through papers to find the correct ones. "Hmmmm, America Between the Wars, huh? Sounds like an interesting class."

"It is. I really like American history, and besides, Professor Wallington knows his stuff. Actually," she giggled, "I think he lived through most of that time period, so it's probably first-hand knowledge. But don't tell him I said that."

"My lips are sealed," Andi said, smiling "I enjoy American Lit, which is often linked to the history and politics of the times, so I can understand your interest in American history." She paused as she scanned the notes. "Okay, these notes are titled, 'Prohibition: The Government's Attempts at Citizen Control.' Ready?"

"As I'll ever be," CJ said.

Andi launched into the material, intoning her words so that the notes read more like a story than a lecture. CJ smiled at her friend's reading, enjoying the subject matter even more than she did with Professor Wallington. Andi, too, found herself caught up in the information and wishing she had paid a little more attention in her history classes while she was in school. After nearly forty-five minutes of reading, she stopped and put down the papers.

"That's all for today's episode," she spoke in a deep, serious voice. "Tune in next week for the exciting conclusion of, 'As the Country Drinks.'" She reached over to the end table to get her water, then drained half the glass to relieve her parched throat.

"Bravo!" CJ clapped loudly and laughed. "Well done!" Andi smiled at the younger woman's enthusiastic response. "Your students must love it when you deliver the lecture."

She smirked. "I don't recall ever hearing clapping, if that's any indication. Want me to read you notes from another class?"

"How about we take a break from school work for a while," CJ requested. "After all, it is Saturday."

"Sure," Andi said. "We can finish tomorrow, if you'd like." Her mind wandered to the sensation of CJ's soles pressed against her leg, and she smiled. She thought back to the previous night, when her sleeping companion gripped her hand so closely while she slept. Her body tingled at the thought of the blonde's nearness and a blush darkened her face.

"What are you thinking about?" CJ asked.

"Nothing," she said quickly. She was glad CJ couldn't see her blush; otherwise, her persistent friend might not have accepted her hasty reply. Andi held her breath, expecting CJ to push the question as if she could read her thoughts. After a moment of silence, she exhaled silently. The two sat in companionable silence.

"Andi?"

"Yes?"

"Can I ask you something?"

"Sure," she said, but feeling less confident than the one-word answer suggested.

"The other day you told me that you know what it's like to be an injured athlete." Her voice was soft and hesitant. "Could you tell me about how you know?"

Andi's heart began to beat rapidly as she listened to CJ's request. A hint of fear crept into her heart, for she knew that a story about her injury would be incomplete without including the part about Liz. *What to do? Things are going so well. Okay. Don't panic. Just open up a little and trust her. Start the story and see how it goes. You can leave the last part out.* CJ's question was met by silence as Andi's mind quickly weighed her options.

"I'm sorry," CJ stammered, uncomfortable with the silence. "I didn't mean to make you feel—"

"It's okay. If we're trying to build a," she paused, "a friendship, then it's okay for you to ask. It's not you making me feel uncomfortable, really. It's me. I'm afraid I'm just not as open as you are, so—"

"Then you don't have to tell me."

"But I want to. Your openness is one of the things that's so wonderful about you, and you deserve that type of openness from me in return." She wrapped her long fingers around CJ's foot as it rested against her thigh. The skin beneath the sock was warm, and she rubbed her thumb against the cloth-covered toes. The motion elicited a slight moan from CJ, which caused Andi to smile.

"You sure?" CJ asked.

"Yeah, I am," Andi said. She took a deep breath then launched into her story. "I was recruited during my senior year in high school," she began. "The swim coach here has a great reputation, and she convinced me that it would be a better fit for me here than at a Division I school. I was kind of a loner in high school, and I didn't want to get lost on a large campus anyway. Plus, I didn't want to swim for a Division I coach who was more concerned with winning than with grades. So I signed on here. I was fairly successful in high school, and I knew that this coach could bring me to the next level. And she did.

"Although I was initially shy and homesick as a freshman, I soon met Martha, who introduced me to other people on campus, so I made a few friends. Once swimming practice began, I met other gals on the team so I had enough of a circle of friends to make me feel more comfortable here. Not that I had much of a choice about leaving, really. My mother certainly couldn't have afforded to send me to school, so it was this or go to work. I stayed. Don't get me wrong; once I adjusted to college life, I really liked it here. I still do, which is why I'm still here.

"Anyway, during my freshman year I did okay in terms of swimming. I had several wins, which made the coach very pleased, but after being the star in high school, I guess I was expecting a little more. My coach was great, though, and she helped me come up with an off-season plan to help me improve.

"I worked my ass off from the moment that first season ended until the start of the second. I spent hours upon hours in the weight room, lifting and getting stronger. My shoulders and back got so broad that I had trouble finding shirts that fit me. But I didn't care. All I cared about was swimming faster, and those stronger muscles helped me to do that. I also ran to build up my wind and got pretty good at that, too. In fact, the track coach wanted me to join the spring squad, but I turned him down. It was not part of my plan for success.

"All that training began to pay off in my sophomore year. As my coach put it, I became the team's 'secret weapon' because none of the other teams expected a sophomore to swim as powerfully as I did. Most of the other teams recognized my name from the previous year but there was nothing spectacular about my swimming then, which disarmed them during my second season. I took them by surprise. I think I took my coach by surprise, too. Everyone was a bit surprised, but I wasn't. I was like a woman possessed. I had found something I was good at, and I worked hard to be the best. Not for anyone else, mind you. It wasn't like I had something to prove to anyone else. I only had to prove it to myself. And I did. I went undefeated during my sophomore year. My coach said she never had a swimmer do that before. I was on top of the world.

"Everything seemed to be working out great. Not only was my swimming going well, but my classes were, too. I made Dean's List four straight semesters, which made my coach even happier. My mother was happy, too. It felt good to make her feel so proud of me. I had also learned to enjoy the freedom of college life. I liked the fact that no one told me what to do, other than my coach, to an extent. I came and went when I wanted, which I certainly didn't do when I lived at home."

Andi paused to take a breath. She had been speaking for several minutes uninterrupted and wondered what CJ was thinking regarding everything she said so far. Usually Andi was much more comfortable as a listener than a talker, so her uncustomary openness put her out of her comfort zone a bit. She exhaled audibly.

"You okay?" CJ asked. Her voice expressed concern. She pressed the soles of her feet against Andi's thigh.

"Yeah," Andi said. She stroked her thumb back and forth several times across CJ's toes before she stilled her hand and simply rested it on top of the warm feet. She feared she would lose her nerve if she remained silent much longer, so she continued with her story.

"By that time, I was also involved in a relationship. My first real one, actually. Liz. We met during the second semester of my freshman year. She was everything I wasn't: outgoing, adventurous, daring, popular. I couldn't believe she was interested in me, especially since she was two years older. Up to that point in my life, I knew I was attracted to women, but I'd never acted on my feelings because...well, for a lot of reasons, one of which was the fact that I had no privacy living with my mother. But when I got up to college, with no one looking over my shoulder, I had the freedom to follow my heart. That led me to Liz."

CJ felt a jolt of jealousy rise up in her throat as she listened to Andi speak. She did not pick up on the sadness in her friend's voice, nor could she see her down-turned mouth or slowly shaking head. She held her breath as Andi continued.

"So, for a while, my life seemed perfect. I was swimming as well as I had ever dreamed of swimming, my classes were great, and I..." Andi's voice trailed off to silence. She closed her eyes as she thought back to that difficult time. CJ tensed as she waited for Andi to resume. Softly, Andi spoke. "I thought it was real. We hung out together, went to the Oasis nearly every weekend with the whole crew to dance and drink dollar beers. At the end of my sophomore year, Liz graduated and moved into an apartment in town with two of her friends. I lived on campus that summer, through a work-study program, so I got to see her all the time. Everything seemed to be going well.

"I kept up my training routine, since it had brought me so much success, and when my junior year rolled around, I was out for records and national ranking. My coach named me captain that season, and I knew the whole team looked up to me and counted on me. All their expectations didn't feel like pressure, though. Rather, it pushed me even harder. By midway through my junior year, I owned all the school records in my events. I worked my body to near exhaustion every day.

"It was on one of those days that it happened. I was walking across the pool deck, like I had done a thousand times before, when I slipped. I fell forward and put my arms out to break my fall, but when my palms made contact with the deck, they slipped, too. You know, there's both good news and bad news with strong muscles. The good news is that strong muscles hold the joint nice and tight. The bad news is that those same tight muscles easily tear when the joint is stressed. I dislocated my right shoulder. The muscles tore.

"The pain was mind-numbing. I can still see myself lying there on the tile, writhing in so much agony I was afraid I *wouldn't* die. My coach came running over, followed by the trainer, and he popped it back into place. Then I passed out."

CJ heard the pain in Andi's voice as she described the injury. Having come off an injury herself only a few days ago, she could practically feel the pain, fear, and heartbreak Andi was sharing. Suddenly, her foot-to-thigh contact simply wasn't enough. She sat up slowly and shifted on the sofa so that she was sitting cross-legged next to and facing her companion. CJ tentatively reached out her right hand and touched Andi's arm. Caressing it softly, she slid her hand up toward Andi's shoulder, then wrapped her arm around her, pulling her in for a hug. Andi stiffened initially at the contact, but immediately relaxed against her friend, whose warmth and compassion shot right to Andi's heart. Neither woman spoke for several minutes, yet their body language bridged the gap of silence. Finally, CJ broke the hug but kept her right hand around Andi's shoulder as the other woman continued to speak.

"When I woke up, I was in the infirmary. Even though I was heavily sedated, I was still really uncomfortable. More than the pain, though, I was scared. I could just tell that I had done something really bad to my shoulder. When the nurse came in, I asked her what was going on, but she only said that I'd have to wait for the doctor to come by. So I waited and I waited for what seemed like forever until he came. He said the MRI revealed three tears, which would require surgery to repair. Three days later I had the operation."

"I didn't know you had surgery," CJ said softly. Her arm was still draped across Andi's shoulders, and she stroked her hand gently over Andi's right shoulder.

"Yeah, a couple inches of railroad tracks on my shoulder. Not very attractive," she shrugged.

"Can I feel...?" CJ asked.

Andi hesitated, then took CJ's left hand and raised it up toward her shoulder. With her right hand, Andi pulled the neck of her T-shirt over far enough to allow access to the scar. She guided her companion's hand under her shirt until she felt the woman's fingers make contact with her skin. CJ's touch was warm and tentative as she traced the raised scar tissue with her fingertips. The scar, still sensitive several years after the surgery, tingled as the younger athlete trailed her fingers up then down its length. Finally, CJ removed her hand from the warmth beneath Andi's shirt. Clasping her own hands, CJ placed them both in her lap, afraid that if she didn't hold them there they would reach out to touch Andi again. Her legs, still crossed as she sat facing the ex-swimmer, pressed against Andi's thighs to maintain contact.

"Wow," she whispered. "I didn't know."

"Needless to say, that was the end of my swimming career. I spent six weeks in a sling, then nearly five months in physical therapy in order to get back most of my range of motion. It's not too bad for day-to-day activities, but I can't throw overhand or play racket sports. And, of course, swimming competitively was out. I was stubborn, though. I had more records to break and races to win, and the injury was not part of my plan. I thought I could work myself back in time to have a season my senior year. All I had was chronic tendonitis that several cortisone shots wouldn't clear up. It was so sore I couldn't even brush my teeth. I finally had to resign myself to the fact that it was over. I never got to swim competitively again." She took a deep breath and exhaled slowly.

The words "it was over" rumbled around in CJ's mind, raising the hairs on her arm. *She knows exactly what it's like. At least I had my four years. I would have been destroyed if this happened to me during my third season.* Things started to click in CJ's mind as she remembered past conversations with Andi. The taciturn woman would change the subject quickly if CJ asked about her swimming career or her scholarship. Back then, CJ attributed Andi's reticence to her reserved personality, but now she knew the rest of the story. The younger woman marveled at Andi's emotional strength.

"Were you able to graduate on time, after missing school during the injury?" CJ asked.

"Yes, I graduated after four years with the rest of my class. The professors were good about letting me make up work. I only missed about two weeks of school from the injury and the surgery. After that, I carried my laptop to class to take notes. I learned to type pretty quickly using my left hand. Martha was a real pal, though. She typed all my longer papers for me because my one-handed method took so long."

"What about Liz?" CJ said. Her voice was soft, and she held her breath waiting for the answer.

"She dumped me," Andi said softly.

"What! She dumped you?" Her voice was loud and almost angry.

Andi smirked at CJ's defensive reaction. "When I was going through all that rehab, I had major restrictions on what I could and couldn't do. Going out dancing and drinking at the Oasis was not on the 'to-do' list. Liz told me that things had 'changed' and that it just wasn't fun anymore."

"Bitch," CJ muttered. Andi grinned at her remark. "Sorry, I should mind my own business and keep my mouth shut."

"You're allowed to express your opinion any time you like, CJ," Andi said. "And if I disagree, I'll tell you. In this case, you're right, though. She was a bitch, very controlling and manipulative. In retrospect, I can see all that clearly, but at the time, I was heartbroken. I had just lost my swimming career, and a few weeks later I lost her, too. For a while, I thought..." She hesitated, then stopped.

"Thought what?" CJ asked.

"That I loved her," Andi said quietly.

"You didn't?"

"No," she said sadly. "Real love is based on trust, respect, and communication, sprinkled with genuine affection and mutual attraction."

"Sounds like a good recipe to me." CJ smiled.

"I think so, too," Andi said. "But that's not what we had at all."

"So you're over her?"

"Yeah, I'm over her. What took me a while to get over was the pain of getting hurt, though, of giving my heart to someone I thought I could trust to hold it gently in her hands. But she didn't." She sighed. "My heart is in one piece now, but I learned not to give it away that easily anymore."

The two women sat in silence, each lost in her own thoughts. Andi felt a surprising sense of relief at having told CJ about that difficult part of her past. While it was tough to begin the story, Andi found that she became more comfortable as she opened up to the other woman; CJ's spontaneous, affectionate reaction further compelled her to expose her feelings. Recalling and speaking about hurtful things in her past wasn't nearly as scary as she thought it might be. Andi had a feeling that her new friend was the one who helped make it feel safe.

CJ sat quietly, letting the impact of Andi's story settle. She never ceased to be amazed at the depths of what lay beneath the grad assistant's calm, steady surface. Andi's presence could be calming like the gentle bobbing of a raft on the ocean or as powerful as an arching wave. There was so much for CJ to discover about Andi, and everything she learned made her yearn for more.

"Jeez," CJ lamented. "That's a lot to lose and a lot to deal with. How did you handle it?"

"I worked out a lot, rode my bike for miles and miles over half the state. Dove back into my schoolwork. Wrote. I keep a journal."

"I know."

"How do you know?" Andi looked quickly at the blonde woman. Her dark eyebrows were knitted together as she considered CJ's response. The journal had been sitting out the whole time CJ was there. *As if she could read it*, she chided herself. *Even if she could see, she's just not like that and you know it.*

"Ahhh," CJ stammered, "you must have mentioned it before." She didn't want to reveal that she wasn't asleep when Andi was reading her journal aloud a few nights earlier.

Andi easily accepted the explanation. "I also spent a lot of time by myself," she continued. "I think I needed to. For a while, with Liz, I let myself get lost in being with her. It made me feel out of control, especially when she ended things. I'm okay being by myself now."

"Does that mean you don't want to get involved again?" CJ asked.

"Not with just anyone, and not just casually," Andi said honestly.

"But if it felt real?" CJ persisted. "What if it *was* real?"

Andi looked at CJ, who was facing her. The younger woman was still sitting so close that her crossed legs were pressed against Andi's. Her soft lips were slightly parted after having spoken. CJ's head was tilted slightly to the left as she waited for an answer to her question.

"That would be the only risk worth taking," Andi said softly. Her eyes, still focused on CJ's lips, watched dimples crease as her mouth moved into a smile.

Andi closed her eyes and imagined what it would be like to kiss those lips. Her own lips parted in anticipation and she leaned a breath forward. *No! Not yet*, she reprimanded herself.

Her eyes shot open, and she shook her head slightly to clear out the tempting vision. *I want to look into her beautiful green eyes and see her say yes. Only then will I.*

The air around the two women teemed with barely contained energy and emotions. CJ sat transfixed by the sensations as she focused her concentration on picking up signals from Andi. At that moment, she wished more than ever that she could see. The heat of Andi's body radiated from mere inches away. The blonde could hear the increased cadence of her friend's breathing and thought for a moment she even felt Andi's breath on her cheek. How long she had taken her eyesight for granted! Now that she couldn't rely on it to read Andi's body language, she felt the full impact of its loss. *Please let me see again*, she pleaded to any higher power that might heed her wish. *I need to look into her blue eyes again so I can be sure. I think I know...but I need to be sure.*

"What?" Andi asked softly.

"Hmmmm?"

"You just looked like you were going to say something, like you had something on your mind."

"I have a lot on my mind," CJ said honestly. "I...I'm very touched that you shared all that with me, Andi. I know you're a very private person, so it means a great deal to me that you trusted me enough to be so open." She unclasped her fingers and reached out, tentatively placing a hand on Andi's forearm. "Thanks."

"Thank you for making me feel comfortable enough to speak openly. It takes two people to communicate." She placed her hand on top of CJ's and smiled.

The moment was interrupted by a loud growling from CJ's stomach. Andi laughed from the depths of her belly, half relieved that the tension was broken. CJ moaned with embarrassment and placed her hands over her face.

Andi chuckled. "Guess we better start dinner."

"HOW LONG HAVE the shiitake mushrooms been soaking?" CJ asked. She sat at the counter, keeping Andi company and talking her through the meal preparation. Her feet swung back and forth as they dangled from the stool.

"About fifteen minutes," Andi said. "How much longer?"

"Until they're re-hydrated. Pinch one and see how it feels."

"That's not going to help me much," she responded. "I have no idea what it's supposed to feel like."

"Bring it over here." Andi brought the bowl over and set it

on the counter. She lifted CJ's hand and placed it into the liquid containing the mushrooms. CJ pinched a mushroom. "They're done," she announced. "Drain the mushrooms, but save about a half cup of that liquid. Then you've got to cut the mushrooms into thin slices. Cut off the stems, though. They get tough." She heard the silverware clatter as Andi opened the utensil drawer.

"Slice them all?" Andi asked.

"Yup," CJ said. She heard the sound of the knife as it cut through the mushroom and scratched the cutting board.

"So," Andi said, "now that you know most of my recent past, how about you do a little sharing?"

"What would you like to know?"

"I don't know. How about what you do in your free time, aside from basketball."

"Let's see, I like to take road trips, you know, a day trip in the car, or an overnight. I love long weekends, too."

"Me, too," Andi agreed.

"There are so many beautiful places within a few hours' ride that there's always something to do."

"One of my favorite trips is over to the White Mountains."

"Oh, yeah! My car has done that trip so many times it can practically steer itself."

"You like hiking?" Andi asked.

"Very much. I love to be out on a trail amongst the pine and balsam trees. When the sun rises and warms the air, it gets fragrant from the tree needles. Their sponginess underfoot is so soft to walk on. No matter what's on my mind or what problem is getting me down, when I'm out there, surrounded by acres and acres of nature, my issues seem so insignificant. I walk out of the woods feeling rebalanced. Know what I mean?"

"Exactly. I spend a lot of time on the trails for the same reason. Being out there makes me feel like I'm part of the earth, not part of humanity. Ever climb Mt. Chickorua?"

"Hmmmm," CJ considered. "I don't think so. It's nice?"

"A steady climb for a few hours with the reward of a 360 degree view at the bald rock top. It's spectacular."

"Maybe you could take me there sometime?"

"Count on it. It's breathtaking in the fall." She stopped speaking as she moved the sliced mushrooms into a bowl. "Mushrooms are sliced," she announced.

"Is the water boiling yet?" CJ heard the pot lid clink as Andi lifted it to look.

"Nearly."

"Okay, then it's time to make the mushroom sauce."

CJ talked Andi through the remaining steps to prepare the

rest of the meal. The grad assistant scurried around the kitchen, closely following her companion's directions, which she delivered from the counter stool. In between CJ's directions and Andi's working, the two women carried on their conversation.

"I have a confession," CJ said. "Know what else I like about the White Mountains?"

"Hmmmm," Andi mused. "Ben and Jerry's is in Vermont, not New Hampshire, so I give up." She chuckled.

"Very funny...but I did visit their factory once. Anyway, what else I like is the outlet shopping in North Conway." She ducked her head sheepishly as she waited for Andi to react.

"No way!" Andi exclaimed. "I thought you loved being out in nature?"

"I do, really, but I don't like to hike if it's a rainy day, and there's always a bargain to be found. They have all the major retailers there. Ever go?"

"Well," Andi sighed. "I admit I stopped at the Nike outlet once, 'cause I needed a new pair of sneakers." She looked up to see CJ grinning. "And what are you smiling at?"

"Nothing," CJ drawled. "Can't a gal smile around here for no reason?"

"There's always a reason," she jested. "Come on, out with it."

"I was just thinking that, after we climb Mt. Chickorua, we could hit the outlets before we head back."

"Once we get to the top of that mountain, you won't want to leave, except maybe to have dinner at this charming old lodge that serves the best brick oven, roasted vegetable pizza."

"Food or shopping—my two weaknesses and you're making me choose?"

"Hey, life is choice," Andi teased back. "So, what do you want?"

"I'll tell you what I want," CJ said. Her voice became soft. "Come here."

Andi looked up when she heard the change in CJ's tone. Her dark eyebrows creased together as she wondered what brought on the sudden change in their bantering. She left the pot she was stirring and walked over to her injured friend, standing in front of the blonde woman still perched on the stool. The fingertips of her right hand touched the top of CJ's knee, letting the younger woman know she was there. CJ reached out and took both of Andi's hands, drawing her friend closer until Andi stood between her bent knees. Andi could feel CJ's inner thighs pressed against her legs.

"What I really want," CJ said softly, "is a hug." She let go of the other woman's hands to wrap her arms around Andi's narrow waist. Her head rested in the crook of Andi's neck. Andi responded by encircling CJ's shoulders with her strong arms. She felt CJ's warm breath against the pulse point in her neck and wondered if the blonde could hear her racing heart. She pressed her cheek against CJ's soft hair and inhaled slowly. After several moments, both women reluctantly broke off their embrace.

"Mmmm," Andi hummed. A small smile played on her lips. "What was that for?"

"Do I need a reason?" CJ said.

"No," she chuckled. "You definitely do not. In fact, you can do that anytime you like."

"Well thanks," CJ responded. "I just might."

"I'M STUFFED," CJ announced. She pushed her chair back from the table and patted her stomach. "I should have stopped after the first bowl."

"Me, too," Andi agreed. "I have to admit I was a bit skeptical about this meal."

"Skeptical?"

"Yes, skeptical. First off, the list of ingredients was a bit unusual, especially the peanut butter part. It's not at all what I'm used to eating. Second, I'm not exactly at home in the kitchen, and I wasn't sure I could pull it off, even with your expert coaching."

"But you did great! It's as good as I've ever made it. Did you like it?"

"I loved it. It's a definite do-over meal, for sure. And *you*," she added, emphasizing the words, "you could be on one of those cooking shows. Your directions were perfect. Amazing." She smiled at her friend, who grinned shyly at the praise.

"You did most of the work, so how about we share the credit," CJ suggested. "I think we make a good team, don't you?"

"Yeah. We really do." She smiled as she considered the implications of that statement. "Okay, partner, I think it's time for you to get horizontal again."

"I feel bad that you end up doing the dishes all the time," CJ said. "I wish there was something I could do for you."

"You don't have to do anything for me, CJ. I don't mind doing a few dishes. Don't worry about it, okay?"

"Okay for now, but I'll think of something." She pushed away from the table and made her way back to the mattress while Andi cleared the table and washed the dishes. As CJ lay on her back, she heard the sound of running water and dishes clattering. She reached over and located the stereo remote and turned on the unit. By touch, she managed to locate the play button, which started the disk that had been left in the unit. An Indigo Girls bootleg echoed from the speakers across the room.

"Good choice," Andi called from the kitchen.

"Just lucky," CJ said. She chuckled. Despite her eye injury, she was feeling pretty lucky. *Things might not be perfect, but they could be a whole lot worse.* She whistled along with "Closer to Fine" as the Indigo Girls' voices filled the living room. A few minutes later, she heard the footfall of stocking feet as Andi walked across the room and flopped on the sofa.

"All done?" CJ asked.

"Yup. The rest can dry in the rack." She stretched out along the length of the cushions with her back resting on the padded arm of the couch. Crossing her long legs at the ankles, she sighed deeply and patted her still-full stomach. "Mind if I lower that a bit?" she asked.

"Not at all. I had it loud so that you could hear it from the kitchen." She handed the clicker to Andi, who leaned over and took it from her. Pressing the remote several times, she decreased the volume of the music so they could carry on a conversation in a normal tone of voice.

"So, when was the last time you were in the White Mountains?" Andi asked. She looked over at CJ, who reclined on the mattress below her. The blonde's hands were laced behind her head while her bent elbows pointed out to either side.

"Hmmmm," she considered. "I guess it was shortly after school began in the fall, but before basketball started. Once we start practices, I usually don't have time for a road trip, other than for games."

"What'd you do while you were there?"

"A short hike to Ripley Falls. The water was really flowing 'cause we had rain the week before. The leaves were just starting to turn so it was quite pretty. I got a great sweater at the Liz outlet, too." She grinned.

"So, did you go…by yourself?"

"No," CJ said. Andi held her breath. "My two roommates went with me." Andi exhaled slowly. "Why do you ask?"

"Ah…I was just wondering who you hung out with, you know, who you liked to spend your time with."

"Kim and Maria, they're my roommates. We've all been friends since sophomore year. And Joanne. You met her at Martha and Karen's party that night. The four of us often go to Oasis on Friday or Saturday nights, depending on when we have games. I have to twist their arms to go hiking, though." She paused to think, then continued. "Sometimes I hang out with a couple of the gals on the team during the season, mostly the ones who stopped by yesterday. We're together all the time on road trips, you know? We all sit together on the bus and tell stories and laugh to pass the time." She stopped again to think. "That's mostly it, I guess."

"Do you...I mean, are you...dating any of them?" Andi asked softly.

"No way!" laughed CJ. "I like them all, but not like that." She paused while images of all her friends' faces flashed before her, then she shook her head to clear the women from her mind's eye. "No, I haven't dated anyone seriously in a while, actually."

"Really?"

"Why does that surprise you?"

"Because you're attractive, intelligent, funny, creative, outgoing..." She stopped short as she realized how quickly she had rattled off a list of adjectives that very well might embarrass CJ. Sure enough, the younger woman was blushing pink as she lay on the mattress. "Sorry, did I embarrass you?" Andi asked.

"A bit." Her cool hands were pressed to her cheeks to defuse the heat under her skin.

"Well, everything I said was true."

"Thanks," CJ said softly. She removed her hands from her cheeks as the blush drained from her face. Andi's flattering comments echoed in her head, and a small grin formed on her lips. As embarrassed as she was at hearing the flattering remarks, she was glad to know the other woman felt that way about her. The fact that Andi was fishing around for her dating habits seemed to hint at the grad assistant's interest. *I'll have to wait and see. Interesting choice of words. See. I wouldn't be lying here, hearing her say all of that if I could see, but my doubts about her interest in me might be answered if I could just look into her eyes and see. Interesting predicament.*

"Earth to CJ," Andi said. Her voice was raised a notch above the level of their previous conversation.

"Oh, sorry," she said. "I guess I drifted for a minute there. I was just wondering...when you were last in the White Mountains." She laced her fingers and rested them on her stomach.

"Around Christmas, actually. My mom wanted to do some shopping in North Conway so I agreed to drive her there and —"

"You went shopping?" CJ teased.

"I didn't say I never shopped. I'm just not crazy about it, that's all," she said.

"So where'd you go? What'd you get?" She stifled a yawn, covering her mouth with her hand.

"Well, my mom is practically a career shopper. You'd like her, in fact. She can sniff out a bargain at a hundred yards. She makes it her goal never to buy anything for full price. I kid you not. It's a matter of pride for her, I think. It's like her own personal victory over retailers who overprice. Anyway, we started at one end of the strip at a shoe outlet and worked our way from one store to the next. We had to move the car after every few stores because she had too many bags to carry very far. She got sweaters for my cousins, baby clothes for the nieces and nephews, Levi's for my uncle, sunglasses for my aunt, kitchen gadgets for the Secret Santa run by her church—the list seemed endless. As far as I was concerned, after the third store they all started looking the same to me. I told her that my being there and taking her around was part of my gift to her, because she knows how I feel about shopping. I'll admit that I did poke around in the L.L. Bean outlet, though. Upstairs, where the hiking and camping equipment is, I found a few things I was interested in. Most of the prices there were pretty good, too. Ever go there, CJ?" She paused as she waited for an answer. "CJ?" she asked again.

Andi sat up from her sprawled position on the couch to get a better view of CJ, who was asleep on the mattress. The younger woman's lips, slightly parted, allowed the sounds of her deep breathing to escape. Her hands, still gently interlocked, remained crossed on her stomach. The soft skin on her cheeks was relaxed, making her look even younger than her twenty-two years. Andi looked at her beautiful friend's profile and smiled. *She finally gets me talking and what do I discover? I'm boring.* She smiled. *That's okay, CJ. I'd much rather listen to you anyway.*

Quietly, she moved off the sofa and padded over to the mattress. Without disturbing the sleeping woman, she lifted the blanket up to CJ's shoulders. She lingered for another moment, enjoying the peaceful beauty of her face, then moved across the room to switch off the lights.

Several minutes later she emerged from the bathroom, having changed into lightweight sweats and a T-shirt to sleep in. Her eyes needed several minutes to adjust from the bright bathroom light to the darkness of the living room. During the interim, she felt temporarily blinded, so she closed her eyes to block out the sensation. She stood there, just outside the threshold, as a great sadness seized her heart. *This is what CJ has felt every day for the last five days. Even if it was just temporary, I don't know if I could cope, but the possibility that it might not return... No! Don't even think that way. Her vision will come back. CJ will be okay again.* She opened her eyes, relieved that she could make out the shadowed objects in the room. Filtered moonlight shone through the windows, cascading enough brightness to guide her across the room.

She turned on the table lamp and picked up her journal before settling on the sofa. Her long legs stretched out to rest on the coffee table in front of her. She placed a pillow on her lap, then rested the journal on the pillow before opening the book to the ribbon-marked page. After reading silently for several minutes, she picked up her pen and began to write. Occasionally her eyes lifted from the page to glance at CJ, still fast asleep on the mattress near her. A gentle smile emerged on Andi's lips.

She filled the page, recalling her conversations with CJ and the ease with which she spoke so openly and honestly. Her heart hadn't felt that light and happy in years. Images of CJ's smile, their tag-team dinner, and personal revelations all came spilling out onto the page as she tried to capture in words the feelings that were beginning to overwhelm her heart. With one last glance at her injured companion, she completed the entry, then marked the page with the purple ribbon. She placed the book on the table, turned off the lamp, and stretched out on her temporary bed. Her last waking image was CJ's profile as she slept bathed in the moonlight.

ANDI'S PEACEFUL SLEEP was interrupted for the second night in a row by CJ's tormented cries.

"No! No, no! Please! Not yet!"

Upon hearing CJ's tortured pleas, Andi bolted off the sofa and sat on the edge of the mattress close to the distressed woman. One of her hands clasped CJ's while her other hand firmly held the woman's shoulder.

"CJ!" Andi whispered. "CJ, wake up." She gently shook the younger woman's shoulder as she spoke. CJ's body was rigid and tense, then shuddered slightly as she emerged from her dream. Out of reflex, she squeezed Andi's hand and sat bolt upright on the bed, banging her body against Andi's as she moved. Andi slid her arm around CJ's back to steady her as she trembled.

"Oh, Andi," CJ cried. She wrapped her arms around Andi's shoulders and buried her face against her neck. The blonde's warm breath on her skin made her body tingle. Her chest, pressed against CJ's, echoed the other woman's racing heart. She tightened her arms around CJ's body and rocked her slowly.

"It's okay," she soothed. "It was just another dream. I'm here." She made soft, calming sounds as she comforted her friend. Her hand stroked a steady rhythm up and down CJ's back. After a few minutes, CJ's rapidly beating heart slowed, as did her breathing. She inhaled audibly and exhaled slowly before releasing her tight grip around Andi.

"Sorry I woke you again," CJ whispered.

"Don't apologize," Andi said. She stroked the trembling woman's soft hair several times, enjoying its silky texture against her fingers. As she raked her fingers through CJ's hair, then drew her hand slowly over the back of the other woman's head, she felt CJ leaning into her touch. "I'm glad to be here for you," she added. "Was it the same dream as last night?"

"Sort of," CJ sighed.

"Want to talk about it?"

CJ shrugged her shoulders and sighed again. The dream that was so intense just moments ago had faded already, and she was loath to bring it back to her conscious thoughts and revive its intensity. On the other hand, the anxiety produced by the dream still lingered. She hoped that talking about it with Andi would exorcise the demon that haunted her sleep of late. She pulled away from the hug but continued to hold Andi's hand as she spoke.

"I think it's the waiting that's getting to me," CJ began. "Every day that I get closer to my appointment with the doctor, I get more and more anxious about what she'll find. I don't know how I'll cope if..." She paused and swallowed hard. "If I lose my sight," she finished softly. "It's only been five days but it feels like forever. I can't imagine—"

"Then don't," Andi interrupted gently. "I know it's hard not to worry, especially when you're here by yourself during the day and you've got nothing but time on your hands, but that's when you've got to be strong and stay positive." She squeezed her friend's hand. "You're an athlete, CJ, so I know you know how to do it. Think of any game you've ever been in where your team's behind. I've seen you out on the court. I know you don't give up. In fact, you dig down deeper and try harder to win. Well, partner, that's what you've got to do now. Attitude is everything, CJ, and you've got to keep your winning attitude with this eye injury. It's only a few more days before you see Dr. Erroll again. Let's take one day at a time until then, okay?"

CJ hung her head as Andi spoke to her. She realized what her friend was telling her was true, but she wasn't feeling especially strong at the moment after that nightmare. Some spark deep within her still smoldered, however, and she was intent not to let Andi think she would be so easily defeated, whether it was on the court or in life.

"I know you're right," CJ said softly. "Sometimes, when I wake up scared but can't open my eyes to escape the nightmare...it's hard, then. You know?"

Andi placed her hand gently against CJ's cheek and lifted the young woman's face upward. She stroked her friend's cheek lightly with her thumb, enjoying the softness of the skin. After a moment, she felt CJ leaning into her hand as it rested against her cheek.

"I know, CJ," Andi reassured her. She reluctantly removed her hand from its warm resting place against CJ's face. "So when you're feeling like you need a little help being strong and positive, all you have to do is ask, and I'll be there for you, okay?"

"Like to give me a little kick in the butt?"

"Maybe now and then. I've been known to kick some butt when it's necessary," Andi teased. "But with you, I was thinking a hug might produce better results."

"Yeah, you're good at those."

"Think so?"

"Definitely." She unclasped Andi's hand so she could hug her again. The feel of Andi's body pressed tightly against her own, held securely by Andi's strong arms, made her feel safe. "You give the best hugs," she whispered. CJ's warm breath tickled Andi's ear and sent tingles throughout her body. After a moment, CJ reluctantly untangled herself from Andi's arms but continued to hold her hand.

"Andi? Can I tell you something else that's bothering me?"

"Of course. Anything."

"How did you handle...you know, when you got hurt and couldn't swim any more...and it was unfinished. You never had the chance to find out what could have been. How did you handle that?"

Andi considered the question. The fears the younger woman expressed were not foreign to Andi, and she sighed inwardly knowing that her emerald-eyed friend was going through a similar hurt. She exhaled slowly and thought back a few years, trying to find words to explain an ache that went beyond the physical pain of an injury.

"When I first got hurt, I thought the pain and rehab would be the worst part, and once I got through that, the rest would be easy. I was wrong. What was even harder was the loss of my identity. I defined myself as a swimmer, a successful swimmer. All my hard work in and out of season was directed toward achieving that goal. My coach, my friends, my family—they all saw me in that light. When I couldn't swim anymore, I lost my identity. I didn't know how to be anything else. That was difficult to deal with." She stopped briefly and looked down at her hand, which CJ still held, then continued. "It was like starting my life over. I had to redefine myself." She sighed audibly. "I'm still working on defining myself." She paused and thought back to that tormented time in her life when her world seemed to be falling apart.

"I also had to deal with losing nearly two years of an athletic career and never knowing what might have been. That was very hard. It still is." She inhaled deeply, then exhaled slowly. "There will always be a question in my mind of 'what if,' and that's tough to live with. What if I hadn't been injured? What would I have achieved? Where would swimming have led me after graduation? Would I still be here?" She looked again at her hand in CJ's and tightened her grip, which was answered by a returned squeeze. She smiled. "I can't change the past, but I did learn from that experience. Whenever there's a situation in my life where I have to make a decision, I always remind myself how 'what if' feels. Then I decide what to do based on if it's better to suffer the consequences of going after something, even if I don't get it, or if I can live with never knowing what could have been."

"What do you usually choose?" CJ asked.

"To suffer the consequences," Andi said. "To some extent, I still hate living with 'what if.'"

CJ sat quietly, reflecting on the older athlete's words. She knew Andi knew exactly what she was going through, and that alone offered her a modicum of solace. The fact that Andi's observations and assessment of dealing with the situation were so on target made her admire her friend even more.

"When I lie here by myself during the day," CJ said, "it's so quiet that all I can hear are my own thoughts and worries running around in my head. This is the first time my team has made the playoffs. That was my dream all through college, and now it will never happen. My eligibility is gone. The WNBA doesn't draft from Division II schools. It's over. The chapter of my basketball career is unfinished and will never be completed. I'll always wonder how it could have been, and will never know the answer. I hate the lack of resolution." She paused to collect her thoughts, and then continued in a soft voice. "I'm almost embarrassed to tell you that. I mean, what you went through was probably worse, since your career was cut short sooner than mine. Here I am complaining when I have no right."

"You have every right to complain, or be upset, or feel unresolved, CJ. I expressed all of those things, too, when I went through it, you know. It's not like I always held it in. Ask Martha and Karen. I cried on their shoulders on more than one occasion. Many other times I just cried alone by myself. So, no, you don't have to feel embarrassed about telling me how you feel. I hope...I'd like for you not to be embarrassed to tell me anything."

"You make that easy."

"Thanks," Andi said softly. "And I wish I had a better answer for you. I know how it is to feel that a situation is beyond your control. Personally, I hate that feeling more than I can begin to tell you. It's too...I don't know...passive. I wish I could offer you resolution, or at least a sense of peace, regarding basketball. I'm afraid that I can't."

"I guess I'll have to accept the lack of resolution in my basketball career and just learn to find resolution and peace in other areas of my life where I do have control."

"That, my friend, sounds like the best plan yet." Andi squeezed CJ's hand tightly. "You came to that conclusion way quicker than I did after I was injured." She chuckled. "I think I'm a bit more stubborn than you."

"You? Stubborn?"

"Are you teasing me?"

"Yes, just a bit."

"Well, I'll let it slide this time 'cause it's getting late," Andi said, grinning. "Are you tired?"

"Kind of," CJ said.

"Why don't you lie back and try to—"

"Please stay," CJ pleaded, tightening her grip on the hand she held.

"I'm right here." She stroked her hand up and down CJ's back. "I'm not going anywhere." She hesitated, then continued. "I promise."

CJ lowered her body to horizontal once again. Andi followed suit, reclining on her side next to and facing CJ. She reached down and pulled up the blanket so that it covered both their bodies.

CJ felt the warmth of her companion's body lying next to her, and she fought hard to stifle the urge to wrap her arms around Andi as she had around her friend's pillow that very morning. She clasped her hands together tightly, resting them on her stomach to keep them in check.

"Why don't you roll onto your stomach," Andi said. "I'll help you relax and fall back to sleep."

The young woman hesitated and parted her lips to ask why, then decided against inquiring and simply turned over. Andi scooted closer to her until their legs were touching. She could distinctly hear the reassuring cadence of Andi's breathing from mere inches away. The next sensation CJ felt was Andi's hand at her lower back. Slowly and tentatively, Andi slid her hand under the T-shirt until her fingers were touching CJ's warm body. CJ moaned softly as Andi's fingertips moved sensually over bare skin.

"My fingernails aren't very long. Hope this feels okay," Andi said.

"It feels wonderful." She made soft purring noises as Andi skated patterns with her fingertips over CJ's back.

Andi lightly and slowly dragged her fingers up the centerline of CJ's spine. She smiled as her touch left a trail of goose bumps in its wake. Continuing her lazy, light touch, she zigzagged a path from shoulder to shoulder over the broad and muscular expanse of the basketball player's back. Andi felt CJ's ribs rise and fall as she inhaled deeply, then moaned audibly as the breath escaped. When she reached the small of CJ's back, she let the pads of her fingers gently brush the fine hairs covering the skin. After playfully petting the downy softness, she once again glided side to side across CJ's back, working her way up toward her shoulders. Each time she swept across the broad surface, her fingers traveled further around the blonde's ribs until she approached the sensitive area near CJ's breasts.

All the while Andi's hand remained in contact with CJ's warm skin, the heat inside the dark-haired woman rose steadily. Andi's objective of relaxing her injured companion had exactly the opposite effect on her own body. The sensation of soft bare skin against her fingers, CJ's musky scent, and the warmth radiating from the woman lying mere inches from her, all served to arouse Andi. She found herself wanting to touch more skin than what her fingers were exposed to on CJ's back. She longed to nuzzle her face into the soft skin between CJ's shoulder blades. She wanted to roll the younger woman onto her back and continue her gentle ministrations on much more sensitive spots on CJ's beautiful body.

CJ's soft moan snapped Andi out of her sensual dreaming. *Stop!* she warned herself. *Not now. Not like this. Too many things are still left unsaid.* She dragged her fingertips down to CJ's lower back and removed her unwilling hand from beneath her friend's shirt. After smoothing down the hem of the material, she placed her open hand flat on CJ's back, gently rubbing the skin through her T-shirt before resting her still hand between CJ's shoulder blades.

"How'd that feel?" Andi said.

"Mmmm. My words could never be adequate to describe how wonderful that felt." She rolled onto her side, facing Andi. "So how about I show you?" CJ reached over to touch Andi's arm. "Roll over."

Andi did as she was asked and rolled onto her stomach. Her previously injured right arm lay at her side while her left arm pillowed her head. The rapid beating of her heart echoed in her ears and she felt sure that her companion, whose body was so dangerously close, could hear it as well.

CJ reached out and gently tucked her hand under the cotton fabric of Andi's T-shirt. Andi inhaled sharply as CJ's touch ignited her bare skin. The sound was not lost on CJ, who grinned at the reaction her touch inspired. Following the same zigzag pattern Andi had used, CJ leisurely worked her way back and forth across Andi's taut muscles. The sensuality of Andi's bare skin combined with her soft sighs continued the arousal Andi's touch began. CJ's body tingled from the stimulating contact. *How long can I continue to torture myself with such sweet pleasure?* CJ wondered silently. She was reluctant to remove her hand from Andi's skin yet she feared that her barely maintained self control was slipping. She sighed, then reluctantly removed her hand from the sweetness of Andi's skin.

"How'd that feel?" CJ asked.

"Like heaven," Andi responded. She rolled over so she faced CJ, whose face was shadowed in the moonlight. "Your touch is very gentle," she added. "Thank you."

"My pleasure," CJ said. *You have no idea how that was my pleasure.*

"Why don't you lie on your back now, and maybe you'll be able to fall back asleep. I'll be right here."

"Okay." She rolled onto her back as Andi suggested and scooted her body closer to Andi's as subtly as she could manage. Her leg lightly touched her bedmate's beneath the blanket, and she reached out her hand and felt around on the mattress before she found Andi's hand. She slid her hand beneath Andi's palm and wrapped her fingers firmly around her friend's. "Is this okay?" she asked.

"It's better than okay," Andi responded. She squeezed CJ's hand gently to punctuate her reply.

Andi felt CJ settle into stillness on the mattress. The younger woman's body radiated comforting warmth beneath the blanket they both shared. Within moments CJ's breathing became deep and steady, a pleasant rhythm Andi had come to associate with

CJ's sleeping. The injured woman's breathing cadence, combined with the warmth and nearness of her sleeping body, served to relax Andi. In between long blinks, she gazed at CJ's face in the soft glow of the moon. Soon she closed her eyes to the beautiful image of CJ's profile only to have it reappear again in her dreams. A smile graced Andi's lips as she slept.

Chapter
Twenty-five

ANDI BLINKED HEAVY eyelids open. She lay on her back trying to focus on ceiling shadows while the sun began its ascent above the horizon. The left side of her body felt pleasantly warm as she emerged from sleep. As a growing awareness revived her slumbering senses, she turned her head slightly toward the source of that warmth. CJ was curled up on her side facing Andi, her body pressed tightly against the older woman's. CJ's head shared part of Andi's pillow. Her breathing, soft and rhythmic, tickled Andi's nearby ear and her left arm was draped gently across Andi's stomach.

CJ's affectionate gesture and body contact made Andi's heart ache with longing. She wanted to take the beautiful woman into her arms, to pull CJ's body even closer so that from head to toe they would be pressed together. *To hell with waiting. She wouldn't be snuggling with me if she wasn't interested in me.* She looked once more at her peacefully sleeping bedmate nestled against her side. CJ's mouth was slightly parted as she breathed softly. *She probably doesn't even know she's hugging me,* Andi observed, contradicting her first thought. *She's so deeply asleep that she's not aware of her arm draped across me. She's hugging me like a kid hugs a stuffed animal — for comfort. In the darkness of the night, after her bad dream, that's probably what she's looking for. Comfort. Security. Don't read anything else into it. It's just wishful thinking.*

Andi breathed in then slowly and quietly exhaled. *But that doesn't mean I can't enjoy it.* Locking the doubts away in the corner of her mind, she focused her senses on the attractive woman cuddled up next to her. She glanced at the wall clock across the room and noted the early hour. *The sun's not up yet, so why should I be? There's too much keeping me right here to move. Might as well enjoy it while she's here.*

With that thought, Andi blinked several times then closed her eyes and drifted back to sleep, feeling comfortable and safe in the arms of the woman who had captured her heart.

IN CJ'S DREAM world, somehow it seemed perfectly natural to her that she could be having a dream yet see herself as a character in that vision. Nothing about that concept appeared impossible in a somnolent world where illusions seemed real.

She saw a light brown horse walk slowly through the meadow, pausing now and then to dip its head to tear out a clump of clover before moving on. The two riders astride its broad back swayed gently with its gait, giving the animal enough rein to reach its long neck to the ground. Cottony clouds drifted overhead on a summer's breeze that slightly ruffled the horse's mane. The splashing sound of a nearby creek drew the animal's attention as it continued across the meadow, guided by the skilled hands of its lead rider.

Two pairs of denim-clad legs hung down the horse's sides, dangling loosely around its saddleless body. Not even a blanket separated the riders from the animal's coarse, light brown coat of hair. The taller woman sat in front holding the reins in her left hand. CJ sat behind, pressed up against the woman, chin resting on the broad shoulder as she looked out toward the river. CJ's arms were wrapped securely around her companion's waist, using the woman's sturdiness to help maintain her own balance while enjoying the physical closeness. Breathing in deeply, smelling the spicy aroma of the other woman's skin, CJ smiled and nuzzled nearer, brushing her cheek against her partner's. The front rider turned her head slightly and smiled in return, placing her right hand over CJ's, which remained around her waist.

"How much further?" CJ heard herself ask in the dream.

"No more than an hour," her riding partner replied. "You okay?"

"Fine. Just a bit tired."

"Hold on to me and close your eyes. If you fall asleep, I'll watch out for you."

"Okay," CJ heard herself reply. She watched herself yawn and close her eyes, resting her head on her partner's shoulder. A small smile formed on her lips as she drifted off to sleep.

In her dream world, CJ watched the woman, yet *was* that woman, both at the same time. She wrapped her arms tighter around her companion who lay beside her and pressed her body closer. The horse and riders faded away as she returned to her deep, dreamless sleep.

ANDI AWOKE ABRUPTLY to the sound of a loudly ringing phone. She tossed off the covers and bolted out of bed, grabbing the receiver before the second ring. Fearing CJ would be awakened by the noise, she made a hasty retreat into her bedroom and closed the door before speaking.

"Hello?" she answered. Her voice was husky with sleep. Rubbing her hand across her forehead a few times, she tried to focus her attention and appear coherent to the caller.

"Andrea? Is that you?"

"Of course, Mother. Who else would it be?"

"You don't sound like yourself. Are you sick?"

"No, I'm fine, Mom. I was just sleeping in this morning. I was up late last night...ah, grading papers. I had a lot of work to do."

"It's not like you to sleep late. You sure you're okay?"

"I'm fine. Really." She paced around the room, peering out her bedroom window. The sun was fully above the horizon, and its warm rays reflected patterns of light through the glass. Patches of shadows and brightness created a collage on the hardwood floor.

"I haven't heard from you in a while, Andi. How come you haven't called?"

"I've had a lot of work to do, both grading students' papers as well as research for my own courses." She hesitated to consider whether to tell her mother more, then decided to include some additional information. "Besides, a friend of mine got hurt last week and I've been helping her out."

"Hurt? A friend? What do you mean?"

Andi proceeded to give a brief report of CJ's eye injury and her subsequent healing process; however, she neglected to reveal that CJ was convalescing right there in her apartment.

"That's too bad," her mother lamented. "When she's feeling better, bring her with you for dinner sometime."

"Sure, Mom," Andi said. She was touched at her mother's kind offer, almost completely forgiving her for the most unwelcome wake-up call.

They continued to talk for several more minutes while Andi's mother filled her in about her job, the house, and the relatives. The grad assistant shuffled around the room restlessly while her mother droned on. Finally, after several minutes of small talk and pacing, Andi politely ended the conversation with the promise that she would call soon.

Emerging from her bedroom, she tiptoed quietly into the bathroom before heading back to check on her companion. With slow and stealthy steps, she padded silently across the floor, hoping to avoid squeaky boards or any other noises that might wake CJ. She rounded the front of the sofa and was just settling down on the cushions when CJ spoke.

"Morning," she said, her voice a singsong greeting.

"Morning to you," Andi said. She couldn't help but smile at her golden-haired ward, whose cheerfulness touched her heart. "Sorry about the phone. My mother felt like chatting."

"It's okay." She yawned and stretched, cat-like, with arms and legs reaching out as if someone was pulling on them. As she extended her arms, her T-shirt inched upward, exposing a smooth, flat stomach to Andi's view. The older woman arched a dark eyebrow in appreciation as a rakish grin crossed her lips. She continued to enjoy the view as her friend talked. "I should be getting up anyway. What time is it?"

"It's after eleven," Andi said. She actually did a double take as she noted the time. She never slept in that late, preferring to be up and about by early morning. Usually she felt lazy when she lounged around in bed. *You don't usually have a beautiful woman lying by your side*, she reminded herself. Her body tingled as she remembered the feel of the younger athlete's body snuggled up against hers as she awakened.

"That's late even for me," noted CJ.

"You don't usually sleep in?"

"It's a luxury I enjoy, but rarely have time to indulge in. Between basketball or schoolwork, it seems like I'm always up early."

"You've got a built-in excuse for a few days. Doctor's orders, remember. You might as well enjoy it."

"Oh, I enjoyed it plenty," CJ observed. A playful grin curled her lips as she recalled the blissful feeling of drifting off to sleep lying so close to the object of her desire. Although she had been upset by the nightmare, the consolation of getting to spend the remainder of the night by her attractive friend's side helped to balance out the effect. "Andi?" she continued. "About last night..."

Andi's mind was jarred to attention at those three words. She stiffened and sat up on the couch. *What about last night? What was CJ going to bring up? Their closeness? The physical contact? Could she sense that I was interested in more? Did I make her feel uncomfortable?* Andi's mind raced with questions in the seconds it took for CJ to continue to speak.

"I'm sorry I woke you up again," CJ began. "I didn't—"

"CJ, please," responded Andi quickly. She moved off the sofa and onto the edge of the mattress. Sitting facing her fair-haired companion, she reached out and took CJ's hand, her voice soft and serious. "Don't worry about waking me up if you need me. I would hate to think that I was lying there sleeping while you were upset, and that you were afraid or uncomfortable about sharing it with me. That's what friends are for, right?" She squeezed the younger woman's hand gently and was answered by a returned squeeze. "Besides, I fell right back to sleep, thanks in no small part to your wonderful back scratches." She tousled CJ's golden hair with her other hand, her heart feeling warm and fluttering from the remembrance of the previous night's sensual touches.

"Well, I still feel bad about waking you. I mean, first I take your mattress so you have to sleep on the sofa. Then I wake you up in the middle of the night with my crazy nightmares. On top of that, you're stuck doing all the cooking and cleaning up afterward. You must be ready to drop kick me out your door by now." The lightheartedness of her last observation did not disguise the hint of worry that her fears might be well grounded and that Andi might indeed be getting tired of having her around.

Andi picked up on her insecurities but was quick to dispel them. "I'm the one who should feel bad, CJ."

"What do you mean? Why should you feel bad?"

"Because you're my guest, and if I've given you any reason to feel that you're in my way or not welcome, then I'm to blame."

"But you haven't! You've been wonderful, Andi. You've made me feel completely at home. You've taken such good care of me."

"Then why would you feel like I'd be ready to 'drop kick you out the door'?"

"I guess... I don't know... I think I'm a little afraid you're doing this because you feel sorry for me, or because you're just too polite to tell me it's time for me to go." CJ hung her head as she spoke, her voice small and insecure.

"Hey," Andi said. She lifted CJ's chin with her long fingers so the younger woman's face was tilted up toward her own. "First off, I don't pity you. Pitying you would be insulting. You're a strong woman and whatever happens, I know you'll be okay. Second, I'm not that polite. Believe me. If you were getting on my nerves, I probably *would* 'drop kick you out the door' and that's the truth." She paused to look at the fair-skinned woman, whose face was so close to her own. Shifting her fingers from beneath CJ's chin, she placed her hand gently on her companion's cheek. With her thumb, she softly stroked the skin near CJ's cheekbone, right below her eye patch. As she did, she could feel the other woman leaning into her touch. "I love having you here, CJ," she assured. Her voice was soft yet sincere. "Do you believe me?"

"Yes," CJ said, nodding her head slowly. "I guess I just needed to hear you say it."

"Then I'm sorry I didn't say it sooner." She continued to caress CJ's cheek with her thumb until the emotional moment was interrupted by a very loud growl emanating from the younger woman's stomach.

"Time for the next feeding," Andi said. She removed her hand from CJ's cheek and rested it on her forearm. "Ready for breakfast?"

"I was born ready!" she teased. "Help me up?"

Andi stood, then reached down to clasp CJ's hands. Pulling the woman to her feet, she continued to hold her hands while her friend adjusted to being vertical and maintained her balance.

"You okay now?" Andi said. She hoped CJ realized she was talking about more than just her balance.

"Yeah, I think I am." She removed her hands from Andi's grasp and encircled the taller woman in a hug. As she stood pressed against her friend's body, CJ felt Andi's arms tighten around her as she returned the embrace. The younger woman inhaled deeply, her senses overwhelmed by the aroma of Andi's hair and skin. She smiled and exhaled slowly. "Thanks for last night, and for talking with me this morning."

"My pleasure." Andi made no attempt to disengage herself from the embrace. With her body pressed up against CJ's, her heart beat rapidly in synchronicity with the younger woman's. For an extended moment they remained that way, then another loud growl erupted from CJ's stomach, causing both women to laugh. Reluctantly, they disentangled their arms. "To the kitchen," Andi directed. "Let's get your stomach happy again." With that, she wrapped her arm around CJ's waist and led her friend across the living room to start breakfast.

"Can you read the comics to me while we're eating?" CJ asked. She turned her face toward Andi as they walked slowly.

"I don't know," Andi teased. "What's it worth to you?"

"Hmmmm. How about a foot massage later?"

"I think that can be arranged," Andi said. She gave CJ's waist as slight squeeze.

THE TWO WOMEN lingered over a late breakfast. As promised, Andi read CJ the funny papers, gamely describing each box of Sunday's color comic strips. After thirty minutes of giggling, more from Andi's presentation than from the comics' contents, CJ reclined on the sofa. Her companion lingered over the rest of the local Sunday paper as a Winton Marsalis CD played softly in the background. Occasionally, Andi read articles aloud when she thought the subject might interest her friend.

The afternoon passed quickly, with Andi reading more lecture notes to her attentive charge, who was determined not to fall behind on her schoolwork during her period of required inactivity. Following the schoolwork, Andi ordered pizza for dinner as a change of pace from her usual cooking routine over the last few days. As she stood in the kitchen, placing the order on the phone, she looked out across her living room at CJ and was reminded of a Friday night, two months prior, when they had shared a pizza as they worked on CJ's research paper. *Two months*, she contemplated. *How did my life get so wrapped up in this woman in just two months?* She shook her head slowly as she considered the answer. *You'd better face it*, she admonished herself, *you've got it bad.*

Once their dinner was finished, both women retired to the sofa again so Andi could continue reading notes to CJ. The golden-haired woman reclined against the padded arm of the couch with her legs fully extended. The soles of CJ's feet pressed against Andi's leg as she sat at the other end of the cushions. CJ rubbed her socked feet back and forth a few times against Andi's leg, enjoying the physical contact and warmth created by the friction. Andi smiled at CJ's dancing feet and continued reading the notes despite the subtle distraction. After nearly a half-hour of narrating the material, the grad assistant placed the papers on the end table and relieved her parched mouth with a long drink of water.

"So, that catches you up with last week's work," Andi announced. "I'll send out emails to your professors tomorrow morning requesting this week's notes as soon as they can send them." She placed her left hand over CJ's feet and rubbed them gently, enjoying the sensation as the younger woman wiggled her toes when she touched a ticklish spot.

"Thanks so much, Andi. I can't tell you how great it's been to get that work and not fall too far behind. I have so many other things on my mind these days. It's nice to have one less thing to worry about."

"Speaking of things you might have on your mind... Can I ask you a question?" She spoke hesitantly, wondering if she should ask at all, knowing she wouldn't relax until she at least brought it up. Of course, the answer to the question might indeed produce more anxiety than simply wondering about the answer, but she had to know. "About grad school..." she began.

"Yes?"

"I remember you telling me a couple weeks ago that you had some offers for grad programs, and I was wondering if you've had any good offers."

CJ sat silently, contemplating Andi's question. She had intentionally avoided thinking about grad school over the last few weeks because of her distractions with the tournament as well as over Andi. More recently, her injury and its possible repercussions kept her mind off her impending grad school decisions. Andi's mentioning it, however, brought it to the forefront of her thinking, but for the first time the decision seemed clear to her. She relaxed her shoulders a bit, unaware she had tightened them upon hearing the inquiry.

Andi construed the silence to mean that CJ didn't want to discuss the topic with her. *What if she's going far away?* she asked herself silently. *What will I do?* She cursed herself again for handling things so badly with CJ a few weeks ago. *Right around the time when CJ might have been making grad school decisions*, she reminded herself. Her heart sank and her shoulders slumped.

"We don't have to discuss it...if you don't want to," Andi stammered. "I didn't mean to —"

"No, it's okay. Actually, I got a really good offer from a school out West."

Andi was crushed at hearing the news. She was glad CJ couldn't see her face, since she couldn't even pretend to hide the disappointment she felt. She heard herself sigh deeply, but the sound was out before she could stop herself.

"But I've decided that I'm going to decline their offer," CJ continued. Having decided at that very moment what to do, she felt surprisingly lighthearted and happy about her decision. *Maybe when the financial reality of that decision sinks in, you won't quite feel so chipper.* Despite the self-reprimand, she felt an overwhelming sense of relief. *I guess I really didn't want to go out West after all,* she realized.

Andi shook her head to clear the fog as CJ's words registered in her brain. *She's staying!* She released a breath that she hadn't even realized she was holding while her heart flooded with relief. She wrapped both her hands around CJ's feet and rubbed them vigorously, giving them the hand-hug she so desperately wanted to bestow on their owner, who was out of arms' reach.

"That's great news, CJ!"

"Why's that?" Her golden-blonde head tilted to the side as she listened for Andi's response.

"Well...ah," Andi stuttered. *Try being a bit more subtle next time,* she chastised herself. "I guess I'm just glad that, ah, you won't be moving all the way across the country." She spoke softly and shyly, dipping her head and contemplating her feet as they tapped nervously on the floor.

"I'm not sure exactly where I'll end up yet. I'm still waiting to hear from the rest of the schools I applied to." She rubbed her feet back and forth against Andi's leg again. "But thanks for reacting that way. It made me feel...nice inside." She smiled self-consciously and turned her face from Andi, uncomfortable about letting the other woman see her when she felt so vulnerable. "Once I hear what the doctor has to say, then I can think more about what I'll do for school next year." Her nervousness reemerged at the thought of the doctor's prognosis.

Andi noticed her apprehension. "Only a few more days now," she encouraged. "Wednesday will be here before you know it." She rubbed CJ's feet affectionately. "Don't forget," she added in an upbeat tone, "I'm sending you lots of good vibes to help you heal."

"Thanks. I could use them." She yawned, covering her mouth with her hand. "Sorry, it's not the company, I assure you."

"No need to apologize," Andi said. She looked at her watch. "It's after 10:00. Want to call it a night?"

"Soon. But first, your foot massage." She rubbed her hands together vigorously and grinned.

"But you're tired, CJ," Andi protested. "I'll take a rain check."

"Nope. A deal's a deal." She shifted from reclined to an upright position with legs crossed, but still leaned her back against the armrest of the sofa, facing Andi. She placed a pillow in her lap, then patted it a few times in invitation. "Come on, lie down and put your feet here."

"You sure?"

"Positive. Unless, of course, you've changed your mind."

"Not me," Andi quickly said. She swiveled around on the cushion and leaned back against the armrest opposite CJ, then carefully placed her feet on the pillow in CJ's lap. "Is that too heavy there?"

"That's fine. Ticklish?"

"Not a bit."

"Comfortable?"

"So far."

"It's only going to get better," CJ promised. She grinned and began to knead the top of Andi's foot with sweeping motions from her thumbs while at the same time her fingertips pressed firmly into the soles.

"Ohhhh, wow," Andi moaned. "That feels sooooo good."

"I'm glad," CJ said. "It's supposed to." She continued kneading with her thumbs and fingers, beginning at the junction of Andi's ankle and working slowly toward her toes. During the first pass, her pressure was moderate, but during the subsequent passes, it became deeper. "Is that okay?" she asked, not wanting to cause any discomfort.

"It's much better than okay. Wow, does that feel good!" Her foot became pleasantly warm from the contact of CJ's hands as well as from the friction created as the younger woman massaged her socked feet. The tingling sensation began in her foot then radiated up her legs and throughout her body. She could feel her muscles relax as she melted into the cushions of the sofa on which she reclined. A contented sigh escaped her lips.

CJ was pleased by Andi's reactions. Although she could not see the contented look on the other woman's face, she recognized Andi's sigh as an expression of blissful enjoyment. She felt the muscles relaxing beneath her strong, skilled fingers as she continued her ministrations.

After several laps of deep kneading the full length of Andi's foot, CJ concentrated on each toe, beginning with the big toe and working her way out. She slowly rolled each digit between her thumb and forefinger while gently pulling to stretch it.

"This little piggy went outlet shopping," she narrated in a singsong voice as she worked on Andi's big toe. "This little piggy stayed home to go to basketball practice. This little piggy ate spicy noodles with shiitake mushroom sauce, and this little piggy had none. And this little piggy laughed and laughed all the way home." She finished her narration as she finished massaging Andi's little toe.

"Is that how your mother recited that nursery rhyme to you?" Andi chuckled. "I've never heard that version before."

"Nah," CJ laughed. "I'm my own storyteller. If I don't like how the story sounds, I make up my own version as I go along."

"Sounds like fun. I liked the story nearly as much I enjoyed the toe massage." She sighed as CJ repeated the toe kneading one more time. "God, CJ. You're really good! Where did you learn how to do that?"

"During my sophomore year I turned my ankle and bruised a bone in my foot. It was really sore, so the doctor sent me to physical therapy for a few weeks to make sure it healed okay. The therapist who worked on me specialized in foot injuries. She also studied reflexology."

"Reflexology? I've heard of that."

"Know what it is?"

"Not exactly."

"I didn't either, before that. But the therapist explained it to me while she worked on me. I found it so interesting that I did some reading about it online, too. I'm no expert, but I'll give you the *Readers' Digest* version of what I know." As she spoke, CJ shifted her hands so that she could reach Andi's heel as well as her Achilles tendon. The blonde kneaded the tissue deeply as she continued to explain. "Reflexology is a type of bodywork therapy that focuses on pressure and trigger points primarily in the foot, but also the hand. The theory is that we all have these energy channels that run throughout our bodies, and that pressing or massaging certain points increases or decreases the flow of energy through those channels."

"You're into energy, aren't you?" Andi observed. "You've made comments in the past about my energy. Do you believe in all that?"

"Most definitely. But not because of any real, concrete proof—and quite honestly, my exposure to it is limited—but rather because I feel it." As she spoke, she placed her hand over her heart. "I've learned to trust what I feel, you know, even if I don't quite understand it."

"You have good instincts," Andi observed. "Sorry, I didn't mean to interrupt."

"It's okay. So anyway, people who practice reflexology believe that a person's organs, nerves, muscles, and metabolic functions are reflected in trigger points in the foot and hand."

"What exactly does that mean?"

"It means certain spots on your feet correspond to spots throughout your body."

"Like what?"

"Hmmmm... It's been a few years since she explained it to me, so I don't remember a lot. Let's see. This area reflects your spine." She ran her fingers up and down the inner area of Andi's foot. "I remember that because, if you look at your foot, that inner edge is actually curved like your spine is curved."

"Interesting." She looked down at her left foot while CJ continued to work on the right one as she spoke.

"And these spots here, if you rub them, it helps when you have menstrual cramps." She kneaded the area on both sides of Andi's foot between her heel and ankle. "The therapist explained a lot of other spots, but I've forgotten them. I just remember how good it felt when she worked on my feet. Not only did the injury heal fast, but I just felt great all over by the time I left the office. I may not understand it completely, but I can't argue with success."

After she worked on Andi's heel, CJ continued to knead both the outer and inner foot before moving on to deeper pressure on the sole. With firm, clamp-like motions, she increased fingertip pressure to the thick pads of Andi's foot. While she worked, she heard her murmur softly, obviously enjoying the special treatment. She finished up the right foot with some gentler friction strokes, then tapped the top of Andi's foot three times to signal the end of that foot's session.

"Time for the other one."

"That was *so* wonderful," Andi said lazily. She raised her arms up and laced her fingers behind her head, fully relaxed and ready to enjoy the attention to her other foot.

CJ worked attentively. Following nearly the same pattern that she had on the right foot, she was rewarded by Andi's soft moans of delight and repeated reminders of how wonderful the foot massage felt. All too quickly, the second foot was completed, and Andi sighed contentedly as her feet and body tingled from CJ's thorough treatment. For moments after, she lay motionless, her body limp and sated, her feet still cushioned in CJ's lap.

"You've spoiled me. I can't tell you how much I enjoyed that!"

"You already did," CJ said. "I heard you purring while I was working on you. It's nice to know I have that effect."

"More than you probably know," she said. The words slipped out before she could stop herself. CJ's head rose, and Andi was glad CJ couldn't see the full red flush coloring her face. She coughed and cleared her throat, not sure what to say to fill in the awkward silence that followed her remark. "So, I bet you're pretty tired now," she ventured. "That seemed like hard work."

"A little. Hopefully, I won't have round three of the nightmare from hell."

"If you want, I could..."

"Would you want to?"

"Sure, no sense in you waking up again and—"

"Maybe it won't happen if you're there."

"I'll be closer so that if you're afraid I could—"

"I would really like that. You sure you don't mind?"

"Not at all. I think...it's a good idea."

"Well, then, I guess I'll go brush my teeth."

"I'll get changed. Can I help you to the bathroom?"

"Sure. Might as well avoid my pinball imitation since you're offering to guide me."

Andi reluctantly removed her feet from CJ's lap and swung

them off the sofa. Her body still tingled from the foot massage, causing a slight head rush as she moved to vertical. Once she regained her balance, she reached down and helped her younger friend to her feet. With an arm wrapped securely around CJ's muscular body, Andi guided her to the bathroom before proceeding on to her bedroom to change.

CJ called out, "Could you bring me a clean T-shirt from my bag when you come back?"

"Sure. Just give me a few minutes."

By the time Andi changed and walked back to the bathroom, CJ had finished washing up and lingered in the doorway as she waited for Andi to return.

"Hope I rinsed all the toothpaste out of the sink," she said. "It's hard to tell."

"Don't worry about it. Here's your T-shirt." She placed the clean shirt in CJ's hand.

"Thanks." She paused, turned around slowly so that her back was to Andi, then pulled her old T-shirt off over her head. Both of Andi's dark eyebrows shot up nearly to her hairline as she watched the beautiful young woman remove her shirt. She drank in the view of her strong, broad back, noting the goose bumps that emerged when her warm skin was exposed to the cooler air. Dipping her eyes, she noticed the fine white-blonde hairs that covered CJ's lower back, the same ones she tickled her fingers through the night before. Out of the corner of her eye she detected a motion and turned to see CJ's profile reflected in the mirror over the sink. Self-conscious about her voyeurism, she was still unable to tear her eyes away from the reflection that revealed even more of the younger woman's beautiful body. Andi gazed at the profile of CJ's small, round breasts and hardened nipples, made firm and erect by the same cool air that raised her goose bumps. Swallowing hard, Andi's heartbeat increased, corresponding to an increase in body temperature, the fire spreading to her heart and between her legs. Then just as quickly as the old shirt was removed, the new one was donned, and CJ turned to face Andi once again, completely unaware of the transformation that had taken place in her flushed, attentive guardian.

"Meet you in bed?" CJ said as she stepped through the door. She felt her way toward the sofa using the backs of the chairs as her guide.

"Okay," Andi squeaked. "Be there in a minute." She closed the door partway, then stepped to the sink to splash her face with cold water for several minutes before she cooled down enough to brush her teeth. *Just keep breathing*, she reminded herself. *You've been in the women's locker room before. There's no such thing as modesty.* She looked at her reflection in the mirror as she vigorously scrubbed her teeth with the toothbrush. *Yeah, but you never got wet just looking at your naked teammates. How the heck are you going to climb into bed next to her now that your body's all hot and turned on?* She answered her own question by dousing more cool liquid on her face. To increase the impact, she removed her shirt and splashed her neck and torso. The shocking effect served to cool down the fire of her raging libido. She leaned on the counter and looked once again at her dripping reflection. *Okay, now keep it under control,* she warned herself. Toweling off quickly, she slipped into a clean T-shirt, then wiped off the sink before heading into the living room.

She tiptoed across the room, noting the complete silence that filled the darkened space. *Wonder if she's sleeping.* Gingerly, she sat down on the edge of the mattress and slid under the covers. She rolled onto her side and looked at the profile of the beautiful woman lying beside her. CJ was indeed asleep. As Andi lay beside her, she could hear the slow, steady cadence of her breathing. The sleeping woman's lips were slightly parted and her face was relaxed and peaceful in the shadows of the darkened room. *All that worrying for nothing. Just roll over and go to sleep.* After a long, lingering glance at her attractive bedmate, she turned slowly to recline on her back, but scooted her body closer to CJ's so that their shoulders touched under the blanket. She reveled in the warmth of that contact until she too surrendered to the night.

Chapter
Twenty-six

ANDI WAS AWAKENED by the sun streaming through the living room window, arcing a path of brightness directly onto her face. Even with her eyelids closed she could feel the warming glow of the newly dawning day. She sighed deeply and opened her eyes, turning her head to avoid the direct glare of the sunlight.

There, as she turned to her left, was CJ. The younger woman lay curled up on her side, facing away from her; however, her shoulders, back, and butt were pressed up fully against Andi's left side. The bodily contact was pleasantly warm, and Andi was unwilling to move from the comfortable cocoon of her shared bed. *No nightmares this time*, she noted to herself. She smiled at her sleeping friend, languishing in her closeness for a few precious minutes before reluctantly leaving her sleep haven to begin her day.

Padding quietly into the kitchen, she flicked on the coffee, then shuffled to the bathroom to shower. Once she'd dried off, she donned a bathrobe and headed to her room to dress. A few minutes later, she emerged, toweling her damp hair as she moved toward the bathroom. With her head covered by the terry cloth, she didn't see or hear CJ, who was just stepping out of the bathroom. The taller woman bumped into her, nearly knocking her to the floor.

"Oh, my God! CJ, I didn't see you." She reached out her hands to grab the other woman, steadying her after the collision.

"I didn't see you either," CJ said dryly. "Sorry, bad joke." She offered a lopsided grin to lighten the moment.

"I'm so sorry, CJ. I thought you were still sleeping. I wasn't paying attention to where I was going. Did I hurt you?"

"I'm not that delicate, Andi. Don't worry. Really. I could hear you coming, but I didn't realize you didn't see me."

"It's my fault. I should have been looking where I was going." Andi wrapped her arm around her shoulders. "You sure you're okay?"

"I'm fine, Andi. Honest."

"How come you're up? Did I wake you?" She kept her arm around CJ as she guided her toward the kitchen's counter stool. Pulling it out, she helped the younger woman get settled on it before moving around to the other side and pouring orange juice. She returned to her companion's side and offered her the glass.

"Thanks," CJ said, smiling as she took the juice. "And no, you didn't wake me. I just woke up. I had a good, uninterrupted night's sleep and I feel great." She turned toward where she knew Andi was standing and offered her a glowing smile. "You are clearly the secret to scaring my bad dreams away." She reached out and clasped Andi's hand, squeezing it gently.

"I've been told I can be a little scary sometimes," she said. "I'm glad you slept well."

"Thanks for sleeping with me, Andi. I really mean that. Just having you there made me feel...I don't know...safe, I guess. It's like you're my eyes, temporarily, so it's good to have you close by." She let go of the taller woman's hand and wrapped her arm casually around her waist, leaning her head against Andi's shoulder.

"My pleasure," she responded. She rubbed up and down CJ's back several times before tousling her hair. "Any time you need me, just ask."

"How about tonight, then?"

"Hmmmm, let me check my planner," she teased. "Let's see. It's Monday night, huh? Well, you're in luck. I'm completely unbooked. Count me in."

"Great!" She gave Andi's waist a gentle squeeze before releasing her. "So, do I smell breakfast?"

"I've always heard that when one of the five senses is limited, the others become more acute. I guess your extra perception has gone right to your nose."

"It's true!" CJ agreed. "Not just about my sense of smell, though. All my other senses seem to be heightened. My hearing, my taste, my sense of touch... Definitely that one." She felt her face become warm and flushed, so she dipped her head to sip some of her juice. Her blush was not lost on Andi, who smiled.

"What you smell is coffee, but I know you don't drink that. As for breakfast, your choices are Karen's banana nut bread, cereal, eggs, or last night's leftover pizza. Any of that sound appealing?"

"I'll pass on the pizza and go with... Hmmmm... I think I'll have the nut bread. That's my favorite."

"Nut bread it is." Andi sliced some, placed it on a plate, then set it in front of CJ. "Milk?"

"Please. So, what are your plans for today?"

"A little triage during my office hours, I suspect. The freshmen got some of their projects back and will be scrambling to figure out how they can improve their writing and research skills in enough time to pass their classes." She snickered as she set the milk glass down right beside CJ's hand. "I also have to assist with an 11:00 class, then I'll be home for lunch. Any requests?"

"Nope. Just your company." She took a bite of the bread, then washed it down with a swallow of milk.

"After lunch I need to spend some time in the library going through journal articles." Andi sipped her coffee as she paused to think. "Oh yeah, and hopefully I'll have some notes from your professors by this afternoon. I'll stop by my office at the end of the day to print them out." She took another drink, then broke off a piece of the nut bread and popped it into her mouth.

"Are you stealing my nut bread?" CJ asked, feigning insult.

"Not stealing, merely sharing." She grinned and broke off another piece. "How about you? What will you do today?"

"Let's see, I usually like to start my day with a run, just to wake up my muscles. Then, I'll grab a quick shower before I head across campus just in time for my 10:00 class. After that I'll—"

"Ahem."

"Oh, right. That was my life eight days ago. I forgot. In that case, I guess I'll just remain horizontal most of the day. I'll make my daily phone call to my mother, to assure her that she doesn't need to drive all the way out here to bring me back home 'where I belong,' then I'll wait eagerly for lunch-time to arrive. After lunch I'll probably take a bath, then spend the afternoon lounging around some more, hoping one of my friends stops by to visit. You know...same shit, different day."

"I'm sorry you're getting a little stir crazy, CJ," Andi said sympathetically, "but you're in the home stretch."

"I know, Andi. I didn't mean to sound like I was complaining. You've been terrific, really. In case I didn't mention it, I had a really great weekend. Thanks for hanging around with me and making everything... special."

"No need to thank me, CJ. I had a great time, too." She reached out and placed her hand gently over CJ's, giving it a squeeze as she lingered there. "Speaking of time, I'd better be heading out." She finished the last sip of her coffee then piled the plates in the sink. "Will you excuse me a minute while I finish getting ready?" She patted CJ's hand before moving away from the counter.

"Go. I'll be hanging out on the sofa." She moved off the stool and used the furniture as guides to return to the living room. Shortly after she settled on the sofa, she heard Andi's steps as she walked across the room.

"Okay, I'm back," Andi announced. She sat on the edge of the cushions where CJ reclined. The injured woman shifted over a bit to make room. Andi stroked the blonde forearm a few times before resting her hand there as she spoke. "The phone and the clickers are right next to you on the coffee table. If you decide you want something special for lunch, call my office before 10:45. Anything I can do for you before I go?"

"Just one thing."

"What's that?"

"How about a hug goodbye?"

"I think that can be arranged."

CJ sat up from her reclined position. Although she couldn't see Andi, over the last few days she had grown aware of Andi's presence when she was near, sensing her pulsing energy. Reaching out her arms toward where she knew Andi was sitting, she enveloped her temporary roommate in a warm, affectionate hug. Andi's hands stroked up and down her back as their bodies remained pressed together in their embrace.

"Mmmm," hummed CJ. "You always smell really nice." She nuzzled her face in Andi's neck and her soft, dark hair.

"It's *CK One*. Do you like it?"

"Very much so. I've noticed you wearing it before."

"Yeah, I usually put some on unless I'm just hanging around the house. It's my one real concession to girlie behavior." Andi chuckled softly, and CJ felt her chest vibrate with the sound.

"Whenever I smell it, it reminds me of you." She inhaled deeply once more, then reluctantly pulled back from the embrace and returned to her reclined position. "I don't want to make you late," she said ruefully. "So, until soon?"

"Yes, until soon, CJ." She smiled. "Until lunch."

Andi gave CJ's hand a final squeeze before she stood from the sofa and headed out of the apartment.

ANDI'S DAY PASSED quickly, filled with questioning students, teaching, and researching. Her trip home for lunch was a welcome break during the day, and before she knew it, she was walking across the green at the end of her day, looking forward to relaxing and spending the evening with CJ. She glanced at her

watch. *Hmmmm, 4:30. Not too bad. What should I cook for dinner?*
She ran through the menus of the previous nights and realized
she had exhausted her very limited cooking repertoire. *Might be
time to raid the freezer and take out one of mom's meals.* She nodded
at the idea, then searched her brain to remember what was
buried in the recesses of her freezer that would make a decent
meal for them. *Did I eat that chicken casserole?* she wondered as
she mounted the steps to the porch leading to her apartment. She
frowned, deep in thought, as she tried to remember. Pulling
open the door leading to her upstairs home, she nearly slammed
into Jen, who was just leaving.

"What the—"

"It's you," Jen said snidely.

"Who'd you expect? I live here."

"Yes, you and your new friend."

"It's temporary. I'm just helping her out."

"Ha! Like I can't see through your Florence Nightingale
routine. You got exactly what you wanted."

"What are you talking about?"

"Her. You've got her not only here, in your apartment, but
right in your bed."

"Oh, please. Don't be ridiculous."

"CJ couldn't stop gushing about what good care you're
taking of her. I'm sure you've been very attentive to all her
needs."

"Shut up, Jen. You can just take your assumptions and get
the hell out of my sight."

"Gladly. At least I won't be putting up with you much
longer."

"And what the hell is that supposed to mean?"

"You'll find out soon enough."

With that remark, Jen snarled at Andi and marched down
the porch steps, walking quickly across campus. Andi watched
her go, still seething from her cutting remarks as well as
wondering about her final comment. She breathed through
clenched teeth, consciously relaxing her jaw to release a breath
she had been holding. Her hands were balled into fists. Slowly
she unpeeled them and relaxed her hunched-up shoulders. Her
face was hot from a rage that threatened to boil over had Jen
remained within striking distance of her fists. *Won't be putting up
with me much longer,* she mused, angry at Jen's enigmatic remark.
*Speaking of putting up, I'd like to put my foot up her ass, that's what
I'd like to do!*

For a long moment she stood in the entranceway, door open,
while she tried to regain her composure. *She doesn't matter,* she

tried to convince herself. *She's an idiot. Ignore her. Don't let her rile you up.* Repeating these phrases to herself silently, she managed to unwind enough to consider heading upstairs. She tilted her head, looking up the flight of steps that led up to her second floor apartment and noticed the door was open. "Shit," she muttered.

She mounted the steps slowly, trying to regain the lightheartedness and anticipation she had been feeling the few minutes prior to her confrontation with Jen. She stepped through the open door, closed it behind her, put down her bag, and walked into the living room.

"Andi?" CJ called.

"It's just me." She tried to remove the anger and bitterness from her voice. Moving toward the sofa, she sat on the cushioned arm opposite of where CJ reclined. She touched the basketball star's feet in greeting to let her know where she was.

"What was that about?" CJ asked. Her voice reflected a note of concern.

"What?" Andi said, stalling for time to think.

"Sounded like arguing."

"Oh. That. Jen and I don't see eye to eye on some things."

"What things?"

"Just things."

CJ sat silently, as if waiting for an elaboration. Her hands rested on her stomach, loosely linked together. Her dimple was hidden, and her face held none of the cheery playfulness she had exuded when Andi left her after their lunch together. Andi remained silent as well. Her head swam with chaotic emotions. She feared that if she attempted to speak, she would say the wrong thing; it was safer to say nothing, and an awkward silence hung between the two women. Andi had the advantage of reading CJ's body language, and she could tell the younger woman was disquieted. The injured athlete sat in darkness, wondering what was going on with her taciturn friend. Finally, after painful moments of emptiness, Andi broke the silence.

"I'm sorry, CJ. I just—"

"No. It's okay, Andi. You don't owe me any explanations. You and Jen seem to have some kind of history. You don't have to tell me about it. You're entitled to your own affairs."

"But that's exactly what I *don't* want you to think it is. We have a history of arguing and disagreements, but that's where it ends. It's never been anything more than that, despite what she wanted."

"What did she want?"

"More than I was willing to give. Can we leave it at that, for now? There's nothing between Jen and me except bitter feelings."

"I'm sorry," CJ said softly. "It's really none of my business." Her voice was serious and sad, holding a hint of disappointment. Andi picked up on her tone and tried to ease her anxiety.

"I don't want you to feel that way, CJ. It makes me feel good knowing that you care enough to ask me those questions. I certainly don't want you to think the feeling's not mutual."

"That's okay, Andi. I'm too nosy for my own good."

"You're not nosy. You're caring." She moved from the arm of the sofa to a spot on the cushion near CJ's hip. The blonde woman shifted over on the couch when she felt Andi sit near her. CJ felt the warmth and pressure of Andi's body as she leaned slightly against her, eager to reestablish a physical connection to repair the emotional distance that seemed to separate them. Andi rested her hand on CJ's forearm, gently stroking the soft skin with her thumb. "I love that about you, and I wish I could express that as easily as you do. I'm trying, even though it might not be so obvious." She paused. "You're a good teacher. I'm trying to learn from you."

"I'm sorry, Andi." She placed her hand over her friend's. "I guess I was just feeling a little out of sorts after Jen's visit. I didn't mean to—"

"What did she say? Did she upset you?" Andi's ire was raised again at the thought of Jen bothering CJ.

"No, she didn't say anything, really. It's just that I associate her with basketball, so she was a reminder of the season and our tournament loss. You know, it's that whole 'unfinished chapter' stuff we talked about." A hint of sadness and regret colored her tone.

"I'm sorry, too, CJ," Andi said. "I didn't mean to make you more upset by clamming up when you asked me questions. I promise, we'll finish this conversation soon. I owe you some explanations for a lot of things, just give me a little more time, okay?" A small measure of pleading in her voice penetrated CJ's heart. The blonde sensed Andi's sincerity, so she allowed herself to be satisfied with the promise.

"Okay," CJ responded. "I'll hold you to it."

"Speaking of holding me," Andi began, "can we end this with a hug and start the evening over again?"

"Sounds good to me."

Andi stayed seated but leaned over to hug CJ as she remained reclined. Reaching her hands down into the soft cushions, she managed to wrap her arms around the sturdy, strong body. CJ buried her face in the space between Andi's neck and shoulder, and Andi felt her warm breath as she sighed deeply.

"You okay?" Andi asked.

"Better now. You still smell good." She breathed in deeply and remained locked in the embrace, the firm pressure of Andi's body pressed against her as she lay stretched out on the couch. After an extended moment, they untangled their arms and separated.

"So, let me get my sweats on, then I'll start dinner," Andi said. She rose from her seat and headed toward her room. "I think I have some of my mother's chicken casserole in the freezer. Does that sound okay?" she called from her bedroom.

"Fine," CJ said. She remained on the sofa, contemplating their discussion. *There's definitely more to things between her and Jen than what she revealed, but it doesn't sound like anything good,* she mused. She felt a wave of relief wash over her. *Jealous?* she asked herself. *You thought the two of them had been together and that bugged you, didn't it?* She laughed at herself silently. *Well, she confirmed that definitely wasn't the case. You'll just have to wait to hear the rest of the story.*

ANDI PACKED THE last of her students' papers into her school bag, glad to be finished with her grading. The work took longer than she had expected, occupying nearly ninety minutes of her time after dinner, time that she would have preferred to spend with her beautiful companion. She sighed and looked over at her injured friend who was stretched out on the sofa with the TV on softly in the background. Zipping up her bag, Andi picked it up off the table and walked across the room, placing it near the door. She then walked softly back into the living room to relax for the remainder of the evening.

"What are you watching?" Andi asked. She paused to consider her statement, annoyed at herself for the thoughtless remark. "Sorry. Poor choice of words. What's on TV?"

"The Food Channel," CJ said. "I'm listening to Alton Brown talk about cheese. Ever watch 'Good Eats'?"

"I don't think so. Is that a hint that I should? Is my cooking that bad?" She feigned insult.

"No! That's not what I was implying. It's a fun show, with lots of food facts, history of different foods, and the chemistry of foods. He gives some cooking tips, but it's not like Emeril."

"Sounds interesting."

"Yeah, it is." CJ shifted on the sofa, moving slightly to find a comfortable reclined position. "Could you do me a favor?"

"Name it."

"Is there an extra pillow around that I could put behind me?"

"Sure. Just sit up for a minute." Andi picked up the nearby pillow as CJ sat up slowly, her legs still stretched out nearly over the length of the couch. As soon as the younger woman moved, Andi seated herself on the cushions where CJ's head had been. She placed the extra pillow on her lap. "Okay, you can lie back down now," she said. CJ lowered her body until her head rested comfortably on Andi's lap.

"That wasn't exactly what I had in mind when I requested a pillow, but I'm not complaining," CJ said. A contented grin lit up her face. "You sure I'm not squishing you? I didn't mean to hog the whole sofa."

"You're fine. Is it comfortable for you, though?"

"Perfect," CJ said. The smile remained on her lips.

Andi watched and CJ listened as Alton Brown explained the steps required to age sheep's milk into the perfect cheese. Andi's feet, crossed at the ankles, were propped up on the coffee table in front of her. The darkened living room glowed from the TV's glare, casting shadows across the room as well as on CJ's face. Andi turned away from the show to look at the woman whose head nested in her lap. The eye patch marred the landscape of her friend's perfect features. Looking at the patch, Andi sighed silently.

She wondered how CJ coped so well handling the darkness that had become her life for the last eight days. Trying to imagine the loss, if only for a few moments, Andi closed her eyes and allowed the darkness of her eyelids to cut off her sight. She sat there, listening, feeling, smelling, her senses immediately on high alert to make up for the one sense that had been temporarily disallowed. As the moments passed, every noise became louder and more distinct as she focused on the source. Every nerve ending in her body tingled from the touch of fabric, cushions, or her young friend's body as it leaned against her. The aroma of the evening's dinner hung in the air, mixed with the earthy scent of CJ's skin. She felt as if a magnifying glass was held in front of her senses to compensate for her eyelids remaining closed.

She wondered what was going on around her even as she sat on her own sofa, resisting the urge to open her eyes and simply look around to satisfy her curiosity. *Did I lock the door?* she wondered. *Anyone could walk up quietly and I wouldn't even know.* She fought the desire to look over at her entranceway to allay her fears. *That's what CJ must feel every day, all day, when I'm not here and she's left alone with the door unlocked. How must she feel during the first few seconds when a visitor opens the door but doesn't immediately identify herself?* The discomfort registered in her heart, and without thinking, she reached out and placed her hand protectively on CJ's shoulder. She opened her eyes as her hand made contact with the younger woman's body, and her magnified senses returned to normal.

"You've been quiet," CJ observed. "What are you thinking?"

"Nothing. Just winding down at the end of a long day."

"Yeah, it feels good just to hang out here, doesn't it?"

As the cooking show credits scrolled on the screen, Andi turned off the TV using the remote, then remained comfortably relaxed on the couch. Her hand rested protectively on CJ's shoulder as the two women sat in silence. The light from the kitchen provided minimum brightness to the room. CJ stifled a yawn, covering her mouth with her hand.

"Tired?" Andi asked. As if moving of their own accord, Andi's fingers traveled from CJ's shoulder to her hair. She laced her long fingers through the short, golden hair that spilled onto the pillow in her lap. The texture was silky and she wrapped the flaxen strands around her index finger, twirling her finger around, then unwinding the silky filaments once again. The soft, blonde hair tickled as she swam her fingers through its slight waves.

"Mmmm. That will put me right out," CJ murmured. "It's so wonderfully relaxing." A contented smile played across her lips. CJ lay still, enjoying Andi's soft touch as she gently played with her hair. As stimulating and enjoyable as the sensation was, CJ found herself fighting the urge to drift off into a sensual sleep.

"Ready to call it a night?" Andi asked. She continued to rake her fingers gently through the soft, golden tresses.

"Yes, though I hate to move," she confessed. "Why don't you take the bathroom first tonight? I had it first last night."

"It really doesn't matter to me."

"Go ahead, then. I'll go in when you're done." She sat up reluctantly so that her living pillow could move. When she felt Andi vacate the couch, she reclined once again. "Would you do me a favor and put one of my T-shirts on the sink?"

"Sure," Andi said as she headed toward the bedroom.

A few minutes later Andi stepped back into the living room wearing sweat pants and a baggy T-shirt, untucked. Her socked feet made very little noise so she announced her presence by tapping CJ's toes as she approached.

"My turn?" the younger woman asked. She shifted to a sitting position, then stood slowly as she controlled her balance.

"Yup. Need a hand?"

"Nah, I'm getting good with the furniture guides. Go ahead and get in bed. I'll be back in a few minutes."

Although she was tired, Andi was not anxious for the night to end. She felt cheated of precious time that she could have been spending with CJ because she'd had schoolwork to do earlier. She searched her mind, trying to think of a way to extend the evening a little while longer before her younger friend fell asleep. *Hmmmm,* she mused. *How about a little music? Something quiet in the background. That way she can still fall asleep if she's really tired.* She moved to her stereo and squatted down in front of her CD collection, looking for something instrumental that would be good background music without lulling either of them to immediate sleep. She chose one, put it in the tray, and set it to play, adjusting the volume before taking the remote control and retiring to bed.

CJ continued to scrub her teeth as she leaned over the sink, brushing well beyond the few minutes it should have taken to do the job well. *Don't want dragon breath,* she chided herself. *She won't want to lie next to me, let alone talk to me, if my breath curls her eyebrows.* With a few final sweeps, she finished brushing and rinsed her mouth. After a few more minutes with soap and a washcloth, she pulled on her clean T-shirt and headed back into the living room. She smiled upon hearing the soft music emanating from the speakers across the room. "I'm back," she announced. She lowered herself to the mattress, then crawled under the blanket.

"I was just relaxing with some music. Is that okay with you?"

"Fine. What are we listening to?"

"Pat Metheny's *Still Life (Talking).* I guess it's a contemporary jazz kind of sound. It's hard to categorize, really. Do you like it?"

"I do. It's different."

"I like to listen to instrumental music when I have to read or grade papers. It's less of a distraction."

"I know what you mean. Whenever one of my roommates has the radio on in the dorm, I find myself singing along and not doing my work." She settled herself under the covers, her right shoulder pressed up lightly against Andi's left. The soft music was upbeat yet relaxing, and she could picture Andi sitting at the table, doing schoolwork, with this music filling the room. "What's the name of this piece?" she asked, noting the haunting melody of the quiet instrumental.

"That's one of my favorite cuts on the disk. It's called 'So Let it Secretly Begin,'" Andi said. She smiled at the title's irony. "So, tomorrow's your last full day before you go back to the doctor, your last full day...here." She ended the sentence with a hint of sadness in her voice as the realization of her words sunk in. While she was anxious for CJ to get a good report from the doctor, she knew that would mean CJ would leave to go back to her dorm. In the last eight days her life had become so intertwined with CJ's that her heart felt a great sadness and loss at the prospect of CJ not living with her any more.

CJ noticed the uncertainty in Andi's voice, the sadness in her tone, and wondered about its cause. Bending her right knee slightly and turning her leg outward, CJ hesitantly leaned her leg against her bedmate's, hoping to add to their contact. She sighed inwardly and relaxed when Andi did not pull away from her touch.

"I guess you'll be happy?" she said, her tone colored by a questioning inflection.

"Yes, I mean, no, I mean...of course, I'll be happy when the doctor tells you your eye is okay and you can go back to your regular routine. But no, I won't be happy to see you go. It's not like I'm anxious to get rid of you. You're low maintenance...very easy to be around."

"Low maintenance, huh? I feel like a Honda." Her voice was serious yet playful.

"You know what I mean, don't you?" She rolled onto her left side and propped her head up on her elbow, facing CJ's profile. "I can just be myself around you. I can talk when I feel like it, and spend long stretches just sitting near you saying nothing and that's okay, too. We seem to like and dislike similar things, yet your perspective is different enough from mine that it's not boring, like when someone just parrots another person's life. You're a complete person by yourself and...you add something special to my life." Her last words spilled out without conscious thought, before she had time to self-edit. As the words crossed her lips, she felt her face blaze with heat, lit by the fire of embarrassment and vulnerability. She swallowed hard, fighting the urge to flee from the bed to avoid facing CJ's reaction. She held her breath as she tried to regain her composure and think of something else to say that would distract her attractive blonde friend from her last few words. Her tongue betrayed her a second time, however, this time by remaining silent.

"Wow," CJ whispered. "That's such a nice thing to say." Despite the fact that she couldn't see Andi, she turned to face the soft-spoken woman, hoping her body language would convey what her eye contact could not. She reached out her hand and clasped Andi's. "The feeling's very mutual. I hope you know that." She squeezed the hand and was answered by a lingering returned gesture. "Things don't have to change that much. I mean, we can still hang out together, right?" In a moment of panic, she wondered if perhaps things would change, and their lives would become two completely separate entities whose paths seldom crossed. At that thought, a great sadness filled her heart.

"I'd love that, CJ," Andi said. CJ felt her heart soar at hearing those words. "I think these past days are only the beginning of something very special."

"You do, huh?" CJ smiled.

"Yeah, I do."

They remained facing one another for several moments, basking in the emotional connection that had been established through speaking from their hearts. As the final track on the CD faded, the only remaining sound was their soft, steady breathing. Finally, CJ broke the spell. "We should get some sleep," CJ said reluctantly. "You've got an early class tomorrow."

"You've got my schedule down already?" Andi chuckled.

"Hey, you've been watching out for me, it's only fair that I return the favor." She smiled broadly, showing a pearly set of perfectly straight teeth.

"I guess you're right," Andi sighed. Using the remote, she turned off the stereo, then stretched out on her back, lying close enough to CJ so that their bodies touched. Her companion remained on her side, her head mere inches from Andi's.

"Night, Andi," CJ whispered.

"Night, CJ. Happy dreams."

With a smile, CJ said, "I'm sure they will be."

Chapter
Twenty-seven

AS DAY DAWNED, Andi found herself once again nestled up against her blonde bedmate. She felt almost disappointed that she slept soundly enough not to remember what was probably a night filled with cuddling near the younger woman. She wished she had been in a half-sleep so she could have stored up seven hours of pleasant sensations similar to what she was currently feeling. Enjoying a few lingering moments in CJ's company, she sighed and finally slipped out from beneath the covers.

Moving quietly around her apartment, she was determined not to wake CJ as she had on previous mornings. Her Tuesday class began at 8:30 a.m., but there was no sense in the injured athlete waking early, too. She moved from kitchen to bathroom to bedroom with the stealth of a skilled tracker, this time keeping more alert for her wandering ward who, she thought, might just emerge from the bathroom and surprise her, as CJ had the previous morning.

Fearing that her usual morning coffee-brewing would awaken CJ, she managed to get ready with enough time to allow for a pit stop at the campus coffee shop. Pausing at the door before heading out of her apartment, she reconsidered her earlier decision simply to leave without waking CJ, then phone home after her class finished. After replacing her book bag on the floor near the door, she tiptoed silently back to the bed where the basketball star slept. She lowered herself slowly to the mattress, then spent an extended moment enjoying the view before her.

CJ had rolled onto her back with her left arm resting casually on the pillow over her head. Her right arm lay across her stomach, loosely clutching the crumpled T-shirt she was sleeping in. The blanket was kicked down around her thighs. Her soft features were relaxed in sleep, making her look younger than her twenty-two years. A contented smile played upon her lips, and Andi wondered what she was dreaming. Seeing her companion smile caused her to smile, too. Andi hesitated about waking her out of what appeared to be a pleasant dream; however, she placed her hand on CJ's shoulder, shaking her ever so gently while whispering her name.

"CJ, are you awake?"

"Huhmmm?" the younger woman responded sleepily. Her head moved slightly, and her body stirred, but she did not appear to be awake.

"I need to leave for class now." She leaned down so that her face was mere inches away from CJ's. Whispering, she said, "I just wanted to say goodbye."

CJ's arms reached up and wrapped around Andi as she leaned down, enveloping her in a sleepy embrace. The young woman's arms felt heavy around her, and Andi could tell that her companion had not quite broken the surface of lucid awareness. She smiled as CJ seemed to fall back asleep with arms wrapped around Andi's neck and shoulders.

Moving gently, Andi slowly unwrapped the younger woman's arms from her body. As she began to move them, however, CJ surfaced briefly, yet not completely, from her somnolent state.

"Stay..." she pleaded. "I like when you're here." She rolled on her side, facing Andi, then grasped her bedmate's pillow, pulling it close to her and nuzzling her face in it. "I love sleeping with you near me."

Andi's eyebrows arched high on her forehead at hearing CJ's admission. She was taken aback at the direct confession, yet quickly chalked it up to slumbering chatter. "I'll be home for lunch, CJ," she whispered. She hesitantly reached out and stroked the golden hair, pausing to rub her thumb gently across the high cheekbone.

A smile appeared on CJ's lips, and she moaned softly at the touch. "Okay," CJ mumbled. "Lunch."

Andi smiled warmly at her, caressing her hair and cheek as she slipped back into a deeper sleep. She felt emboldened by the younger woman's contented reaction to her touch and continued to stroke her gently. Reveling in the silkiness of her hair, she fingered the tousled tresses, raking her fingers gently to push back some unruly strands to expose CJ's striking face. Moving her hand from hair to cheek, she held her palm against the soft, warm skin for a moment before traveling back to stroke the flaxen strands once again.

After several moments, she reluctantly removed her hand from CJ's hair. Sighing, she stood, gathered her things, then headed out the door with one lingering glance over her shoulder at the sleepy woman who had captured her heart.

ANDI HEARD THE stereo as she mounted the stairs to her apartment and she smiled, recognizing the Pat Metheny CD she had played the previous night. She stepped through the door and quickly announced her presence.

"Hey," she called, then proclaimed happily, "lunch has arrived."

She moved toward the sofa where CJ reclined. As she sat down on the edge of the cushion near CJ's hip, the injured athlete shifted her body to allow enough room for her tall friend. Andi reached over for the remote and lowered the volume slightly.

"Do you like this disk, or are you listening to it simply because I forgot to take it out?"

"Both," she said, smiling brightly up at Andi.

"I picked up subs today."

"Great. I'm hungry." Almost on cue, her stomach growled loudly. With her palm, she rubbed it with circular motions as if to quiet the demanding beast within.

"Gosh, CJ, you didn't have breakfast. You must be starving!" She mentally slapped herself in the head for not remembering that her temporarily blinded friend would not be able to rummage through her fridge to get her own breakfast. "I wanted you to be able to sleep in and rest this morning, but I didn't think about your breakfast. I'm so sorry!"

"That's okay, Andi," she said good-naturedly. "I actually managed to feel my way around enough to snag an apple and pour a glass of juice. You might want to check the counter. I think I spilled some."

"Don't worry about that. I'm such a dope."

"Really, it's okay about breakfast." She paused, then spoke more softly. "I was kind of hoping to say goodbye to you before you left though. How come you didn't wake me?"

"But I did. I mean, I tried." Andi looked quizzically at the blonde. "Don't you remember? I came over and sat on the edge of the mattress. You even gave me a hug and...told me not to go." Her voice softened as she remembered CJ's confession; however, she omitted that from her recap.

"Sometimes I'm a very deep sleeper. My roommates always tease me about it. The last two nights I've slept so well. I guess I was just very relaxed." She could feel her face redden so she looked away.

"Come on, then. Let's feed you," Andi said. She clasped CJ's hands and helped her up, continuing to hold her hands while the other woman gained her balance. Andi placed her hand on the small of CJ's back, guiding her to the counter stool where they would eat lunch.

"So how was your morning?" CJ asked.

"Uneventful, which is good. The class went well, and I managed to get some work done in my office before heading back here." She pulled out the stool and helped CJ settle on it before walking back into the living room to retrieve their subs. "How about you?"

"Same old," she said. "I have no idea what time it was when I got up." She sniffed the air as Andi unwrapped the subs and the aroma of eggplant Parmesan filled the air. "God, that smells good."

"Here," Andi said, placing the food in front of the hungry woman. "Eat up while it's still warm." She watched as CJ dug into the sandwich hungrily, feeling guilty all over again about her breakfast error. After she unwrapped her own sandwich, she joined her friend at the counter to eat.

"Coach stopped by about an hour before you got back," CJ said between bites.

"That was nice of her." She mumbled a bit as she spoke with half a mouthful of food. Swallowing, she continued. "What'd she have to say?"

"She talked about some interesting recruiting prospects she is working on. Asked me if I heard of any of them, and I actually did recognize one of the names. A senior from a high school not far from my old school." She stopped talking to take another bite, chewing quickly, then swallowing so she could continue. "We also talked a little strategy, you know, like 'what if' stuff. What would I have done differently if it was me calling the plays in the tournament." She chuckled, then took a bite of her sub. She smiled as she chewed, clearly amused by whatever she was thinking.

Andi found her smile contagious and waited eagerly to hear its cause. "What did you tell her?"

"I answered her question, that's for sure." She chuckled again. "But perhaps more directly than she was anticipating. I mean, I didn't say anything disrespectful, because you know that I really like Coach and think she's good at what she does, but I think my perspective as a player was eye-opening for her." She took another bite before continuing. "Initially, I thought I pissed her off because she didn't say anything. I wish to hell that I could have seen her face. Sometimes, when she got mad at practice, this little vein in her forehead would start to pulse and I knew enough to get out of her way. But today I couldn't see her anger meter, so I didn't know what to do."

"So what *did* you do?"

"I just shut up and waited for her to say something. After what seemed like fifteen minutes, but was probably fifteen seconds, she spoke."

"And?"

"She said she agreed." She took another small bite of the sub and smiled. "It gave me a real feeling of satisfaction to hear her agreement. She quickly followed it up by adding that hindsight was always 20/20, but I think that was because I bumped her off balance a bit." She took a long swallow of water, having gobbled the first half of her sandwich so quickly. "She also asked about you."

"Me? What about me?" She felt defensive, but didn't know why. *Probably lingering annoyance at Jen*, she said to her internal question. *I wonder if that bitch said anything. Was it just coincidence that Coach stopped by the day after Jen did?* Andi was uncomfortable with the coincidence and tried to put it out of her mind.

"Just asking about you. Said she heard you've been taking real good care of me. Of course I confirmed that." CJ grinned widely at Andi, not realizing that the intended compliment made her caretaker a bit uncomfortable.

"Oh?" Andi said weakly.

"Yeah, I told her that you were the best. Oh, and she wants me to go see her after I get checked out by the doctor, assuming everything's okay. Said there's something she wanted to discuss with me, but wouldn't tell me what."

"No ideas?"

"None. I tried to get it out of her, but she said she had a meeting in fifteen minutes and would rather talk to me about it another time. I told her I'd stop by on Thursday, the day after I see the doctor." She tore into her lunch once again with her usual enthusiasm, seeming more unfazed by the coach's request than her companion was.

"I'll be curious to hear what she has to say," Andi noted, frowning. She looked at her watch. "Speaking of meetings, I have to meet with my department Chair in twenty minutes." She looked up and saw disappointment paint CJ's face. A note of sadness filled her own heart as she considered that this was the last lunch she and her injured ward would share. She wished she could extend it, to prolong any time in CJ's company, but she was compelled to leave much sooner than she had hoped. Eager to erase CJ's disappointed look, she came up with a compromise that might make up for her early exit from lunch. "I don't have office hours this afternoon, though. I could be home by 4:00. How's that sound?"

"Great!" CJ responded, her smile lighting up her fair complexion.

"It's a date," she said, cringing at her choice of words. CJ continued to smile.

THE TWO WOMEN lay shoulder to shoulder on Andi's mattress, CJ's thigh turned out to the side in order to make additional contact with her bedmate. Rain pummeled the roof outside, beating a steady rhythm over their heads. Thunder rumbled occasionally, and lightening pierced the sky, illuminating the early spring evening. In sharp contrast to the noises of nature outside, the apartment was dark and quiet inside. Even through closed eyes, Andi could see the brightness of the lightening as it split the sky and lit up the living room. She felt CJ twitch after especially loud cracks of thunder.

"So, what time is your appointment tomorrow morning?" Andi said.

"I have to meet the doctor in her office at 10:00. At least I don't have to go back on a stretcher in the ambulance." She smirked with relief, recalling how the doctor refused her request to walk to Andi's apartment on her own two feet. Her smirk quickly turned into a frown, however, when she remembered that a simple walk across campus to the infirmary was not quite so simple for her these days. "Actually, I don't know how I'll be getting there, though."

"I'll take you, CJ. I cleared my schedule tomorrow morning because I thought you might need some help and, well, I'd really like to go with you, if you want some company. If I had to sit in my office with students, I wouldn't really be concentrating anyway."

"That would be great. I'd like you to come with me. I could use the company."

"Nervous?"

"Yeah, I am." She sighed deeply, then paused before continuing to speak. "I've really been trying to stay positive about everything, you know? Because when you start to think you're defeated, it always ends up happening. And most of the time I think to myself that everything's going to be okay, that I'm going to look back on this whole experience and know the only thing I lost was my chance at the big tournament, not my eyesight. During those times I remind myself how much I've gained from this whole thing, too." She reached out and clasped Andi's hand. "But then there are some times when this nagging voice of doubt creeps in, and I worry that when the doctor takes off my eye patch, I'll still be...in darkness. I try to push those thoughts out of my head, but sometimes, when I'm alone, by myself in darkness, it's hard. It's kind of like how a scary movie is so much scarier when you watch it at night, then the next day, when the sun comes up, you wonder what scared you so much the night before. Only with me, the sun hasn't come up for the past nine days so my fear remains. Does that make any sense?"

"Yeah," Andi said. She squeezed the blonde woman's hand gently. "I can totally understand your fear, and I think you're very brave." CJ let out a little snort-giggle, indicating that she didn't agree. "No, really," Andi insisted. "You've been wonderful. You're never moping or moody, and you don't sit around with a 'poor me' attitude. Geez, you're ten times better at dealing with your injury than I was at dealing with mine. I was like a bear with a sore ass for weeks on end." She snickered as she recalled her impatience and grumpiness. "Martha and Karen would have never been able to live with me in close quarters the way I'm able to live with you." *And to enjoy it so much.*

"Well, you're too kind. And I really don't feel that brave. In fact, nearly every day, when you're at school, I come real close to taking off this patch and opening my eyes because I can't wait another minute. I just have to know. But I don't. I chicken out every time." Her voice turned sad, with a note of self-disappointment.

"That doesn't make you less brave, CJ. It just proves that you're smart by doing exactly what the doctor told you to do in order to heal."

"Yeah, well, I'm still afraid."

"Of what?"

"Of the pictures in my head fading," she said sadly. Turning on her right side, she bent her elbow and propped up her head on her hand, facing Andi. She reached out and placed her hand on the older woman's arm, resting it there while she continued to speak. "The first few days after the accident, while I was lying here by myself, I had a lot of time to think and remember. Whenever my mom called, or a friend visited, or every time I thought of someone who is important in my life, I got this picture in my mind of that person. Initially, the picture was practically three-dimensional, sharp and clear, with deep, rich colors. Then, after a few days, it started to look more like a photograph, kind of flat. After a few more days it would take me a few minutes to get the picture fully in my mind, and the colors in the picture started to fade." Her voice became soft and infused with sadness. "When that happens, especially during one of my scared times when the doubts creep in, I worry that, if I lose my sight, I'll eventually lose the pictures in my head, too."

Andi felt her tremble at her side. "Those pictures won't ever go away, CJ." She reached down and touched the younger woman's hand as it rested on her arm. Stroking it reassuringly, she continued talking. "Even if you were to lose your sight—and I'm optimistic that you won't—you won't lose your memories of people. Your mind's eye will always be able to see them."

"Sometimes, when I'm on the phone with my mother, I try to picture her—her wavy hair, her rosy cheeks, the way she squints her eyes when she's concentrating—and it just seems that, I don't know, like I can't fully recreate her picture in my head anymore."

"You've been away from home for four years now. Perhaps some of what you're feeling comes from simply not seeing your mom every day, like you did when you were growing up."

CJ was silent for a moment as she considered Andi's explanation. "I suppose you're right. I hadn't thought of it that way." She paused to think more about Andi's theory and to apply it to the faces of others who appeared in her mind. The hypothesis fit each case, except for one. She sighed. "There's only one person that doesn't fit with."

"Who's that?"

"You."

"Me?"

"Yeah, you. One of my favorite images of you is when we returned from sledding that day, and we were standing on your porch downstairs. The sun was setting and the sky was red, orange, and purple—simply beautiful. I was looking over your shoulder at the sunset, and then I looked at you. Your dark hair fell softly, nearly touching your shoulders. The wind and cold had turned your cheeks to pink, which only made the blueness of your eyes stand out even more. I had always noticed them—how could I not—but I had never seen them look so crystal blue. You were smiling, not just a little grin, but a full, toothy smile, like you were really happy."

"I was."

"Well, that's the picture of you I keep thinking of, to remember, but some days, that, too, seems faded." Sadness tinged her voice. "I don't want to lose your picture. I don't want to forget your beautiful face."

"Oh, CJ," Andi whispered. Her heart ached at her friend's sadness yet raced from the flattering compliments. She turned toward CJ and tugged at her hand, which was still resting on her arm. "Let me help you to remember."

Andi moved CJ's hand off its warm resting spot on her arm

and placed it on her cheek. She held it there for a moment, inviting the younger woman to explore, and then Andi slowly let go. CJ's palm remained where Andi had placed it, temporarily immobile, trembling lightly against the grad assistant's warm skin.

Slowly, CJ moved her hand and placed it on Andi's head. Beginning at the crown of dark hair, she slid her palm down the silky strands of ebony as they cascaded over her ear and fell nearly to her shoulder. As she moved to the ends, she rubbed the locks between her fingers, luxuriating in the soft texture. She moved upward once more, this time raking her fingers into the dark tresses, gently rubbing her scalp as she traveled north to the top of Andi's head.

From there, she moved down onto Andi's forehead. Using only the tips of her fingers, she dragged them down slowly until she reached her eyebrows. Her motion then shifted left to right as she skated her fingertips side to side across Andi's forehead, pausing at her temples, then returning to the center again. Her exploration continued at Andi's dark eyebrows, tracing their arching shape from center outwards, stroking lightly over the soft hairs.

Andi felt CJ's tentative touch grow more confident as the younger woman slowly explored her face. She never had been touched in such an intimate way before, and although her invitation to CJ was meant to relieve the injured woman's anxiety, Andi could feel her own mounting. She forced herself to stay relaxed although her body was feeling anything but calm.

CJ's fingertips drifted very lightly to Andi's eyelids, which twitched slightly at the touch. She dragged her fingertip slowly down the crest of the older woman's nose before gliding back up again to run her thumb and forefinger gently down the slope of each side. As her fingers spread out onto Andi's left cheek, CJ rested her palm gently against the warm skin, pausing for a moment before sliding her palm lightly down until Andi's chin rested in her hand. Once at her chin, CJ reversed the position then dragged the back of her hand gently up Andi's left cheek. Enjoying the feel of the woman's soft skin against her knuckles, she caressed her cheek slowly several times before gliding back down to her chin.

Using her thumb, she traced small arches back and forth across Andi's chin. On one of the passes, she grazed her friend's lip and Andi couldn't prevent a sharp intake of breath. CJ hesitated for a moment, then continued her exploration. Alternating between her thumb and forefinger, she traced her fingers across Andi's soft, full lips. Andi parted them slightly as

CJ moved across their silky surface.

Andi felt her body heat rising at the touch. Her heart thumped loudly and rapidly in her chest, while her breathing accelerated to keep pace with her growing excitement. *What have I invited?* she asked herself. Her willpower and self-control teetered on the brink as the intimate touch continued. Just when Andi thought she would go out of her mind with desire, CJ stopped. She touched Andi's cheek one last time, then moved her hand away, replacing it once again on Andi's arm.

"Thank you," CJ whispered. "You're in my mind's eye again, just like you were that afternoon." She sighed contentedly and pressed her hand around Andi's arm.

"My pleasure." Her heart continued to thump loudly for several minutes as the fire in her body slowly subsided.

"Night, Andi," CJ whispered. She snuggled closer to her caretaker, still holding her arm.

"Sleep well." She reached over and stroked her friend's hand for several minutes until she recognized CJ's sleep breathing begin. Sighing silently, she closed her eyes, enjoying the closeness and warmth of her sleeping companion.

As she lay with her lids closed, her own mind's eye envisioned a picture of a certain golden-haired, emerald-eyed basketball star. She smiled at the image of her beautiful friend, content in the knowledge that CJ's face would be the first thing she would see upon waking the next morning. With that thought, she slipped into a contented sleep.

Chapter
Twenty-eight

"STEP," ANDI WARNED. She paused as she reached the wide stone platform that led to the eye doctor's office. CJ walked to her right, just slightly behind her. The injured athlete's left hand was firmly wrapped around her guardian's bicep. Andi watched as her friend reached forward with her toe to gauge the distance to the step.

"Just one?" CJ asked.

"Yes, then about six feet to the door, all flat." She glanced to her right, watching CJ step hesitantly up and then pause, waiting for her guide to give her further directions. Andi moved forward slowly, leading her toward the entrance. "Here, let me get the door." She pulled the heavy glass open with her left hand, then moved her right hand to the small of CJ's back, guiding her through a doorway that was too narrow for them to pass through side by side. Once inside, Andi reached for her friend's hand and replaced it on her bicep.

Pausing at the office window, she gave the smiling assistant CJ's name, then moved slowly across the waiting room to claim two chairs for them. Just as she was about to help the younger woman to sit, the waiting room door opened and Dr. Erroll poked her head out.

"Come on in," the doctor said. She smiled and nodded a greeting to Andi, which the grad assistant returned. The middle-aged woman watched as Andi carefully led her younger charge into the room. With a wave of her hand, Dr. Erroll silently directed Andi to where she wanted CJ to sit. Andi hoped the doctor didn't pay any attention to the whispered encouragements that she offered as she guided CJ toward the seat.

"Andi, you could take that chair," Dr. Erroll directed. "I need to move around a bit where you're standing." She smiled apologetically at the tall, dark woman.

"I'll be right across the room, CJ," Andi said, bending close to her and speaking softly. She gave the hand another squeeze before releasing it and moving to her seat.

"So, CJ," Dr. Erroll said as she seated herself on a rolling chair at a small desk next to CJ, "how'd your week and a half of bed rest go?" She opened her folder and began scribbling notes. "I didn't get any messages from the receptionist that you called, so I take it there were no problems?"

"It went fine," CJ said. "I was more than a little stir crazy, but it was a hundred times better than being at the infirmary." Her face lit up with a smile, directed at her friend who she knew was sitting across the room. "Andi made sure I was horizontal nearly all the time, right, Andi?"

Andi's dark eyebrows shot up nearly to her hairline at CJ's last remark. A blush colored her face, and she desperately hoped the doctor wouldn't read too much into the comment. She managed to offer a half-quirked grin at the smiling doctor, who swiveled in her chair to look at her as she waited for the confirmation to CJ's statement.

"She was very good," Andi choked out. *Good comeback*, she chided herself silently. *That'll certainly clear the air.* She sighed deeply, glad when the doctor turned back to her patient.

"No pressure? No pain? No headaches?" the doctor asked.

"Nope. Other than this patch over my eyes, I feel pretty good."

"Well then, let's see if all that expert care helped you to heal." She shot a quick glance back at Andi, grinning at the dark flush that returned to the grad assistant's cheeks. Before turning back to her patient, she rose and dimmed the lights in the room, casting them in shadowy darkness.

CJ held her breath as she felt the doctor's fingers removing the patch. Her heart pounded so fast she could hear the rush of blood pumping in her ears and racing through her body. Her stomach clenched and churned, and her hands maintained a white-knuckle grip on the arms of the chair. *Please, oh, please*, she prayed silently.

Andi leaned forward and shifted to the end of the chair as she watched the doctor slowly remove the patch from her friend's eyes. Her heart raced in anticipation, anxiously awaiting a reaction from CJ that would indicate her vision was restored. Although the room was cool, she began to perspire as she waited nervously. She linked her hands as in prayer, pressing them together as if to squeeze out the pent-up energy for which she had no release.

"Keep your eyes closed when I take this away," the doctor directed. "I'll tell you when to open them." She lifted the eye patch from CJ's face, then put it off to the side. "Tip your head back slightly," the doctor said. "These drops will add some lubrication since you haven't opened your eyes in a while." Once finished, she placed her hand gently on the tense muscles of CJ's forearm. "Okay. I want you to open your eyes slowly. Just raise your lids a bit," she instructed. "You'll be very light sensitive after so many days with the patch even though I dimmed the lights."

CJ's eyelids fluttered perceptibly as she lifted them slowly for the first time in ten days. Their weight felt heavy to her, as if during that time she had lost control of the muscles whose job it was to shade the emerald eyes that they protected. Through the filter of her eyelashes, she slowly became aware of brightness that initially was not associated with a specific person or object. The shapes were just that, abstract, undefined matter. Her vision was blurry, as if she was looking at the world underwater. Despite the lack of clarity, she felt encouraged.

"When you're ready, you can open your eyes a little more," the doctor encouraged. "Go slowly, though," she warned, "and blink a little, to keep your eyes moist."

CJ fluttered her eyelids, each time raising them a bit more. Gradually, the nondescript shapes and fuzzy objects began to sharpen as the muscles in her eyes, so unaccustomed to functioning properly, were finally called on to do their job.

"Look up at me," the doctor said. CJ raised her head at the request. Her eyes strained to focus on the face of the doctor seated in front of her. Doctor Errol smiled.

"Wow, I can actually see you, Doc."

"The blurriness will go away in a few days. Your friend here," she said, indicating Andi by pointing her thumb over her shoulder, "did a good job of helping you heal."

CJ leaned to her left, straining her blurry vision, and willing her fuzzy eyes to focus on the woman whom she knew sat across the room. Looking around the doctor who sat in front of her, the image of her dark-haired protector slowly came into view. The picture wasn't clear, but even so, CJ knew it was Andi. An electric smile lit up her face. For the third time since walking into the office, Andi's faced reddened, betraying her emotions.

"Let me get a better look at those eyes now," the doctor said. She opened the drawer of her examining table and removed the instruments she would need to complete CJ's eye exam.

"HOW ABOUT WE celebrate with lunch, my treat?" CJ asked. She turned to look at her friend through the lenses of the dark glasses the doctor insisted that she wear, even though the sky was overcast.

"Sure. I don't have to be back to my office 'til one o'clock," Andi said. "But you don't have to treat."

"Are you kidding? After all the takeout and all the meals you cooked for me, this is the least I can do. Where do you feel like going?"

"Hmmmm." Andi frowned in thought, trying to gauge her hunger. "How about Eat-a-Pita? They always have good food."

"Yeah! I could go for a Southwestern Chicken wrap with spicy fries." She rubbed her hands together and licked her lips in anticipation.

"Are you ever not hungry?" Andi teased. She bumped her shoulder gently into CJ's, being careful not to throw her off off balance.

"Nope," she said honestly.

Andi shook her head and smiled at the blonde athlete as they walked back to her car.

THE POPULAR CAMPUS lunch spot was crowded by the time Andi and CJ arrived. As they stepped inside, Andi walked close to CJ, protective of the injured woman's tenuous balance and still-blurry vision. Spotting a table off to the left, Andi lightly touched CJ's elbow and steered her over to the spot.

"How about you save this table, and I'll go order the food?" Andi asked.

"Sure."

Andi grinned. "Still goin' for the Southwestern Chicken wrap with spicy fries?"

"You bet," she said, nodding. "My mouth's been watering for the past fifteen minutes."

"I'll be back in a few." Smiling, she headed for the counter.

Andi waited in line, noting the influx of students who walked in shortly after she and CJ arrived. Checking her watch, she concluded that the last morning classes had just finished up and students were eager to eat and relax before beginning the afternoon sessions. She turned around to check on the basketball star, smiling as she spotted her across the room. CJ faced toward her, her eyes obscured by the sunglasses, so Andi waved once. The blonde gave no indication that she saw the motion, which Andi attributed to her still-blurry vision. She sighed deeply, then shuffled forward in line.

A few minutes later, Andi made her way back toward their table, carrying a tray of food and trying not to bump into other customers in the crowded restaurant. As she neared their spot, she noticed that CJ was engaged in a lively conversation with two women seated in the empty chairs at the table. She walked up to them and placed the tray near CJ, and nodded at the women.

"Hey, Andi," CJ said. "These are two of my friends from the dorm. I'd like you to meet Marci and Ellen." She pointed to each of the women as she spoke.

"Hi," Andi said. She shook their proffered hands.

"Well, your lunch is here," Marci said. "We'll let you get to it."

"You're welcome to join us," Andi said.

"Thanks for the offer," Ellen answered, "but we're headed over to the library. I just stopped in to get a soda."

Marci piped in, "When we saw CJ, we came over to say hi. Anyway, it's great to see you around, CJ. I'm really glad that you're okay."

"Thanks," CJ said. "It's good to be back. I'll catch you gals later." The two women vacated their seats and, with a final goodbye, headed out of the restaurant.

"Here you go," Andi said. She took CJ's sandwich off the tray and placed it in front of her. "I got you a Diet Coke, too. I thought that's what you prefer."

With a grin, CJ said, "You remembered correctly. I'm starved!"

"Well there's a surprise," Andi teased

"Mmmm," CJ murmured as she chewed her food. "This is great! And it's nice to be able to eat my lunch and not have to worry about making a mess of myself because I can't see my food."

"You never made a mess of yourself," Andi chided.

"How about the vegetable fried rice? I had an impossible time keeping that rice on the fork long enough to make it to my mouth. I know I had it all over my lap."

"Oh, yeah, but that was my fault," she said sheepishly. "I should have known better than to choose rice. But I helped you eat it, didn't I?"

"That you did. How could I forget?" CJ said softly. She was close enough to Andi to notice a hint of red coloring in her cheeks. She smiled, remembering how she and the grad assistant shared one spoon and one big bowl of Ben & Jerry's ice cream.

"So," Andi began, "what are your plans for the—"

"CJ!" Coop bellowed from across the small room. Grinning broadly, the wiry basketball player strode over to where CJ and Andi sat. "Hey CJ, how the hell you doin'?" She patted the blonde athlete firmly on the shoulder a few times in greeting. "Hi, Andi," she added. Andi nodded a silent hello.

"Hi, Coop," CJ said. "Good to see you, and I mean that literally."

"So, are you incognito with those glasses there, or what?"

She smiled at her teammate. "Who'd have thought I'd ever be glad to look at your goofy face," she teased, "but I am."

"And that's supposed to be a compliment?" Coop said, feigning insult. She stood with her hands on her hips, glaring at CJ for all of five seconds before she busted out laughing. "Jeez, it's good to see you, too. I guess things went well with the doctor?"

"Yup. I'm good as new, thanks to Andi's expert care." She shot an affectionate glance at the blushing brunette across the table.

"She still has some restrictions," Andi chimed in.

"So you won't be joining us for a game of pick-up this afternoon?" Coop asked.

"Unfortunately, no, but maybe I'll wander by just to say hi to everybody."

"Great! We'll be meeting around 4:00. Maybe I'll see you later." She clapped CJ on the shoulder again in farewell. "See ya, Andi," she added as she made her way across the room.

"Your adoring public can't seem to get enough of you," Andi teased. This time CJ's face darkened from the remark.

"Yeah, right. So, how's your sandwich?"

"Pretty good. Want to try?"

"Sure, if you're sharing." She took the sandwich Andi offered, had a bite, then returned it to her blue-eyed friend. Chewing thoughtfully, she nodded slowly, then swallowed. "That is good. I'll have to get that one next time."

"Welcome back, CJ," said a sandy-haired guy who was walking past their table with a tray of food.

"Thanks, Tom," CJ said as he continued on to his way. Andi looked over at her. "He's in my sociology class," CJ explained. "So, what are your plans for the rest of the day?"

"Back to my office for a few hours, then off to the library for some work. Nothing exciting. And you?"

"I'm going to head over to my afternoon class, I think. If I get a seat up front, I can at least hear the professor even if he is a little blurry. It'll give me a chance to see if there's any other work I need to make up. Thanks to you getting notes for me, I feel like I'm in pretty good shape with most of my schoolwork. Thanks again," she added, placing her hand gently over Andi's for an extended moment before removing it to continue eating.

Andi looked down at CJ's hand before glancing up quickly to her eyes, still obscured by the sunglasses. Her whole body tingled from the warmth of the younger woman's touch. *God, I wish I could see her eyes.*

CJ continued to chatter while Andi sat listening, enjoying the liveliness of her voice. CJ had a *joie de vivre* about her that Andi both enjoyed and admired. She smiled at the attractive woman, her heart filled with a mix of warm affection and building desire. After a short time, they both finished their food.

"How about I drop you off near your class?" Andi suggested. "I have to move my car anyway. No sense wearing yourself out on your first day back."

"Sure," CJ said. She was eager to find any excuse to spend more time with Andi.

They walked out to the car, then drove the short distance across campus to the building where CJ's afternoon class was held. Andi pulled up to the front of the old, brick building in order to shorten the distance that CJ would have to walk. Putting the car in park, she shifted in her seat, turning to face the blonde athlete. CJ likewise turned.

"Thanks for the ride, and for joining me for lunch, and for ten days of the best, most healing attention I could have ever had," CJ said. Her voice, soft and sincere, reached out and touched Andi's heart. "I don't even know how to begin to thank you, Andi." She placed her hand on Andi's thigh.

"You've already thanked me about a hundred times in the last ten days, CJ," Andi said gently. "You're very welcome," she whispered. "It was my pleasure." She patted the younger woman's hand before resting hers on top of it. Searching through the dark sunglasses, she attempted to catch a glimpse of the emerald eyes behind the shades. "Want me to walk with you to the classroom?"

"Nah, I'll be okay from here." She sighed, not wanting to exit the car and walk away, ending what had become a pattern of life that was intertwined with Andi's. "So, can I call you later?"

"I'd be disappointed if you didn't," Andi said softly. She smiled and was rewarded with a beautiful smile in return.

"Well then, until soon?" CJ asked.

"Until very soon."

CJ turned forward in the seat and gripped the door handle, then turned back abruptly and threw her arms around Andi's neck. Squeezing gently, she buried her nose in the soft, ebony locks, breathing in the aroma of Andi's perfume mixed with her earthy scent. Strong arms wrapped around her in return and pulled her close for an extended moment before reluctantly releasing her. With one final glance into the pools of Andi's azure eyes, CJ exited the car and headed off to her class.

Andi sat in the car, watching her friend walk away. *You might be walking off to class, CJ,* she thought as she silently addressed the retreating figure, *but you won't be walking out of my life. Not this time around.* She shifted the car out of park and pulled out of the lot.

"KNOCK, KNOCK," CALLED a familiar voice. Andi looked up from her desk to see Martha's head poking out from around her partly open door. "Can I interrupt?"

"Always." She stood, leaving her work behind, and stepped quickly across the small office. Embracing her friend warmly, she said, "I've been thinking of you."

"Good things, I hope," Martha countered.

"But of course." She stepped back and waved her friend in. Offering Martha the chair in front of her desk, she sat on top of the desk facing her friend. Her feet dangled as she spoke. "So, how's Karen?"

"Same old. Good, but busy. How's CJ? That's what I came over for, not that I don't always love to see you," she teased.

"She's okay," Andi sighed. She briefly summed up their morning appointment.

"Bet you're relieved."

"Quite." She inhaled deeply, then exhaled slowly. "I didn't realize how tense I was the whole morning up until the visit." She rubbed her neck a bit, kneading out the knots that lingered despite the doctor's positive report. "I think I held my breath from the moment we walked into the doctor's office until she finished her exam." She shook her head slowly side to side. "I don't know what I would have done if—"

"Don't even say it," Martha interrupted. She held up a hand as if to stop the words. "Don't make yourself more tense. It's over, and it's good news. Enjoy it, okay?"

"Yeah, you're right."

"How about joining us for dinner tonight?"

"You sure? You just told me how busy Karen was."

"It was her idea. You can fill her in on everything, and we can catch up with you, too. I feel like it's been a while since we talked."

"That's my fault. I've been busy with—"

"No blame necessary. I didn't mean it that way at all, just that we missed you." She smiled and was answered by a grin from Andi.

"Sure, I'd love to have dinner with you both. What time and what can I bring?"

"Six o'clock and just your smiling self." She stood from the chair and turned to leave. "You know, if you think you want to invite CJ..."

"Not that I don't want to, but I think she probably wants to see her roommates and catch up with her friends." A hint of disappointment colored her voice. She opened her mouth as if she was about to speak, hesitated, then stopped.

"What?" Martha asked.

"I was wondering, could I ask you a favor?"

"Sure, but ask while you walk me downstairs. I have to be across campus in fifteen minutes for a meeting."

Andi smiled and grabbed her jacket from the back of her chair before following Martha out the door, closing it behind them.

"HEY, CJ, CAN you pass the chow mein?" Kim asked.

"Uh huh," she mumbled with a mouthful of food and handed the white cardboard box to her roommate. Kim nodded her thanks.

"Bet you haven't had Ming's in a while," Maria said. She dug her fork into a big plateful of food and looked over at the blonde.

"Actually, Andi ordered take-out one night," CJ said. "This is great, though. I really appreciate you girls getting this tonight."

"We're glad to have you back," Kim said and then went on to tease, "Not that it wasn't a whole lot easier to share a bathroom with just one other person."

"But the bathroom was a lot cleaner when that third person was around," Maria quickly added. She focused an exaggerated glare in Kim's direction, then smiled and winked at CJ.

"What can I say? I never claimed to be the cleanest," Kim said, "but at least I don't snore." She returned Maria's teasing glare from across the table.

"I can see that things haven't changed much in my absence," CJ said. She looked from one roommate to the other, clapping them both on the shoulders. They broke their stares to look at their friend. "It's soooo good to be home," she added sarcastically.

"Now that you're all spoiled from Andi waiting on you hand and foot," Kim mocked.

"But don't think you're going to get that kind of service

from us," Maria warned in a half-teasing, half-serious tone.

"I wouldn't dream of it," CJ said. *I only want that kind of attention from one person.* An image of a tall, dark, blue-eyed woman appeared in her mind's eye.

Kim said, "So, we wanted to have a little welcome back party for you here tomorrow night. You up for some company?" She continued chewing her dinner as she waited for a response.

"Sounds like fun," CJ said. "Who's coming?"

"The usual suspects," Kim said. "You know, some of your teammates, the softball and lacrosse gang, Sue, Jo...who am I leaving out, Maria?"

"Coach, or Jen?" CJ said. She looked at her roommates for a reply.

"Neither, but if you want—"

"No," CJ interrupted. "Just friends would be great. I'd like to ask Andi, too."

"Sure." Kim shrugged. "I figured you'd invite her, so I didn't bother to call her."

CJ said, "Thanks, you two, for arranging everything."

"No problem," Maria answered. "It'll be fun, and I'm sure you're anxious to 'see' everybody. Get it?" She elbowed CJ gently as she grinned.

"I get it," she said, groaning. She rolled her eyes at the pun.

Maria said, "If you think of anyone else you want to invite, let me know. We told everybody to come by early 'cause we didn't know if you'd be up for a late night."

"Yeah, I'm out of practice for that. I don't think I've been up past eleven in nearly two weeks."

"That's just when I'm getting rolling," Maria said. "But if you're tired, you can duck into your room and—"

"And we'll continue the party without you!" Kim exclaimed. She laughed as CJ rolled her eyes.

"You're real pals." CJ grinned and shook her head slowly as she looked back and forth between her two roommates.

"No need to thank us," Kim said. "We only want what's best for you." She smiled and batted her eyes at CJ.

"I'll try to keep that in mind," CJ said, sarcastically.

"SO, GLAD TO have the apartment all to yourself again?" Martha asked. She sank down deeper into the soft cushions and propped up her feet on the coffee table. Sipping at the steaming mug of coffee, she looked up at Andi, who sat across the small living room on the other sofa.

Andi slowly sipped her own coffee, enjoying the strong taste of the hot *café au lait*. She looked from Martha to Karen, debating about how to reply to the question. Her half-hearted smile revealed the answer.

Karen smirked. "You're pleading the fifth, I take it."

"Oh, stop with the lawyer lingo, will you," Andi said. "No, I can't say that I'm glad to see her go." She sighed. "I mean, of course I was sorry she had the eye injury that was keeping her there, but I have to admit I really enjoyed her company." She shrugged and took another sip of her coffee.

Martha blurted out, "So did you tell her you've got the hots for her?"

"Martha!" Andi said. Karen snorted in laughter, nearly spraying her mouthful of coffee across the room.

"Well? Why not?" Martha asked. "Weren't we all sitting here about two weeks ago while you lamented not kissing her back? Seems to me like you probably had several prime opportunities to tell her how you feel about her, with her sleeping in your bed and all."

"It hasn't been good timing," Andi said, defending herself from Martha's onslaught. "I was worried about her, and she had other, more important things on her mind, like wondering if she'd ever see again."

"True," Martha said. She nodded in agreement and took a swig of her coffee. "So, now that all those worries are off both of your minds, when are you going to tell her you have the hots for her?"

"You're incorrigible," Karen said, shaking her head. "And they call lawyers barracudas." She poked Martha playfully. The shorter woman sat with her arms crossed over her chest, a smug expression playfully lighting up her face.

"She just needs a little encouragement," Martha said, nodding to indicate Andi. "I'm only trying to help." She grinned at Andi, who squirmed on the sofa across the room.

"Just ignore her, Andi," Karen said. "Take your time and do what feels comfortable."

"I noticed you didn't say 'do what feels good'!" Martha chuckled.

"Maybe they're one and the same," Karen answered. She looked at her partner and raised her eyebrows. The couple grinned at each other.

"Oh, you two." Andi frowned. She shook her head slowly as a half-grin appeared on her lips. "I plan on telling her soon." She fidgeted on the cushions, staring into the light brown liquid in her mug. "I don't want to take a chance of losing her again," she added softly.

"Does this have anything to do with that favor you asked me earlier?" Martha said. A knowing grin appeared on her face.

"Kind of," Andi said sheepishly.

"Could be the perfect opportunity."

"Let's hope so," Andi sighed.

CJ RECLINED ON her bed, making a concerted effort to block out the noise from the stereo down the hall. The deep bass buzzed in her ears like the annoying hum of an insect. *So good to be back in the dorm,* she thought ironically. *I wish I were at Andi's...with Andi.* She sighed deeply and closed her eyes. *I wonder what she's doing now.* She smiled, recalling what had become a familiar routine for the two women. Looking at the blue digital numbers on the alarm clock near her bed, she linked the hour to the previous ten days' routine. *Hmmmm. She's probably just finishing up her papers, or maybe sitting on the sofa writing in her journal.* She thought back to that first night, when Andi read out loud part of her journal entry, in which she revealed her feelings. *I guess by now a phone call won't interrupt her too much.* She reached over and picked up the receiver, then dialed the number she had memorized months ago. After the fourth ring, the grad assistant's answering machine picked up. A wave of disappointment filled CJ as she waited for the announcement to finish.

"Hi, Andi," she began. "It's CJ. I just called to see how the rest of your day was. I'll be up for a little while yet, so if you're not too tired when you get in, please give me a call. Don't worry about waking me. I was just thinking about you and I'd really..." She hesitated, not quite sure if she should complete her thought. Deciding against it, she concluded her message. "Well, I guess I'll talk to you later."

She pressed the off button and put the cordless phone back on the base. Turning on her side, facing the phone, she snuggled down deeper under the blanket as she focused on the blue numbers of the clock. *Hope Andi doesn't miss her T-shirt.* She lifted the fabric to her face and inhaled deeply, enjoying Andi's earthy scent as her mind's eye filled with images of her friend.

ANDI PUSHED OPEN the door to her apartment and was greeted by an unaccustomed silence. Out of habit, she glanced over at the mattress where CJ had stayed for the previous week and a half, but was saddened to see the vacant spot. With CJ no longer there, the emptiness of her apartment mirrored that of her heart. She stepped into the room and sat on the sofa, sighing deeply.

A flashing light to her left drew her attention to the answering machine. She shifted over on the cushions and hit the play button. The first sounds of CJ's voice caused her heart to accelerate even as a smile formed on her lips. The smooth, melodic tones helped fill the void of the woman's absence.

Andi checked her watch, then headed to her bedroom, deciding to get ready for bed before returning the call. As she took a quick shower and brushed her teeth, she allowed the sweet anticipation of talking with CJ to build, filling her with both the warmth of affection and the heat of desire. Less than ten minutes later, she crawled under the covers and stretched out on the mattress that remained in the living room. She immediately missed the warm presence of her blonde bedmate, so she rolled onto her side, hugging CJ's pillow close to her body as she picked up the phone to dial.

CJ WAS JUST drifting off when the ringing phone jolted her awake. She shook her head to clear the haze of sleep from her brain, then quickly cleared her throat before lifting the receiver. "Hello?" she said, speaking softly into the phone.

"Hi, CJ. It's me," Andi said. CJ closed her eyes in sensual pleasure as the deep, rich tones washed over her. "I hope I'm not calling too late."

"No, not at all," she said hastily. "I was hoping you'd call."

"I just got in a few minutes ago. I was at Martha and Karen's for dinner. They asked about you and said to send you their regards."

"That's nice. I hope you returned the greeting."

"Yes, I did. I filled them in on your doctor's visit." Andi added quickly, "I hope you don't mind."

"No, that's fine. What'd you have for dinner?"

"Always thinking of food, huh?" Andi teased. "Some burgers on the grill with a big salad. We just hung out and talked. It was a relaxing night."

"Sounds good."

"How about you? How'd you enjoy your first day back?"

Andi listened as CJ chattered about meeting up with some of her classmates and professors, hanging out at the gym while watching her friends play a pick-up game, and finally eating dinner with her two roommates. CJ's lively vocal inflections made it easy for Andi to picture her younger friend smiling and moving her hands in animated gestures to accompany her stories. Just hearing that voice created a virtual three-dimensional image of CJ in Andi's mind. She smiled, completely content to listen to her talk as long as she wanted.

After nearly thirty minutes of conversation, most of if coming from CJ, Andi heard the younger woman stifle a yawn. Andi turned and glanced at the wall clock across the room, noting the lateness of the hour. As much as she didn't want to end their phone call, she knew CJ must be tired from her long day. She sighed and reluctantly decided to do what she knew was best for her friend. "I heard that yawn," she chided gently. "I think your long first day back has worn you out."

"Yeah." CJ tried in vain to stifle another yawn. "I'm too used to being horizontal, I guess. Being vertical for most of the day just took it out of me."

"Then I'd better let you get some rest." She wished she could simply roll over and say goodnight to CJ, *and maybe give her a hug, too*, she thought, smiling.

"Hey, I almost forgot," CJ said. "Kim and Maria are having a little party for me tomorrow night and, well, I was hoping you would come."

"You sure you're not tired of me?" Andi joked, though a bit of insecurity crept into her heart. "You haven't seen your friends in nearly two weeks, but you had to put up with me for the last ten days."

"I'd hardly call that putting up with you. I enjoyed every minute of it." She blushed at her bold admission, glad Andi couldn't see her. "So, no, I'm not at all tired of you, and I'd really love for you to come. If you want to," she added softly.

"Then I'll be there," Andi said simply. *As if I could say no to you*, she added silently.

"Great! They'll be starting early, since they know I'm out of late-night shape. You can come by anytime, though. I'll be here."

"Then I'll be seeing you tomorrow," Andi said. "So, until soon?"

"Yes, until tomorrow," CJ whispered.

Chapter
Twenty-nine

CJ AWOKE SLOWLY from her interrupted and restless sleep. Rolling over and focusing her fuzzy, green eyes on the blue digital numbers near the bed, she noted the early hour before closing her eyes with the hopes of reclaiming more sleep. *At least I can still see,* she thought, comparing her immeasurable gain of vision to the annoying loss of sleep. Less than five hours ago she was nearly bounced out of bed by the blasting stereo down the hall, and it was only with much concentration as well as a pillow over her head that she had been able to fall asleep again.

She sighed, wishing for the hundredth time that she were at Andi's apartment with the dark, lean woman who made her heart race. Last night's phone call helped to ease her separation anxiety, and she was glad Andi's voice was the last one she heard before finally falling asleep. The purloined T-shirt she slept in, however, had been a poor substitute for the woman she would have rather had wrapped around her body. *You better get a grip on that wishful thinking,* she warned herself.

Raising the soft cotton material to her face, she breathed deeply and inhaled the scent that was uniquely Andi's. It held a mix of *CK One,* her favorite perfume, as well as an outdoor, earthy scent that immediately helped conjure Andi's image in CJ's mind. She smiled as she remembered past nights waking up next to Andi, curling up against her, or draping an arm across her as they slept. *She never pulled away. Maybe she liked it, too. But she's got to make the first move this time. I already put my heart out there once. Why should I do it again and risk getting rejected?*

Because you want her, that's why! her honest alter ego said. *Admit it, you want to hold her and touch her and kiss her and—*

Okay, okay. I confess. I do want all that. I just need to be sure that she does, too, this time. If I wait for her, then I'll know for sure. I can wait. I can be patient.

Ha! So patient that you planted a kiss on her when she wasn't expecting it and scared her away?

All right, all right. I learned my lesson from that one. I've been good, haven't I? And now that I can see again, it'll be easier. I was lost before when I couldn't look at her face or read her eyes, but now I'll know better how she feels. I won't be so in the dark.

Ugh! Now who's using the corny puns? You better get back to sleep. Your brain obviously needs more rest.

She breathed in deeply, then exhaled slowly, making a concerted effort to relax her body and shut out the warring voices in her head. She replaced the internal noise with a picture in her mind's eye, that of Andi's face framed by the pastel backdrop of sunset. The last images she saw before she drifted back to sleep were the blue pools of Andi's eyes.

FOOTSTEPS APPROACHING FROM down the hall quickly drew Andi's half-hearted attention away from the papers she was correcting. As the noise grew closer, she envisioned a certain attractive basketball star striding into her office with an electric smile that could light up the room. Her heartbeat accelerated, and she found herself shifting to the end of her chair, ready to pounce out of it to welcome her friend. *With what, a hug?* she asked herself. *Are we at that point where we hug each other hello and goodbye?* She smiled at the image. *I'd like that*, she acknowledged to herself, nodding her head slightly. She snapped out of her daydream as the footsteps echoed just outside her partly open door, then gradually became softer as the person continued down the corridor.

Disappointment painted Andi's face as she dropped the pen on her desk and slumped back in her chair, forgoing even the slightest attempt to feign interest in her work. She sighed deeply and remained immobile for another minute or two before finally harnessing enough motivation to get back to work.

Admit it, you miss her like crazy. Her eyes widened and two dark eyebrows arched high onto her forehead as the truthful reality of that confession sunk in.

It's true. I can't deny it. I don't want to deny it. I just hope I didn't blow my opportunity.

You had ten days of having her all to yourself, her alter ego countered. *What the heck were you waiting for?*

The timing wasn't right. She had other things on her mind.

And so did you, some of the time. Sensual things. Erotic things…

Okay, okay. But only some of the time. The rest of the time I was worried about her vision —

And also worried maybe she changed her mind about you. That maybe, now that she's out of your apartment, she'll realize she doesn't miss you so much after all. Maybe she'll just go back to her life before you dissed her. You're still worried about that, aren't you?

Andi attempted to ignore the battling thoughts in her head. She worried that perhaps her unbidden deliberations were more on target about her deepest fears than she was willing to admit. She rubbed her eyes and pinched the bridge of her nose as she tried to regain control of her thoughts again.

Soon, she sighed, ending the battle. *I'll talk to her soon.*

"KNOCK, KNOCK," CJ said. She stuck her head around the partly open door.

"Come in," said Leslie Malardie, the women's head basketball coach. She swiveled her chair around to face the blonde, then stood, extending her hand. "So it's true," she smiled. "I ran into Coop yesterday afternoon and she told me the good news."

"Yeah, Coop's not one to keep secrets," CJ said with a grin. "Not that this is a secret," she added. "It's good to be back."

"I'm really happy for you, CJ." Coach Malardie returned to her seat, motioning for CJ to take the chair across from her desk. "I've had to deal with a lot of players' injuries over the years, but nothing like that before." She shook her head slowly. "The possible repercussions were so much worse than the typical broken bone or torn ACL. I'm really glad you're okay." She looked up at CJ with sincere brown eyes.

"Thanks, Coach." She could see that the auburn-haired woman was genuinely relieved. CJ not only liked her coach but also had great respect for her. In the seven years since she first signed on as head coach, the woman in her mid-forties had taken a down-and-out team and turned them into a conference powerhouse. Leslie Malardie had an uncanny eye for seeing her players' potential as well as for helping them achieve that potential. CJ never regretted her decision to forgo a shot at a Division I school for the sake of playing for Coach Malardie.

Coach checked her watch. "So, do you have a few minutes to talk, or do you have to run to class now?"

"No, I'm free for the rest of the afternoon. You said that you wanted to talk to me the other day."

"Yes, I do." Her tone became more serious as she shifted forward to rest her elbows on the desk. She steepled her fingers as she spoke. "You'll be graduating soon," she began. "Have you decided what you'll do after that?"

"Grad school, I hope," CJ said. "But I kind of put it out of my mind for the last few weeks, you know? First there was the tournament, and I really needed to focus on that, and then, well, my whole eye thing." She paused and looked at her coach, who nodded in silent understanding. "I had one really good offer for a school out west. Tuition, housing, stipend..." She paused as she was reminded of her impending deadlines for committing to that school. *To think I was this close to packing up and leaving here two weeks ago, just to run away, from Andi. And now all I want to do is run back to her,* she mused. She shook her head to dislodge the daydream, then looked up at her coach, whose concerned expression confirmed that she had in fact noticed CJ had zoned out. "So, to finally get around to answering your question, I haven't made any final decisions."

"Well, I hate to add complications to what is obviously a big decision for you, but," she paused, looking directly at CJ, "I was wondering if you'd consider staying here."

"Staying?"

"Yes, as in doing your graduate work here."

"But I wanted to go to school where I could coach, too."

"Ah, but that's where I come in," Coach Malardie replied, smiling.

YOU CAN'T WALK in with flowers, Andi reprimanded herself. She looked at the small bouquet, now soaking in a vase on her kitchen sink, that she had picked up along with a six-pack after work. *It's a party, not a date, you know. Everybody else will walk through the door and hand her a six-pack, and you want to hand her flowers? Jeez, why don't you just wear a sign that says 'I love CJ'?* She stopped dead in her tracks as the words echoed in her mind. Her eyes grew wide and her mouth gaped as the silent thought registered in her brain. Reaching for the counter, she leaned against it for support as a tremor rippled through her body. *Love? Do I...? Could I...?* She blew out an audible breath of air and tried to rein in her senses. *How did that happen?*

It just sneaked up on you. She knocked down all your defenses with one look into those emerald eyes and then it was all over for you. Huh! she laughed at herself. *And you think you're so tough.*

She closed her eyes and pinched the bridge of her nose with her fingers, concentrating. Although her initial reaction to the revelation was certainly shock mixed with fear, the more she thought about it, the more she warmed up to the idea. *Love? Love.* She rolled the word around in her mouth, sampling its flavor and finding she enjoyed it. In fact, if she was honest with herself, it felt really nice. Her heart thumped deeply as a picture of her heart's desire appeared in her mind. She smiled, nervously at first as if the image could read her thoughts and sense her fear, then more confidently as her eagerness grew. *Love! But I'll just keep it to myself for now*, she mused. A smile lit up her face. She picked up the beer and walked across campus toward CJ's dorm.

"HEY, JOANNE!" CJ called. She stepped across the crowded living room to greet her friend.

"Hiya, CJ," Joanne said. She smiled broadly, then handed the basketball star some wine coolers. "I'm glad we've got something to celebrate here tonight. You feeling okay?" she asked loudly, projecting her voice above the conversation and music that filled the small room.

"Still a little light sensitive," CJ said. "That's why the lights are dimmed."

"Ah." Joanne nodded, smirking. "And I thought you were just trying to create a little ambiance."

"It's either this or wear sunglasses inside, so dimming the lights seemed like a better idea."

"Whatever works."

"Want one of these?" CJ asked, referring to the wine coolers.

"Sure," Joanne accepted one from the pack and unscrewed the cap.

"Can you put the rest of these in the fridge for me? I think I hear the door." CJ handed the bottles back to Joanne and reached over for the doorknob. Pulling open the door, she greeted the small group of friends who were waiting to gain entrance. "Hey, Sara, Jude, LaShawna, Becky!" She smiled at each woman and returned hugs from all her teammates. "I'm so glad you gals could come."

"Last time, we saw you, but you didn't see us," Becky jested, "so we wanted to even things out."

"We didn't want to deprive you of the view," joked LaShawna. She struck a pose in front of CJ, then dissolved into laughter with the rest of the women.

"Go!" CJ said, pointing to the kitchen. "I can tell you all need a beer." She smiled at her friends as they headed across the crowded room. She turned back to shut the door and nearly closed it on Andi, who stood motionless and silent at the threshold.

"Change your mind?" Andi teased. "I could go back

home..." She pretended to turn around.

"No you don't!" She grabbed Andi's hand and pulled her into the living room before hugging her warmly. "I've been waiting for you," she said into Andi's neck. *All my life,* she added silently. "Don't be doing a disappearing act on me," she scolded. A flicker of insecurity crossed her heart, so she squeezed Andi tighter, extending the hug.

"You don't have to worry about that, CJ," Andi whispered. Her lips brushed up against the silky flaxen tresses as she spoke softly into CJ's ear. She felt the younger woman tremble at the contact.

"I—" CJ began, "I really need to talk—"

"There you are!" Coop hollered. She stepped up to the two women, who quickly broke off their hug. "I found the guest of honor," Coop added. She wrapped her arm around CJ's shoulder and offered a big grin to her teammate. "Courtney was just saying how she hasn't even seen you yet." She reached over and grabbed the assistant softball coach by the arm, pulling her toward CJ. "See, Courtney," Coop continued, "I told you I could find her."

"Hi, CJ," Courtney said. "Sorry I didn't get over to see you after the accident. We had two-a-days for softball, and I was working on a project for my psych class."

"Don't worry about it," CJ said. "I had other guests and lots of good company." She turned to Andi and smiled, noting the blush that colored her skin.

"I'll go put this beer in the fridge," Andi said softly. "You catch up with your friends here." She tore her eyes from CJ and nodded her greeting to Courtney and Coop before heading toward the kitchen.

CJ's FRIENDS DRIFTED in and out of the dorm throughout the evening. The small living space was filled with women who had come not only to celebrate the basketball star's restored vision, but also to kick back and unwind as the spring semester drew to a close. CJ was constantly surrounded by well-wishers and acquaintances eager to laugh with the personable woman and enjoy her company. Andi was glad to find that she recognized several of the women there, including her friend Sue, the lacrosse grad assistant whom she had not seen since their night out at the Oasis many weeks prior.

Although both CJ and Andi appeared to be preoccupied throughout the evening with their respective conversations, each visually sought out the other across the crowded room. Emerald eyes danced when they scanned the room and found Andi returning the attention. Azure eyes relaxed and smiled when they searched the crowded room and locked on CJ, who reciprocated the gaze. The fleeting glimpses were accompanied by shy smiles and coy grins, a continuation of the nonverbal expressions that ached to be spoken.

As the evening wore on, Andi looked around but could not find CJ amongst the sea of friends. She stood on her toes, adding two inches to her six-foot frame, but still could not locate her. Before she had time to wonder anymore about where she was, CJ slipped up behind her. Placing her hands on Andi's slim hips, she leaned against Andi's back and whispered in her ear. "Can I monopolize your attention for a few minutes?" Andi's ebony locks brushed up against her face as she inhaled the other woman's aroma.

"Of course," Andi said. CJ's warm breath tickled her ear, and the heat of the younger athlete's body caused her own body to tingle. She turned to face the woman who made her heart race and found herself mere inches away from CJ's attractive face. She silently cursed the dimmed lights that made it difficult for her to see CJ's verdant eyes. Arching one dark eyebrow in silent question, she invited her companion to speak.

"It's too noisy here, though. Come on," she added, taking Andi's hand. "Follow me."

After a quick stop in her room to retrieve their jackets, she and Andi slipped out undetected and headed for the fire escape stairs. Andi followed silently, curious about where CJ was leading, but willing to follow her without question. CJ mounted the steps two at a time, with Andi at her heels, until the two women emerged on the roof of the dorm. The basketball player pushed the door open, then looked back over her shoulder at her companion, who stood right behind her.

"It's quiet out here," CJ said in answer to Andi's questioning glance. She walked silently across the tarred roof with the dark-haired woman at her side, stopping when she reached the waist-high cement wall that rimmed the rooftop. She leaned her palms on the flat surface and looked out across campus. Andi stood so close that their shoulders brushed up against each other.

Some of the buildings on campus were lit up, their windows glowing like jack-o-lanterns on an autumn night. Small clusters of students walked across the gravel paths along the green. The crunching of their footfalls and the sound of their laughter drifted up to the rooftop as their silent observers stood watch. Stars glittered in the heavens, adding to the soft glow of the moon, whose light was obscured by a cloudbank drifting through the inky, indigo sky.

For long moments the two women stood motionless as sentinels of the night. Finally, Andi turned to face CJ, leaning her side against the low wall. She wanted to reach out and touch CJ, run her fingers through her companion's golden hair, lean against her—anything to establish a physical connection. Instead, she waited to hear what CJ had brought her up to the rooftop to say, burying her hands deeper into her pockets and away from the nearly irresistible temptation before her. She continued to gaze at CJ, raising an eyebrow in silent question. Feeling the weight of Andi's stare, CJ returned the eye contact. Once again Andi regretted the dimness of the moonlight, which obscured the beautiful emerald eyes from her scrutiny.

"I spoke with Coach this afternoon," CJ began.

"Oh?" Andi stood straighter, her complete attention focused on the woman before her. Her heartbeat raced as quickly as her mind. She anxiously wondered if her fears about Jen's threats had come to fruition.

"I kind of wanted to talk to you about—"

"Does this have anything to do with Jen?" Andi interrupted.

"Kind of, I guess," CJ said. She looked quizzically at her friend, curious about Andi's sudden change in posture and body language.

"Crap," Andi fumed. She turned her head away from CJ and raked her fingers through her hair as an outward gesture of her inner turmoil. "You should have heard it from me first," Andi began. "I should have spoken to you when Jen first—"

"Andi, what are you talking about?" CJ moved to stand directly in front of Andi. Placing her hands on Andi's broad shoulders, she forced the other woman to return her gaze. "Did you know that Coach was going to offer me an assistant coaching position because Jen's leaving?"

"What?" Andi exclaimed. "Coach offered you a position? Jen's leaving?" She stood straight, no longer leaning against the wall for support. Her hands had popped out of her pockets, and her mouth was agape. She feared that CJ would hear the rapid thumping of her racing heart.

"Yes to both questions," CJ said. She removed her hands from Andi's shoulders but kept her eyes locked on the blue ones before her. "If you're so surprised to hear that, then what is it that you think I should have heard from you first?" She tilted her head and arched honey-brown eyebrows, her face open and questioning.

Andi released the breath she had been holding, silently wishing she'd had enough sense to keep her mouth shut. Instead, she found herself with two seconds to reply and nothing to say to the woman before her.

"Never mind?" Andi offered weakly. "Just forget I said anything. It's just a little misunderstanding." She looked away from CJ, embarrassed and unable to maintain eye contact.

"Oh, no you don't," CJ snapped. "You've dodged your last question. Just say it." She stood with her hands on her hips, eyebrows pinched together in annoyance, with an expression Andi had rarely seen on her striking face.

"But, CJ—"

"No buts!" CJ interrupted. She held up both hands to forestall further talk, then rubbed her fingers across her temples, clamping her eyes shut to think. She then opened angry emerald eyes and glared at Andi. "After all this time, after everything, you still don't feel comfortable talking to me?" Her voice rose to a higher register, the hurt clearly coloring her words. When Andi didn't immediately reply, CJ turned as if to go.

"Wait!" Andi cried. She reached out and grabbed CJ's arm, preventing her from moving further. CJ's head dropped as she looked down at her feet, waiting to hear what Andi had to say. "I do feel comfortable talking to you, CJ," Andi spoke softly. "Please believe that," she whispered. "It's just...I don't know. It's a long story and—"

"Just start with the *Reader's Digest* version, then," CJ requested. She still had not looked up from her feet as she stood in front of Andi.

Andi's heart was saddened at the thought that she was the cause of the hurt her friend was feeling. Andi wanted to reach out and hug CJ and tell her how much she meant to her. Instead, she continued holding her arm, although her grip lessened to one of mere physical contact, a connection Andi really needed at the moment.

"A while ago," Andi began, "when I started going to your games and we were hanging out together, Jen kind of...threatened me."

"What?" CJ's head snapped up, and she looked directly at Andi. "What'd she say to you?"

"That fraternizing with students isn't allowed. And..." Andi paused.

"And what?"

"And my grad assistant position could be in jeopardy." She looked deeply into CJ's eyes, then turned away sadly. As much as she hated having to tell her young friend about Jen's threat, she found she was greatly relieved at finally being open. She sighed at feeling unburdened.

"That bitch!" CJ fumed. Her eyes were squinted in anger and her cheeks flushed with heat. She tore her eyes away from Andi's face and looked out across campus, balling her fists as she stood.

"I didn't say anything to you because I thought she was all talk," Andi continued. She looked up at CJ's profile as the angry younger woman continued to stare into the night. The muscles in her jaw jumped as she clenched her teeth in an attempt to clamp down on her anger. "And she was your coach, too. I didn't think it was right to say negative things about her to you, especially during the season." Her voice got softer as she continued. "Besides, she was just trying to hurt me."

"Hurt you?" CJ asked. She focused her gaze once again on Andi, the anger boiling just beneath the surface of her control. "Why?"

"About a year ago, she expressed interest in...wanting to get involved." She dropped her eyes from CJ's scrutiny. "I really wasn't interested, so I kind of ignored her come-ons. Once she started getting more direct with me, I had to be more direct with her. She took it very personally." She looked up again at CJ, who hadn't shifted her gaze. "I didn't want to hurt her feelings. But I know when it feels right." She paused, looking deeply into CJ's emerald eyes, "And it didn't feel right with her." She arched her dark eyebrows, asking a silent forgiveness. Looking once more at her feet, she kicked an invisible stone with her toe. Meekly, she looked up again at her younger friend. "I'm sorry, CJ. Can you understand how it wasn't easy for me to tell you all that, and why I didn't bring it up sooner?"

CJ sighed audibly and looked back over Andi's shoulder to the lights across campus. Her friend's words had penetrated her heart, and she tried to make some order out of her mixed feelings. She was bitterly angry with Jen for being so conniving and spiteful, and she found herself balling up her fists again in reaction to that feeling. Then she thought of Andi's obvious unease at having to tell her about the assistant coach whom Andi knew she liked. *Used to like*, she amended silently.

"I didn't want you to get hurt," Andi said, her voice half-pleading. CJ's silence left her uncomfortable and she desperately wanted to make things right between them again. "Nor did I want to be the one to cause you that hurt," she added.

"I appreciate that, but you can't always protect me," CJ said. She turned to face Andi again. "All you can do is speak honestly, and then be there for me after."

"I can do that," Andi said softly.

"You already have, many times over," CJ quietly responded. She exhaled slowly and released her fists, letting the mounting tightness in her shoulders slip away. The tension between her and Andi during the past few minutes made her uncomfortable, and she was anxious to resolve the issue and get past it. She stepped closer to Andi and reached out, placing her hand on Andi's forearm. She hoped that reestablishing the physical connection would bridge the emotional one as well.

"I'm really sorry, CJ," Andi whispered. Her eyes filled up, then glistened with tears that threatened to fall.

"Listen, if we're going to get—" CJ broke off suddenly before the presumptuous statement crossed her lips. A quick glance up at her dark-haired friend left her unsure whether or not her companion had filled in the incomplete sentence. She continued before Andi had a chance to think too much about her implication. "I really need for you to be open with me, okay?" She squeezed Andi's arm and was answered with a nod of the dark head. "Do you trust me enough to do that?"

"Yes," Andi said. Her voice was soft yet filled with conviction. As she heard herself utter the single-word reply, she knew in her heart that she believed it, totally and completely. She smiled shyly at CJ, hoping her answer would touch the athlete's heart and eradicate the last remaining tension between them.

CJ simply nodded an acknowledgment at Andi's sincere response. Somehow she understood the depth and significance of the blue-eyed woman's reply, and her heartbeat increased. She sighed deeply, relieved to have overcome that emotional challenge and still feel connected to the woman of her heart.

"So, are we okay?" Andi asked. She placed her hand over CJ's as it rested on her forearm.

"Yeah, we're okay." She grinned at Andi as her heart filled with warmth for the attractive woman.

"So, since we're out here where it's quiet, I was wondering if—"

"Here she is!" Coop shouted. The wiry basketball player came bouncing over with her other teammates in tow. "Becky was right. She was stargazing." She approached CJ and Andi, grinning, then tilted her head back to look up into the heavens. The other team members struck a similar pose.

"Yeah, we were just stargazing," CJ fibbed. She looked at Andi and winked quickly. She indicated the tall woman by her side with a thumb gesture in her direction. "Andi bet me that I couldn't name ten constellations."

"Oooohhhh! Bad bet," Jude said. She shook her head slowly from side to side. "CJ knows all the star patterns by heart."

Andi said, "I'm beginning to learn that CJ knows a lot more

than she lets on." She arched a single dark eyebrow and smirked at her friend.

"So what'd you lose?" Coop asked, addressing the grad assistant.

My heart, Andi thought to herself. She smiled. "I believe I owe CJ dinner," she said aloud to Coop's question. She looked over at CJ and grinned.

"That's not too bad," Coop said. "At least you'll get a dinner out of it yourself."

Andi nodded in acknowledgment.

"Jeez, I'm cold out here," Jude complained.

"Me, too," Becky added. "I didn't bring my jacket."

"I'm going to head back in." Jude nodded in CJ's direction. "Aren't you cold?"

"Just a little," CJ said. "You go on in. We'll be there in a minute."

Andi teased, "Yeah, CJ still needs to identify a few more constellations before she earns herself that dinner." She waggled her eyebrows up and down as she looked at her emerald-eyed friend.

"Okay. We'll see you downstairs," Coop said. She rubbed her arms briskly to warm herself as she walked quickly across the roof. Her teammates followed, and all of them disappeared behind the fire door. Once again, the two women were alone on the darkened rooftop, surrounded by the soft sounds of the night.

"You were about to say something before," CJ said, "right when Coop and the others came out. What was it?" She tilted her blonde head and smiled softly, waiting for Andi to reply.

"I was just wondering if you had any plans this weekend." She looked down at her feet, then back up at CJ. "Do you?"

"Just laundry and school work. Why do you ask?"

"Well, I was just wondering..." Andi paused, dropping her eyes once more from CJ's expectant gaze. She took a deep breath and looked back up at her emerald eyes. "I was hoping you might spend the weekend with me."

"With you?" CJ smiled broadly. "What do you mean, with you? Doing what?"

"I'd rather it be a surprise," Andi answered. "It involves a little road trip, though."

"A road trip! To where?" She wrung her hands excitedly and stepped up closer to Andi.

"If I told you that, it wouldn't be a surprise," Andi teased. "I can get you back early on Sunday, if that'll help." She was willing to make any compromise necessary, just as long as CJ agreed to go.

"Hmmmm," CJ said. "I'm intrigued by the mystery." She stroked her chin as she continued to grin at Andi.

"So?"

"Of course! I'd love to go."

"Great!"

"What should I bring?"

"Just an overnight bag and casual clothes. Can you meet me at my place around 3:00 on Friday?"

"Sure, I'll be done with classes by then."

"Good. We'll leave that afternoon." She smiled at CJ, her heart glowing at the prospect of spending the weekend together.

"No hints?"

"Nope," Andi said. She crossed her arms over her chest and grinned. She lingered over CJ's dancing eyes, enjoying the strengthened emotional connection she felt between them. Several minutes passed in silence as they got lost in the intense eye contact.

CJ sighed. "So, I guess we better head back inside before they come looking for us again." She began to step across the rooftop when a hand on her shoulder stopped her in her tracks.

"Not so fast, stargaz," Andi said. She turned and leaned against the cement wall, facing her younger friend. "If you expect dinner, you'd better show me the secrets of that inky sky."

CJ smiled. She stepped back to her side and, placing a hand on Andi's shoulder, tilted her head upward, and began to point out the patterns in the heavens.

Chapter
Thirty

THE TREES LINING the one-lane dirt road obscured what little daylight was left as Andi drove the car slowly over the washboard surface. Similar dirt roads cut off to the left and the right as they rolled forward, and CJ could make out cabins through the canopy of trees. Driveways were marked discreetly with small signs attached to tree trunks. Andi's Jetta traveled slowly down the bumpy lane, kicking up dust in its wake, then turned right into a driveway with a wooden sign, "M & K's Place," tacked on the large white birch at the foot of path.

Halfway down the long dirt driveway, the tree-darkness gave way to the brightness of an evening sunset as the small, lake-front cabin came into view. Through the partly open car windows, CJ smelled the fragrance of pine and balsam needles mixed with the scent of the lake water. She breathed in deeply, filling her lungs with the wonderful aromas.

Andi pulled the car near the house, then slipped it into park. She turned in her seat to face CJ. "We're here."

"It's beautiful!" CJ said. She bestowed a full smile upon Andi.

"You should see the front of the cabin," Andi said, rolling her dark eyebrows upward. "That's where the real view is. Come on." She winked at CJ, then opened the car door, stretching as she exited the vehicle. She waited for the basketball player to walk around to her side before she headed toward the front of the house. "We'll bring the stuff in this door." She pointed, indicating the door in the back near where they parked. "I'll show you the view first, though."

They rounded the pine needle path leading out to the front of the cabin and the lake. The dark wooden building was a mere one story high, but because it was built on land slightly elevated from the water, the view was panoramic. A screened porch offered protection from seasonal bugs while the small deck adjoining it provided an unobstructed view of the wide lake. Twenty wooden steps led down to the dock, which reached out over the water. The sun was just ducking behind the mountains that rose up and guarded the far side of the lake. The sky was painted red, orange, pink, and purple in its wake. Both women paused on the deck, enveloped in silence, to enjoy the view.

"Is that what I think it is?" CJ asked. She pointed to a covered Jacuzzi in the far corner of the deck.

"It is. If Martha filled it last weekend, perhaps we'll get a chance to use it. Interested?" Her dark eyebrows rose in invitation.

"Definitely!" CJ grinned. "Can we walk down to the dock?" She touched Andi's arm and moved off the deck toward the steps leading down to the lake.

"Sure. I need to turn on the hot water heater first, though. Otherwise, you'll be taking a cold shower." She smiled at CJ and nodded, indicating the steps. "You head down. I'll catch up with you in a minute."

CJ turned and walked down the wooden steps leading toward the dock. As she descended, the colorful sunset filled her vision. The pastel sky was iridescent overhead and was equally glowing in the mirrored surface of the still water. The verdant band of trees on the mountains across the way was the only sign of green in the otherwise dazzling scene before her. As she stepped out onto the dock, the vibrations from her footsteps sent small ripples out into the water, blurring the multicolored reflection. To her left, the shore of the lake curved about a hundred feet from the dock, which blocked her view of the neighboring house and dock. To her right, the shoreline stretched out as far as she could see.

The cackle of a loon echoing across the lake drew her attention to a black and white diving bird as it ducked under the water, then surfaced several yards away. Its cacophonous noise was answered by another loon, possibly its mate, which was not too far from it. Their boisterous calls rolled across the water, which amplified the sound. CJ stood on the dock and smiled at their diving antics.

A chill rose off the water as the evening sun nearly disappeared behind the tall mountains. CJ shivered and goose bumps rose on her skin. She crossed her arms over her chest and vigorously rubbed her arms through the long sleeve T-shirt, hoping to create enough friction to warm her chilled skin.

So distracted was she by the view, the birds, and the cool evening air, that she didn't hear Andi approach.

Andi silently moved up right behind CJ, not wanting to disturb her younger friend's obvious enjoyment of the view. "Cold?" she whispered. She spoke softly, placing her mouth very near CJ's ear.

CJ felt the warm breath as Andi spoke. She shivered again, but this time from Andi's closeness. Leaning back slightly, she felt her companion's body a hair's breadth away.

"Good thing I turned on the hot water heater," Andi said, purring into CJ's ear. She placed her hands lightly on the basketball player's hips before leaning gently against her.

CJ felt dizzy from the sensation. The warmth against her back caused by Andi's closeness was in sharp contrast to the coolness of her face and chest caused by the night air blowing off the lake. Through the light cotton of her T-shirt, she felt the press of Andi's breasts against her back as well as the heat of Andi's skin so near her own. She inhaled sharply at the contact, the previous chill quickly replaced by rising heat coursing through her body. Impulsively, she grasped Andi's hands in her own and drew them around her stomach, effectively wrapping herself in the arms of the woman behind her. She left her hands over Andi's and relaxed into the embrace, stepping back slightly and leaning her body fully against Andi, who responded by resting her chin on CJ's shoulder. The two women remained silent as they looked out across the lake, watching the dazzling sunset unfold before them.

"What are you thinking?" Andi whispered softly.

That my heart might explode if it beats any faster, CJ thought to herself. *That I want to turn around and face you in this embrace, and look into your eyes to know what you are thinking.*

Instead, CJ said, "The sunset reminds me of that evening after we went sledding, when we stood on your porch at the end of the day." *When I wanted so badly to kiss you,* she added silently. "Remember, I described that picture of you that I carried in my mind? The one I envisioned when I couldn't really see you? That's what this sunset reminds me of. Only in that image, the sunset was behind you."

"Then if you turn around, I'll have the same view of you as you had of me that night," Andi said, "with the spectacular sunset behind your face." Andi loosened her arms enough to allow CJ to turn and face her. Slowly, she moved around, her heart racing. Andi's hands dropped gently to her hips as she turned, keeping her a short arm's length away. CJ's golden hair shone against the backdrop of sunset pastels. The beauty of the evening sky and the radiance of the mirrored water paled in comparison to the face before her. The glow of the sky illuminated Andi's view enough to reveal CJ's emerald eyes lightly flecked with gold.

Andi gazed into her face, her eyes lighting on each eye in

turn. With attentive care, she studied the patterns of kaleidoscope colors that blended to form the most striking eyes she had ever seen. Her mouth opened slightly, as if poised to speak, but no words were uttered as she gazed at CJ's open face. Her face flushed as the blood coursed through her body, and desire rose in her heart.

CJ couldn't tear herself away from Andi's azure eyes. She felt the weight of their attention as they focused solely on her. The light touch of Andi's hands on her hips served to maintain her connection to the dark-haired woman as well as to tease her with physical contact. She feared that the sound of her rapidly beating heart would betray her feelings. The heat of passion rose in her body, and she locked her eyes on Andi's to stay grounded in the blueness before her.

"And what are *you* thinking?" CJ whispered. Her hands rested lightly on Andi's forearms. Andi first responded to her question with a smile that lit up her eyes. CJ gazed deeply into crystal eyes whose azure hues reflected the dazzling purples of the setting sun. She tilted her head and arched a honey-brown eyebrow, inviting further explanation for the smile.

"I'm just enjoying the view," Andi said. Ignoring the sky, the mountains, and the lake, she kept her eyes locked on CJ's. "For far too long I've missed this," she whispered. "It's so wonderful to look into your eyes again."

Her words brought a smile to CJ's face. "What do you see there?" CJ asked softly.

"The green earth coming back to life after a New England winter. The iron will of a determined heart. The passion of a soul not afraid to experience life's fullness. The kindness of a woman who tempers strength with gentleness."

"Your words are poetry," CJ whispered, smiling. Reaching up, she stroked Andi's soft cheek before gliding her hand down and resting it on Andi's upper chest near her companion's heart. "Your heart's racing."

"It's beating for you. It has been for some time now." Andi smiled and spoke silently to the emerald eyes looking back. *May I?* The blue eyes pleaded wordlessly, accompanied by arched eyebrows and a tilt of her head. Andi's body leaned forward slightly, her mouth parted as she waited for a sign.

CJ's eyes twinkled, not blinking for fear of breaking the almost palpable connection. A slight, nearly imperceptible nod of her head conveyed CJ's response before she leaned forward, pressing her hand more firmly against Andi's heart.

Their bodies moved together with their lips a mere breath away. They moved slowly, but not out of fear. Finally sure of each other and the moment, they had no need to rush. With one more gaze into one another's eyes, they slowly lowered their lids to replace the contact of their eyes with that of their lips.

CJ's body was electrified by their first soft kiss as Andi's moist, full lips tentatively touched her own. Her body tingled with the promise of anticipation finally being realized, yet the sensation surpassed even her wildest dreams. CJ wanted to laugh, sing, jump, and wave her arms, celebrating her long-held desire finally coming true. Instead, she channeled all those feelings and emotions into the kiss, hoping that the object of her desire would feel it, too.

Andi's body nearly vibrated from the touch of CJ's warm, soft lips pressed gently against her own. The world faded away around her as the spotlight of her attention focused solely on the woman she didn't ever want to stop kissing.

Softly, gently, they came together and lingered, as one would savor the first taste of a much-desired meal. Light lip-touches, like small samples of food, introduced them to the first taste of shared pleasure. Their lips met, embraced, then parted briefly before they reconnected to taste each other again and again. Each soft meeting whetted their appetites for further feasting as their kisses lingered and lengthened. After waiting so long for this moment finally to arrive, neither was willing to rush through their banquet of delicate kisses. After several minutes of delighting in gentle, sensual kisses, they paused for a moment to digest their newly shared passion. Their bodies remained pressed together with foreheads lightly touching. Racing hearts and rapid, shallow breathing were outward signs of their mutual ardor.

Andi was first to break the silence. "I've been wanting to do that for a long time." Her forehead continued to rest against CJ's. Her eyes remained hidden as she focused all her senses on the woman before her.

"What took you so long?" CJ chided playfully. Her smirk went unnoticed by Andi, whose eyes were still closed.

"I was afraid," Andi said shyly.

"Of me?" She moved her forehead away from Andi's, then lifted the other woman's chin, inviting her to make eye contact once again. A flutter of long, dark eyelashes preceded the emergence of the blue eyes.

"No, not of you," Andi reassured. She smiled kindly and touched CJ's cheek.

"Of what, then?"

In the past, this type of direct, personal, emotional question would have made the reticent woman dodge the inquiry or retreat into silence; however, the openness and honesty that she saw on CJ's face deserved nothing less in return. "At first, I guess I was afraid of Jen's threat." She shrugged as if to downplay her anxiety.

"Still?"

"No. I realized she's all talk. She's just bitter."

"Is there more?"

"I used to be worried I'd lose my position for getting involved with a student, but..."

"But what?"

"Technically, you're not my student. They might frown on what's between us, but I don't think they could dismiss me. Besides, you'll graduate in a few weeks, and it would be easy to be discreet until then."

"Anything else?"

Andi's eyes dropped to look at her feet as she nodded slowly. *Might as well just say it. You've come this far.* She looked up to meet CJ's eyes, which were gently inviting her to continue.

"I thought I blew it. After that night when you went running out... Well, I thought that after that, you might have changed you mind about me." She spoke the last word in a mere whisper then paused before speaking again. "I was afraid of falling..." She tilted her head slightly, arching her eyebrows in a gesture that begged for understanding and gentleness for her vulnerable heart.

"Was? As in, past tense?"

"Mostly."

"If I promise to catch you if you fall, will you trust me enough to let go?" CJ whispered softly.

Andi's heart skipped when she heard the impassioned plea. Her lips parted as if poised to speak, but rather than use them for that purpose, she leaned in again and answered CJ's question with a passionate kiss. Her hands moved up to cup CJ's cheeks, drawing the other woman's mouth firmly to her own.

A soft moan rose from CJ's throat as Andi deepened their kiss. Her right hand remained against Andi's heart while her left hand tangled itself in her soft, dark tresses. Their bodies pressed against each other once more as their kisses continued. Another soft sound erupted from CJ as she parted her lips, inviting Andi to further intimacy.

Andi's tongue responded to the invitation by licking lightly against CJ's lower lip, which was warm and moist under her touch. Hesitantly at first, she moved her tongue across the surface of CJ's lip before pulling back again to kiss her deeply. When CJ responded in kind, once again parting her lips in invitation, Andi obliged by trailing her tongue slowly across CJ's upper lip. Her ministration elicited a soft moan from her partner, which further inspired her passion. Drawing her own tongue back, Andi opened her kiss to CJ and was answered by an exploring tongue.

Their warm, wet tongues continued a dance that their bodies envied. Delving deeper into each other's mouths, they intimately explored with lips and tongues. With racing hearts, they surrendered to the feelings that each woman had unsuccessfully tried to control. Their hooded eyes no longer noticed the deepening colors of the sunset, and the cool night breeze no longer chilled their skin. Instead, soft moans filled their ears as their bodies heated further by their rising passion. After several moments of reveling in passionate kisses, their lips parted, their mouths breathless. Blue eyes gazed deeply into green eyes as their rapidly beating hearts pounded in unison.

"Wow," CJ whispered.

"Wow, indeed." Andi leaned forward to press her forehead against her companion's. Reaching down to CJ's waist, she wrapped her arms around the muscular athlete, enveloping her in a warm embrace. CJ responded by wrapping her arms around Andi's neck and holding the taller woman firmly against her own body.

"I could stay like this all night," CJ sighed.

"Mmmm, but then we'd both be frozen in the morning." She pulled back slightly to kiss CJ's forehead. "How about we build a fire in the fireplace instead?" As if on cue, CJ's stomach growled loudly. "I think I'd better feed you, too," Andi added grinning. Taking CJ's hand, she led her off the dock and back up the stairs to the cabin. "Let's unload the car and make dinner. I'll start a fire."

"You already did," CJ smirked. She squeezed Andi's hand more tightly and followed her up the steps.

"I'M IMPRESSED." CJ grinned. "You keep telling me that you don't know how to cook, but that soup was fantastic!" She stood at the sink with dishcloth in hand, drying the bowls Andi was washing.

"I have to confess, Karen coached me," Andi said. She added more soap to the sponge, then rubbed aggressively inside the pot. "Not only did she write down the recipe, she also talked me through all the steps for assembling it. I'm definitely not a creative cook, but at least I can follow directions." She rinsed the pot and placed it in the rack to drip.

"Well, thanks for going through all that trouble." She smiled, touched that her companion had planned such a wonderful get-away. She looked around the small cabin, which was warm from their cooking as well as from the fire in the hearth. Andi had presented her with a bouquet of coral roses, then set the dinner table using them as a center piece. CJ lifted up the pot from the rack and dried it, still smiling as she daydreamed about their kisses on the dock.

"That's the last of it." Andi grinned mischievously, arching a dark eyebrow as she looked at CJ and continued to splash her hands in the soapy water.

"I don't like the looks of that," CJ protested. She held up her hands in front of her face. "Whatever it is, don't."

"Okay," Andi teased. "But you don't even know what I was thinking..."

"Well then, what were you thinking?" CJ said, going along with the tease.

"I was just going to splash you with water as an excuse to touch you." Andi shrugged. She took her hands out of the water and dried them on the towel.

"You don't need an excuse." She stepped closer and poked Andi playfully in the stomach.

"Come here, then," Andi said. With a quick twist of her wrists, she rolled the dishtowel and gently looped it over CJ's head and around the back of her neck. With slow deliberation, Andi tugged gently on both ends of the towel, drawing her companion nearer. All the while, her twinkling gaze never moved from the emerald eyes before her. When CJ's body was pressed up against her own, she leaned in and placed a slow, lingering kiss on CJ's slightly parted lips.

"Andi, you definitely don't need an excuse for that."

"Thanks, I'll keep that in mind," Andi said, grinning at her blushing friend. "Come on," she added, nodding her head toward the living room, "let's go sit in front of the fire."

MORE THAN AN hour had passed since they finished dinner and stretched out on the couch in front of the fireplace. Andi had added several seasoned logs to the flames, including some pieces of apple wood, which smelled pleasantly smoky and sweet. The fire was blazing with the logs glowing brightly, bathing the room and the women sitting near it in golden light. Their cheeks were pink from its warmth.

"So, have you thought more about Coach Malardie's offer?" Andi asked. They sat facing each other, leaning back against the padded arms of the small sofa. Andi's long legs, bent slightly at the knees, stretched out along the inner cushions and pressed up against CJ, who rested her forearm on Andi's knees, lightly stoking her thumb against the muscular quads.

"I still can hardly believe it," CJ said. Her legs were extended on the outside of Andi's body and held securely from sliding off by Andi's powerful arm, which was wrapped around CJ's calves. "I can't believe she offered the assistant coach's position to me."

"And why not!"

"There are a lot of talented people out there. I've never even coached before."

"Hey, don't sell yourself short." She squeezed CJ's leg for emphasis. "You're a student of the game, and those type of players make good coaches. Combine that with your people skills, and you're a winner! I think you'd be perfect for the position. Question is, will you accept?" She asked that with trepidation, desperate to know the answer, but afraid of how she'd feel if CJ decided to decline the coach's offer.

"Well," CJ began, using her fingers to count off her points, "first, I'd get to work on my Masters and not have to pay for it. I know the professors in the history department, and I think I'd enjoy continuing to take classes from them. Second, I'd get to coach, which I always wanted to try. And I really like Coach Malardie. We worked well together when I played for her, so I think it'll be okay being her assistant. Our philosophies are the same, you know?" She paused while Andi nodded her understanding. "Third, I know a lot of the returning players, and I'm really comfortable on this campus, so that level of familiarity feels good, too. Fourth, well, there's something else that makes me want to stick around."

"Oh? What's that?"

"More like, 'who's that.'" She paused and pointed at Andi. "You."

"Me?"

"Surprised?"

"Flattered," Andi said, smiling. "But those other reasons you listed, those things are important to you, aren't they? Because as much as I want you to stay—"

"You want me to stay?"

"Of course. Now more than ever." She leaned forward and caressed CJ's cheek. "But those other factors have to be a good fit for you, otherwise you won't be happy here."

"But they're all a good fit. Don't you think? Based on all those reasons I listed?"

"Yes, I do. But I can't pretend to be completely objective," she added, grinning. "I can't ignore my own reasons for wanting you to stay."

"And what might those reasons be?" CJ said playfully.

"The adventure of us," Andi said with twinkling eyes.

"Sounds intriguing."

"I was hoping you might think so." She winked and smiled at her companion, who returned the grin.

They sat in companionable silence, listening to the roaring fire and the crackling wood. The sofa was comfortable, and CJ felt totally relaxed by the warmth of the blaze as well as by Andi's physical nearness. She smiled, wiggling down deeper into the cushions as her eyelids grew heavy. After a few moments, she stretched and yawned, reaching out to the sides with her arms.

"Sorry," she said, quickly covering her mouth. "This fire is just so relaxing."

"That's okay. We can call it a night."

"I don't want to move from in front of the fire, though." She wrapped her arms around Andi's leg and leaned against her muscular quad.

"The good news is that you won't have to. This is a pull-out sofa bed. Quite comfy, I might add. I often sleep out here when I visit Martha and Karen. Why don't you take the first shower, and I'll set up the bed?"

"I could help," CJ offered. She slid her legs over the side of the sofa and stood slowly, stretching again as she rose.

"Nah, it'll only take me a minute. You go on, but leave me some hot water!"

CJ grinned over her shoulder as she walked toward the bathroom. She emerged ten minutes later to find the bed made and the sheets turned down in invitation. Candles of various shapes and sizes were placed around the room, adding their soft glow to that of the blazing fire. She stood in the center of the room and turned slowly, looking at the candles as well as the flowers, which had been moved from the kitchen table to the mantle above the fireplace. A shiver of anticipation rose in her body.

"How was your shower?" Andi asked. She emerged from the kitchen and walked over to CJ. Slipping up behind her, she gently kneaded the muscles in her neck and shoulders.

"Mmmm. Great. I left you some hot water, too." She smiled and turned, looking into her companion's blue eyes.

Andi pointed to the bed near the fire. "Climb in. I'll be out in a few." She turned toward the bathroom, then abruptly spun around and kissed CJ soundly on the lips before turning on her heel once more. By the time CJ had opened her eyes, the bathroom door was closing. Her body shivered involuntarily as she climbed into the bed and burrowed under the comforter to wait for Andi's return.

Moments later, CJ's attention was drawn away from the fire as her sexy companion stepped out of the bathroom wearing a large, white T-shirt that hung mid-way down her long thighs, revealing bare legs that appeared to go on forever. CJ swallowed hard as she stared unashamed at Andi's thigh muscles as they flexed when she walked toward the bed. CJ's beating heart pounded in her ears.

"Is there room in there for me?" Andi stood at the side of the bed, head tilted with one dark eyebrow arched.

"Perhaps a little," CJ teased. She pulled back the covers to allow Andi to climb in.

Andi slipped beneath the comforter and snuggled up next to CJ. For the first time since they had shared sleeping space, her bare skin touched CJ's similarly naked legs. The skin-on-skin contact sent tingles throughout her body, causing her to quiver.

"You're cold," CJ said.

"I guess I'm still a bit damp from the shower."

"Come here, then. I'll warm you up."

CJ rolled on her side to face her bedmate. Although there were no lights on in the room, the firelight cast enough brightness for her to see Andi's face clearly, and her pupils had grown larger while the blue of her eyes darkened to that of the sky in early evening. The glowing firelight twinkled in the blue irises, creating the effect of starlight in an evening sky. Only the desire for more physical contact caused her to look away from Andi's captivating eyes. CJ closed her own eyes and slowly wrapped her arms around the lean woman, eager to continue what they had begun earlier on the dock.

As Andi was pulled into the embrace, she buried her face against CJ's neck. The silky, flaxen tresses tickled her as she snuggled in closer. She lingered there for a moment, reacquainting herself with the perfume that was CJ's essence. Breathing in deeply, her body tingled and she felt drunk on the aroma. The fair-haired woman's scent was a woody, herbal combination that reminded Andi of an autumn day in the forest. She inhaled again, filling herself inside and out with the woman enfolded in her embrace.

Lying beside CJ, with the younger woman's arms wrapped securely around her, Andi was reminded of the final few nights in her apartment when she had slept beside her blonde friend.

The feel of the athletic body beside her flooded her again with a renewed wave of desire. Andi's cheek rested against CJ's skin, and she felt the pulse point in CJ's neck begin to beat faster, revealing that she, too, was enjoying the embrace. Turning her head slightly, Andi placed her lips gently on the beating pulse. Feeling CJ's heart beating against her lips only served to heighten her desire. She kissed the rapidly beating skin softly, then again, before gently nipping the tender skin beneath her mouth. A moan escaped CJ's lips and she tilted her head back, offering her neck to Andi.

"You like that," Andi said. Her words were more a whispered statement than a question. CJ responded with another guttural moan. "Mmmm," Andi said. "Me, too." She continued to kiss and nip her way up CJ's soft neck, following her beating pulse until she reached her jaw. As Andi raised her cheek up and gently rubbed it against CJ's, she whispered very softly into the ear that was so near her mouth. "I love the way you smell," she murmured. Her statement elicited another moan from CJ. Andi's breathy whisper released warm air against CJ's ear, causing the other woman to shiver. The tip of Andi's tongue flicked out against the warm earlobe, drawing forth a whimper from the object of her attention. She licked the soft lobe again, then sucked it into her warm mouth, triggering a muttered cry from CJ.

"You like that, too," Andi said softly. Her breathy voice tingled against the moist lobe near her mouth. CJ's rapid breathing was audible. "Tell me what else you like," she whispered.

"Your lips. Kissing my lips," CJ gasped between breaths. She turned her head to meet Andi's mouth. Wrapping her arms around Andi's neck, CJ drew her closer, searing her lips with kisses. Warm, wet lips pressed together again and again while tongues continued to reacquaint themselves. Playful bites intermingled with deep passionate kisses.

CJ's hands rubbed up and around Andi's broad back, alternating between flat hand and fingertip touches. Andi's long fingers tangled and teased their way through CJ's blonde locks, occasionally lowering to the younger woman's neck to draw her even closer for another deep kiss. Their roving hands continued to explore even as Andi pulled back slightly and broke off the kiss. Her breath was jagged and her molten eyes locked on CJ's as the firelight danced in the emerald eyes.

Andi felt herself being swept up in an avalanche of emotion that quickly neutralized her self-control. Her passion, having been dormant for so long, erupted through her veins, coursed through her body, and heightened her senses. She knew the power of that passion and didn't want CJ to be frightened by her arousal if she wasn't ready for taking that next step. Looking deeply into CJ's eyes, she searched the other woman's soul for a sign.

CJ attempted to catch her breath as she saw Andi's face hovering right above her. She watched as Andi drew air through open, moist lips made even deeper red from their passionate kisses. As she looked at those lips, she wanted desperately to pull Andi's face back down to her and continue to lavish attention on her moist, inviting lips; however, she hesitated, shifting her gaze upward to light on Andi's eyes.

Andi's irises were darkened with passion, and CJ felt them boring into her soul, exposing her heart completely. Andi looked at her with longing and desire, with a promise of unsurpassed passion that CJ had never felt before, and she quivered with anticipation. Then CJ saw the blueness change slightly, revealing a softening, almost questioning plea. Two dark eyebrows rose slowly as she tilted her head slightly. The combination of passion and reverence that mixed within the blueness stirred CJ's heart. She smiled, finally understanding.

"Yes," CJ whispered.

Andi closed her eyes briefly as a smile lit up her face. Slowly, she lowered her mouth once more to capture CJ's lips in a slow, passionate kiss.

CJ slipped her hands down to the hem of Andi's T-shirt and sneaked them beneath the thin material, lifting it up to expose her broad back as she drew it up toward the dark head. Andi shifted her body to allow CJ to disrobe her. After the shirt was tossed carelessly to the floor beside the bed, Andi similarly took off CJ's sleep shirt, dropping it over the side of the bed to join the other one.

They embraced, for the first time completely naked together. Hands rubbed against backs and feet rubbed against calves while their tongues and lips continued exploring. Andi delighted in CJ's firm, well-developed muscles. Her toes traced the outline of heart-shaped calves, tight and strong from sprints up and down the hardwood. Her hand stroked down CJ's side, slipping sensuously across her hip before sliding around to stroke her firm, round glutes. CJ reciprocated by stroking Andi's lean, flat stomach before inching up and brushing fingertips across her ribs. Andi momentarily tensed from the tickle spot before relaxing once again under her gentle hand.

Emboldened by CJ's soft moans, Andi skimmed her hand across the outside of CJ's abs before gliding up slowly to her ribs. As she stroked the firm skin beneath her hand, she softly touched the side of CJ's breast with her thumb. A sharp intake of breath followed by a soft murmur betrayed CJ's pleasure.

"I love touching your body," Andi said in a deep, throaty whisper into CJ's ear. "The first time I saw you on the court, sprinting and jumping, I couldn't take my eyes off you. And now, finally to touch your body... Do you know what it does to me?"

"What?" CJ gasped. She could barely focus on the verbal response because her body was going mad with the desire brought on by Andi's caresses.

"It turns me on. *You* turn me on." She nipped once again at the base of CJ's neck before returning her attention to the blonde woman's waiting lips.

Andi kissed her way from CJ's lips and across her chin before dragging her tongue slowly down the side of her neck, stopping to nip at the soft skin beneath her lips. As she traced her tongue over CJ's collar bone, her hand slid up to cup the younger woman's small, firm breast. The touch elicited a whimper from CJ, who threw back her head, further exposing her body to Andi's gentle caresses. As Andi slowly stroked circular motions around the small swell, CJ's breathing quickened and she panted. Emboldened by the response, Andi softly dragged her thumb over the nipple, which instantly grew hard from her touch. A louder moan emanated from CJ as she arched into Andi's hand. Using thumb and forefinger, Andi rolled and teased the pink nipple as it pebbled beneath her touch.

"I love the way your body responds to my touch," Andi said breathily in CJ's ear. She returned her mouth to meet CJ's, devouring her lips with passionate hunger.

CJ's body brimmed with desire that was slowly pushing her over the brink of control. With strength driven by ardor for the woman lying next to her, she wrapped her arms around Andi and rolled her over, pulling the lean body on top of her own. The weight and press of Andi's skin all over her was electric. Her fingers danced over the broad back while her mouth delivered fervent kisses to the woman lying on top of her. A soft moan escaped CJ's lips. "God, you feel so good," CJ panted. Bending one knee slightly, she pressed it between Andi's straddling legs.

This time it was Andi whose desire expressed itself with a moan as CJ's thigh pressed against her hot center. Swollen with arousal, the pressure of CJ's muscular leg against her nearly sent her over. She bucked her hips against CJ's thigh as if finally scratching an itch that she had been trying to ignore. She moaned again as she climbed higher.

The feel of Andi's hot wetness on her leg made CJ throb. Sliding her hands down Andi's back, she pressed them against Andi's glutes and pulled the firm cheeks harder toward her in an attempt to satisfy her peaking desire. Andi responded by pressing her thigh more firmly against CJ's core. The younger woman could feel her wetness gliding on Andi's toned thigh.

The two lovers rocked their hips in unison, creating a rhythm of passion that spiraled them higher. Whimpers escaped and their lips parted momentarily as both ached for release.

Sensing CJ's need, Andi moved her hand between their slick bodies, which glistened with desire. Pressing through the damp, blonde curls, she slid her fingers over CJ's swollen clit. The moment she touched that bundle of nerves, the young athlete cried out, pressing her hips toward Andi's hand.

"Ohhhh," Andi moaned in response. "So wet..."

"For you," CJ gasped. She continued to buck against Andi's long fingers, trying to hasten her new lover's slow and deliberate pace.

Andi hastened to stroke in rhythm with CJ's grinding hips. She felt CJ growing harder from the stimulating touch while at the same time the muscular body quivered and tensed as CJ neared the edge. Sensing the impending climax, Andi accelerated the stroking, her hand now coated with CJ's wetness. Faster and faster the younger woman's body drove against Andi, her breath coming in rapid, panting gasps. Just as Andi thought CJ was going to peak, the other woman stopped.

"Together," she panted. She slid her hand down and grasped Andi's wrist, then looked deeply into the blue eyes hovering above her own. "I want. To come. Together." The words spilled off her tongue in gasping breaths as she fought her body's urge to give in to the desire she barely had strength to contain much longer. A look of understanding passed between them before CJ released Andi's wrist and threaded her fingers through dark, curly hair made equally wet from Andi's mirrored desire.

When CJ's fingers found the engorged clit, Andi cried out and leaned heavily against CJ's body. Her hips once again resumed the rhythm of passion. Their whimpers echoed as their hands sought out intimate pleasures escalating them higher and higher until they could no longer hover at passion's peak. Powerful orgasms rocked them simultaneously as each woman's body jolted and quaked from the powerful aftershocks. They lay in each other's arms, fingers still pressed against the other's sex, as their bodies shuddered their mutual release.

They remained that way for several minutes, too spent to move and lacking the desire to separate from one another. Gradually, their racing hearts and rapid breathing subsided while their bodies, glowing with dampness, began to cool. They withdrew their hands, but remained locked in an embrace that neither wanted to release.

Andi's face was buried in the hollow at the base of CJ's neck where she breathed in the younger woman's heady scent. "You're incredible," she murmured into CJ's ear. She followed the pronouncement with soft kisses on her cheek.

"It was you," CJ said. She lifted Andi's hand to her lips and kissed it softly.

"I guess it was us —"

"Together," CJ added.

"Yes, us together. An excellent idea." She lowered her lips once more and sealed her words with a kiss before rolling off CJ's body and onto the mattress.

The crackling fire once again became the loudest noise in the small cabin. Its warming heat felt sensually pleasant against their glowing skin as both women lay naked and prone before the blazing hearth. Neither wanted to relinquish physical contact so their bodies still pressed against each other, fingers intertwined, as they lay side by side, completely sated. The blanket, kicked off in the heat of passion, was mounded in a heap at the foot of the bed.

CJ sighed softly before rolling on her side to face Andi. She reached down to pull up the comforter, then snuggled against her lover. She tucked her head against Andi's broad shoulder, tossed her leg possessively over Andi's thigh, and rested her hand gently on the bare skin over Andi's heart.

Andi stroked the flaxen hair, weaving her long fingers through its silkiness. Occasionally her hand drifted down to CJ's back, lightly touching the athlete's soft skin. She felt CJ's warm breath against her neck as the breathing became deep and regular. After a few moments, she looked down at CJ's face. The tranquility of sleep had returned to her features and her lips parted slightly as she breathed. The sight reminded Andi of those nights in her apartment when she watched her friend fall asleep, wishing so desperately that she could be right where she had since ended up. Without disturbing the sleeping woman, she leaned over and kissed CJ's forehead. Andi fell asleep with a contented smile on her lips.

Chapter
Thirty-one

CJ'S EYELIDS FLUTTERED several times before opening. She hummed softly as she stretched her arms and legs, which were still wrapped possessively around Andi's body. The steady, rhythmic beating of Andi's heart beneath her hand nearly soothed her back to sleep again. She yawned, rousing herself from the most pleasant rest she ever had. Tipping her head back, she focused sleepy eyes on her lover's face.

"Hey," CJ smiled.

"Hey, yourself." Andi grinned and wove her fingers through golden tresses before stroking lightly up and down CJ's back.

"Did I wake you?" CJ asked.

"Nah. I've been up for about a half hour."

"Just lying here?"

"Just watching you." Her statement earned her a hug from CJ, who buried her face against Andi's neck. The warm breath tickled Andi's skin. After an extended moment, she pulled her head back enough to see Andi. A smile decorated CJ's face.

"What are you smiling about?" Andi asked.

"You. Me. Last night." She arched her honey-brown eyebrows up and down, still grinning at Andi, whose arms remained wrapped around her. "I woke up during the night, and at first I was confused because I thought it was all a dream, but—"

"You've had those kind of dreams about me?" Andi interrupted.

"I'll never tell," CJ whispered coyly. She stretched up and kissed Andi softly on the lips. "So I'm smiling because I'm glad it wasn't a dream."

"Me, too." She tightened her arms around CJ, drawing her closer for a hug. "Your skin is chilled." She vigorously rubbed her hands over CJ's exposed shoulders, creating friction to warm her.

"That's 'cause I seemed to have lost my T-shirt last night," CJ teased.

"You didn't seem to be too cold last night, though," Andi teased back.

"The fire was roaring and—"

"And?"

"A certain someone made sure I was pretty hot, even without my T-shirt."

"It was my pleasure, I assure you."

"And very mutual," CJ said.

They shared several soft, sensual kisses before CJ's stomach announced her hunger.

"I guess you're hungry," Andi noted. She rubbed CJ's belly as she grinned.

"You stimulated my appetite," CJ said seductively.

"But didn't I leave you satisfied?"

"Very much so, but—"

"But?"

"It was so sweet, you left me wanting more." She pressed her lips softly against Andi's, deepening the kiss until her stomach roared again.

"I think it's time to feed the beast," Andi said. "I brought muffins from the bakery in town. Interested?" A pair of dark eyebrows arched in question.

"I think I could be tempted. Although I'm quite comfortable right where I am." She grinned and nibbled her way up Andi's neck to her chin. Almost immediately her stomach growled again, turning her provocative smile into an embarrassed grimace. "What time is it?"

"Nearly eleven," Andi said. She reached out to stretch, cat-like, before draping her long arms around CJ again.

"I haven't slept this late in...I can't even remember when. Of course, I never had such good reason to before." She reached up and kissed Andi again before her stomach erupted with more gurgling. "Okay, okay," CJ quipped, addressing her demanding stomach. "I'll feed you already." She turned to face Andi before continuing. "I guess I'll be taking you up on the muffin offer after all."

"Good. I have some ideas for the day, so we can head out after we eat."

"Plans? Like what?" CJ asked, excited and intrigued.

"You'll just have to wait and see."

"You're just full of surprises, aren't you?"

A single ebony eyebrow arched in response as a smirk crossed Andi's lips.

"THE TOWN HASN'T changed much since the last time I was here," CJ said. She strolled next to Andi, occasionally brushing shoulders with the taller woman as they meandered through the streets of the quaint New England town. As much as she wanted to hold Andi's hand as they walked, she knew that type of public affection would turn a few heads, and she didn't want to do anything that would make her companion uncomfortable. To avoid the temptation to clasp Andi's hand, CJ dug her own hands into the pockets of her faded blue jeans, replacing the yearned-for physical contact with eye contact instead.

"When was the last time you were here in Woodstock?" Andi asked.

"Four years ago. I came during freshman year with some of the girls on the team. For some reason, Coach canceled a Saturday practice, so we drove out here to do some Christmas shopping."

"It's pretty here around the holidays."

"Yeah, it really was. There were a few inches of snow on the ground, and all the shops had wreaths and holly around the windows. By late afternoon, when the sun was going down, they turned on the holiday lights, and the whole town looked like one of those miniature scenes that you'd set up under the Christmas tree."

"Hmmmm. You're right, it does look like that."

"After we shopped, we had dinner at the Inn down the road. It's a really nice place and we lucked out with the early-bird dinner special, 'cause none of us had much money. The food was great, but the best part was afterward. We didn't feel like going back to our dorms, so we sat in the lobby of that big, fancy hotel, in their comfortable chairs in front of a huge, roaring fire and just hung out and talked for hours. We acted like we knew what we were doing, so people probably thought we were staying at the Inn. Nobody said anything to us." She giggled at the recollection.

"Sounds like a fun day," Andi said. She grinned, secretly pleased with her decision to end their day together with dinner in that very same Inn.

"It was the second best time I've ever had in this town," CJ said.

"Second best?"

"It became second best compared to today," CJ said softly. She bumped her shoulder against Andi's as they walked, then favored her companion with a dazzling smile. "Thanks so much for bringing me here. I'm having a great time."

"Me, too." She smiled warmly at CJ as they strolled along in silence. After half a block, Andi paused in front of an artisan's shop. Placing her hand gently on CJ's forearm, she halted the basketball player with a request. "Do you mind if we go in here? My mom's birthday is next month, and she likes these glass sun catchers that they sell."

"Not at all," CJ said. "It looks like an interesting place."

"It is. They have handmade things by local craftspeople and artisans, some of it very unusual." She held the door open and allowed CJ to enter before her, smiling as their bodies brushed together in the narrow threshold. "The sun catchers are in the back," Andi said. "Why don't you look around, and I'll find you back here in a few." She smiled at CJ, who nodded her assent.

CJ wandered around the small shop looking at the beautiful, handcrafted items. A solid cherrywood jewelry box with an intricate inlay pattern caught her attention, so she walked over to the counter to inspect it further. The wooden surface was polished smooth, highlighting the pink-brown tones of the unusual grain. She lifted the lid slowly, only to discover that the box itself was only part of the treasure. Inside, pens were displayed, each one unique in design and shape. Some of the bodies were made of wood, others metal, and a few were enameled in deep, rich colors. The latter caught her eye. Carefully, she lifted up a sea-green enameled pen, whose primary color was flecked with darker crystals of emerald and gold. The pen felt heavy in her hand, yet as she moved it into writing position, the balance and weight were perfect. Borrowing a pad of paper that was obviously left on the counter for just that purpose, she began to write Andi's name. "Find something you like?" Andi asked. She stepped up beside CJ and placed her hand on the small of her lover's back.

Warm breath tickled her companion's ear as Andi spoke, and CJ found herself shuddering involuntarily at the contact. She could barely refocus her thoughts to answer the whispered question. Finally finding her voice, she responded. "I've never seen a pen like this before." CJ turned and placed it in Andi's hand for her inspection.

Andi turned it over, then held it up to look at. "Yes, it's very unusual. Heavy, too."

"But it feels perfect to write with," CJ added. She blushed as Andi glanced down at the paper and noticed her name written there in CJ's neat script. "And I love the color," she continued. "It reminds me of—"

"Your eyes." Andi held the pen up and looked back and forth between it and CJ's eyes. She smiled at the match.

"Can I help you ladies?" a man's voice interrupted. Both women turned toward the deep voice. "That's an excellent choice," he added, indicating the pen.

"Yes, it is," Andi said. "I'll take it."

"Andi—"

"Consider it an early graduation present," Andi offered softly. She turned back to the man behind the counter and addressed him. "Do you have a box for it?"

"I'll bring one out for you," he said before walking into the back room to retrieve it.

Once he was out of earshot, CJ spoke again. "But you don't have to buy me anything, Andi." She rested her hand gently on Andi's arm. "This weekend is wonderful enough. You don't have to do anything else."

"But I want to," Andi said. "Let me get it for you?" Her azure eyes softened as two dark eyebrows arched up to reflect her request.

The sweet look and soft voice were more than CJ could resist. She sighed softly and smiled, nodding her head in assent. "It's beautiful," CJ said. "I love it."

"I'm glad. Besides, every grad assistant needs to have a special pen. You can use it to take notes in class or when you're scouting recruits." She smiled and winked at CJ just as the salesman emerged from the back room with the box. Taking both the pen and Andi's credit card, he completed the purchase. Within minutes, the two women were back on the sidewalk, strolling toward the next interesting shop.

"Thanks again," CJ said softly. She wrapped her arm around Andi's shoulders and gently squeezed her close. "I'll give you a proper thank you when we get back to the cabin." She winked at Andi, then released her from the sideways embrace.

"I'll look forward to it," Andi said, grinning. She paused, looking down at her watch. "We better get going so we're not late for dinner."

"But the car's this way," CJ said. Her honey-brown eyebrows crinkled in confusion as she pointed in the opposite direction from where they were headed.

"I know, but the Inn is this way. We have dinner reservations in fifteen minutes." She grinned devilishly at CJ, enjoying the younger woman's reaction to her surprise.

"The Inn? But how—"

"Coincidence, really. But it worked out perfectly, don't you think?"

"You're amazing." She shook her head slowly, locking eyes with Andi. Impulsively, she threw her arms around the taller woman's neck and pulled her in for a hug. Andi warmly returned the embrace before walking toward the Inn with her arm linked through CJ's.

"LOOKS LIKE THERE'LL be another beautiful sunset tonight," CJ said. She glanced over at Andi, who drove the Jetta slowly down the dirt road toward the cabin.

Andi looked away from the road long enough to make eye contact with her companion. She smiled. "Perfect for an evening paddle," she said.

"Paddle?"

"Yes, as in canoe. Can you canoe?" Andi laughed at herself. "Say that ten times fast."

CJ smiled at the tongue twister. "I'm better in the front of the boat, where I don't have to steer," CJ answered. "I haven't been out in one in a while."

"I'll take the back, then. We'll paddle up the lake, and I'll show you some spectacular sights. This is the most still time of the day, as far as wind goes. The water will be like glass, and the paddling should be easy. The colorful sunset will be a bonus."

"Sounds good to me."

They brought their things into the house before emerging once again and walking to the dock. Andi carried the paddles and life jackets. After retrieving the upside-down canoe from the sawhorses near the dock, they carried it to the water's edge and set it down. Andi placed their equipment inside the boat then steadied it against the edge of the dock while CJ climbed in. Once she was seated, CJ returned the favor as Andi settled into her seat. The basketball player turned around to bestow a full smile on Andi before she pushed away from the dock and began to paddle.

The watercraft glided over the lake, leaving behind tiny ripples in its wake. Their paddles, stroking virtually in unison on opposite sides of the boat, made soft splashes as the wood broke the surface of the water. Although initially cool from the evening air temperatures, they quickly warmed up from their moderate paddling effort and the canoe floated smoothly.

Once further away from the shoreline and the trees, the sky opened up and the women were surrounded by the brightness of another stunning sunset. Yellows, oranges, and reds painted the heavens and reflected onto the water's surface, giving the impression that the canoe and its two passengers were floating across the sky.

When they were out near the middle of the lake, Andi called

softly to CJ. "Stop paddling for a minute," Andi requested. She lifted her paddle and rested it in the bottom of the canoe. CJ twisted around in her seat to watch Andi, then followed suit with her own paddle. The canoe rocked for a moment while they got resettled, then the small boat became as motionless as the women in it. Mirroring the sky above, the yellow-orange water outside the boat was completely smooth.

The smell of the lake water mingling with a hint of pine wafted to CJ's nose, and she inhaled deeply. She closed her eyes and smiled, finding herself completely at peace. In her mind, the only thing that could have improved the moment was if she had been facing Andi, or better yet, sitting next to the blue-eyed woman, yet she knew that was impossible in the precariously balanced canoe. She breathed in deeply again and conjured up a picture in her mind's eye of the attractive, dark-haired woman.

Andi's voice interrupted her reverie. "What do you think?"

"Perfect," CJ said softly, thinking of her mental picture as well as the scenery. "It's so peaceful out here, and the sunset is simply amazing."

"Yes, it is. It's a perfect night for a paddle. Thanks for coming with me."

"You don't have to thank me. I'm enjoying it, too."

A splash on the side of their boat drew their attention, and a black-headed loon pushed through the water's surface. Emerging with red eyes wide open, alert to the women and boat before him, he let loose with a yodel that startled both paddlers. After his short outburst, he dove back under the water, leaving circling ripples behind in his wake.

"I've never seen a loon up close," CJ said.

"Their markings are so striking. Last year a family of loons lived near the cabin, and every evening, right after dinnertime, they swam by the dock. Martha, Karen, and I would take the lawn chairs down to the water's edge and wait for them to go by. They had two little babies that were so cute. Sometimes the babies would ride on the parents' backs."

"Do you come here often with Martha and Karen?"

"As Martha puts it, I have an open invitation to come up any time, with or without them. I have to admit that I really like it here. Not that campus is crazy-busy like a city, but it's nice to get away from people and deadlines and stress."

"You're lucky. This is a great retreat."

"You're lucky, too. I'm allowed to bring a guest." She arched an eyebrow and grinned at CJ, who had turned in her seat to smile at Andi. "So, are you about ready to unwind in that hot tub?"

CJ smirked. "Silly question."

"Let's head back." They retrieved their paddles and began stroking. Andi steered from the back of the canoe, directing their path back toward the dock just as the sun dipped below the hills across the lake.

THE TWO WOMEN stretched out shoulder to shoulder in the hot tub, reveling in the heat of the bubbling water and the awareness of their mutual nakedness. With heads tilted back, they gazed up at the stars, basking in the glow of the moon as it peaked above the mountains across the lake. Andi slipped an arm around CJ's shoulders, pulling her closer.

"This has been another perfect day," CJ said. She closed her eyes and breathed deeply against Andi's skin, inhaling a heady mixture of woods, spices, and outdoors. "Our walk through town, my beautiful pen—did I mention how much I love it?" She opened her emerald eyes and focused on Andi's face once again.

"Only twenty-five or so times," Andi said. She smiled down at the woman in her arms.

"Well, make it twenty-six. Whenever I'm writing with it, I'll think of you."

"Don't start daydreaming in class now."

"Nothing wrong with a little daydreaming now and then." She shifted nearer to Andi. "And the paddling was spectacular. To see that sunset in the sky above and reflected in the water below was just...I can't even find the words to describe it." She paused and crinkled her nose and brow as she thought. "It was like being a part of forever. Thanks so much for taking me out on the water with you." Bringing Andi's hand toward her mouth, CJ placed small kisses on each knuckle before turning the hand over to kiss her palm.

"I'm glad you liked it."

"I loved it. And dinner... Being at the Inn with you was wonderful."

"The dinner was excellent," Andi agreed. "But the company was even better."

"So you like my company?" CJ asked flirtatiously.

"Isn't it obvious? I love to be near you."

"How near?"

"Very near."

"This near?" CJ shifted her position and moved her leg over Andi's legs, straddling her lover's thighs with her knees, which rested on either side of the seat upon which Andi sat. After briefly rising out of the water to expose her breasts to Andi's devouring gaze, she slipped down below the water again and lowered herself onto Andi's lap.

"God, you turn me on," Andi whispered. Her heart ached with desire as she gazed at the beautiful body before her, the moonlight glistening off the younger woman's wet skin. CJ's eyes opened slowly, revealing eyes dark green with yearning and passion. Andi reached up and slid her palm behind CJ's neck, gently pulling the younger woman's lips down to her own. She paused when CJ's face was just a hair's-breadth away and looked deeply in her companion's passion-hooded eyes.

Their lips met in a frenzy of passionate kisses that elicited plaintive cries from both women. All day long, CJ had wanted to touch Andi, to reach out and wrap her arms around her tall lover and cover her mouth with kisses, yet their day in public as well as her apprehension of coming on too strong prevented her from acting. However, being so close to Andi, touching her provocatively, and hearing the blue-eyed woman respond to her touch moved her to act on previously restrained feelings.

When they finally pulled their lips apart, both women gasped. Their breath came in ragged bursts, and a plaintive moan escaped from Andi's lips. *Did my heart ever beat before I met her?* Andi wondered silently. She panted. "What you do to me..." She leaned her forehead against CJ's as her rapidly beating heart pounded in her ears. "God, I want you." Every nerve in her body tingled with arousal.

"I am yours," CJ whispered. She opened her emerald eyes to peer into deep pools of blue. The offering, so simple yet so meaningful, touched Andi's heart ardently, rendering a spoken reply unworthy. Substituting action for words, she pressed her lips to CJ's to convey the passion of her feelings through the intensity of her kisses.

After several minutes, CJ reluctantly leaned back, breaking the contact. "I never knew a hot tub could be so much fun." She rested her head against Andi's forehead and was held close in a loving embrace.

Andi responded with a throaty chuckle that vibrated against CJ's chest. "There's something wonderfully erotic about water," Andi said.

"So that's why you became a swimmer?" CJ teased. "Being around nearly naked wet bodies all the time?"

"Certainly one of the perks of the sport," Andi replied. She placed her hand on CJ's cheek, drawing the other woman's face closer for a kiss before CJ rolled off Andi and onto the seat next to her. "I have to remember to thank Martha for filling up the hot tub last weekend."

"It was certainly a treat. Much as I hate to say it, though, I think I've got to get out now. As it is, I'm so relaxed I'm not sure I have any bones left in my body, due in no small part to you," she added, kissing Andi once again.

"True. I think we exceeded the fifteen minute max."

"More at issue is what we were doing during those fifteen minutes, wouldn't you say?" She grinned.

"Quite right." Andi returned the grin, arching one dark eyebrow as she spoke. "Besides, I don't want to drown in this hot tub and miss out on a little bit of heaven on earth with you right here." Her remark earned her an emphatic hug from CJ, who remained sitting shoulder to shoulder with her arm wrapped tightly around Andi.

"We can always take this party inside," CJ suggested. She was so wrapped up in Andi's passion that she didn't want the evening to end.

"I'll stoke the embers and get the fire going again. It'll be a chilly run from here to the cabin."

"I'm sure I can count on you to warm me up once we get there," CJ teased.

"That you can."

CJ SAT BACK in bed, propped up against the pillows, watching Andi, who sat at the foot of the bed near the fire, drying her ebony locks in front of the roaring blaze. As Andi bent forward, shaking her head and raking her fingers through her dark tresses, CJ watched the cotton T-shirt creep up her back, exposing the upper swells of her butt as well as the soft, fine hair on her low back. Never before had CJ felt so emotionally and physically connected to another person. She shivered as she thought about their hot tub kisses a half hour earlier, and she craved more intimate contact with the attractive body before her.

As if reading her mind, Andi turned toward CJ, smiling softly as blue eyes met green. "It's pretty dry now," she said. She stood, then added two more logs to the fire before coming around to the side of the bed and crawling under the blanket, which CJ held open in invitation.

Andi shifted onto her side, her body tucked up against her golden-haired companion. With her elbow bent and her head resting on her hand, she gazed at the woman lying by her side. CJ's green eyes were partially hidden beneath eyelids that were half closed as she reveled in her lover's nearness. A smile tugged on her slightly parted lips, and Andi heard her increased breathing and saw the rising flush color her face.

She slid her hand under the hem of CJ's T-shirt and raked her fingers slowly around her flat stomach, eliciting a soft happy-noise from the younger woman. Her fingers trailed up to CJ's ribs, gliding softly in arching half-circles underneath CJ's breast. Andi felt her arch slightly to the touch, murmuring her pleasure.

CJ's arm snaked out and slid around Andi's back, stroking light touches in zigzag patterns. Andi responded with a soft hum accompanied by warm breath that tickled CJ's ear. Suddenly the small distance between their two bodies became too great for either woman to bear. Andi was the first to close the distance, rolling further toward CJ, then pressing against her as she leaned up to kiss the woman of her desires.

With the wanton desire of one whose passions were quickly spiraling upwards and nearly out of control, Andi rolled over on top of CJ and straddled her hips, her body pressing against the younger woman's. They continued to exchange passionate kisses for several moments until Andi slowly pulled back, breaking their lip contact. She looked down into emerald eyes wide open in both disbelief and eager surprise.

CJ looked up into azure eyes, lit from within by a fire of burning desire. Had she not felt equally turned on by Andi's assertiveness, she might have pulled her eyes away from the blue ones that peered into her soul. Rather, she locked eyes with Andi and smiled seductively, encouraging the ebony-haired woman with her eye contact as well as her body language. She arched a single, honey-brown eyebrow, inviting Andi to continue.

With both hands positioned on the bed near CJ's shoulders, Andi hovered over her, maintaining enough physical contact with her legs and hips to tease the woman beneath her. Her dark hair, backlit by the roaring fire, hung down, framing her face. Slowly, she lowered her torso until she was practically touching the muscular body below her. Two cotton T-shirts separated their skin, yet Andi felt her breasts pressing against CJ's aroused nipples. She lowered her face further until her lips hung just above CJ's. With pounding hearts and lips moist with anticipation and desire, they breathed each other's air.

"I want to feel your body against mine," Andi said. She continued to gaze into CJ's eyes, waiting for a response. Dancing green eyes smiled their assent. Andi sat up and with one, swift motion, pulled the white T-shirt over her head, tossing it onto the floor. She watched as CJ's eyes widened and took in the beautifully toned, bare body before her. When CJ attempted to follow the motion with her own shirt, Andi stayed her hand.

"Let me," Andi whispered. Kissing CJ softly, she gently pressed the younger woman back down onto the bed. Then, with slow, worshipful motions began to undress her. Slipping her hands under the hem of CJ's T-shirt, she lifted the light, cotton material upward, dragging her fingertips against CJ's smooth body as she moved. Her flat stomach was exposed as Andi lifted up the material.

As the pale skin of CJ's abs came into view, Andi paused in her motion to gaze upon the smooth expanse. Moving one hand from the T-shirt's hem, she dragged it back slowly over CJ's firm stomach. Her light touch elicited another murmur from the younger woman. Teasing her fingers over the skin's surface, she lightly brushed the white-blonde hairs that covered her companion's belly. She leaned down to kiss it once, dipping her tongue into CJ's navel before slipping her hand back beneath the shirt's hem to continue what she had started. She smiled as CJ squirmed beneath her ministrations. She wanted to bring exquisite pleasure to CJ, to convey her love through worshiping hands and devoted lips.

"Raise your arms for me," Andi requested in a whisper. CJ lifted her arms as asked, pausing to trace Andi's cheek with her knuckles before resting both her arms above her head on the pillow. She was unaccustomed to giving up so much control to a lover, yet she sensed that she could trust this woman who gazed down upon her with a heated mix of tenderness and desire.

Even through the light cotton of the T-shirt, Andi could see the rapid rise and fall of CJ's chest as her breathing continued to come is short gasps. Her peaked nipples pressed against the thin material, announcing her arousal. CJ's lips were slightly parted, adding a breathiness each time she exhaled. Her body wiggled slightly as she watched and waited.

Andi slowly dragged her hands under the material, against the outer sides of CJ's breasts, then up the exposed undersides of her arms, which remained over her head on the pillow. With one gentle tug, Andi doffed the sleepwear then leaned up over CJ's body, her firm breasts teasingly close to the younger woman's mouth. Lowering her face to speak softly into her ear, Andi whispered, "Close your eyes and keep your hands where they are." She pulled back to look once again at CJ's face.

The green eyes gazed up at her, questioning the request while blue eyes gazed back with passion and intensity. After a brief moment, a look of complete trust crossed CJ's eyes before they closed.

"Focus your senses," Andi said. "Just feel me touching you." Two honey-brown eyebrows arched as a grin raised CJ's lips, but her eyes remained closed. Andi leaned down and whispered in a sultry voice, "No peeking." The warm breath tickled CJ's ear, causing her to shiver despite the heat of the fire and desire.

When she was sure that CJ's eyes were shut, Andi shifted her weight back, once again straddling the basketball player's hips. The sight of CJ's naked body beneath her own, as if in perfect offering, served to arouse her. She smiled as she thought about what she'd offer in return. *My heart and soul, if she'll have them,* she thought silently. She pressed her warm, wet center into CJ's golden curls, grinding lightly against the younger athlete's body.

CJ responded immediately by arching her hips under Andi's weight, trying to press herself against her lover's core. She fought against the urge to open her eyes and gaze at the lean body that rocked on top of her. Desperately she wanted to reach out and pull that body fully down on top of her own, to touch the body fueling her desire like none had ever done before. Abiding by Andi's request, however, she kept her eyes closed and her arms where they were, focusing her senses on Andi's warm, wet pressure.

Tickled by those golden curls beneath her, Andi felt the wetness of her building arousal, but when CJ's hips began to move faster, accompanied by her increased breathing and soft moans, Andi intentionally slowed the pace to light contact. She watched CJ's fingers clench and open as they rested tensely on the pillow over her head. The delay was near agony for Andi as well, since the rubbing had increased her own desire for release; however, she was not finished elevating CJ's passion.

CJ moaned softly when Andi decelerated her grinding hips. She could have easily slipped over the edge of a pleasant orgasm if the rocking had continued. Instead, she felt her sex throbbing against the pressure of Andi's body as her companion continued to straddle her. When Andi's body nearly stilled, CJ fought off the temptation to open her eyes to look at the woman who could light up her body with such apparent ease.

Andi simply sat back and watched CJ become still beneath her. The pale, muscular body glistened lightly, and her chest rose and fell with her rapid breathing. Andi looked with longing at the younger woman's breasts, slightly smaller than her own, and fought off the urge to lower her lips to them. She waited, wanting CJ to feel the weight of her adoring gaze. Andi knew that, in the absence of her physical touch, CJ would know she was watching her, caressing the muscular body with her eyes. She looked at the younger woman's face, the lids still blocking the emerald eyes behind them.

CJ's body tingled from Andi's stimulation, but the cessation of the other woman's touch continued to arouse CJ's curiosity and desire and cause her imagination to wander. She envisioned Andi's eyes roaming over her body and was completely turned on by the thought. Thrusting her hips again, she tried to indicate her desires to Andi, who watched CJ's body obviously craving her touch.

CJ's writhing and squirming had their desired effect. As much as Andi enjoyed the view before her, her wet and tingling body demanded a more active role. Placing her hands on the bed near CJ's shoulders, Andi her lowered mouth until it hovered over her lover's breast. Softly, she blew on the pink nipple, watching in delight as it immediately responded. CJ's glistening skin combined with the warm breath caused it to harden perceptively, accompanied by its owner's throaty moan. Then, starting several inches away, Andi touched her tongue to the light skin beneath her. Dragging her warm, wet tongue around the erect nipple in ever-narrowing circles, Andi slowly approached the hardness that ached for her touch. Just before she arrived at her destination, she lifted her tongue from her lover's skin.

CJ's moan expressed more disappointment than Andi could bear, so she gently lowered her lips to the hypersensitive nipple. Upon contact, CJ inhaled sharply, her body electrified from the touch. Andi's patience was fast coming to an end as her lover moaned and writhed beneath her mouth. Responding to CJ's urgings, Andi sucked and bit gently on the tip of the erect nub, evoking a sharp cry from her lover. Lowering her other hand, Andi gave equal attention to CJ's other breast, rolling the nipple between her fingers.

CJ's body was on fire as Andi continued to suck and stroke her. Arching her hips up off the mattress, she pressed her need against Andi's hot center. With eyes squeezed closed and hands clenched tightly over her head, she wondered how long she could endure. When Andi's mouth moved to the other breast, CJ felt ready to explode. In one swift motion, she arched her back and dislodged Andi, effectively rolling her over and lying on top of her before the dark-haired woman knew what happened.

"Hey!" Andi protested.

"Sorry," CJ panted, "but you exceeded the fifteen-minute rule in the sweet-torture pact." She straddled Andi and gazed upon her with deep green eyes alive with passion. "My turn," CJ added seductively.

She lowered her mouth to Andi's breast and licked the pebbled nub with abandon, eliciting whimpering moans from the woman beneath her. She wanted to devour her lover, to take Andi within her own body, to feel her inside, to share one place, one heart. With equal time devoted to each breast, CJ moved back and forth between the erect nipples, sucking and gently biting the tip in her attempt to consume Andi's body. Andi arched into her touch, lacing her fingers through her lover's hair and holding on so that CJ wouldn't tease her by ceasing her ministrations. As she writhed beneath the strong, muscular body above her, Andi managed to bend her knee slightly, bringing her thigh in contact with CJ's wet, hot center.

CJ moaned loudly when Andi's muscular thigh pressed against her throbbing sex. Immediately, she rubbed against Andi's leg, her slick arousal further exciting the woman beneath her. Her arms shook from the exertion of holding herself up as she rocked and ground her core against Andi. She released Andi's tender nipple to catch her breath as well as to make a request. "Touch me," she begged through panting breaths. She raised her body off Andi's slick thigh just high enough for Andi to slide her hand between them.

With a knowing touch, Andi's fingers gladly took over what her thigh had begun. Her touch met with silky wetness and heat, sparking a soft cry from the younger woman. As her thumb stroked CJ's engorged bundle of nerves, Andi slid her finger into the warm passage of her lover's desire. She felt CJ's body shudder as she plunged deeper before withdrawing slowly.

CJ felt herself balanced on the precipice, knowing that another moment of Andi's touch would thrust her over the edge. Shifting her weight to balance herself on one very shaky arm, she lowered her hand to the apex of Andi's legs, dragging her fingers through passion-dampened ebony curls. As her fingers parted Andi's folds and found their mark, her lover cried out softly beneath her. CJ slipped inside the silky, warm passage, and her finger was squeezed as Andi arched to press her deeper within.

"Come with me," CJ whispered. Her body began to tingle all over and she knew that the wave of her release was about to crash. With a final caress of her thumb against Andi's hard clit, her body exploded with her lover's, both women's aftershocks rocking their bodies against each other as they held on, riding out the waves. For several minutes they trembled in each other's arms, whispering reassurances and holding on tightly to sustain their intimate connection. After the quaking eventually subsided, CJ's spent body collapsed on top of Andi's. Their slick, hot bodies molded together as they wrapped arms and legs around each other.

"You. Are. Incredible," CJ managed to say before her breathing finally returned to a somewhat normal rate. Her cheek was pressed against Andi's chest and she could hear the older woman's heart still beating quickly. *She completes me,* she thought silently. *She's what I've waited my whole life for.*

"Unbelievable. You," was all that Andi could manage to respond. She placed her hands on either side of CJ's face and gently pulled, urging CJ to shift upward so that she rested fully on top of her own body. Gazing at CJ with deep blue eyes, she brought their lips together in a tender, passionate kiss. "You are the other half of my soul," Andi said softly.

As their lips parted, a single tear rolled from CJ's eye and dropped onto the pillow. Despite the relative darkness of the room, the emotion was not lost on Andi.

"CJ?" Andi whispered. She stroked the blonde's cheek with the back of her fingers. "What?" Dark eyebrows arched, pleading for a response.

"I..." She paused, closing her eyes hard as another tear followed the first. She opened her eyes again to find concerned eyes gazing back at her.

"Is something wrong?" A hint of worry colored Andi's words.

"No. Not wrong." She shook her head a bit from side to side. "Just the opposite."

"Tell me," Andi invited. She smiled slightly.

"I..." Again CJ paused, biting her bottom lip as she struggled to give voice to her feelings. Andi watched the nervous gesture, then kissed CJ's lips again, silently willing her the courage to open up. Andi's offering seemed to strengthen CJ's resolve. Closing her eyes, she released a deep breath, then opened her eyes again and looked at Andi with a noticeable, newfound sense of peace.

"You can tell me anything," Andi said.

"I love you," CJ whispered. She blinked back another tear, then locked her eyes on Andi's. "I couldn't share such an intense, passionate evening with you and not feel that way or not tell you." After revealing her feelings, CJ's heart raced as her anxiety mounted. Her ears echoed with her quickly beating heart, and she found herself counting its beats as she waited for a response from Andi. By the time she reached seven, Andi spoke.

"I love you back," Andi said softly. Her lips formed a contented smile and her deep blue eyes twinkled below arched eyebrows. Saying those words was easier than she thought it would be, and the warm flush and tingling feeling that flooded her body confirmed that her words were indeed accurate. Suddenly she felt giddy and grinned broadly. "I really do," she added, punctuating the statement with a searing, passionate kiss.

CJ responded by throwing her arms around Andi's neck and pulling her close, covering her lover's face with kisses. The effect was ticklish to Andi, and she began to giggle.

CJ paused her kisses to gaze into Andi's eyes. "Do you have any idea how happy I am?"

"As happy as I am right about now, I hope." A smile decorated her face. Breathing a contented sigh, she kissed CJ's lips once more before moving to her lover's side and wrapping her arm and leg around CJ's muscular body.

Outside the cabin, the moon's glow cast indigo shadows through the branches of the pines and birches. Pinpoints of starlight decorated the velvet sky, reflecting their fire in the still waters of the lake below. A shooting star dashing through the heavens was the only movement in the otherwise still night. Gaia's cycles continued that night as they had since the dawn of life. Inside the cabin, however, the women's lives had changed forever.

Chapter
Thirty-two

THE CABIN ECHOED with the gentle rhythm of rain beating off the rooftop. The pattern, steady and regular, blended subtly with the slowly beating hearts of the women sleeping inside. With bodies still wrapped together in love's embrace, they remained lulled in sleep by the consistent, soothing rhythms around them.

A crack of thunder made Andi stir. She wrapped a protective arm more tightly around the flaxen-haired woman in her arms, smiling as CJ murmured softly. A second rumble caused dark eyelashes to flutter before opening slowly to expose crystal blue eyes to the rainy morning. Her face lit up as she gazed fondly at her beautiful bedmate.

What did I do to deserve this? Andi wondered silently. Her heart overflowed with happiness as her eyes caressed the striking face beside her. She smiled and softly kissed CJ's forehead before enveloping the slumbering woman in her strong embrace.

Andi's loving gestures were not unnoticed by the drowsy woman in her arms. With her cheek pressed against Andi's chest as they embraced, CJ heard her lover's accelerated heartbeat. The tender kiss followed by the affectionate hug warmed CJ's heart and roused her from another wonderful night's sleep. She yawned and stretched before rewrapping her arms securely around Andi's tall, lean body. Tilting her head back, she opened sleepy emerald eyes to gaze up at Andi.

"Hey lover," Andi said.

CJ smiled. "Mmmm. I like the way that sounds."

"I like the way it feels." Andi arched two ebony eyebrows and grinned.

CJ shifted up enough to meet her lover's lips in a soft kiss. Her fingers brushed Andi's cheek, and she reveled in the contact. Andi slid her hands down the younger woman's sides, pulling her body up so that they were face to face. They greeted the morning and each other with lingering, adoring kisses that reaffirmed the passion of the previous evening. After several moments, their lips parted, yet they maintained intimate contact with their eyes.

"The rain on the roof sounds so relaxing," CJ murmured. She broke away from Andi's gaze and rested her cheek against her lover's chest once again, comparing its steady thumping to the soft patter of the precipitation.

"Perfect day to lounge around," Andi said. She sighed contentedly and snuggled closer to CJ's warm skin.

"I wish the weekend didn't have to end."

"Me, too," Andi agreed. "But I promised you that I'd get you back to campus in enough time for you to finish up your work."

"Right. Back to the real world." The younger woman's tone held a hint of sadness.

They remained quiet and still as the rain beat a steady pattern on the rooftop, interrupted occasionally by the rumble of thunder echoing across the lake. Both were loath to leave not only the bed in which they slept, but also the cabin in which their love was finally brought to life.

"You're quiet," Andi said softly. "What are you thinking?"

CJ remained silent for an extended moment, gathering her thoughts to form words with which to share her fears and dreams. Andi brushed CJ's back with the tips of her fingers, wordlessly encouraging her lover to share what was on her mind. Finally CJ lifted her head and looked into Andi's blue eyes before speaking. "How will things be when we leave here, when we get back to campus?" Her voice was soft, almost timid. Her head was tilted slightly to the side as she gazed at Andi with questioning, emerald eyes.

"How would you like things to be?" Andi asked. She smiled and continued to brush her fingers up and down CJ's back before tangling them in her golden hair.

"Like they have been this weekend. I want there to be an 'us' when we get back."

"Did you think there wouldn't be?"

"You said yesterday —"

"That we should be discreet 'til you graduate. But that doesn't mean I don't want to be with you. I do. More than anything. I would like to make things work between us."

"I do, too," CJ said. She looked up shyly before continuing. "I meant what I said last night, when I said that I love you."

"I know you did." She placed her hands on CJ's cheeks before gently drawing the younger woman's face up and kissing her tenderly. "And I meant it when I said that I love you back."

She smiled reassuringly. "That won't change when we leave this cabin and get back to campus. Except—"

"Except what?"

"Except to get stronger over time," Andi reassured.

"It's funny," CJ began. A small grin tugged at her lips. "I feel like I've known you all my life and have been waiting for you to come back to me."

"Yeah?"

"Yeah. So what took you so long?" She poked Andi playfully in the belly.

She shrugged. "I detoured at the school of hard knocks. But I'm here now, and I'm not going anywhere."

"I'll hold you to that."

"You can hold me anytime."

"I LOVE BABY animals, especially puppies and kittens," CJ said. She sat sideways in the passenger seat, facing Andi as she drove. CJ's arm rested across the backs of the seat while her fingers tangled in Andi's dark locks.

"I love that first cup of coffee in the morning," Andi said. She leaned her dark head into CJ's gentle touch, humming quietly as the younger athlete played with her hair. "The first cup is always the best, especially if I splurge and use some light cream." She paused, then continued. "Your turn again."

CJ pouted. "I hate the fact that we had to leave the cabin." She looked over at her dark-haired lover with gloomy, emerald eyes and down-turned lips. "I wish the weekend didn't have to end."

"And I hate to see you sad," Andi said. She reached out and gently stroked CJ's cheek before resting her hand on the blonde woman's thigh. "We'll come back again, I promise. And we'll take other fun road trips, too."

CJ placed her hand over Andi's and intertwined their fingers, squeezing gently. Her thoughts lingered on their wonderful morning in the cabin and how they lounged together in bed after Andi built up the fire. A smile crossed her lips, and her body tingled as she recalled making love as they listened to the roaring of the fire and the pounding of the rain. It had been hard leaving the warmth of Andi's arms in order to pack up and clear out of the cabin by noon, but she'd reluctantly agreed since she had a few hours of schoolwork waiting for her when she got back to campus. She sighed audibly, still disappointed, but accepting their inevitable return.

"You okay?" Andi asked. Concerned eyes searched CJ's face.

"Yeah." She sighed again. "I'm okay. I'm sorry that I got droopy about leaving. I don't want to end such a great weekend on a sad note."

"It's not sad, CJ. Just think of it as the beginning, not the end."

"The beginning?"

"Yes. The beginning of us." Andi smiled broadly and winked.

"Good point." Her eyes brightened, and a smile spread across her lips. "So, is it my turn?"

"I believe that it is." She squeezed CJ's hand gently.

"I love hot tubs," CJ said suggestively. Her honey-brown eyebrows danced up and down as she grinned at her lover.

The women continued to talk and listen to music to pass the time on their return trip. As quickly as the weekend had passed, so, too, did their drive. By early afternoon, Andi pulled the Jetta back onto campus and drove slowly toward CJ's dorm. She parked the car and turned off the ignition before shifting in her seat to face her companion.

CJ sighed. "I suppose I should get out of the car now. I don't know how I'm going to get any work done, though. My mind will be on you." She smiled at Andi while reaching out and clasping her hand.

"I'll be thinking of you, too." She winked at CJ and grinned, hoping to cheer up her friend. "Work for a couple hours, catch up with your roommates, then call me when you climb into bed later tonight. I want your voice to be the last thing I hear before I fall asleep, so that you will be in my heart and in my dreams."

"Can I hug you, or would that be indiscreet?" CJ asked.

"I think a hug would be just fine." CJ returned Andi's smile then leaned across the car to embrace her. She buried her face against Andi's neck, breathing in deeply to memorize her scent. After several moments of holding each other close, they reluctantly parted.

"I suppose a passionate kiss would fall into the 'indiscreet' category," CJ mused.

"Unfortunately, yes. I'll take an IOU for the next time we're together, though."

"You can count on it. So, until soon?"

"Yes, until very soon," Andi said.

ANDI SAT ON her sofa with the phone cradled between her ear and shoulder while she unlaced her sneakers and waited for Martha to pick up on the other end. After the third ring, her friend's cheery voice greeted her.

"Hello darlin'," Martha sang.

"Aren't you taking a chance with that kind of greeting?" Andi teased. "I could be a phone solicitor or something."

"I've got caller ID, remember?"

"Oh yeah," she said sheepishly. "So, how are you?" she asked, her tone more spirited.

"We're fine. Question is, how are you? How'd your special weekend go?"

"Perfect! I just called to thank you sooooooo much for letting me use the cabin. It was just... Everything was so... I can't even begin..."

"Must have been good. The English major is speechless," Martha teased. "See if you can string together enough words to tell me what happened."

"One or both of us might blush."

"Nuff said," Martha hastily remarked. "I'll take that to mean you told her how you feel and the feeling was mutual?"

"Very mutual. And very wonderful."

"Kaaaa-ren," Martha called. Andi listened as her friend shouted to her partner from across the room. "Andi got laid. You owe me ten bucks."

"Hey!" Andi choked out. "You're acting as a bookie for my love life?"

"I'm just teasing you," Martha said. "So, things went well, huh?"

"Better than well," Andi gushed. "I'm so incredibly happy. I feel like...she's exactly what I've been waiting for."

"Well, we're excited for you, Andi. It's good to hear you sound so happy. You deserve to be. CJ's a lucky woman."

"I'm feeling pretty lucky myself. So, can I buy you lunch tomorrow to thank you for the cabin?"

"I'd love to meet you for lunch, but please don't feel like you owe me anything. Just seeing you happy will be sufficient payback."

"Great! I'll walk over to your office at noon, okay?"

"I'll be ready."

"Tell Karen I said hi, and I'll see you tomorrow."

"I will. Talk to you later."

ANDI STEPPED OUT of her bedroom wearing sweats and a T-shirt, her hair still damp from her recent shower. She padded across the living room and stretched out on the sofa before turning on the table lamp and picking up her journal. With her back resting against the padded arm of the couch and a pillow placed on her lap, she opened the ribbon-marked page to her last entry. She reread it before dating and beginning a new page.

> *I feel like my life has begun this weekend. I love CJ and she loves me back. It's really that simple, yet I made things so complicated for so many weeks while I agonized over what to do. Right from the start I should have taken a lesson from CJ and followed my heart like she followed hers. Lucky for me, her heart was still willing to take a chance with me when my heart finally got brave enough to admit what I was feeling. Now that I've acknowledged it, not only to myself but also to her, I feel so incredibly happy! Our weekend together was unbelievably passionate, sincere, comfortable, fun — it was everything I could have ever hoped for. She is everything I could ever hope for. She's the one. After this weekend together, I have no doubt that she is what I've been waiting for my whole life. Now that we've found each other, I don't plan on ever letting go.*

Andi's writing was interrupted by a phone call. She quickly closed her journal and placed it on the coffee table, then reached for the phone, eagerly anticipating the sound of CJ's voice. She was not disappointed.

"Hello?" Andi answered.

"Hey, lover."

"God, what you do to me when you say that." Andi's body tingled with thoughts of her blonde lover.

"It's very mutual, I assure you."

"You're calling earlier than I expected," Andi said. She looked at the clock on the wall and noted the time. "Finish your work already?"

"Yup. I was motivated by a phone call that I was eagerly anticipating making. So, what are you doing?"

"Just got out of the shower and was writing in my journal. How about you?"

"I can't stop thinking about this weekend," CJ whispered softly.

"Me either."

A knock on Andi's door made her swing her legs off the sofa and sit up abruptly. Her eyes widened at the sound.

"Someone's knocking on my door. Stay on the line with me while I walk down to answer it. And hold onto that thought," she added, her tone playful. She opened her apartment door and descended the stairs, then looked through the peephole in the door. A smile decorated her lips as she pulled the door open. CJ stood outside, smiling.

"I'd rather hold on to you," the blonde said. She clicked off her cell phone, stepped through the open door, and closed it behind her. The two women fell into each other's arms, melding their bodies into a passionate embrace.

CJ's warm breath tickled Andi's ear as she spoke. "I really wanted to see you. I just needed...you."

Andi pulled back from the embrace just enough to kiss CJ tenderly on the lips before taking her lover's hand in her own and leading her up the stairs.

Chapter
Thirty-three

ANDI TUNED OUT the keynote speaker, whose prosaic baccalaureate address didn't capture her attention nearly as much as did thoughts of her lover, who sat with the other graduates on the great lawn. Andi's seat in the bleachers provided her with a perfect view of the object of her desire, which went along with the fantasies preoccupying her mind. She smiled, daydreaming about the last few weeks since their trip to the cabin and the love that had developed and deepened. She wanted to take that microphone out of the keynote speaker's hand and shout to the world that she loved CJ. She grinned mischievously at the thought.

"Well?" Martha asked. Her question was emphasized with an elbow to Andi's ribs, causing the grad assistant to pop out of her reverie.

"Sorry," Andi said sheepishly. "I wasn't paying attention."

"Thanks, Captain Obvious," Martha teased. "I could tell. I asked if it was me, or if this guy was a bit dull."

"He's dull, all right," Andi said. She looked at her watch for the tenth time, anxious for the ceremony to be over. All the faculty members of the college were expected to attend, so she sat amongst them, with Martha at her side. Both women were clothed in the mandatory dark gowns and capes reflecting their degrees. The only advantage to their duty assignment was the bird's eye view of CJ.

As if reading Andi's thoughts, CJ turned and looked up toward the faculty section where she knew Andi was seated. She waved inconspicuously. After Andi returned the wave, CJ signed 'I love you' to her before touching her heart with the same hand. Andi's heart raced and her face flushed, causing her to grin.

"I saw that hand jive, and you're blushing!" Martha said. "I'll bet you're glad that," she paused to look at her watch, "in a matter of minutes CJ will officially not be an undergraduate anymore."

"Quite." Andi sighed. "I was never big on public displays of affection anyway, but I'm afraid that even our eye contact and body language give us away."

"You're right about that," Martha said. She feigned injury after Andi elbowed her lightly.

"That's because you know the truth. I don't think anyone else was paying attention to us. Everybody else was too worried about finals and other end of the year stuff."

"True," Martha agreed. "It's all history now, though. You can say and do what you like together — within reason, of course. If you start romping naked across the Great Lawn together, I think you'll force the administration to override its 'don't ask, don't tell' policy, though."

Andi grinned. "I wasn't planning any naked romping — at least not in public. I'm really not looking to drape myself all over CJ when we walk across campus either," she added, her voice more serious. "It's not about that. I just don't want to feel like I have to hide something that has become so important to me, and I don't want CJ to feel that way either."

"You don't have to explain anything to me, girlfriend. Your life is my life, remember?"

"I know. Speaking of which, what's Karen doing while you're here?"

"Probably home cooking or cleaning. Her folks are stopping by this weekend on their way to Boston for vacation. Speaking of vacations, when are you and CJ headed out of town?"

"Three days from now, and counting," Andi said. "Before we go, we have to move CJ's stuff into her new place. Coach Malardie got her a room in the graduate dorm for the summer."

"Hopkins Hall?"

"Yeah. It's not bad, for a dorm."

"Roommates?"

"Nope." Andi grinned. "Coach arranged for her to have a single. She promised CJ about twenty hours work a week this summer so that she can afford to stay on campus. She's also signed up for two classes."

"Sweet. I guess both of you are happy about that. So after you move CJ, where are you gals headed off to?"

"CJ wanted to go to Provincetown for a few days. She said that after weeks of being 'discreet,' she wants to walk down the street holding my hand for all the world to see. We'll take our bikes, hang out on the beach, and just blend in with thousands of other people just like us."

"Sounds like fun," Martha said. "Hey, look, CJ's row is next." She pointed to the black-gowned students who stood and walked obediently in the prearranged order to receive their diplomas.

Andi sat forward on her seat, peering around heads to watch as CJ shook the dean's hand before being handed her document. She smiled broadly at the administrator, then turned back toward the spectators and waved. Her emerald eyes found Andi in the crowd, and she smiled when they made eye contact before CJ exited the platform.

Andi sat impatiently while the remaining students received their diplomas, then processed out across the green led by the full professors and other school dignitaries. When the last student exited, Andi followed the rest of the faculty and marched out to join the celebrating crowds. After saying goodbye to Martha, she walked over to their designated meeting spot to wait for CJ.

Within a few moments CJ came bounding across the lawn with a woman in tow. She had blondish hair, starting to gray, and though she was much shorter, she resembled her daughter. CJ's arm was linked in the older woman's arm as she walked briskly to keep up with CJ's considerably longer legs. Andi smiled and waved a greeting as the two women approached.

"Congratulations!" Andi announced.

"Thanks!" CJ said. The athlete unlinked the older woman's arm and faced Andi, reaching out and pulling her close for a hug. Her surprised lover returned the hug, quirking a grin over CJ's shoulder at the woman who had walked over with CJ and stood watching as the two women embraced. After an extended moment, they stepped apart and CJ spoke.

"Andi, I'd like to you meet my mother, Terry," CJ said. "Mom, this is Andi."

Andi stepped forward and offered her hand to the older woman. CJ's mother's handshake was warm and firm. Her emerald eyes, so like her daughter's, looked deeply into Andi's.

"Hi, Mrs. — "

"Please," she interrupted, "call me Terry. It's a pleasure to finally meet you." She smiled up at Andi, still holding her hand firmly. "CJ's told me so much about you," she added.

Andi used every bit of her self-control not to turn and look at her lover to interpret the meaning of Terry's seemingly casual remark. She blushed slightly and grinned. "Good things, I hope," she managed to squeak out.

"Very good things. I wanted to thank you personally for taking such good care of CJ after her eye injury. She couldn't rave enough about how attentive and welcoming you were." Terry finally released Andi's hand and shifted her arm around

CJ's waist. "CJ tells me that you'll be joining us at the restaurant," she added. "I'm glad. It'll give me an opportunity to show my appreciation."

"It was my pleasure, Mrs.—I mean, Terry. And thank you for including me in the celebration."

"CJ wouldn't have had it any other way. I'm glad you're coming." She turned and faced CJ. "Shall we? We're meeting the rest of the family in thirty minutes. With all these people trying to leave, we're likely to hit traffic." Andi stepped forward next to CJ's mom, who stood between the two tall athletes. As they walked, Terry gently placed her hand on Andi's arm before addressing her in a voice loud enough for CJ to hear. "So, can I count on you to keep an eye on CJ this summer?" Terry asked. "Sometimes trouble has a way of finding my daughter, if you know what I mean," she added, winking at Andi. "This is the first summer that she won't be home. I'll feel better if I know that you're keeping an eye on her."

Andi bit the inside of her cheek in order to stifle a laugh. She dared not look at CJ for fear of giggling out loud. She swallowed and regained her composure before she responded. "I'll take good care of CJ, I promise," Andi said. Her voice was sincere, even if her idea of that job description was slightly different than CJ's mother probably had in mind.

CJ simply walked along next to her mother, grinning to herself at Andi's innuendo.

Epilogue

One year later

ANDI PUSHED OPEN the door to her apartment and slowly walked to the center of the large room, her footsteps echoing in the empty space. Now that the last of her boxes had been loaded in the van, the place looked much bigger than she remembered. She turned slowly in a circle, looking at the fireplace, the empty bookcases, the kitchen, and the windows that looked out across campus. Sighing deeply, she thought back to the last time the apartment had looked this way, when she moved in just over two years ago. She shook her head slowly. *So much has changed.* Back then, the apartment had been her cocoon while she healed and re-created herself following her injury and her breakup. Her new living arrangements would serve a similar purpose by marking another turning point in her life.

She smiled when she thought of her new life with CJ and how she had redefined herself yet again, not just as an individual, but also as an integral half of a committed relationship. *A soulmate, as CJ puts it.* Their first year together had been a wonderful bonding of partners whose hearts and energies were focused on the same goal—a loving life together. The prospect of falling asleep and waking up every day next to her blonde lover filled her heart with soul-warming joy. So enraptured with the image was she that Andi didn't hear her soulmate as she quietly stepped into the room.

CJ walked up behind Andi and slipped her arms around the taller woman's lean waist. Her chin rested on one broad shoulder as her body pressed its full length against that of her lover. CJ smiled when Andi rubbed her hands affectionately on the younger athlete's arms before intertwining their hands. She nuzzled her face against the ebony locks, enjoying the fresh, herbal scent that mixed with Andi's unique aroma. They stood silently for several moments before CJ finally spoke.

"You okay?" she asked. Her voice was soft and her breath tickled Andi's ear.

"Fine," Andi said. "Just making sure I didn't forget anything." With that said, she still made no further move to look around the apartment for forgotten possessions. The women remained motionless.

"Second thoughts? Regrets?" CJ asked.

"None." Her voice was confident and direct. She turned in CJ's arms and placed her hands gently on the younger woman's cheeks. With their noses nearly touching, Andi gazed deeply into her lover's emerald eyes and smiled. "I've already promised you all my tomorrows. Living together is the next step in our commitment and I'm absolutely thrilled about it, my love." She punctuated her statement with a passionate kiss that left no doubt about her feelings.

"I will always love you, Andi," CJ whispered.

"Until forever," Andi said.

The End

Maya Indigal is the pen name of a devoted fan of lesbian novels. A teacher by day, she spends her free time reading voraciously, writing when she's able to, and communing with nature while in her kayak, on her bike, or in her garden. She and her partner live in the Northeastern USA, sharing their home and hearts with several adopted cats. This is her first novel.

She can be reached at indigal@optonline.net

Printed in the United States
31447LVS00002B/25

9 781932 300314